Sky of Diamonds

Anderson Gentry

Cover Design by Hanna Al-Shear

CRIMSON DRAGON PUBLISHING

Contents

Crimson Dragon Publishing
Willow, Alaska
https://crimsondragonpublishing.com

Sky of Diamonds

Prologue

Tarbos, 2356 CE

A tense but long-lasting peace followed the
First Galactic War. While diplomatic relations were
established between the Confederacy and the Grugell
Empire, the relationship remained tentative.

Aided by the newfound ability to calibrate scanners
to function during subspace transits, cross-border
traffic became somewhat more enthusiastic. In a
robust display of market economics, each side swiftly
discovered that the other had commodities worth
trading for. An illegal but brisk trade developed, with
Grugell wines, art, weapons, and other goods coming
into the Confederacy, and Confederate electronics,
computers, and other high-tech equipment flowing
into the Empire. The Confederate Navy set up a
regular patrol along the Grugell frontier, but intercepting smugglers along the billions of cubic light-years
of space was hopeless. More disturbing, the Navy had
for some time suspected that cloaked Grugell ships
routinely violated the border.

The Navy still patrolled the area, with Task Force
947 maintaining a presence at "Alpha Station," an area
of space between the closest settled worlds on either

side. To support this operation, a major naval base was established on New Wichita, an agricultural world on the Confederate side of the line.

It was a Confederate Navy medical cruiser, the CSS Charity, which was present at the incident that first gave evidence to an ancient, almost forgotten legend, and provided the first hints that there was a guiding influence that may have manipulated events in human society for a thousand years.

The years following the "Ionescu incident" saw the Confederacy distracted by a sharp increase in pirate traffic out of the unaffiliated Rim Worlds, as the human presence in the Galaxy began its second wave of expansion outside the borders of the Confederacy itself.

—Morris/Handel, A History of the First Galactic Confederacy, University Publications, 2804 CE

Following are selected excerpts from Morris/Handel, *A History of the First Galactic Confederacy*, University Publications, 2804 CE, and selected popular news media from 2350-2354 CE.

Morris/Handel: 2350, Subspace Scanning

Interstellar travel had for years been hampered by the inability to use standard scanning technology while in subspace transit. From 2341 to 2350, the Confederate Navy Department poured billions of Confederate dollars into research, which paid off in 2350 with the development of a series of algorithmic software filters that were able to translate the seeming gibberish of subspace into data that the human mind could comprehend. Ships could now detect other ships in subspace, and while transit speeds made it impossible to identify or interact in any way with ships on tangential courses, the capacity made tight-formation jumps and convoy operations much easier. Ships on parallel trajectories were now able to track and trade messages with each other.

Within three Standard Years, the Navy discovered that the Grugell had managed to steal the technology, swiftly erasing the tactical advantage. Thus, the technology race continued.

Affiliated Galactic Press, Mountain View, Tarbos, January 1, 2354

In a press conference held this morning, Secretary of the Navy Roland Adams revealed that armed and cloaked Grugell frigates have intruded on Confederate space twice in the last Standard Year. Both ships were discovered only due to the partial or complete failure of their cloaking systems.

The transit of armed ships into Confederate space is a direct violation of the Treaty of Honshu, which allows only unarmed ships under diplomatic beacon. The president has issued a formal complaint to the Grugell emperor by hyperphone.

Morris/Handel: Unaffiliated Worlds

Prior to the passage of the Eminent Domain Act in 2408, entrepreneurs were free to open habitable worlds as private corporations. While the Rim Worlds were frequently cited as examples, the three Rim planets of Wilson, Last Chance, and Jinx were not settled in any organized fashion, but rather grew in place as an ad hoc society of smugglers, escaped convicts, Navy deserters, and various other brands of misfits.

Roman Holiday, on the other hand, was opened to settlement as a private corporation, registered as such with the Confederate government. Run by a shadowy cabal of individuals known only as "The Organization," Roman Holiday's local laws took the normal libertarian politics of the Confederacy one step farther. The world's three cities developed rapidly as meccas for gambling, prostitution, and general vice.

Transcribed from the *Navy Times*, a Confederate Navy internal newspaper, August 23rd, 2354:

Item: Three new ships have been commissioned into active service in the last month: the medical cruiser Charity and the destroyers *Robert E. Lee* and *Polena Tesch*.

The *Charity* is the first in her class, with a crew of four thousand and the latest in medical technology. The new *Charity*-class ships will provide medical support to major task groups. Three more ships of this class are in construction.

The *Charity* is currently in shakedown and will be assigned to TF947.

The *Robert E. Lee* is a *Reuben James*-class frigate...

Book One
Blood Red

Tarbos

The years following the First Galactic War saw an unprecedented expansion into previously unknown space. As the Confederacy grew, so did the length of the border with the Grugell Empire. Despite the establishment of diplomatic relations with the Empire, there were many cross-border incidents.

It was during this period that several thorns began to make themselves felt in the Confederacy's side. The establishment of several colonies on the generally ignored planets of Wilson, Last Chance, and Jinx, known as the Rim Worlds, provided a safe haven outside the Confederate border for escaped convicts, murderers, traitors, and renegades from both Confederacy and Empire. All three worlds, situated as they were on the outer edge of the Galactic arm, were notoriously poor in water, metals, and other resources. The inhabitants of those worlds resorted to raiding on small colonies and undefended freighters to support what industries they managed to create.

Perhaps more surprising was the discovery of a unique retroviral disease that had given rise to an ancient, almost forgotten Earth legend, and the fact that carriers of the disease still lived and traveled throughout the Confederacy even in the modern era.

One such carrier was later discovered to have been
influencing human history and events to his own
benefit for well in excess of a thousand Standard Years.

*—Morris/Handel, A History of the First Galactic
Confederacy, University Publications, 2804 CE*

Chapter One

I have learned not to think little of any one's belief, no matter how strange it may be. I have tried to keep an open mind, and it is not the ordinary things of life that could close it, but the strange things, the extraordinary things, the things that make one doubt if they be mad or sane.

—Bram Stoker

Wallachia, 1462 CE

It was a bright day in early spring, with a hint of winter's chill still in the air. The Carpathians brooded over the tiny village as they had for centuries, caps of white still glinting on their peaks this April day. The wind regularly brought whispers of war to the valley, but to a teenage boy, the talk of war was a distant matter, hardly of any concern at all.

"Belos!" It was his mother, calling for him from the back door of their tiny hut, a rude, thatch-roofed, two-room affair down a side alley of the tiny village. "You must go to the well for water! Hurry, boy!"

"I'm coming, Mother!"

As he hurried towards the hovel he shared with his mother, he heard the drumming of hoof beats. Riders frequently came and went through their tiny village, but this sounded different. Many horses were pounding down the road.

Belos ran to the hut, retrieved the bucket from his mother's proffered hand. "Mother! There are riders coming into the village!"

His mother shook her head. "And your father away, fighting in Vlad's Crusade," she spat and cursed. "Evil plagues the land these days, Belos!" She stepped out, listened. "They're stopping in the village square. Well, come on, boy, let's go see what they want of our poor town."

In the village square, a rider in mailed armor was just now unrolling a scroll, which he read in a booming voice:

"The Lord Vladimir Tepes commands that all males aged fifteen summers and older are to join his army under the banner of the Dracul to war against the infidel Turks, against the army of the barbarian Suleiman Bulut. All of you as such, in this village, will join our march at once. You will gather here in one hour." He rolled up the scroll and tipped up his helmet's visor to reveal a hawk-like face, long moustaches dangling. "Well, what are all of you looking at?" he snapped. "Get moving!"

Belos walked his crying mother back to their rude hut. "But, Mother," he assured her, "Father is in Vlad's army. I will find him and fight at his side, and when the Turks are beaten, we will come home together!"

"I will pray for it to be so, my son," his mother sobbed.

But it was not to be.

At the edge of Grugell Space, 2356 CE

"There he is! There he is! Target main batteries and fire!"

An uncharacteristically agitated Group Commander Tottalas-trik VI shouted orders at the flagship crew, who hurried to comply. While the helm officer drove their battle cruiser at the tiny alien ship, the weapons officer slaved the weapons systems of the three accompanying frigates to his own console and targeted the tiny, fleeing yacht. One long, clawed finger stabbed down on a stud, and nine bolts of green energy lanced out after the private ship.

"Sir, he's about to cross the frontier," Subcommander Gorbagittid VII pointed at the view screen, where the flashing lights of the frontier marker buoys were now visible.

"Fire again! Get him before he crosses the frontier!" the group commander screeched. "Get me a reading on his engine signature, and stand by homing torpedoes!"

The first volley missed, but the second barrage lanced three beams of green flame through the tiny ship. The yacht was sent tumbling end over end, trailing sparks, spewing gases into space. It tumbled out of control, barely missing one of the flashing border buoys as it crossed the border into the Confederacy.

"That's a hit!" the weapons officer shouted. "Multiple hits! Enemy ship appears to be out of control, Group Commander! Ship is burning, sir, scans show engine failure, multiple fires on board."

"Good!" Tottalastrik ground out through gritted teeth. "Let the Confederacy deal with the remains of that monster. Whatever he is, he must have come from there." He turned towards the helm console. "Take us back to station. Signal the Imperial Navy Command that the monster has been destroyed, and that his ship was blasted back into Confederate space."

The task group turned away. Behind them, a small but obscenely expensive private yacht wallowed out of control, trailing a comet's tail of sparks and flame.

Chapter Two

Space Dock Alpha, in orbit around Tarbos, two weeks earlier

Captain.

Jared Gellar still loved the sound of the word.

He took one more look in the mirror before leaving his quarters for the last time and was generally pleased with what he saw. The dark green Confederate Navy uniform still fit perfectly, and the silver eagle of his newly achieved rank shone brightly on his chest above the Medical Corps branch insignia.

Gellar was tall at a bit over two meters, and still as trim as the day he had entered the Academy, sixteen years before. His close-cropped hair was iron gray, his eyes the blue of Arctic ice. He smiled at himself in the mirror. At first appearance, he projected the image of unswerving authority, but under that veneer laid an irreverent streak and an irrepressible sense of humor. A 'lifer' in the Confederate Navy, he'd never taken the time for a wife or family, and had never regretted it. The adventures he'd had as a medical officer, a practicing physician in the Navy, had provided him with as full a life as he could ask for, and today was the high point. Today was the day his career had been building up to for sixteen years; today was the day he assumed command of the medical cruiser, Confederate Star Ship *Charity*.

He ran a hand over the stubble of gray hair on his head, picked up his bag, and left staff quarters on Space Dock Alpha for the last time. The CSS *Charity* was on final approach, her outgoing commander overdue for retirement on his home world of Caliban.

Striding briskly down the bustling, white-painted corridor towards the lift shaft that would float him up to the docking bay, he was whistling an old tune from his childhood when a familiar voice speaking in a horrendously affected Scottish brogue stopped him.

"Are ye really in such a hurry to leave, Jared? Och, pardon me, I mean Captain Gellar, *sir*!"

Gellar turned to face his old Academy classmate, Commander Angus MacKay.

"Angus, you old devil, you can still call me Jared. Well, at least in private. In public, of course, you should stand at attention and address me only as 'sir.'"

MacKay grinned, a twinkle of humor in his green eyes. Short, almost as wide through the shoulders as he was tall, red-haired, and red-faced, MacKay looked for all Space like a madly happy, grinning orangutan. His beard grew in so fast as to require shaving at least twice a day, his hair was as bristly as a thistle from his homeland, and his huge hands hung down to his knees. MacKay was of a sort that was beginning to become the exception to the rule in these days of Confederate expansion, having actually been born and raised on Earth. He'd come a long way from his native Scotland.

"Ye lucky, lucky bastard," he teased Gellar. "A promotion and a new command all in the same month, even; ye lucky, *lucky* bastard!"

"No luck to it, old friend. Just the Confederate Navy's inevitable recognition of talent, brains, charisma, and natural leadership ability." Gellar winked at his friend, who feigned a coughing spasm.

"Och, man, ye'll have me losin' my lunch on the deck here!" MacKay threw back his head and laughed his customary, booming laugh, with the full-throated passion of a Highlander. "Well, man, ye'll have to let an' old friend escort ye to the docking bay."

"I wouldn't have it any other way, Angus. Shall we?" Gellar agreed, indicating the way to the lift shaft.

Moments later Captain Gellar and his Highlander friend were at the docking bay view port. Gellar watched his new command come into dock with all the quiet pride of a new parent.

The *Charity* was a command to be proud of, one of the Navy's newest hospital ships. The main section was entering the docking bay now, a snow-white bulb sixteen hundred meters long by three hundred and fifty wide, built around the inevitable mass tunnel of the Gellar Star Drive, actually invented by a distant ancestor of Captain Gellar. With a crew of four thousand, the *Charity* was the first in its class, only two years in commission.

"Old friend, 'tis a day to be proud of, and that's a fact," MacKay breathed. "She's a beautiful lass, she is." He clapped his friend on the back with a hand as hard as granite.

"She is, isn't she?" Gellar replied, entranced.

A tone sounded, and the two friends watched as the docking umbilical snaked out to *Charity*'s docking port. To the left, a green light went on over the docking port entrance, and the door hissed open. Gellar turned to his old classmate.

"This is it, old buddy," he said, extending his hand. "I'll miss you, you bristle-pated, knock-kneed, Scottish baboon."

"Aye, and I suppose I'll miss ye as well, ye pasty-faced, space-born donkey's arse," MacKay replied, completing the ritual with a gap-toothed grin. He gripped his friend's hand hard, shook it once, and then, straightening as much as his simian physique would allow, saluted his friend smartly.

"Fair winds, lad, and safe journey."

Gellar returned the salute gravely. "And to you as well, Angus." MacKay winked, and the spell was broken. "Now, laddie, I've got the ER watch in ten minutes, so I'd best shift meself. Ye get on board ye're new baby, there. And good luck—ye'll need it." With another booming laugh, the Scotsman spun on his heel and stumped away, bellowing an ancient song from Earth:

> *"You may talk o' gin and beer*
> *When you're quartered safe out 'ere,*
> *An' you're sent to penny-fights an' Aldershot it;*
> *But when it comes to slaughter*
> *You will do your work on water,*
> *An' you'll lick the bloomin' boots of 'im that's got it.*
> *Now in Injia's sunny clime,*
> *Where I used to spend my time*
> *A-servin' of 'Er Majesty the Queen,*
> *Of all them blackfaced crew*
> *The finest man I knew*
> *Was our regimental bhisti, Gunga Din."*

Gellar grinned as the booming shout of the Scot's "singing" faded around a corner.

Well, it's time, he told himself. Needlessly straightening his tunic, he stepped over the threshold and walked through the docking umbilical into his new command.

The umbilical opened into a cavernous bay that held two shuttles, with bay doors at the far end. As Gellar entered, a gray-haired master chief petty officer blew a blast on a pipe to welcome him.

A good portion of the ship's company, probably everyone who wasn't standing an essential watch, was assembled in formation in the bay. Rank after rank of green and white uniforms stood lined up, at attention. *Impressive*, Gellar had to admit.

Just inside the bay, a commander in Navy green was standing next to a white-haired captain in undress whites. This would be his predecessor, Captain Andrew Clark. Gellar walked up to the officers, saluting as he approached. "Permission to come aboard, sir?" he requested formally, with the required address of the outgoing Captain.

"Granted, of course," Captain Clark replied, smiling. He remembered all too well the excitement of assuming command, but the only thing that appealed to him now was his overdue retirement. He returned Gellar's salute. "Welcome aboard, Captain, and congratulations." He turned to the rather youthful commander beside him. "May I introduce you to Commander Wils Hoff, your executive officer?"

Hoff was young for a commander at thirty-four, but he'd already seen twelve years of duty on various types of combat and support ships with the Fleet. Tall, rangy, and athletic, with piercing gray eyes and light brown hair, Wils Hoff was the sort who would rather be in space than in port, and that was something he'd never shared with his outgoing commander. He knew his new captain by reputation, and knew him to be of the same inclination. He snapped off a smart salute, which Gellar returned, and then stuck out his hand. "Welcome aboard, Captain. You'll like it here."

"I already do, Exec," Gellar answered.

"And this, Captain Gellar, is Master Chief Bosun's Mate Anders Gillespie, the ship's senior chief petty officer. I frankly don't know how the *Charity* would run without him."

"Pleased to meet you, sir." Master Chief Gillespie was short and broad-shouldered with grizzled gray hair and eyes the color of blued steel. His handshake was hard, his calloused palms like machine tools.

"I've heard of you, Master Chief," Gellar noted. "Wasn't it you on the old dreadnought *Ranger*, in the—"

"Yes, sir, that's me." Gillespie cut him off, looking slightly embarrassed. "It wasn't that big a deal, sir. I just did what anyone would have done in my place."

"It was a big enough deal for a Distinguished Service Medal, Master Chief. Hell, I read about that rescue in the Academy. I'm damn glad to have you on the *Charity*."

"Thank you, sir." *Another new Captain to break in*, Gillespie thought to himself wryly.

The change of command ceremony was brief. In front of the assembled ship's company, Captain Clark accepted the ship's flag from the ship's master chief and handed it to Captain Gellar, who handed it back to Master Chief Gillespie for return to storage in what was still called a sail locker. Salutes were exchanged, and Gellar addressed his new command briefly as Captain Clark took a place behind the formation.

"Officers and crew," Gellar began.

"I'll keep this short and simple." There was a small scattering of applause, which Gellar greeted with a smile. "On Earth in the days of oak ships and canvas sails, the saying was, 'On this day, England expects each man to do his duty.' That is what I expect of each of you, to carry out your assigned duties to the best of your abilities. In return, I will carry out mine—to ensure that each of you has the tools needed to do your jobs, to save lives, to deliver medical care to those in need."

He stood at parade rest, a position as old as uniformed service, and rocked back and forth on his heels as he spoke.

"I've seen our orders," Gellar continued. "We're bound for the far edge of Confederate territory, to join Task Force 947 on the edge of Grugell space. This is considered hazardous duty. I'm sure you'll all welcome the Navy's generous hundred and fifty dollars a month hazardous duty pay." A chorus of chuckles greeted that remark.

"Relations with the Grugell are tense at best. As with all medical ships, the *Charity* is unarmed and unarmored, and as medical professionals, we are bound by oath to provide medical care to any in need, no matter where they are from. This means human and Grugell alike."

"People," he concluded, "we've got the Fleet's newest medical cruiser, a first-rate crew, the best doctors and nurses in the service. We're not just going to follow the standard; we're going to set a new standard."

"We leave space dock in seventy-one hours. Let's get to work. Dismissed!"

A round of cheers broke out, and the formation broke up, the crew breaking up into groups of twos and threes to return to quarters, recreation centers, and duty stations—or for long-awaited shore leave.

Captain Clark walked up to Gellar, smiling. "Jared, that was a damn fine speech."

"Thank you, Andrew," Gellar responded. Now that the formalities were over, the two slipped into the easy informality of conversation between equals.

"It's Andy," Clark replied, "And by the time you take this ship out again, it will be plain old *Mister* Clark, instead of Captain. I'm two years overdue to retire, Jared. The Navy's too short of medical officers." He shook his head. "Well, you've got a fine ship and a fine crew. You're getting one of the best navigators in the Fleet, and a master chief petty officer who's been in the Navy since I was in grade school. You'll have a great tour. I wish you all the best of luck, Jared. Safe journey."

"And you too, Andy. Thanks."

Commander Hoff walked over to shake hands with his outgoing captain. "Jared, you're also getting a first-rate exec. Best I've ever worked with," Clark added. "Good luck, Wils. You'll be happy with your change of command evaluation, I think."

"Thank you, sir. Safe journey," Hoff replied. With a smile and a handshake for Gellar and Hoff both, Clark turned and strode from the hangar bay to the docking umbilical entrance. His personal effects were already packed and en route to the station's transient quarters. In twenty-four hours, Clark would be officially retired and bound for his home on Caliban.

"Well, Exec." Gellar turned to his new second-in-command. "Shall we head for the bridge? On the way, you can fill me in how our re-provisioning and re-supply schedule looks for the next three days."

In addition to overseeing loading supplies, foodstuffs, and replacement personnel, Gellar spent the next three days meeting key members of the *Charity*'s crew.

His chief surgeon was Captain Andrea Moses, a short, stocky Navy Medical Corps veteran ten years Gellar's senior.

Chief navigator, always a key job in a starship, was Lieutenant Commander Morely Bice, a man whose reputation for making sense of half-documented star systems and predicting arrival times to within minutes was known throughout the Fleet.

Marine Lieutenant Colonel Christine Sandelescu was tall, raven-haired, black-eyed, statuesque, and extremely striking; as the commander of the ship's Marine contingent, she was also chief of security, an important position even in a space-going hospital. Sandelescu left one with the impression that she was not to be trifled with. In her quarters was a trophy from the Academy's women's kickboxing team, where she had taken first place in the Confederate Championships in her senior year.

Master Chief Petty Officer Gillespie was one of the few Navy NCOs to beat the thirty-year retirement mandate, having managed to stay in the Navy for almost forty years by dint of sheer competence, and also by his reputation as the hero of the *Ranger* incident.

Gellar had last witnessed the fitting-out and provisioning of a starship for patrol four years earlier, when he was chief medical officer aboard the CSS *Borealis*, a cruiser assigned to the First Fleet. First Fleet was home-based on Tarbos, a posting that Navy officers competed for. Being home-based at the Confederate capital yielded ample opportunities to be noticed by the senior Flag officers, and had the added benefit of ample recreational opportunities while in port. Unfortunately for this tour, Task Force 947 was part of the Third Fleet, home-based on New Wichita, a truly dull agricultural planet.

On the last afternoon in port, Gellar closeted himself in his quarters and reviewed the composition of Task Force 947, currently at what was known as 'Alpha Station' on the Grugell border.

Task Force Commander: Rear Admiral Horace Wright Crittendon.

Flagship: Dreadnought CSS *Arcadia*, second dreadnought to bear the name, commanded by Captain Adolf Guttenberg. Gellar had served with Captain Guttenberg before, when both were assigned to Seventh Fleet. Guttenberg had been the exec on the *Borealis* when Gellar was chief medical officer. *A familiar face*, Gellar thought, *if not really a friendly one. Maybe the old Prussian bastard has grown a sense of humor in the last few years.*

There was also a Fleet carrier, the CSS *Wasp*, commanded by Captain Minoru Tosake. Two wings of fighters, one of planetary strike craft, a squadron of minesweepers, various liaison, and support craft filled out the carrier's complement. The carrier provided invaluable screening and long-range strike capability, as well as planetary strike assets for what was otherwise a purely spaceborne force.

Two heavy cruisers, the CSS *Rudway* (commander, Captain Aleksander Pyotrovitch Gregov) and the CSS *Rangely* (commander, Captain William Jefferson Davis.)

The usual screen ships, four destroyers and six corvettes, and a replenishment group of two munitions ships, two tugs, a medical cruiser, and a heavy repair/reconstruction ship rounded out the Task Force. TF947's currently assigned medical cruiser, the CSS *Mercy*, was due to rotate into overhaul when relieved by the *Charity*.

Gellar was surprised to see one note that was in the TF947 data supplied by the *Charity*'s central computer. As long as TF947 was at Station Alpha, Rules of Engagement Bravo was in effect, rather than ROE Alpha, as in the rest of the Confederacy. Under ROE Bravo, Confederate Navy units were authorized to shoot first at any ship a commander deemed as hostile.

Interesting, Gellar concluded.

The *Charity*'s bridge was a joy. The captain's command chair sat in the center of the hemispherical chamber, facing an enormous view screen. To his front were the helm and navigation stations. The exec had a station to his left rear, security to the right rear. At the rounded rear wall were stations for engineering, signals, scanning, and tactical. The last station was somewhat perfunctory, as the *Charity* was unarmed and unarmored.

Exactly seventy hours and fifty-eight minutes after the change of command ceremony, Gellar was seated in his bridge chair, giving his first conning orders to the helmsman on watch.

"Clear all moorings."

A moment later: "Sir, all moorings are clear. We are clear to leave spacedock. Inertial dampers are on-line. All decks report secured for space."

"Very well. Navigation thrusters, back one third."

The great snow-white length of the ship began to back slowly out of the orbital berth. Blinking navigation lights winked on fore and aft, port, and starboard. Gellar looked up at the main screen, set now to show readings from the aft scanner. Outside the great frame of the dock's entrance, the stars shone steadily.

On an impulse, Gellar flipped up the small personal viewer set into the arm of his bridge chair and scrolled through the exterior scanners until he found the portside forward scanner. As the ship floated backwards, he focused the scanner on the view ports overlooking the docking bay near the retracting umbilicals. A tiny, red-haired figure stood at one of the larger view ports. Gellar increased the magnification. A grin spread across his face as he recognized the simian form of Angus MacKay, standing at attention and holding a salute as the *Charity* backed out of spacedock.

"Thank you, old friend," Gellar said in a whisper. He flipped the tiny screen back down again.

"Clear of space dock, sir. No ship traffic within ten kilometers," the helm reported a moment later.

"Very well." Gellar looked at the navigation readout. "Navigation thrusters, ahead full. Come to course one one five, positive one oh two."

"Coming around now, sir. Sir, we are on course, one one five by positive one oh two."

Regulations required the use of only navigation thrusters within ten kilometers of spacedock. Gellar watched the numbers on the main screen tick off slowly.

"Engage main engine. Ahead one third," he finally ordered.

"Star drive engaged, sir. Engine room answers ahead one third. Drive fields are building normally."

The *Charity* began to pick up speed, a faint but noticeable *thrum* echoing through the ship. The ship's cavernous mass tunnel began ingesting the faint ends of spaceborne matter, hydrogen atoms, and the odd iron filing, converting them to pure energy with almost one hundred percent efficiency, and converting the mass to thrust by means that Gellar never understood.

"We are at the space beacon, sir," Navigation reported. Helm chimed in: "Confirm, we are past the space beacon. Free to maneuver. All decks report secured for subspace."

"Thank you, Ensign. Ahead full."

"Engine room answers ahead full, sir," Helm repeated.

At full drive, it took the *Charity* four minutes to reach the subspace transit. A faint ripple vibrated through the ship, front to rear, and then the *Charity* leaped into subspace, bound for the border of Confederate space to make their rendezvous with Task Force 947. Captain Gellar was certain an exciting mission lay ahead. His expectations were to be played out tenfold.

The Goat Locker, near the chief's quarters

While the ship's officers had their wardroom, where meals were served and general lounging and socializing took place, the ship's chief petty officers had a smaller lounge located near the chief's quarters that was known, for reasons long forgotten, as the Goat Locker. Master Chief Gillespie and several other non-commissioned officers sat in the lounge now, watching the ship's departure on a large viewscreen set into the aft bulkhead.

"The Old Man seems to know his stuff," a chief gunner's mate commented.

"Anyone can drive a starship out of space dock." Gillespie snorted.

"Have you met with the new cap'n yet, Master Chief?" a voice called from the back of the room.

"Yeah," Gillespie answered, not taking his eyes from the viewscreen, currently set on the forward navigation scanner. "He seems all right, for a doctor. I'm not too sure about having a doc for a ship captain, but, I have to admit, Captain Clark did OK. This guy's pretty young, though. We'll see."

"Long as he remembers that the chiefs are the ones who get all the work done," a chief engineer's mate observed.

"Roger that." Gillespie chuckled.

A tall, hard-muscled figure in an off-duty gray coverall strode into the Goat Locker, looked around once, and nodded to Master Chief Gillespie. "Afternoon, Master Chief," he drawled, rendering the proper informal gesture of respect to the ship's ranking chief. He was Marine Gunnery Sergeant Paolo Anthony, the senior NCO of the ship's Marine contingent and, as a gunnery sergeant, the equivalent in rank to a Navy chief petty officer.

"Heading out again, eh?" Anthony noted somewhat rhetorically, taking a seat on the far end of the lounge couch from Master Chief Gillespie. "Good. I hate being in dock."

"Don't we all," Gillespie noted.

Anthony scratched his bristled head—like most male Marines, he wore his light brown hair in a style that had been known as "high and tight" since time immemorial. "Captain spotted you right off, Master Chief. Hero of the *Ranger* and all that."

"Damn. I wish people would forget about that. It wasn't that big a deal. And after thirty-six years, you'd think..."

On the viewscreen, the star field gave way to the weird, shifting patterns of subspace before the scanner filters adjusted.

"Under way," Anthony said.

"OK, everyone, show's over," Gillespie called. He stood up and switched off the big display screen, and then turned to face the assembly of *Charity*'s senior non-commissioned officers. "We've all got work to do, so everyone who's on watch, let's get to it. Gunny, you pull a late one last night?"

"Boarding exercise on the space dock's simulation suite. Figured I'd run one since we were in dock and all. Some of my kids want to try for Force Recon. I'm sure not going to discourage them." Anthony had himself served eight years in the Marine's elite commando force, and encouraged his troops to strive for that goal themselves. "And, of course, as poor spacies in the big city for a few days, the only time I could book the suite was from oh-three-hundred to oh-eight. I had a bunch of ragged-assed, sleepy Marines to run through the boarding exercise. The 'Good Guys' won, but only because the opposing force screwed the pooch on their defense. So, as part of the after-action review, I got to have a few young Marines for breakfast this morning."

The master chief laughed at that last. He had held similar 'counseling sessions'—more commonly known as ass-chewings— many times in his forty-year career. "Good deal. OK, I'm heading for my office." Gillespie's office was on Deck One, only a few steps from the bridge.

He hadn't thought much about the *Ranger* incident in quite a while, in spite of the framed Distinguished Service Medal on his office wall. It was a memory he'd rather leave thirty-six years in the past, where it belonged.

Chapter Three

A heavily damaged private yacht

The Grugell ships had done their job well. A few kilometers inside the border, a small private yacht drifted aimlessly, still trailing sparks and smoke into the vacuum of space. The lone occupant of the yacht lay in semi-conscious delirium, grievously wounded and burned to the bone by the fire that had swept his ship.

His burns alone would have killed almost anyone else, but this man was unwilling—indeed, unable—to die so easily. But the pain of his burns rendered him almost comatose, and as he moaned in his fever, memories assailed him, memories of other injuries, other burns, long before...

As morning drew near, the Turks had stormed the wall at last to set the great house ablaze. His followers scattered, prodded by his silent commands cracking like whips on their backs. *Go! Save yourselves! Seek me out when this battle is done.* He drove them away with thoughts that stung them like darts, and when that was done, he'd turned to face the Turkish heathen by himself. Their leader had broken the door of the house down himself and leaped into the entryway. A great, curved scimitar flickered in the firelight as the sweating warrior clutched it in his right hand, while a torch flickered in his left.

"Show yourself, monster!" the Turk had shouted, and like a shadow flowing from the very flags of the floor, he had obliged. "In Allah's name, die!" the heathen screamed, and sprang for him.

"You think I am to die so easily, Suleiman Bulut? Come then and try it! Die at my hands as your father did. I have fought your kind in all too many battles, but this one last Crusade I will still swear to see through to the end." He formed his hands into talons and struck at the infidel barbarian.

"It is not I who will kill you, monster," the Turk had gloated, parrying with the great sword, "but this!" The torch had jabbed into his face, making him scream in agony and reel away, smoke rising from his hair. "And them!" the Turk roared in triumph. Four of his warriors rushed through the doorway, carrying earthenware jugs. They dashed the jugs at him, shattering them against his cloak, covering him with oil. Bulut threw the torch at him, setting him ablaze from head to foot.

He had staggered, screaming, towards the window as the Turks roared in laughter at his pain. A lunge, and he was through the glass, blazing like a comet as he fell a hundred, two hundred feet into the river, far below.

It had taken time for Ionescu to recover. A year of regenerating flesh, bone, and skin while the Szgany followers tended him, fed him from their own bodies when necessary. Such devotion those Gypsies had shown him! Ionescu never knew what desire drove the Szgany to seek him out, why the call of a strong master inspired them to such faithfulness, but their service proved ever so valuable in that interval. For that, Ionescu would protect and safeguard them for hundreds of years afterwards.

When he recovered, though, a cold dish was to be served to Suleiman Bulut.

His revenge, that time, that had been sweet indeed, as he healed, recovered, walked again. And when Suleiman Bulut grew old, what joy Ionescu had taken in hunting down Bulut's grandchildren, taking and then killing his daughters, one by one, tightening a circle of death around the old, old man until at last he'd stood before his elderly enemy and laughed at the man's helplessness before striking him down.

The dreamed memories comforted him now, like a warm blanket. As he dreamed, his ship tumbled aimlessly along the edges of the Grugell frontier.

Fourteen days into the *Charity*'s journey

"Captain," the signals watch officer called from her bridge station, "I'm getting a faint signal. Sir, it's on a Confederate frequency."

"Bearing?" Captain Gellar yawned. It had been an uneventful trip so far, to say the least. He swiveled his bridge chair around to face the signals station.

"Ten degrees off the port bow, sir, twelve degrees positive."

"What sort of signal?" Commander Hoff wanted to know.

"Coming in a little stronger now, sir. Let me fiddle with it a little bit."

The ensign on signals watch was a good operator. She picked up a set of headphones, placed them on her head, and twirled several dials for a few moments.

"Sir, I have it. It's an automated distress beacon—computer says it's a private yacht, identification unknown but manufactured in the Confederacy."

"Exec?"

"Standing Order Twelve, sir," Hoff answered instantly.

Standing Order Twelve was a Confederate Navy regulation: Any CN ship detecting a distress beacon will investigate that beacon to the exclusion of all other duties.

"Very well. Helm, adjust our course to close on the beacon's source. Ahead full. Signals, do we have any range data?"

"Not yet, sir. Signal strength is weak, and that would normally indicate range of at least several light-days, but their signal strength may be down if they're damaged. Aspect is too bow-on to get a cross bearing. I should know more in another hour or so if we continue to close."

"Very well, Signals, thank you. Tactical, focus all forward scanners on the signal's source. Let me know as soon as you get a visual."

"Aye aye, sir."

"Sir, we are heading directly for the Grugell border. At present speed we'll hit the frontier in," Commander Hoff consulted the navigator's position chart, "six hours."

"Well, Standing Order Twelve doesn't include violating the Grugell border. If we hit the border, we'll resume our original course and report this to the admiral when we make our rendez-vous. *He* can sort out the diplomatic tangles."

Commander Hoff chuckled. "That's why he makes the big bucks, sir."

Five hours later, Gellar ordered the *Charity* to drop out of subspace as the forward scanners had finally picked up the source of the beacon, a tiny, sparkling dot just outside the zone defining the Grugell border. The flashing marker buoys were even in visible range beyond the craft.

As the scanners automatically adjusted magnification, the sparkling dot in space resolved into a small, private yacht, smoking in the aft section. The unmistakable marks of a Grugell anti-proton blaster dotted the yacht's hull.

"Captain," Ensign Ruark called from Tactical, "I'm showing someone still alive on the yacht. Structural damage is serious, but the ship should be salvageable. No sign of the Grugell ship anywhere in scanner range."

"You've got signs of someone alive?"

"Sir, I think so."

"You *think* so?"

"Yes, sir. Really strange readings, here, like someone's hurt really badly, but they're not fading. They've picked up noticeably since I first detected them."

"What do you mean?"

"Sir, it's almost like ... whoever it is on that ship is, well, *healing.*"

Before Gellar could consider that, the tactical watch officer spoke up again. "Captain, this far out there won't be just one Grugell ship. It's probably a task group centered on a battle cruiser at the least."

Commander Hoff agreed. "Call it five or six ships, sir. There will be the flagship, probably a battle cruiser, then two light cruisers, and two or three frigates. Maybe a carrier, too. That's standard for a border task group for the Grugell Navy."

"Their frigates are small enough to carry cloaking devices," Gellar mused. "They could be watching us right now."

"Roger that, sir. They won't cross the frontier with a cruiser or bigger, but Fleet Intelligence figures they sneak across in cloaked frigates once in a while. One lost his cloaking device to a malfunction in the middle of a convoy last year," Hoff said.

"I bet that was embarrassing."

"Forget embarrassing, sir, that ship's commander probably got disintegrated. He had two heavy cruisers escort him back to the border. He's lucky they didn't blow him out of space."

Gellar considered the situation. The risk was considerable; relations with the Grugell had been touchy at best recently. The *Charity* was within visual range of Grugell space and easily in range of a Grugell battle cruiser's main batteries. Task Force 947 was several days away under maximum drive. If there were to be an incident, the unarmed and unarmored *Charity* would be a sitting duck. There were treaties between Confederacy and Grugell that rendered dedicated hospital ships inviolate even in a shooting war, but Gellar had little faith in the Grugell's propensity to abide by treaties.

Nevertheless, he had taken an oath, as had every professional health care worker on this ship. They were required, by ethics, regulations, and Confederate and treaty law, to render assistance, and here in front of them, such assistance was required. There was really no decision to be made, not at all.

"Well, Exec, tell Tracking to get a tractor beam on that yacht. Bring her into the hangar bay. Inform Dr. Moses to bring an emergency team down; in fact, I'll go down myself. I want to see who was wandering around in a private yacht on the edge of Grugell space." He stood up. "Mr. Hoff, you have the deck. Mr. Bice has the conn," Gellar announced as he headed for the exit. "As soon as we get that yacht aboard, get us on a course that will take us at least a parsec straight away from the border before we turn back to our rendezvous with TF947."

It was only a few steps to the lift that took Captain Gellar to Deck Four, where the entrance to the hangar was found. Striding briskly, he quickly covered the distance through the now-familiar corridors, arriving at the entryway to the hangar bay to see Lieutenant Colonel Sandelescu and two Marines waiting by the airlock.

Sandelescu noted the footsteps behind her and barked at the Marines.

"Attention on deck!" The Marines snapped to attention. Gellar waved them off impatiently.

"As you were, as you were. What's going on?"

"Sir, they're bringing the yacht in now," Sandelescu pointed out crisply. The Marines relaxed a fraction of an inch.

There was a view port in the airlock door. Gellar took a look through.

The yacht was long, slim, sleek, and expensive. The narrow, charcoal-gray fuselage hung between streamlined pylons that supported *two* Gellar Star Drive tunnels. This private yacht was not only expensive, but with two Gellar drives it would be faster than most of the Fleet's single-seat fighters, and maneuverable as well. The hull was sleek, obviously designed for atmospheric transit as well as space travel, which was unusual. Standard practice in private yachts involved docking at skyhooks on settled planets, but this yacht was evidently—expensively—outfitted for dirt landings as well.

"Now there's a *rich* man's toy," he commented.

This rich man's toy showed the scars of a Grugell anti-proton blaster. Smoke still poured from a large hole in the rear of the main fuselage, and another in the front, which probably hit the cockpit. One of the Gellar drives was punctured through as well. This rich man was lucky to have escaped with his life.

As the invisible tractor beam settled the yacht to the floor of the landing bay next to one of *Charity*'s two small landing shuttles, the giant doors closed, and ventilation systems kicked in. Fresh air blew into the cavernous chamber, and ventilators sucked the billowing black smoke through purifiers.

"Sir," the security chief announced, "We have registration data on the yacht coming in now."

"So, who's our billionaire?" Gellar wanted to know. The air pressure in the bay had come up now, and damage parties were racing out to the yacht with firefighting equipment. The airlock door he was looking through slid open.

"*Trillionaire*, as it happens. Sir, this is the SS *Black Dragon*, registered to a citizen of Earth, Bel Ios. His occupation is listed as a trader in fine wines."

"That Bel Ios? I've heard of him. A trillionaire recluse, isn't he? He's almost never seen in public, *that* Bel Ios?"

"It would seem so, sir," Sandelescu affirmed.

"Well, Commander, shall we go see how our wealthy visitor is faring? If we can help him out, maybe he could donate a new battle cruiser or two to the Fleet—he can sure afford it." Taking the Marines by surprise, he spun on his heel and strode into the bay. Perturbed at being caught out, the Marines hurried after their captain, scurrying to take the lead position with their M65 rifles held at the ready.

A medical team led by the chief surgeon, Dr. (Captain) Andrea Moses, was just preparing to enter the yacht as Gellar walked up. Doctor Moses was short, slightly heavy, with short brown hair shot through with gray, but in an emergency, she was a dynamo. Seeing her in action was an education in itself.

The chief petty officer in charge of the damage party met them at the open port. He had smudges of soot on his uniform and one on his face, but seemed unharmed.

"Sir." He turned to the captain and saluted. "Fire's out. It's not pretty inside, sir. Fire pretty much ate up the main compartment. Only one pilot aboard." He turned to Captain Moses, a grimace on his face. "You're the doc, Ma'am, but me, I don't see how he could make it. Two of my boys are in there with him now."

"I'll have a look," Moses replied. "Captain Gellar, care to join us?"

"Of course!" Gellar replied. The relationship between a medical cruiser's captain and the chief surgeon was always delicate; the chief frequently forgot that the captain was, by regulation, a doctor as well, and on a hospital cruiser like the *Charity* the captain had to deal with the chief being his equal in rank and generally senior in time in grade. That alone required a high level of diplomacy.

They entered the ship, with the Marines leading the way. The port entered into a corridor, which led forward to the cockpit and aft to the living quarters. The CPO in charge of the damage party pointed forward. "They're in the cockpit, sir." Gellar stopped for a look around. The corridor seemed unharmed, but the smell of electrical fires was still strong.

Two of the firefighting team members were crouched next to a hunched figure on the floor of the burned-out cockpit. The Grugell blaster had indeed hit the ship right at the bulkhead that separated the cockpit from the rest of the ship, and the compartment had been pretty well consumed. Captain Moses hurried to the blackened figure on the floor, reaching into her bag for a med-scanner.

Incredibly, the charred form spoke.

"No... drugs..." The voice was a barely audible hiss.

"What was that?" Moses gaped, incredulous.

"No... drugs... allergic... reaction." The words came through an all too obvious haze of agony.

"Are you Bel Ios?" Gellar asked.

"Yesss…" The word trailed off into a whisper.

"OK, we have to get him to Emergency. Everybody, out of the way!" Captain Moses barked, taking charge of the situation. "You two," she pointed at two of her assistants "get that litter over here. You," she pointed at a young female medic "call ahead and tell ER One to be standing by. Patient has third, oh hell, third- and fourth-degree burns over entire body surface. Tell them to prepare a hyperbaric retention field, genetic analysis, and grafting gear, and get Doctor Wilson awake Get moving!

"Wilson's our best man on burns," she said to Gellar. "Not that it's likely to do much good."

Everybody scrambled to do the chief surgeon's bidding. Gellar smiled despite the obvious desperation of the case. He knew the hallmarks of a top-flight chief surgeon when he saw one. The medical techs gingerly lifted Ios onto the litter and, activating the grav-field nullifiers, floated him out the port and towards ER One.

"He isn't going to make it," Captain Moses announced. "Not burned like that."

"How can he possibly be *conscious*?" Gellar asked. "He's got to be in agony. Anybody burned half that bad should be comatose."

Moses shook her head. "I've never seen anybody burned that badly who was alive, much less conscious. I don't know what we can do other than try to keep him comfortable. He'll be dead within the hour." She walked off frowning, her attention focused now on the ship's only patient.

Lieutenant Colonel Sandelescu emerged from the smoking ruin of the yacht. "Nobody else inside, sir. Our guest was alone on his ship," she reported.

"Very well. Dismiss your men, Colonel," Gellar replied absently. "Why would he be out here on the fringe of Grugell space alone?"

"Don't know, sir. Maybe he tried to work a deal with the Grugell for some of their wines?"

"They have wine?"

"I'm told it's pretty awful, sir. I wouldn't know, personally." Gellar looked sideways at his normally inscrutable security chief. She showed no trace of a smile, but a twinkle played in the corner of her eyes.

"All right." The captain grinned. "All right. I'm going back to the bridge. Have one of your Marines keep an eye on our guest, for now. I'm not certain everything's completely kosher with Mr. Ios."

"Sir," Sandelescu replied, saluting. Gellar returned her salute with a wave, and then returned to the bridge. The remainder of a long, boring watch beckoned.

Chapter Four

En route to ER One

Bel Ios was, amazingly, conscious, although it wasn't apparent to the medics bearing his litter through the corridors. As he lay on the litter, floating through the ship, a raging conflict coursed through his battered system.

The searing pain from his burns was agonizing, but he could deal with it. It was only pain. The heathen Turk had burned him over a millennium before, as well as his would-be killers in England centuries after that. He had been burned by a terrorist bomb in France, by an explosion on the first colony on Hecate. He had been injured in a dozen different ways in a hundred or more wars and battles, but never as badly as this. Still, he'd recovered before, and given a little time and a little sustenance, he'd recover now.

What was proving difficult to control was his rage, and his hunger. Rage at the foul, ichor-filled alien beings who had attacked him, rage at the necessity of turning to mortal humans for help, rage at the damage his body suffered. His hunger was overwhelming; his body had extensive repairs to make, and his system screamed for sustenance. And here, all around him was what his body required. Over the smell of his own, ancient, scorched body he drank in the delicious, salty scent of food, and his cravings threatened to overwhelm him. He longed to leap from the litter and strike about him, to kill and feed, to rage unchecked among these mortal humans, but that would mean his final death here, on a military ship.

Control, he reminded himself over and over, *Control your urges. An opportunity will present itself.*

He already knew where the opportunity lay. The tall woman in the Marine's uniform, in the hangar bay—her mental aura was familiar to Ios. Indeed, very familiar. *One of mine!* his mind exulted on making the briefest feather-touch of contact. *One of the Followers, one of my Szgany, one of my children. What odds? I'd thought them long extinct.*

He relaxed a fraction, his rage cooling now. A fortuitous time lay before him now. All he had to do was regain his strength. He willed himself to relax, forced his mind into semi-torpor, allowing his thoughts to drift, back to another time, another burning…

Flames licked at the ancient monastery he'd chosen for a hiding place. Damn that Hemmings—that damned Englishman had tracked him even here!

Ios—he'd gone by Ionescu still in that long-lost day—rose up from his resting place. The smell of smoke filled the old monastery. He must flee before the old pile was consumed, but how? His senses reached out. Too soon! He could feel the sun beating on the outside of the ancient stone pile, seething on the stones, scorching the very tiles on the roof like acid. The scorching, golden death waited for him if he dared step outside the old stone building, and yet leave he must, as the interior was ablaze. Furniture, wood paneling, carpets, even in the old stone building there was more than enough to burn.

And Hemmings had done his work well, moving through the abandoned monastery as Ionescu slept, spreading kerosene throughout the building before striking his match. All around Ionescu the flames spread, eating the carpets, the tapestries, and the drapes. A large drapery fell, burning, and the sun poured in through a filthy window. Ionescu was forced to dance back away from the killing rays.

Oh, for a few weeks more, a mere few weeks of being flattering and charming at court, Ionescu told himself bitterly, and Victoria herself would have been under my control. With that done, enthralling her young son Edward, next in line for the throne, would have been child's play. Ionescu would have been the power behind Britain for generations.

That bastard Hemmings, he had to interfere! And now, he had nowhere to turn as the flames licked at him, setting his clothes to smoldering, licking at his hair, tearing at his flesh.

He could hear his enemy calling to him from outside, cajoling him, "Come out into the sunlight, Count Ionescu, come out or you shall surely burn!" Hemmings was no doubt standing safely in a beam of sunlight. How Ionescu longed to strike him down!

He'd staggered this way and that, with no way to escape, until he'd spotted a grate set into the ancient flagstones on the floor. His fingers had torn to bloody shreds against the hot metal, but finally he'd ripped the grate free and flowed into the hole, into a long, dark drain that opened finally into the malodorous and yet blessedly cool and dark sewers beneath London.

There had been no revenge that time, no sweet recompense for the injuries he had suffered. A girl selling flowers in the evening's dim light at the edge of the Thames had served to fuel him for his flight across

Europe, into the mountains he'd sprung from. He retreated there to hide, to emerge a century later with a new identity, his old attempt to corrupt England Herself forgotten. That time, he'd lost utterly and been forced to flee in disgrace.

Gamblers who play for great stakes stand to suffer great losses, and in Victorian England Ionescu had lost greatly. But it had been only that once.

A Grugell battle cruiser

Group Commander Tottalastrik had tendered his report, only to receive a terse message back from the Imperial Navy Command:

> YOU ARE TO PURSUE THE CRIMINAL IOS AND DESTROY HIM BY ANY MEANS NECESSARY. YOU ARE ORDERED BY AUTHORITY OF THE EMPEROR TO USE CLOAKED SHIPS IN CONFEDERATE SPACE. LONG RANGE SCANS INDICATE IOS SHIP PICKED UP BY A LONE CONFEDERATE NAVAL VESSEL. LAST KNOWN COORDINATES AND COURSE FOLLOW.

Tottalastrik was surprised. The Emperor Himself evidently wanted Ios dead.

Violating the Confederate border in a cloaked frigate wasn't exactly a routine matter, but it wasn't terribly uncommon, either. There were precedents.

Well, that's what group commanders were for: to carry out the difficult missions. He stabbed the button on his desk that summoned his personal aide.

"Tookliktak," he ordered, "it seems we are to pursue Ios even into the Confederacy. Get me a channel to the commanders of the three screen frigates. We'll transfer to Commander Kitrickstak's frigate; it has Flag quarters."

His aide looked at him blankly for a moment while the order sank in. Tottalastrik grinned evilly. "Go on, boy, get moving. We don't have all day to plan our invasion of the Confederacy, you know."

The Goat Locker, 1948 hours

The first few days under way were always stressful on any ship's non-commissioned officers, with the usual replacement of personnel bringing a leavening of fresh-faced new crewmen straight from their trades courses.

Eschewing a proper meal in the chiefs' mess a deck below, Master Chief Gillespie instead opted to build himself a thick ham sandwich from the supplies the ship's cooks kept stocked in the Goat Locker's capacious refrigerator. He took his sandwich, retrieved a cold Forestian ale, and seated himself at a table facing the viewscreen.

Second-rate space opera again, he noted with some chagrin. The entertainment system was tuned to a typical bit of light entertainment, having mostly to do with spies, high-speed air-car chases, and scantily clad young women. Several younger chiefs were gathered around watching. Gillespie preferred more cerebral entertainment; the Earth playwright Cord Andell was his favorite, and the ship had a small stock of his plays rendered into video. But Gillespie diplomatically surrendered to majority preferences for the most part, telling himself that it was, after all, in the interests of morale.

Besides, Gillespie had spent the last few hours badly distracted by something he couldn't quite put his finger on. Memories from the *Ranger* incident were preying on his mind.

What was it about the present that dragged his mind so back to the past?

He had been a young man, a boy really, when it had all happened thirty-six years before. The Dreadnought *Ranger* was assigned to Task Force 947.6, patrolling a section of the Grugell Frontier.

Nobody even knew how it started. Nobody ever found the killer. But a series of murders had taken place on the Ranger. They'd found the first body stuffed into a storage cabinet on Deck Four, near the engineering spaces. Crewman Second Class Genny Lindt had her throat torn out, and, strangely, no blood was found anywhere around the body, or anywhere else on the ship. And no blood remained in her body.

Two more bodies had been found in the next three days, all in similar circumstances.

Gillespie had been an engineer's mate third class then, just a fresh-faced kid with only four years in the Navy, and he wasn't involved in any investigation. On a ship with a crew of five thousand five hundred, he hardly knew what was going on at all.

But when the ship's Marine contingent began to close in on the killer, everyone got involved. Especially when, to avoid being taken alive, the murderer had set off an explosion on the ship that blasted the starboard weapons wing clear of the main body of the old dreadnought.

Over a hundred people were caught in that weapons wing, and the damaged, drifting structure was bleeding air. Thirty crewmembers had already been lost either in the explosion or blown into space when the wing blew clear.

Gillespie had run to the nearest airlock on the starboard side, and looking out through the port in the airlock door he could see the drifting wreckage only a few hundred meters away.

"We've got to get those people out of there," he shouted to the gathering crowd.

"Nothing we can do, son," a senior chief gunner's mate told him.

"I don't believe that," the young petty officer snapped. "There's got to be a way."

Racing to a nearby firefighting station, Gillespie found what he needed: an oxygen mask, a pressurized, fireproof coverall, a pair of heatproof gauntlets, and a heavy, pressurized CO2 fire extinguisher.

Back to the airlock he ran. "Can we get the docking umbilical over there?"

"Only if someone pulls it over somehow—there's no docking port on that wing and no tractor to haul the umbilical in. Won't do any good."

"It might." Gillespie turned to a pair of crewman-firsts that stood nearby. "You two, run to the nearest emergency locker and get me a spool of three-centimeter line and a Jacob's ladder."

Ten minutes later, he was ready. The senior chief tried to stop him, but Gillespie ignored the orders of his superior NCO and slammed the airlock door shut, scowling through the heavy polycarbonate window as he adjusted the oxygen mask. Then, with a slam of his hand on the activation plate, he blew the emergency seals on the airlock door.

The nylon and plastic Jacob's ladder was made fast on one end to the cleats on the airlock doorframe, which also made up the frame of the docking umbilical. A roll of three-centimeter nylon line was tied to the other end, and Gillespie trailed the rest of the line out behind him. He looked towards the wrecked weapons wing, drifting in space, moving slowly farther and farther away—it looked to be only about two hundred meters, and he had three hundred meters of line and fifty of Jacob's ladder. He aimed himself as best he could at the wing, pointed the fire extinguisher back at the *Ranger*, and fired a blast of CO2 into space.

A wild ride followed. He found himself blown towards the wrecked wing like a comet, racing in towards the severed portion of the ship. The absolute-zero cold of space was rapidly creeping into the heavy firefighting overall, but he had a job to do, and the cold was only cold. There hadn't been time to find a proper ENV suit.

He slammed into the severed face of the wing's bulkhead with shattering force. He spit some blood into the oxygen mask and gasped at the sudden pain of three broken ribs.

To his good fortune, there was a broken structural beam just to his left. He made the line fast to that, and began to haul in the small remaining amount of slack. Now, at least, the wing was made fast to the main body. Now he had to see to the rescue.

He pounded on the bulkhead until at last he heard a tapping in reply. A heavy, airtight door was nearby, and by going hand over hand along projecting bits of wreckage he managed to get over to it. A glance through the heavy poly viewing port showed a number of crew in the corridor behind the door, and they looked near panic.

Gillespie pressed the faceplate of the oxygen mask to the port and shouted, "I've got the wing tied off to the ship. I'm going to try to snake the docking umbilical over here to this port. Can you help make it fast from the inside?"

His answer came as a frantic nod from a chief gunner's mate inside the port.

Hand over hand again, the six meters to where the line was tied off. The nylon line had gone taut but held; the wing's movement away from the *Ranger* was halted.

Good thing they still teach line handling at the NCO *Academy,* Gillespie told himself. *I'd have never thought it would come in handy, but here we are.*

His luck was holding. Someone on the *Ranger* had read his mind, and the docking umbilical was already snaking loose from the airlock. He wedged himself in behind the broken beam, grabbed the line with both gauntleted hands, and began to heave.

It took four minutes, with his skin beginning to tighten with frostbite all around the seams of the suit. His oxygen level was running low as well; the mask's small, compressed emergency supply was only good for a few minutes. But in the end, he got the umbilical strung out to the severed wing, and managed somehow to wrestle the end of it to the airtight door. Using the line, he secured the umbilical from the inside in six places to the doorframe, and then went hand-over-hand again inside the heavy, steel-banded nylon snake back to the airlock door, laying the Jacob's ladder straight for the rescued crew to hand-over-hand back to the *Ranger*. He could already feel the hissing of air pumping into the umbilical as he frantically made his way back to the ship; as he reached the *Ranger*, the airlock door popped open. Air blasted out from the door into the under-pressure umbilical, but he managed to hang on to one of the passageway's reinforcing steel bands until several hands reached to grab his arms, dragging him into the ship. He collapsed on the deck, tore the oxygen mask from his face—and tore a strip of skin with it, where the heavy polymer had frozen to his skin. Gasping the wonderfully warm, fresh air of the ship, he pulled himself halfway up on one elbow before his strength failed him and he was driven into unconsciousness.

Gillespie awoke from a deep coma three days later to learn three things: The very senior chief who had told him his efforts would be useless had led a party of rescuers through the under-pressured, leaking umbilical to bring the trapped crew-members to safety; that he was now not an engineer's mate third class, but a bosun's mate second, and finally, when he overcame the pain of healing star burn and third-degree frostbite to turn his head, that there was a Distinguished Service Cross pinned to his pillow—the Navy's highest peacetime award.

A few weeks later, when the crippled dreadnought had arrived in spacedock, Gillespie also discovered that his name had become, overnight, a household word throughout the Confederacy.

But the identity of the murderer on the *Ranger* had never been discovered. It was presumed he'd died in the blast.

Nobody ever really knew.

And now, thirty-six years later, Master Chief Gillespie couldn't figure out why this long-ago memory was haunting him again, after all the time that had passed.

0600 hours the next morning

A persistent chiming greeted Captain Gellar when he stepped from his private shower. Grunting his annoyance, he padded over to the comm panel, dripping water on the carpet. He picked up the handset.

"Captain speaking," he barked.

"Captain, this is Doctor Moses. You'd better see this. Our patient is in Room 601."

"Very well, give me ten minutes." He set the handset back in its cradle.

He's still alive? Gellar thought with some amazement. *I wonder why they moved him from* ER *to a room?*

He picked up the handset again, this time punching the code to 'page.'

"Executive Officer, call the captain's quarters. Executive Officer, please call the captain's quarters."

He was dried off and halfway dressed when the handset chimed again. "Captain speaking," he answered.

"Exec here, sir. What's happening this early?"

"Exec, meet me in Room 601. Our Mr. Ios survived the night. I guess Doctor Moses has something to show us."

"On the way, sir. I'm on the bridge, I'll be there in five minutes," Hoff answered.

As it turned out, they met in front of the door to Room 601 exactly four minutes later.

"Good morning, Captain," Commander Hoff greeted Gellar. "He's survived? I wouldn't have bet a penny on it."

"Me either, Exec, but Doctor Moses seems pretty uptight about it. Shall we have a look?" Gellar indicated the door. They went through, wondering what to expect, but nothing in either's experience could have prepared them for what they saw.

Bel Ios, trillionaire recluse, lay on his back in the white-sheeted bed. Around him, the faint shimmer of a mild force field held in a hyperbaric atmosphere. His charred clothing had been removed the night before, and a hospital gown covered his torso, while his face...

No, it can't possibly be, Gellar told himself, leaning in for another look.

His face was over halfway healed. Charred flakes of skin were peeling from the new, pink skin that was growing rapidly over the burned patches. The V-necked hospital gown revealed the same thing on Ios' chest.

"Ever seen anything like it, Captain?" Doctor Moses' voice came from the corner of the room. She was somewhat disheveled. Gellar assumed correctly that she'd been sitting there all night.

"No, I don't know what to think," Gellar replied. "Is he... human?"

Doctor Moses stood up, stretching. She walked over, pulling Gellar to a corner of the room and speaking in a low voice. "Well, his baseline readings are human, but there are some abnormalities, to put it mildly. His metabolism runs at an abnormally fast rate, but his hemoglobin levels are abnormally low." The chief surgeon turned to face Gellar directly. "We're talking, low as in 'incompatible with *life*.' And look at his face."

Gellar looked over at the bed. Ios' face was odd, his nose narrow and almost beaklike, his jaw long and angular, and his high forehead led into a receding hairline. *Even his hair is growing back already*, Gellar noted belatedly.

Doctor Moses continued: "He's got skeletal deformities, especially craniofacial malformations, that I'm at a loss to explain. His muscle tissue is, well, extremely dense—our friend here, healthy, would be considerably stronger than any three of Colonel Sandelescu's young Marines. And his spinal cord is almost twice as large in cross-section as normal."

"Twice?" Gellar gaped at the sleeping figure. "What you're describing isn't possible! He'd have to have, what, fifteen, twenty different mutations at multiple loci?"

"More like forty."

"So, what is he? Is he human?" He walked back to the bed, leaning to examine Ios' face more closely.

He jumped suddenly as Ios' eyes snapped open. The eyes were deeply bloodshot and had a strangely feral look to them.

"You are Captain Gellar." A deep, sepulchral voice emanated from the burnt figure. It wasn't a question so much as a statement.

"Yes, I'm the commander of this ship. Do you know where you are?"

"Yes, Captain, your Doctor Moses was most forthcoming. I'm on the Confederate Navy Medical cruiser *Charity*. I understand you have my yacht in your hangar bay?"

"Yes, we do. It's severely damaged but salvageable. My engineering department will be doing an evaluation later today."

Ios nodded once, grimacing. "Then it seems I owe you my gratitude, Captain."

"Can you tell us why the Grugell attacked you, Mr. Ios?" Commander Hoff asked.

"I suppose I wandered over their border, and they took offense," Ios offered. "I am aware that it is against Confederacy law to violate the Grugell frontier, but I've been having some difficulty with my navigation computer. Perhaps, Captain, your engineers can advise me on repairs?"

"Yes, I'll speak to them. If you'll excuse me, Mr. Ios, I need to return to my bridge. I'm pleased you are recovering well, sir. I'll speak with you again soon. Exec?" Gellar motioned towards the door.

In the corridor, Commander Hoff gaped at his captain. "Sir, what the bloody hell... How could he... I mean, how could anyone possibly heal that quickly? He was burned to the *bone*—I saw him!"

"I don't know, Wils," Gellar replied, startling his exec with the use of his first name. "I'll tell you what, though. Get hold of Colonel Sandelescu. I want one of her Marines outside that door. Oh, and find some excuse to call Doc Moses out of there—from here on out nobody goes in there alone. I don't know what the deal is with the mysterious Mr. Bel Ios, but something just isn't right."

"Yes, sir, I'll see to it."

Chapter Five

The bridge, 1038 hours

"Sir, I've got a message coming in." The call from the signals watch officer tore Gellar out of a bored semi-haze.

"From TF 947?"

"No, sir," the young ensign replied. She bent over the panel, whispering with the petty officer on the signals panel. "No, he claims to be the commander of a Grugell task group. Sir, he's sending a video signal, and requesting to speak to the captain."

"Very well." Gellar got up and stretched. "We're still pretty close to the border. Transfer it into the conference room. Let's see what they want."

A small conference room was just off the bridge, connected by a hatchway just to the left of the main entrance. Gellar headed that way, seating himself before an auxiliary signals panel on the conference table. He tapped a stud on the panel.

"OK, Signals, put him through."

The pinched, snow-white face of a Grugell officer swam into view on the panel's small viewscreen.

"You are the captain of the Confederate ship I have on my scanner?"

"Yes, I'm Captain Gellar. This is the medical cruiser CSS *Charity*. Who are you?" Gellar was a bit put off by the Grugell captain's tone.

"I am Group Commander Tottalastrik VI. We are in pursuit of a dangerous criminal, and our scans indicate you've picked up his ship."

"You're in violation of treaty, Group Commander, if you're close enough to scan our ship. You are in Confederate space, without a diplomatic passport."

"Captain." Tottalastrik folded his long white fingers together in front of his face. "You are aware that the treaty allows border crossings in the event of hot pursuit, I'm certain. We are in pursuit of the criminal Bel Ios of the Confederacy."

"Criminal?" Gellar was startled for a moment, but only a moment. "What did he do?"

Tottalastrik actually looked confused for a moment. "It's hard to describe, Captain. We suspect he is carrying illegal mutagenic agents. He is accused of biological warfare against the Grugell Empire."

"Come on, now, Group Commander, biological warfare? One man, listed in our records as a trader in wines?"

"Trader or no trader, are you harboring this criminal on your ship?"

"Group Commander, Bel Ios is on our ship. He is recovering from severe burns suffered when, it appears, a Grugell anti-proton blaster struck his ship. This is a hospital, Group Commander, and any patient in our hospital is afforded full protection under interstellar treaty and Confederate law. Also, Mr. Ios is a Confederate citizen, and we are in Confederate territory. If you wish to press any sort of charge against him, the Empire will have to seek extradition in the Confederate courts."

"Captain, you are harboring a monster."

"I have no reason to think so," Gellar lied.

"I will give you a reason, Captain. Please wait one moment. My communications staff are preparing to beam you a video stream taken earlier this week on the Grugell border planet Itstek."

The scene on the small viewer shifted suddenly to a force-field-contained cell, very similar to the ones in the *Charity*'s tiny brig. Evidently a hand-held camera was used, for the picture wavered several times, scanning roughly back and forth across the seemingly empty cell.

With startling suddenness something dropped into view from the ceiling.

It obviously had once been a Grugell, but no longer. What must have been a truly blood-curdling shriek issued tinnily from the panels' speaker as the creature slammed itself against the force field, throwing a shower of sparks.

Very little was known of Grugell biology and evolution, but Gellar had no problem imagining that a very early ancestor of the race may have looked something like this. The creature stood on all fours, gasping in exertion from trying to break the field. Black, stiff hair rose in a mane from its head, tapering down its back to a point above the hips. Brushes of stiff black hair ran down the rear of all four limbs and sprouted from the clawed fingers as well. The normally self-possessed face of a Grugell was replaced by some-thing out of a nightmare, a fanged, wolf-muzzled monstrosity with glowing, crimson eyes.

As Gellar watched, the horrific thing melted to the floor as though its skeleton were suddenly transformed to liquid and flowed to the back wall, up to the ceiling, and out of sight. A prolonged hiss came from the cell, lingering after the thing had disappeared from view.

The picture broke away, and the face of Tottalastrik swam back into view.

"He left three of these things on Itstek, Captain. They are—were—three former miners, citizens of the Grugell Empire, with families to support. The one you saw was Portamastok III, a shift chief with four wives and sixteen children."

Gellar shook his head, distracted for a moment by the candid description of Grugell polygamy. "And you claim Ios did this? How?"

Tottalastrik looked doubtful for a moment, an expression Gellar had never seen on a Grugell before. He rubbed his chin with one black-clawed hand and looked away for a moment before replying. "I'll be honest with you, Captain, we don't know how he did it."

"Then how do you know *that* he did it?"

"Captain, how we know it is none of your affair." Tottalastrik leaned forward. "I am making a formal request that you turn him over to us to face Grugell justice."

"I'm afraid I can't do that, Group Commander."

"You are aware that you are under the main batteries of a Grugell frigate, Captain?"

"I figured as much, since our scans don't pick up any ships in the area. You're obviously running cloaked. You are also aware that you are not only on the wrong side of the border and in violation of treaty, but also that we as a designated and marked medical ship are protected by that same treaty? Even in the event of war, Group Commander, your own laws forbid you to fire on us." Gellar grinned at the screen. "What is the penalty for breaching an interstellar treaty in the Grugell Navy, Group Commander?"

Tottalastrik looked as though he'd just swallowed a liter of something bitter. "Very well, Captain. I will consult with my superiors regarding the necessary extradition proceedings."

"And, I trust, you will return to your own territory?"

The Grugell commander terminated his signal without reply.

Gellar got up and walked back to the bridge, where the tactical watch officer was just shouting out a contact report:

"*Grugell frigate decloaking*, five kilometers to starboard! He's turning away, turning to starboard, I got a bearing change." The lieutenant looked up at Gellar. "Sir, he just popped up out there out of nowhere. Looks like he's heading back for the border now."

"Very well. Keep an eye on him, make sure he keeps going."

"Sir," Commander Hoff pointed out, "a group commander in the Grugell Navy is the equivalent of a rear admiral. That boy is in command of a task group. If he only brought his cloaked ships, figure that's at least three frigates."

"He may have only brought one since he's taking a chance by crossing the border, Exec."

Hoff looked doubtful. "I don't know, sir. Recommend we maintain tactical alert status until we rejoin the Fleet."

"Very well, Exec, that's a good idea. We'll just be a little paranoid as long as we've got Ios with us. Alert Status One, all exterior scanners to be operating and manned on all watches until further notice. Helm, all ahead full. Let's pick up the pace a little bit. The sooner we get Ios off this ship, the better it suits me."

Five kilometers to the *Charity*'s port side

"Commander Gopratisk's frigate just came out of cloak as ordered, sir."

Tottalastrik waved a hand at his flagship's commander to acknowledge the report. Gopratisk would make a show of proceeding out of the area in plain view, while the other three frigates under Tottalastrik's command let the Confederate hospital ship proceed, dropping in its wake under cloak to follow. His orders were simple: *Follow the Confederates. If the monster Ios takes his ship out of their hangar, destroy him.*

Room 601

It had been many years since Ios, as even he now thought of himself, had been around so many people.

So many years, he thought, *so many years gone by since I've been so badly hurt. Not even at the hands of the heathen Turk was I so badly burnt as by those evil-spirited, foul-blooded aliens.*

His injuries had been severe, but his system was coping well. But his body had drawn on the last of its already depleted reserves to accomplish the healing, and he was dangerously close to losing control.

The temptation! All around him, he could smell the sweet, salty tang he craved. Every one of these Navy doctors and nurses came in and out bearing the wonderful smell, trailing a hot aura of the delicious scent. He could hear their pulses rushing in their veins, their hearts pounding to drive the life-giving fluid throughout their bodies. And his hungers in other areas were growing as well, as his body regained its strength. An hour previously, a pretty young nurse had come to take a blood sample—*Ahh, the irony!* Ios told himself—and he had almost been beside himself with raging, primal lust.

To feed the body is one thing, he thought, *but to feed the baser appetites of the soul is another, and it has been nearly a century. I've secluded myself for, perhaps, too long.*

Still, I must keep myself in check! His hungers would not override his survival instincts, not yet. *That captain is a smart one, and this Doctor Moses suspects something.* Ios' hearing, more acute than anyone could possibly suspect, had heard every nuance of the whispered conversation in the room as he feigned sleep. *I must contrive to keep them from discussing my conditions further.*

It will not be easy. They are strong-willed people.

Ios' weak telepathic ability had tickled at both minds, only to find two of a kind—highly disciplined, intelligent, and iron-willed mentalities. His abilities in this respect were limited. *I cannot control these two. I can only influence.*

He forced his body to relax. *Bide your time*, he told himself. *There is one of mine on this vessel. Her blood speaks to me. I must will this one to this place.*

His eyes closed; his face relaxed. Outside the room, a Marine glanced through the tiny viewing window in the doorway.

"Hmmph," the Marine grunted. "Asleep again."

He couldn't have been more wrong.

Chapter Six

The wardroom, 1645 hours

Lieutenant Colonel Sandelescu rarely shared a meal with anyone else in the crew, and this afternoon was no exception. After ordering and receiving her customary evening salad and turkey (cloned) sandwich, she skirted a table of four chattering ensigns to take her tray to her usual seat at a table against the back wall of the compartment.

Damn dry stem-cell meat, she thought for the hundredth time after taking a bite of the sandwich. The Navy had pioneered the technology decades earlier, and now every ship carried a variety of stem-cell cultures from which to grow a variety of favored portions of meat. The nutrient broth for the process was easier to store and took up less space and energy than an equivalent freezer space for frozen meats, and the Navy was in love with space saving—on starships that often ran as much as three kilometers long and one wide.

Sandelescu took another bite, chewed briefly, swallowed with a grimace, and picked moodily at her salad. While few people complained, if asked most would tell you that the cloned meats just didn't taste the same, even though the Navy biologists that ran the project insisted that there was no measurable difference. *There are three ways to do everything*, Sandelescu thought wryly. *There's the right way, the wrong way, and then there's the Navy way.*

She pushed her tray away, thinking suddenly of the ship's "guest," currently in a bed on Deck Six.

Maybe I'll go pay our visitor a call, she thought. *Sure nothing keeping me here.* She cast a final disparaging look at the remains of her supper before tossing the tray in the cleaning port and leaving the wardroom.

Room 601

And so, this child of my children's children still answers my call, even if she knows it not, Ios told himself, somewhat smugly.

He opened one eye to peer at the back of the Marine guard's head, just visible through the small view port in the door. The young man's mind was clear, hard, disciplined. *Such strong people,* he thought. *Were this Marine commander not one of my own blood, I'd have no hold over her at all.*

He didn't have long to wait. Within ten minutes after he sent his telepathic call, the raven-haired form of the Gypsy woman appeared in the open doorway.

"Good afternoon, Mr. Ios," she said, looking about the room somewhat uncomfortably.

"Good afternoon, my dear. Won't you please sit down?" He extended a long-fingered hand towards the chair next to his bed.

"Thank you." After a moment's hesitation, she perched herself stiffly on the edge of the seat.

"You are a Marine," Ios pointed out, examining Sandelescu's blue uniform.

"Yes, sir, I am. I'm Lieutenant Colonel Sandelescu. I'm the commander of the Marine contingent on the *Charity,* and I'm in charge of security."

Better and better still, Ios thought. "You? Such an attractive girl in such a serious position." He reached for her hand, feeling her flinch away. A telepathic nudge calmed her.

"Sir, I just wanted to —"

"You wanted to question me briefly. You are concerned as to any possible security risk I might pose for your ship," Ios interrupted.

"Well, yes."

"Dear, I assure you, I intend nothing more than to heal my body, have my ship repaired, and be on about my business."

"I'm sure you are, sir. However, you are known to have been in Grugell space only recently, and you understand how I should evaluate any possible risk."

"Of course."

"Can you tell me what you were doing in Grugell space?"

"Of course, dear. I visited a mining colony; I believe it was called Itstek. I do visit Grugell border settlements regularly to trade Confederacy wines for Grugell, ah, beverages."

"And, sir, you do have the proper permits for cross-border trading, and for dealing in intoxicants?"

"You already know that I do, do you not?" Ios replied with a wolfish grin.

"Actually, yes. I had my clerk pull your licenses from our database earlier today."

Ios patted Sandelescu's hand; she had forgotten he had placed his palm over her left hand, his touch being feather-light. On the index finger of that hand, his fingernail began to slightly elongate, growing in a few seconds to a claw-like point. A drop of clear fluid gathered on the tip of his finger, just under the nail.

"And yet you asked, in order to see my face as I answered." His grin broadened.

"I suppose—ouch!" She jumped slightly as his fingernail scratched her skin slightly. The drop of liquid fell from his fingertip onto the slight break in Sandelescu's skin and, as though it were sentient, flowed immediately into the scratch and disappeared.

"I'm sorry—did I hurt you, my dear?" Ios crooned.

"No... It's just a scratch..." A whirling dizziness assailed the Marine suddenly, passing only in moments, leaving a strange lassitude.

"Yes, it is. And now, my dear Colonel, you will listen carefully to me," Ios droned hypnotically. "Look into my eyes, child."

Sandelescu turned to look into eyes that glowed now like coals. Trapped, like a bird faced with a cobra, her will was gone.

"You, my dear, are one of mine, flesh of my flesh, blood of my blood. Have your parents, your grandparents, told you any tales of the Old One? Of old Belos, the Master?"

"No."

Ios shrugged. "It matters not. Your blood remembers me. I am the Old One, child; I own your mind, your soul, and now I own your body as well. Flesh of my flesh now, indeed. Now, there are things I must tell you, and instructions that you must carry out for me before I depart this room, this ship. Listen carefully!"

Ios went on to explain at some length, while Colonel Sandelescu sat, enthralled, her will no longer entirely her own.

Room 601, 1800 hours

Two hours into the second watch, Captain Gellar again found his footsteps heading for Deck Six. As ordered, a Marine was standing post at the door to Room 601. Gellar knocked once and walked in.

A surprise! Lieutenant Colonel Sandelescu was seated in a chair at Ios' side, listening intently to something Ios was muttering in a low voice. Gellar announced himself politely.

"Good evening, Mr. Ios. Colonel," he added, nodding to Sandelescu.

"Captain." Bel nodded. Not even a scar was visible now on his long, angular face.

"Mr. Ios," Gellar greeted him. "I see you're feeling better."

Bel Ios stretched a bit in the hospital bed. He raised one arm to rub an incredibly long-fingered, sharp-nailed hand along his pointed chin. "Why yes, Captain," he replied. "I'm feeling very recovered. In fact, I'm anxious to return to my ship! I've much to put to rights." *And there is much I must prevent your repairmen from examining too closely.*

"I'm sure you do, Mr. Ios. My engineering department is completing an evaluation of your ship's damages now, and they inform me that we have most of the parts on board to complete your repairs. We will of course have to bill you at standard rates for parts and repair work, in accordance with Navy regulations."

Ios waved a hand in annoyance. "Of course, Captain, I can easily afford that."

"I'm sure you can, sir. There is one shortfall, however. One of your Gellar tunnels is beyond repair with the parts we have on hand. We'll have to complete the job when we rendezvous with Task Force 947. The Fleet repair ship will have the parts you need. In fact, it would be much easier for you to take your ship to the repair ship to have your repairs finished there."

"Is there no way to speed the process, Captain? I'd be quite willing to pay for a shuttle to bring the parts to us."

"I'm sorry, but Naval regulations prohibit it," Gellar informed him. "Shuttles aren't allowed to leave a formation outside a planetary system."

"I see," Ios replied, looking somewhat disappointed.

"I see you've struck up a friendship with my security chief, here."

"Yes, I have indeed." Ios reached out one of his strangely claw-like hands and patted Sandelescu's arm where it rested on the armrest of the chair. "She's a charming young lady." Gellar blinked at that. He hadn't heard *that* term ever used to describe his stern, no-nonsense security chief. Colonel Sandelescu smiled somewhat absently, but offered no comment.

"Mr. Ios," Gellar began, "I really have to ask you, my own curiosity as a medical doctor—"

"Of course, Captain." Ios interrupted. "You're wondering how I healed so quickly?"

"Well, yes. You have to admit it's a bit unusual."

"More than a bit, yes, Captain?" Ios grinned, revealing oddly pointed, interlocking teeth. A strange sparkle entered his still bloodshot eyes. *A trick of the light?* Gellar wondered.

"The answer is simple, Captain, although it was expensive." Gellar raised his eyebrows. "Nanotech robots," Ios added. "There is a facility that answers to neither the Confederacy nor to the Grugell, on a small system at the edge of the Confederacy-Grugell border. This facility has both Confederate and Grugell castoffs in residence, renegades I suppose, who have made a specialty of supplying technology that is, to put it mildly, frowned upon in other parts of the settled Galaxy."

"And where exactly is this 'facility'?" Gellar asked. "One of the Rim Worlds, or somewhere else?"

"Of course, Captain, I may not tell you that, as you know," Ios chided.

"And you, Mr. Ios, understand that I am required to ask nonetheless."

"Of course. But we digress, yes?" Gellar noted that Ios had a strangely formal manner of speaking, and an almost hypnotic way of crooning his sentences. *Could that be the reason for the bemused expression on Colonel Sandelescu's face?*

Ios continued. "At any rate, the nanotechs. On this facility, of which I really must speak no further, I paid an astronomical sum to have a quantity of nanotech devices injected into my body. These nanotechs, Captain, are capable of regenerating skin, flesh, bone, similar to the way auto-repair droids mend unmanned space platforms."

"Our bioscans indicated nothing of that kind, Mr. Ios. How is it that we didn't detect these nanotech devices?"

"I imagine they are shielded in some manner, Captain. Does Confederate law not proscribe the creation of cybernetic organisms? I am certain that devices such as these are in fact illegal. I admit to their existence for two reasons only. First, you obviously know there is something unusual in the manner of my speedy recovery, and second, the nanotechs are obviously beyond the ability of Confederate science to detect."

"You understand that I am required to file a report of this conversation with Third Fleet Intelligence when we reach the Task Force we're assigned to. However, since we cannot detect these nanotechs, I can't hold you here for any reason. I'd like you to stay in this room for the night, and if Doctor Moses approves your recovery, in the morning you'll be free to leave medical care. I'll have you assigned to guest quarters until your yacht is repaired."

"Yes, of course."

"Then, Mr. Ios, I'll say goodnight. Good evening to you as well, Colonel."

"Good evening, sir."

I have to talk to Doc Moses about that, Gellar thought as he left the room. *Nanotechs? I've never heard even a rumor of any such thing!*

Strangely, though, the thought was forgotten by the time Gellar reached the lift shaft.

The hangar bay, the next afternoon

"Hey, Audrey, hand me that plasma coil."

Engineer's Mate Second Class (EM2c) Tomas Guerra and EM1c Audrey Ophell were busily engaged in repairing the *Black Dragon*'s control suite, and flirting at the same time, as they generally did when they were assigned a task together.

"So, Aud, are you gonna be by the Deck Four lounge tonight after shift?"

"Why?" Ophell teased. "You got something in mind?"

"Me?" Tomas feigned an innocent look. "No, not me. I'm just curious."

"Yeah, right. Hey, did you hear something?"

The two techs paused for a moment, and then resumed their banter.

Two meters away, in the main cabin, Bel Ios froze as the two paused, then relaxed slightly as the conversation began again. They had not yet examined anything in the cabin, and that was good. But now, Ios determined to make sure that these two would not report anything untoward they found on the *Black Dragon*.

He floated forward towards the hatch to the control suite. Reaching the open hatch, he let his senses flow outward, into the control suite. The sensations that assailed him were almost irresistible! *But now, now, at last,* he thought. The two minds before him were young, malleable, accustomed to accepting orders. He reached in with his awareness, touching the male and shutting his mind down, touching the female and putting her into a fugue state, before gliding into the cabin.

EM2c Guerra slumped to the deck deep in coma, and before EM1c Ophell could react a fist clamped shut on her mind, leaving her aware but unable to react. A strange lassitude settled over her, and she closed her eyes for a moment. She opened them again at a shuffling sound. The sight before her was horrifying at some deep level, but all she could manage now was mild surprise.

Her friend, Tomas Guerra, was laid out on the deck, and crouched over him was a horrible figure, batlike, hissing. Its face dropped to Tomas' neck, pausing only for a few moments before turning to her. Eyes shone like coals in the pointed, elongated face of the thing as it drifted towards her. "Ahh, yes," a deep, chuckling voice sounded, "and so young, too!" A claw-like hand reached for her, and began unfastening her coverall as the face dropped to her neck. The pinpricks of white-hot pain made her flinch slightly, but then another wave of languor washed over her. She slumped to the deck, barely conscious, as the clawed hands found their way inside her clothing.

Ophell gasped as the engineer's coverall was suddenly stripped away from her body, and then the dark form flowed over her, entering her, surging inside her, and the teeth fastened again in her neck.

She knew nothing more after that.

The chief surgeon's office

"I tell you, Andrea, something's not right here!"

An upset chief nurse was something every doctor hates to face, and Andrea Moses was no exception. She leaned back in her huge, plush swivel chair behind an expansive desk of black polymer, unconsciously distancing herself from her angry chief nurse.

"We can't just let this man walk out of the ward! It's not responsible!" Commander Julia Cartwright was red-faced with consternation.

"And why not? You've seen his chart. He's completely healed."

"In twenty-four hours?"

"Yes, in twenty-four hours," Doctor Moses snapped. "We can't hold a healthy man in the ward against his will, no matter how quickly he heals."

"But... it's just not possible!"

"Sit down, Julia. Sit down, and let's just relax and talk through this a little, OK?" An appeal to reason won through, and Chief Nurse Cartwright dropped into a chair. "Julia, we've worked together for almost twenty-five years now, right?"

"Yes, something like that."

"And we've both seen lots of strange things, right?"

"Yes," the chief nurse admitted.

"So, this is another one."

"I'm sorry, Andrea," Cartwright replied. "I just don't buy it. Nanotechs? Who's ever heard of such a thing?"

"It's technologically feasible, you know that."

"And illegal."

"So? If we can't detect them, we can't charge our Mr. Ios with violating the Cybernetics Act, now can we? And can you think of any other reason for his recovery?"

"So where is our esteemed guest now, anyway?"

"I don't know," Doctor Moses answered. "He's not a prisoner, you know. He can go anywhere he likes, except the bridge and the engineering spaces. Maybe he's looking over the damages to his yacht. Maybe he's wandering the greenhouse space. Who knows?

When was the last time you got down to the greenhouse, Julia? You're looking a little pale"

"It's been a while," Cartwright admitted.

"Get down there for at least an hour after your shift ends," Doctor Moses ordered. "Got to get your sunlight, even if it is artificial. You need your Vitamin D."

"Yes, ma'am."

Deck Four lounge

Ios followed the corridor around the slight curve of the ship's bulb-like forward section. Somewhere up here would be a lounge, a nightclub really, and Ios was still hungry.

A thumping sound coming from a large double hatchway betrayed the lounge. Ios entered, looked around cautiously.

The Deck Four lounge appealed mostly to the younger members of the crew, thirty or so of whom were in the lounge now, mostly in their off-duty clothes. A music system blasted a heavy bass synthmusic into the darkened compartment, and dim red and blue lights were strung along the upper half of the bulkheads. A heavy smell of sweat, perfume, and alcoholic drinks pervaded the room.

Perfect, Ios thought.

He took a seat in a corner, facing out over the room. Putting his acute senses to work, he began scanning and evaluating the female clientele in the lounge.

One, a petite blonde girl, was engrossed in conversation with a young man with round glasses. Ios sensed the heavy smell of sexual excitement from both; he'd have no luck there.

Another woman, tall and brown-haired, sat alone at the bar. Ios focused on her, watching intently. But after a moment a tall

Marine sergeant came in, greeted her warmly and sat on the stool next to her. No good.

An hour passed, then another, as Ios slowly sipped at a glass of red wine. People came and went as the evening went on, until finally a commotion in the far end of the lounge caught Ios' ear.

"Didi, you've had enough," a female voice protested.

"You let me be th' judge of that!"

Ios sought out the source of the slurred reply. It was a tall but slightly heavy woman, older than most of the crewmembers in the lounge, with a few streaks of gray in her black hair. Her scent was tinged with the tang of a habitual and heavy drinker.

Perfect, he thought.

The woman's companion rose from her chair and left in disgust, trailing the hot scent of anger as she swept out of the lounge. Ios rose slowly, walked across the lounge to where the black-haired woman was trying to signal the drink server droid.

"All alone?" Ios' face shifted, gentled, softened. He damped the fire of his eyes, forcing them to a neutral black. His hands shortened, and his chitin chisel nails retracted to almost normal.

"Yes, I am now," the woman slurred. "You wan' sit down?"

"Indeed, I would. Let me get you something," Ios smiled.

"Thanks. You're a handsome fella." The woman laid a hand on Ios' arm. "Where you work? I don' 'member seeing you before."

"I'm a passenger, dear lady," Ios replied.

"Name's Didi," she hiccupped.

"And you may call me Belos," Ios said. He looked briefly into the woman's alcohol-befuddled mind, knowing exactly which libidinous switch to trip.

"Good, I'll do that."

She tossed back the drink Ios ordered her with startling speed and gave him a smile that had probably been dazzling a few short years earlier. "Well, you wan' hang 'round here all night?"

"I have a lovely bottle of Corinthian wine in my stateroom," Ios informed her. He looked around quickly. Nobody was paying any attention to him, or her.

"Corinthian, eh? Soun's like good stuff. Le's go, Handsome, it's your lucky night." She grabbed Ios' hand and pulled him towards the exit.

Chapter Seven

The bridge, the next morning

What was it I was going to talk to Doctor Moses about?

Captain Gellar was a little concerned with his own absent-mindedness. *I'm not usually this forgetful,* he chastised himself. *What's wrong with me today?*

He twirled his bridge chair around to face the signals station. "Ensign Lynch, any traffic from TF947?"

"No, sir, not since yesterday evening."

"Thank you," Gellar replied absently.

"Everything all right, sir?" The exec was always attuned to the finer details of shipboard life, as a good executive officer should be. Wils Hoff was an exceedingly good executive officer.

"I guess I'm a bit distracted, Exec," Gellar answered. "This thing with our guest, Mr. Ios, I suppose. Have you ever seen anything like that?"

"No, sir, not in sixteen years in the Navy. But then, I'm an engineering puke, sir, not a doctor." The exec grinned at the last remark. Navy regulations required a non-medical type as the second-in-command on medical cruisers, to provide a tactically proficient backup to the doctor in command.

That was it! The nanotechs! How could I have forgotten that? Gellar gave himself an internal kick. "OK, then, as an engineer. You think that nanotech story of his is on the level?"

Wils Hoff stood up and stretched his lanky frame, and then rubbed his chin thoughtfully. "Damned if I know, sir. I do know that nanos are already used now in electronics fabrication—that's the only economically practical way to build computers using quark-quark switches." Subatomic switching technology had revolutionized the computer world in the last fifty years. Gellar's pocket watch now had more computing power than entire ships had carried only a few decades earlier, and that breakthrough in quark-antiquark switching had been made using nanotech machines to manipulate subatomic particles directly.

"OK, Exec, do a search of known systems along the Grugell border, and see if there are any systems that might be hiding a habitable planet that fits what the esteemed Mr. Ios told us."

"Yes, sir. You thinking that the Navy ought to look into this little enclave?"

"If we can find it, Exec. If we can find it." Gellar stood up. "While you do that, I'm going to go see how our guest is doing." He walked towards the passageway. "Mr. Hoff has the deck. Mr. Bice has the conn."

The hangar bay

Gellar was surprised to find Lieutenant Colonel Sandelescu at the doorway to the hangar bay containing the SS *Black Dragon*.

"Good afternoon, Colonel," he greeted the younger officer. The Marine looked up at him blankly for a moment before her eyes seemed to focus, and then she snapped to with her usual brisk salute. "Ah. Captain. Good afternoon."

Gellar ignored the salute, staring at his security chief. "Is everything all right inside? I was just wondering how Mr. Ios' repairs were going."

Colonel Sandelescu paused for a moment, frowning as though she was thinking. "Oh!" she burst out suddenly. "Yes, sir, everything's fine. Mr. Ios is in there now, looking over his ship. There's a repair crew already at work."

"All right. I'm going to have a look for myself. Care to accompany me, Colonel?"

"Yes, sir."

They entered the hangar bay, and Gellar was surprised at the temperature, which seemed several degrees cooler than the passageway. *Odd,* he thought. *Environmental seems to be on the blink in here.*

He walked quickly towards the scorched and battered yacht. Stepping up to the open hatchway, he banged one fist quickly on the edge of the hatch and called, "Permission to come aboard?"

A tall figure appeared suddenly, as though out of nowhere, startling Gellar.

"Of course, Captain. Enter freely—please be at ease in my home." Ios' deep voice seemed to roll out of the very bulkheads of the yacht. Gellar could see now how Ios seemed to appear out of nowhere in the dim interior of the yacht, dressed as he was in a black, high-necked tunic, black trousers, and shined black shoes. He even wore a hooded black cloak, very similar to those affected by Grugell officers. *Another trade item?* Gellar wondered. *It is chilly in here.*

"Thank you, Mr. Ios." He stepped into the yacht. "Your home, sir?"

"Indeed, Captain, the only home I have known for some time now. I owe you my thanks for aiding me in repairs." He stretched out one long-fingered hand to indicate the two engineers' mates working busily at a console at the front of the room. "These two have proven most satisfactory."

The two young crewmen ignored their captain, remaining focused on their task. Gellar chose to ignore the slight breach of protocol. He'd never been a stickler for military fuss and feathers, anyway.

"So, they're doing a good job?" Gellar turned to the security chief. "And these two would be?"

"Engineer's Mate Second Class Guerra and Engineer's Mate First Class Ophell, sir."

"Thank you, Colonel." Gellar spun on one heel and walked to where the two were busily working. "Good work, you two," he announced. "Are you keeping your section chief updated on your progress?"

EM1c Ophell looked up at him for a moment with a blank expression on her heart-shaped face. *Odd,* he thought. *That's the same expression that Colonel Sandelescu had.* "Oh, yes, pardon me, sir," the young crewman finally said. "We're keeping Senior Chief Tracy updated. We'll have the mainframe, navigation, and environmental back on line today, and then we'll start on structural repairs once we can talk to the ship's computer."

"Good. Carry on."

He turned and was startled to find Ios standing immediately behind him. *The man moves like a shadow,* he told himself. *Maybe it's time I got to understand our guest a little better.*

"Mr. Ios," he began, "may I offer you a tour of the *Charity*? I'm fairly new to the ship myself—only a little over two weeks in command—but I think I can give you a pretty comprehensive showing of the Confederacy's latest in medical cruisers."

"I'd be pleased to accept, Captain. I would find that fascinating. Naval architecture is a particular interest of mine."

"Good!" Gellar hadn't really expected Ios to accept. "If you'll just allow me a moment to notify the bridge, I'll be right with you."

Ios inclined his head in a sort of half-nod. "Of course, Captain. I await your convenience."

There was a comm panel near the entrance to the hangar bay, so Gellar headed in that direction. He picked up the handset and tapped the direct code for the executive officer's bridge station.

"Bridge, Executive Officer speaking."

"Exec," Gellar faced directly at the panel, placing his back to the yacht in the hangar bay, "this is the captain. I'll be escorting Mr. Ios on a tour of the ship for the next hour or so. Page me if there are any messages." He glanced around as casually as he could, to see Ios standing patiently by the ramp to his yacht, maybe fifty meters away. He lowered his voice. "How is that search coming along?"

"Sir," Commander Hoff replied, "We're still looking through long-range scan data, but our initial results show that all systems and planets along the Confederate-Grugell frontier are mapped and claimed by one side or another. The 2420 Non-Aggression Pact specifically mapped out the border systems and established the border around all known habitable worlds, even marginal Class III and IV planets. If there's a secret planet of renegades out there, I'd bet serious money against it being anywhere along the border."

"How about the Rim Worlds?"

"Not likely, sir. They're pretty backwards. I'd bet against any ground-breaking technological capability out there."

"Very well, Exec. I'll be back on the bridge in an hour or so."

He laid the handset in its cradle and resigned himself to an hour of being diplomatic to the *Charity*'s weird guest. Turning towards Ios with what he hoped was a friendly smile, he raised a hand to the entry and called, "Shall we begin, sir?"

The bridge

Commander Hoff's search for rogue systems had been fruitless, but his curiosity got the better of him. He brought up the ship mainframe's search feature again. The information search feature allowed him to access the main databases, updated every time the ship was in space dock—in this case, only two weeks earlier. The main databases contained virtually all the encoded information available to humanity.

Hoff brought up the text string search and tapped in FIND BIOGRAPHICAL DATA PROPER NAME BEL IOS. The computer almost instantly brought up one biographical summary and several minor links to other information. *Damn, these new quantum systems are fast*, Hoff thought, his engineer's mind exulting in any use of new and interesting technology. He tapped the screen on the biographical summary entry, and watched as the screen scrolled out a surprisingly small entry:

IOS, BEL	(NO IMAGE)
D.O.B.:	UNKNOWN
NATIVE PLANET:	UNKNOWN
CITIZENSHIP:	CONFEDERATE
MARITAL STATUS:	SINGLE
KNOWN ALIASES:	NONE
OCCUPATION:	TRADER, ENTREPRENEUR
PRESENT RESIDENCE:	UNKNOWN
CRIMINAL RECORD:	NONE

NOTES: Registered owner of SS Black Dragon, private yacht, built by H.H. Masters Shipwrights, Earth.

Registered dealer in wines and liquors, confederate intoxicants trading authority, license current

Present whereabouts unknown

The last comment drew a smile. *Not anymore*, Hoff told himself. *So, our Mr. Ios is more of a mystery man than we'd suspected, eh? Let's see what else I can find out.*

The other information links led only to a couple of popular culture 'gossip' items, one with a picture of an undamaged *Black Dragon* sitting on a landing pad on Forest, and an entry in a wine dealer's trade journal.

I wonder about the aliases?

Hoff brought up the main data search screen, and entered, FIND HUMAN GIVEN NAMES *BEL*

The computer screen immediately scrolled out the answers:

ABEL, ALBEL, ALLIBELLE, ANNABELLE, BEL, BELLE, BELOS, BELVAR, BELVEDERE, MARYBELLE…

The list produced a host of names. Hoff grimaced, and narrowed the search:

FROM RESULTS FIND BEL*
BEL, BELLE, BELOS, BELVAR, BELVEDERE…
FROM RESULTS FIND MALE NAMES
BEL, BELOS, BELVAR, BELVEDERE…

Belos?

He tapped away again, dropping the name search and bringing back the general data screen. FIND BIOGRAPHICAL DATA PROPER NAME BELOS IOS

Three links popped up. Hoff tapped the first one.

IOS, BELOS	(NO IMAGE)
D.O.B.:	?/?/2106
D.O.D.	22/6/2199
NATIVE PLANET:	EARTH
CITIZENSHIP:	CONFEDERATE

MARITAL STATUS:	MARRIED, SPOUSE MARIE FERRENZIG IOS
KNOWN ALIASES:	NONE
OCCUPATION:	TRADER, ANTIQUE AND ART DEALER
PRESENT RESIDENCE:	N/A
CRIMINAL RECORD:	NONE
NOTES:	NONE

No help there. He tapped the second link.

IOS, BELOS	(SEE IMAGE)
D.O.B.:	31/10/1966
D.O.D.	16/5/2029
NATIVE PLANET:	EARTH
CITIZENSHIP:	ROMANIA, EUROPEAN UNION
MARITAL STATUS:	UNKNOWN
KNOWN ALIASES:	NONE
OCCUPATION:	MERCHANT, SPICES AND WINES
PRESENT RESIDENCE:	N/A
CRIMINAL RECORD:	NONE

NOTES: Wounded in terrorist bombing of Arc de Triomphe, Paris, 2014. (See notes of attending physician)

Well, at least this one's got a picture, Hoff noted. *Let's have a look.* He tapped the link to the photograph, which promptly popped up in another browser window.

Hoff staggered to his feet, gasping, and took an involuntary step backwards, almost stumbling over his bridge chair. Staring at him from the screen was the unmistakably weird countenance of the *Charity*'s 'guest,' Bel Ios.

Realizing that the bridge watch was staring, he snapped, "As you were!" The crew hurried back to their duties. Hoff seated himself again, staring in disbelief at the screen.

It can't be him. That picture is three hundred years old!

He saved the record to his personal space on the computer's storage bank before he proceeded. *Attending physician's notes? This should be interesting.* He tapped that link.

> NOTE FOLLOWS:
>
> (Translated) Subject was wounded in the Bastille Day bombing of the Arc by elements of the Islamic Stateterrorist organization. Injuries sustained included second- and third-degree burns over two-thirds of body surface, punctured and collapsed left lung, penetrating wound in left chest, left abdomen, left leg, and scalp. Condition initially rated as Severe/Critical. Patient remanded to Hospital of Paris May 1, 2014, 2355. Patient was re-evaluated at May 2, 2014, 0900. Injuries mostly healed, left lung functioning normally, patient displayed extreme vigor. Patient was released 2056, May 2, 2014.
>
> Follow-ups unsuccessful. Patient's address of record was falsified. No further record.

Hoff stared at the entry for a moment.

This isn't possible, he thought. He looked back at the picture again.

Shaking himself out of his amazement, he dropped the record and brought up the search screen again.

FIND BIOGRAPHICAL DATA PROPER NAME BELOS IOS*

The same entries popped up as before. Hoff tried another tack.

FIND BIOGRAPHICAL DATA PROPER NAME BELOS IO*

Sixteen links.

FROM RESULTS FIND CITIZENSHIP ROMANIA

One link. Hoff tapped the legend, "BELOS IONESCU

IONESCU, BELOS	(SEE IMAGE)
D.O.B.:	?/?/1465
D.O.D.	?/?/1521
NATIVE PLANET:	EARTH
CITIZENSHIP:	WALLACHIA (ROMANIA)
MARITAL STATUS:	UNKNOWN
KNOWN ALIASES:	NONE
OCCUPATION:	LANDOWNER
PRESENT RESIDENCE:	N/A
CRIMINAL RECORD:	NONE

NOTES: Major landowner in Carpathian Mountains near Transylvanian border. Known ties with several major Gypsy families. Noted for reclusive nature.

With a certain apprehension, Hoff tapped on the image link. An old woodcut popped up, depicting an Eastern European land-lord in an archaic, high-necked outfit. But it wasn't the clothing that riveted Hoff to the screen. Crude as the old woodcut was, the artist had possessed a certain talent. The visage on the screen was unmistakably that of Bel Ios.

This is too weird, Hoff thought. He saved the last record to his own storage as well, erased the search and turned his panel to scroll the standard 'Ship's News' screen. As a tidbit about the evening's menus in the Deck Nine mess hall rolled past, he glanced at his pocket watch. *I'll have to tell the captain about this. I wonder where they are now?*

Chapter Eight

Radiology

"Didi, are you all right?" Senior Chief Warren was more than a little exasperated at his assistant. Old for a radiology mate first class at forty-one, she'd been passed over for promotion to chief at least twice. A bad drinking habit combined with a penchant for showing up for duty hung over made her a liability to the department.

"I'm all right, just dizzy."

"Rough night last night again, Didi?"

"No, not like you think. Met this really weird guy in the Deck Four lounge. I guess I did have a little too much to drink, because I don't remember all that much, but he must have been a real animal."

"I think you've already told me more than I want to know, Didi." The senior chief snorted.

"No, not like that! Look, look here, I noticed this when I was getting ready this morning." She pulled back the high collar of her whites to show the left side of her neck.

"What the hell? Is that a bite mark?"

"Sure looks like it, doesn't it? Itches like hell, too."

"You should go get that checked out, Didi."

"Nah, I can't bother with that. It's just a scratch. It'll be fine. I've got work to do, Senior Chief."

"You say so."

"I think I'll stay the heck out of that lounge for a while. Bette Gillian has been telling me I need to lay off the sauce anyway."

"She ain't the only one, Didi," Warren reminded her.

Deck Four, near the greenhouse

"My first deployment was on one of the older ships, the CSS *Hyparion*, that still had to spin radially to provide artificial gravity," Gellar said to Ios as they neared the end of the tour. "It wasn't much fun trying to work in a zero-gee command compartment. Space travel is a lot easier these days with pseudo-grav floorplates and ships built along more traditional lines, with decks built laterally around the tunnel instead of radially."

"I've wondered, Captain, about the name of our standard star drive?" Ios looked expectantly at Gellar.

"Yes." Gellar grinned. "He was my five-times great-grandfather, or something like that. Unfortunately, most of the vast Gellar fortune was gone by the time my father was born, so now us Gellars have to work for a living. When old Hiram sold the drive patent to Peebles, he sold the whole works for a lump sum—no residuals. A few generations of inheritances, and it was all gone."

Ios looked vaguely disappointed. "How sad for you, Captain."

"No regrets on my part, Mr. Ios. Well, at least not very many. I mean, even today a billion and a half is still a lot of money to most of us. But I love the Navy, I love being out among the stars. I wouldn't trade my life for anything."

"I envy you, then, Captain. And you may have my assurances, not even wealth will free you from all desires."

"You and I would seem to be kindred spirits in one respect, Mr. Ios. You've chosen to make your home among the stars, as well." Gellar was gently probing, but for what he wasn't yet sure.

"Chosen? Perhaps. There are reasons for my lifestyle, Captain, and anonymity is paramount among them. While I may be a well-known name in Galactic society, my face is known to only a select few. I prefer to be able to pass unnoticed in a crowd, which would not be possible were I to tie myself to one planet, one world."

I can't imagine anyone ever forgetting your *face*, Gellar told himself silently. "I see. Well, Mr. Ios, you've seen our finer dining facilities, the Officers' Club, about everything Navy regulations allow me to show you. Right around the corner, though, is my favorite spot on the ship."

They rounded a bend in the corridor, and as they made the turn a passageway hatch opened in front of them, disgorging two female crewmembers in somewhat abbreviated sunbathing costumes. Ios coolly watched the two young women walk away down the corridor, lost in conversation. He turned to raise a bushy, arched eyebrow at Gellar. "I begin to understand why, Captain. What is this marvelous place of yours where such attire is routinely worn?"

The door had slid silently closed as they approached, so Gellar tapped the panel next to the frame, and the double door slid open again, revealing the bright, artificial sunlight of the huge, open greenhouse within.

Ios let out a gasping hiss, startling Gellar. The trillionaire recluse threw his hands up in front of his face, staggering backwards away from the light. Gellar tapped the panel again, closing the doors. Ios backed away still further, scuttling to the opposite side of the corridor, crouching as though in agony. Claw-like hands drew his thick black cloak tight around his lean form.

"Mr. Ios!" Gellar exclaimed, following the hunched figure. He reached to touch Ios' shoulder. "Sir, are you all right?"

Ios had been taken totally by surprise by the burst of artificial sunlight, and the agony was overwhelming. Knowing that the ship was in deep space, sunlight was the last thing he would have expected. Ios wasn't aware that the latest generation of Navy ships all carried greenhouse decks, both to provide an additional source of oxygen for what was basically a contained ecosystem, and to provide the crew with a source of synthesized sunlight, which aided in stabilizing their circadian rhythms in the eternal night of deep space.

But Ios had no need of artificial sunlight. He had lived the vast majority of his life in an unending night.

"Mr. Ios," Gellar insisted, his voice finally breaking through Ios' agony. "Sir, are you all right? I'm a doctor, remember. What's wrong?"

"I do apologize, Captain," Ios finally replied, his voice trembling slightly. He was struggling to maintain control, his baser instincts screaming at him to either flee or strike dead this fool who had blasted the killing sunlight at him. "I'm afraid I suffer from a rather severe photophobia. It's a rather odd paranoia that has worsened since I've been living in my yacht. I suppose that's another of the reasons I live as I do."

Ios straightened up, his eyes red and tearing, his face brick red. Gellar gaped at him—it looked like severe sunburn, but Ios had only been in the light for a second or two at the most.

And then, as Gellar watched, the redness faded, passed in a wave from Gellar's face, leaving a few patches of flaky skin that peeled away and drifted to the deck.

"If you'll excuse me, Captain, I find that I'm suddenly quite exhausted. By your leave, I would like to return to my quarters." Ios looked almost embarrassed.

"Of course. Would you like me to escort you?"

"No, that won't be necessary, Captain. Please accept my apologies. I wish you a good evening."

"And a good evening to you as well, Mr. Ios. I'll look in on you in the morning."

Ios turned away and walked down the corridor towards a lift shaft that would take him to Deck Three, where the guest quarters were located. He seethed with rage, and more than rage. His body had only just recovered from the fire, and now he had been blasted with sunlight, that deadliest of all things to him, and his system was too taxed to recover.

The previous evening and this afternoon's feedings had only been tidbits. He would need to feed again, and soon. Fortunately, he knew how that might be accomplished, and who might be able to assist him. As he walked, he put out a silent call.

The bridge

"Exec, the strangest thing just happened," Gellar began as he walked onto the bridge.

Hoff jumped in before Gellar could finish the sentence. "Pardon my interrupting, sir, but you've got to see this." Hoff grabbed his captain by one arm, practically dragging him towards his computer panel.

"If it was this important, Exec, why didn't you page me?"

"Sir, you were with Mr. Ios. Just look, you'll understand."

Quickly, Hoff explained his databank search, and brought up the entries on the various incarnations of Belos Ionescu/Bel Ios.

"Exec," Gellar stammered, as stunned as Hoff had been, "This isn't possible."

"I know that, sir. But healing from third and fourth degree burns in twenty-four hours isn't possible, either, is it?"

"No, you're right. But then, what the hell is possible about Mr. Ios?" Gellar reached down and picked up a handset from the exec's station, hitting the 'Page' button. "Doctor Moses, please call the bridge. Doctor Moses, call the bridge please." He replaced the handset in its cradle.

"So, Mr. Ios is a damned immortal of some kind?"

"You tell me, sir, you're the doctor. All I know is what I see on that screen." He pointed at the twenty-first-century photograph. "That, sir, was taken in a hospital in Paris the year before the Third World War started. That man, Belos Ios, was wounded severely in a bombing attack on the Arc de Triomphe in Paris that year. He walked out of the hospital the next day. That's the same man, sir; I'd stake my pension on it."

"The picture's pretty good. If it's not him, then it's a dead ringer. And the thing about him healing that quickly…You know, if he's got some kind of supercharged immune/regenerative ability, then he might not age normally, either. Nanotech robots, my eye—why didn't I see through that faster?"

The handset chimed. Gellar picked it up. "Bridge, Captain speaking."

"Captain, this is Doctor Moses."

"Doctor Moses, I've got something I want you to see."

"Funny you should mention that, Captain," the voice in the handset answered, "because I've got something down here in the lab that you've got to look at. Can you come down?"

"Of course. Is this something to do with our guest?"

"I'm afraid so."

Gellar turned to his exec. "Wils, can you pull this up on the panel in the main lab?"

"Yes, sir!"

"Very well, Doctor Moses, the exec and I are on the way now." The two officers left the bridge quickly. Gellar barely remembered to call over his shoulder as he walked through the passage: "Mr. Bice, you have the deck. Lieutenant Saferly, take over the conn."

Chapter Nine

Security office

Marine Major Othello Sutt was used to his boss's stern demeanor and taciturn nature, but even he was startled when Lieutenant Colonel Sandelescu suddenly stood up in the middle of typing out a training report, announced, "I've got an errand to run, Major. I'll be back in an hour or so," and left the office.

"Yes, ma'am," he answered.

Sandelescu strode purposely down the corridor, into a lift shaft that floated her to Deck Three. She proceeded to the guest quarters, her neuronic paralyzer banging against her hip as she hurried down the empty corridor. Arriving at last at Suite 301, the VIP quarters, she tapped quietly on the door. The door panel slid open to reveal the dark form of Bel Ios.

"Come in, my dear," he breathed. The Marine went into the VIP suite, and the door slid shut behind her.

"My master," Sandelescu whispered, her breathing fast and shallow, her eyes glazed.

"Yessss," Ios hissed, "your master. Your blood speaks to you, my child. As it speaks to me."

"Yes, my master."

"There is something I must ask you to do for me, my dear child. This is a giant hospital, isn't it? There will be a blood storage facility, yes?"

"Yes, my master."

"We will wait here until late in the night, and then you will take me there."

"There will be a third watch on duty there, my master. This is a Navy ship; the facility will be manned even then."

"Then" Ios chuckled darkly. "I will deal with them as well. It is as well that I have the ones who work in that place in my grasp, even as I do the ones who repair my ship." He reached out to run his hand along Colonel Sandelescu's cheek, her neck, her collarbone, and finally lower into her uniform tunic. "Until then, my child, I have another need which you may fulfill."

Fulfill your needs while you may, ancient monster, a voice deep inside Sandelescu's head snarled. *This thing you've given me grows strong. You won't be able to control me much longer.*

For now, Ios' iron will seized her like a small bird in a mailed fist. She had no choice but to submit.

But only for the moment.

The main medical laboratory

Captain Gellar and Commander Hoff entered the lab to find Doctor Moses and her chief nurse, Commander Julia Cartwright, hovering over a computer panel.

"Oh, Captain," Doctor Moses said, looking up. "Commander," she added, nodding to the exec. "You two really need to see this." She motioned them over to a vapor hood in a corner of the lab, where a small lamp and a petri dish waited.

"Captain," the chief surgeon began, "when Mr. Ios was in the ER, we took several blood samples. It's part of our routine procedure, right? Right." Doctor Moses was in her element now. "OK, well, I've already shown you the blood gas and hemoglobin numbers. There's nothing routine about our Mr. Ios' blood, or anything else. But this is where it really gets weird. Julia?"

"Captain, I had already finished most of the blood work when I decided to get a spectrograph analysis of Mr. Ios' blood. Since there were so many things that seemed odd about him physiologically, it seemed like a good idea to look a little harder at his blood chemistry."

"Yes, makes sense."

"Well, this doesn't. Watch what happens when you apply a UV source to Mr. Ios' blood sample." She reached into the vapor hood and flipped the UV lamp on, directing the beam onto the petri dish that Gellar could now see contained a few cc's of blood.

The blood hissed and bubbled, dissolving in a catabolic reaction that left only a black, tarry mess in the petri dish, and a puff of dark gray smoke that billowed up into the hood, finally being sucked into the exhaust fan.

"What the hell." Commander Hoff gaped. Gellar's mind was drawn back to only a half-hour before, when the doors to the greenhouse had slid open and Ios recoiled in agony. Ios' voice came back to him now:

I'm afraid I suffer from a rather severe photophobia. It's a rather odd paranoia that has worsened since I've been living in my yacht. I suppose that's another of the reasons I live as I do.

"Oh, hell," he breathed. Quickly, he gave an account of the events to the others.

"Photophobia?" Doctor Moses snorted after Gellar finished. "I should bloody well say so! UV light would burn him like an open flame, if this is any indication."

"Well, Doc, there's something else you should see. Wils?" Gellar motioned towards the computer terminal on the lab desk. Commander Hoff was quick to comply.

"So," Captain Gellar asked once Hoff had run through his search results, "it seems our guest is an unusual character indeed. Wils, get hold of Colonel Sandelescu, and have her post two Marines in the hangar bay."

"Sir, should we be asking Mr. Ios about any of this? Frankly I'm half inclined to slap him in a security cell until we reach the Fleet."

"No, Wils, we can't do that. He's a free citizen of the Confederacy, no matter how strange, and he hasn't done anything illegal that we know of. The Grugell have some video of a supposed monster that Ionescu supposedly created from one of their own, but we have no way of knowing if Ionescu was involved or if the video is even real. There's no law against being a damned immortal, as far as I know, as long as you pay your taxes on time."

Gellar scratched his head. "I have to think about this. There's something about this that is nagging at my memory, but I can't place it. Good work, everyone." He pulled out his pocket watch, glancing at it. "It's almost 1800. I'm going to the wardroom to get some dinner; I suggest all of you do the same. I have a feeling we'll be needing our strength."

The blood storage facility, Deck Two, 0130 hours

Pharmacist's Mate Second Class Andrew Chin was bored. An incident in the Deck Four lounge, involving a broken floor lamp and six broken glasses, had earned him the wrath of the chief in charge of his section, and so Chin had been stuck on the late watch in, of all places, the blood storage unit.

Nothing ever bloody happens here, Chin told himself bitterly for the thousandth time. *This is what I get for landing on the chief's shit list.* He dusted off the counter for the fortieth time that night, finishing up just as the entryway hatch slid open and the ship's security chief walked in.

Chin snapped to attention.

"Ma'am!" the young tech blurted. "Beg pardon, Ma'am, didn't expect to see you this late. Is there something I can do for you?" His voice trailed off at the sight of Colonel Sandelescu's companion. This could only be the ship's rumored guest, Bel Ios.

The tall, weird figure moved around the strangely silent security chief, his voice a hiss through clenched, interlocking teeth.

"Yess, young man, it is late, isn't it? There is something you can do for me this late evening." He reached for Chin, and the young tech backed away instinctively. But Ios' arm kept coming, a cracking, creaking sound coming from the bones and muscles of his arm as the hand reached, impossibly, a good three meters to pin Chin against the bulkhead. Ios flowed around the counter, his eyes glowing like coals. "Yes, you can do something for me indeed. Tonight, and in the nights to come. Are you on duty here every night?"

Chin could barely manage a nod. He felt all too acutely the chitin-tipped fingers gripping his neck, the claw-like nails poised over his jugular. "Yes, yes, every night this week," he stammered.

"Ahhh," Ios hissed. He smiled grotesquely, displaying long, interlocked canines. "Good. Good. You will do very well then." He drew closer, and his jaws fastened onto Chin's neck.

The hangar bay, the next morning

Master Chief Gillespie had been an engineer's mate long before in his career, and though he was now the master chief on the *Charity*, the ship's top enlisted man, he maintained a technical proficiency in all matters of ship's design. It was inevitable that he would find a reason to inspect the ongoing repair work on the *Black Dragon*.

He strode into the hangar bay, waving a greeting to Gunnery Sergeant Anthony, who was talking to his two troops assigned to the bay.

"Morning, Master Chief," the Marine called. He snapped off a perfect salute as the master chief walked up, which Gillespie returned with panache.

"Morning, Gunny. Great day to be in space, huh?"

"Finest kind, sir." The Marines had the odd habit of calling everybody of higher rank *Sir* or *Ma'am*, not just officers, as was the Navy tradition.

"Got some of my troops inside?"

"Yes sir, two of 'em. Hey, White, who's inside working today?"

"Guerra and Ophell, Gunny."

"Good kids," Gillespie observed. "I'll go in and see how they're doing, Gunny. What's with the troops?"

"Captain's orders, sir."

"I haven't talked to the Old Man yet today. I guess I'll have to go up and see him. Damn doctors, they never remember to keep the ship's master chief in the damned loop."

"Charlie Fox, sir," the Gunnery Sergeant observed, invoking the oldest of all military euphemisms for a screwed-up situation.

Gillespie walked up the ramp to the yacht and leaned in the open hatchway. Both engineers' mates were busily working away on an open panel in the main cabin. One of them—Guerra— looked around, and Gillespie waved him off. "Keep working, Guerra. I'm just having a look around."

"Yes, Master Chief."

The repairs were obviously coming along very well. The main cabin had been pretty much put back to rights. The living area was mostly restored, the smoke smell gone. Gillespie walked to the control suite and ran a couple of diagnostic routines on the navigation and helm computers. Everything there seemed normal. He walked back to the main cabin.

"Good work," he commented. "Guerra, you come up for First pretty quick, don't you?"

Guerra looked blank for a moment. "Uh, yes, Master Chief, six weeks."

"Keep up this kind of work, and you'll get it. Nice to get a few extra bucks in your pay account every month, eh?" He turned to the girl, Ophell. *Cute little thing*, he thought in a corner of his mind. "You too, Ophell. Damn good work. You two are really making time."

"Thanks, Master Chief."

"I'll just have a look around the rest of the yacht. Carry on."

There wasn't much more to the *Black Dragon*. A tiny engineering compartment containing the engine readouts and instruments was at the very rear, just behind an even tinier lavatory compartment with a stall shower, sink, and a privy, and a bedroom with a fairly large bed and two wardrobes. There was a hatch in the floor of the main cabin, and out of curiosity Gillespie opened it and had a peek. It was a modest cargo compartment, containing only two undamaged cases of Corinthian wine. *I bet it's good stuff, too*, the master chief thought wryly.

He left the yacht with a nod to the two young petty officers.

"Fancy-ass ship, eh Master Chief?" Gunnery Sergeant Anthony was still just outside.

"Rich man's toy, Gunny."

"Guy must make planetfall pretty regular, though."

"How's that?"

"Didn't you notice?" Gunnery Sergeant Anthony's powers of observation were finely honed by his seventeen years in the Corps, especially his time in Force Recon. "No galley. No provisioning at all, except for a water tank and that little reefer unit in the main cabin. How do you suppose this guy eats between systems?"

"Beats me, Gunny. Maybe he gets drive-through."

Anthony laughed. "Could be, sir. But hell—even in the Sol and Tarbos sectors it's a good six weeks between settled systems, minimum. Out here on the border, you can go twelve to eighteen weeks easy without hitting a settlement, even at max drive. It's just sort of weird, you know?"

"Maybe he likes dehydrates, Gunny. He's got a cargo bay. Dry-cake is good for you." Gillespie repeated the timeworn boot camp truism.

"Could be, Master Chief." Anthony shook his head. "I guess some people might actually like that crap. Who knows? Hell, he probably eats dry-cake the whole way. Hell with it. I've got a section to run, I'd better get moving. You have a good one, Master Chief." The Marine snapped off a perfect salute, spun on his heel, and marched from the hangar bay.

Gillespie nodded to the Marine guards and walked to the comm panel that the captain had used the day before, punching in the code for the bridge.

"Bridge, Ensign Foss speaking." The signals watch officer.

"Ma'am, this is Master Chief Gillespie. Captain up there?"

"Yes, he is, Master Chief, wait one." The panel clicked and hummed briefly as the call was switched to the captain's station.

"Captain here. Morning, Master Chief."

"Sir, I got some stuff to talk to you about," Gillespie said. "You got a few minutes?"

"You bet, Master Chief. Meet me in the bridge conference room, give me ten minutes."

"Aye aye, sir. I'm on my way."

Eight and one-half minutes later, Master Chief Gillespie walked into the bridge conference room and was surprised to find not just the captain, but also the chief surgeon, chief nurse, and the exec seated around the oval table.

"Come in, Master Chief, sit down. What's on your mind?"

"Sir," Gillespie began, taking a seat at the table, "there are two Marines down there watching my engineering people fix that Mr. Ios' yacht. Sir, I need to know if there's a security issue involving this guy."

The officers all shared a look. "There might be, Master Chief, but we're not sure what the issue is."

"Then why are there two jarheads babysitting this guy's boat? Sir, you got to keep me in the loop on this stuff, that's what I'm here for."

"You're right, Master Chief, of course. It's all developed very quickly, but you're right, I should have filled you in, and I'll take care of that right now." Gellar quickly brought the master chief up to date.

"Sir, you ought to have let me know about this right off," Gillespie chided the captain. "I'll admit, in forty years space-side, I've heard some stories, but nothing like this character. But there's better ways to keep an eye on someone than having a gaggle of Marines follow 'em around, know what I mean?" The master chief leaned back in his chair, in his element now.

"What do you have in mind, Master Chief?" The exec was curious, at least.

"Well, sir, I got two chiefs that were in the Corps before they branched over to the Navy to go into drive systems. These boys worked in covert ops, sir. I also got a young kid that was in the Special Branch of the New Albion Army, did three years there before going Fed. You want this fellow Ios shadowed, these guys can do it. I can put a senior chief in with the kids you got working on his ship, too." He snapped his fingers. "That reminds me, sir." He turned to Gellar, "One of the Marines, a gunnery sergeant named Anthony, he nosed around that yacht. I had a look around, too, and you know what's odd about that expensive little boat?"

The group stared at Gillespie. "Are you going to make us wait for it, Master Chief?" the chief surgeon asked testily.

Gillespie made brief eye contact with the Chief Surgeon and was gratified when she looked away first. Officer or no officer, he had forty years' time in service and not many people could withstand his direct stare for long. He turned to the captain again, deliberately ignoring the chief surgeon. "Sir, there ain't no galley on that boat. No food lockers, no storage, no microwave cookers, no nothing, no kidding. There's a little tiny reefer unit in the main cabin, a drinks cabinet like, and it's empty. Nothing in the hold but two cases of wine, sir."

Gellar observed the interchange between Moses and Gillespie with some concern. It had the appearance of an ongoing pissing match. A little conflict was to be expected from two strong personalities, but when two of those personalities were among the ship's senior leadership, it had the potential to affect their duties. If it was going to interfere with operations, he'd have to put a stop to it.

"Maybe he likes dry-cake, Master Chief." Gellar was beginning to reach an idea he couldn't quite grasp.

"No dry-cake in the hold, either. And besides, sir, ain't nobody likes dry-cake that much. It doesn't make good sense."

"So, question is, what does our friend eat between planetfalls?"

"Beats me, sir, I just know what I saw, and what I saw was no damn galley."

"OK, Master Chief, good ideas. People, let's compartmentalize this thing. Master Chief, get your two former jarheads learning what Ios does when he's out wandering around, and put your best senior chief in on the repair project. Neither of 'em knows about the others, and the Marines don't know about any of them."

"Aye aye, sir, I'll see to it right away." *Maybe this doc won't be a bad captain after all.* Gillespie was a little happier now with the way things were shaping up. Something was still nagging at him, though; something he couldn't quite place.

"What's the name of that boy's yacht?" he asked suddenly.

"The *Black Dragon*," Gellar answered. "Why, Master Chief?"

"I'm not sure, sir. Sounds familiar, but I can't remember where I've seen it before. I'll remember it eventually. Probably a news report—he is the richest guy in the Confederacy, after all."

"Sir," the exec asked, "shouldn't we let Colonel Sandelescu in on this?"

"No," Gellar thought, reminded suddenly of the security chief sitting in the chair next to Ios' hospital bed. "No, not right away. She can leave her Marines in place. Ios would probably smell a rat if they stood down suddenly anyway. No, none of this leaves this room—everybody clear on that?" There were nods all around the table. "Good. Carry on, everybody. I'll be on the bridge for the rest of the watch."

Chapter Ten

The blood storage facility, 1130 hours

Lieutenant Carol Jones was the officer in charge of the blood storage facility. A medical supply officer by training, she chafed at the boring duty, but at least she had a free hand as OIC to exercise her relentless pursuit of the perfect inventory management system, which would—she hoped—finally get her out of shipboard duty for good, and into a coveted teaching billet at the Academy on Tarbos.

But what she found this morning wasn't pleasing at all. Storming out of the cold storage room, she collared the chief petty officer in charge of the day troops. "Chief Litchswark," she barked, "why is my count off nine units this morning?"

"Ma'am?"

"You heard me. There are nine units missing, all from the latest dated collection." For all the Navy's vaunted medical technology, there were some instances in which there was no replacement for stored, typed, and matched human blood, and so all Navy ships had active donor programs that were "highly encouraged" by commanders.

"Nine units, ma'am? They all matched up yesterday, right?"

"You know they did."

"Well, let me have a look." Chief Petty Officer Litchswark tapped away on the computer keyboard on his desk for a few moments. "Nobody signed anything out, and it doesn't look like any of the medical decks asked for anything either."

"No shit. We've only got one patient. So where did it go?"

"Beats me, ma'am. We'll have to check with the mid-watch and late watch techs, see if they know anything."

"Get 'em in here right now. If you have to wake 'em up, wake 'em up."

Twenty minutes later, Pharmacist's Mate First Class Elwood and PM2c Chin were standing at attention in front of Lieutenant Jones' desk.

"OK, what do either of you know about nine missing units of typed blood?"

Both techs looked at the OIC blankly. Elwood spoke up quickly: "Nothing on mid-watch last night, ma'am. Nobody in or out, nothing from Surgery, nothing from Emergency."

"What about you, Chin? Anything happen overnight?"

Chin was sweating and pale. "No, ma'am."

Lieutenant Jones stood up and leaned over her desk, staring into Chin's pale face. "Chin, you look like you're about to pass out," she said. "Are you all right?"

"Ma'am, I... I mean, last night, I..." A fist closed down over Chin's mind.

"Chin? What were you going to say, Chin?"

PM2c Chin's eyes rolled back in his head, and he slumped to the deck, striking his head on the corner of the lieutenant's desk. Blood spurted from a minor scalp wound.

"Oh, crap." Lieutenant Jones grabbed the handset off her desk's comm panel. "ER One, I got a head wound here, in the blood storage office. I need a litter up here. Right, five minutes, roger that." She banged the headset down and barked at PM1c Elwood. "Don't just stand there, damn it, go and get a bandage or something."

The chief surgeon's office

The handset on Chief Surgeon Moses' desk chimed just as she stepped out of her private bathroom. *Isn't that always the way,* she thought, and grabbed the handset. "Chief Surgeon," she answered.

"Andrea," came the voice of Chief Nurse Cartwright. "Can you come down to ER One? There's a boy down here you should take a look at."

"On my way," Moses replied.

ER One

It was normally only a thirty-second walk down the corridor to ER One from the chief surgeon's office, but the note of urgency in Nurse Cartwright's voice prompted Doctor Moses to make the walk even more quickly. On her arrival in ER One, she found a young pharmacist's mate on his back on an exam table. The chief nurse, a young doctor whose name Moses couldn't recall, and an emergency med tech were hovering over the unconscious boy.

"All right, make a hole," she barked.

All but the chief nurse obediently stepped out of Moses' way. She bent over the young crewman. "What's up with him, besides the scalp wound? I assume there's something else?"

"Well, he's anemic," Cartwright replied, "but there's more. Look here."

With a grunt of annoyance, Moses reached into a pocket for the reading glasses she needed for close-in work due to her refusal to submit to laser vision correction. She leaned in to examine the spot on the boy—Chin, the tag said—that Cartwright was indicating on his neck, just over the jugular.

Two neat puncture wounds, right over the big vein. The wounds were recent, no more than twenty-four hours old, and untended.

"How did this happen?"

"We don't know, ma'am," the young doctor on watch replied. "He came in for the scalp wound. We found this when we started the exam."

"Has he been out the whole time?"

"Since he came in. There's no evidence of any epi- or subdural bleeding, so I couldn't tell you why he's out. The wound isn't that bad, but the kid's out like a light."

"Where's he work?" Moses was beginning to get a bad feeling.

"Blood Storage. That's his OIC sitting over there."

"Blood Storage?" Moses straightened up and strode quickly over to the young lieutenant seated in the waiting area. The younger officer snapped to her feet as Moses walked up.

"Lieutenant, do you know how he got those wounds on his neck?" she asked.

"Ma'am?" the younger officer looked puzzled. "Wounds on his neck? He fell and hit his head."

Moses took her glasses off and rubbed the bridge of her nose. "When was he last on duty?"

"He's working the late watch this week, ma'am. He was on shift last night."

"In Blood Storage." *And we've got a very suspicious, apparently immortal guest, who is walking around the ship somewhere with fatally low hemoglobin levels.* Moses went into the ER office and picked up a handset, punching the code for the bridge. Captain Gellar was in the ER within five minutes.

"Get a Marine guard in here," he snapped, on examining Chin's neck wounds. "This patient is under guard during all three watches, got that? Where's a handset?" Moses pointed towards the office. Gellar strode in and hit the "Page" button.

"Colonel Sandelescu, come to ER One immediately. Colonel Sandelescu, to ER One immediately." After a moment's thought, he paged again, this time for Master Chief Gillespie. Both of them had to be brought into the picture now. The first order of business was to find Bel Ios, who was now a primary suspect in an assault as well as the theft of nine units of blood. For what reason, Gellar couldn't imagine.

Guest quarters

The dreamtime brought back memories again, spurred by his recent injuries and the uncomfortable feeling of his secrets slowly eroding in close contact with so many humans.

Paris, lovely as always in the evening, even cheapened as it was now with flashing neon lights. Ios remembered, decades before, a wonderful café on a corner that was now occupied by an American chain restaurant, 'Pizza Hut.' Barbarians.

He strode the evening streets, enjoying the warm spring air, enjoying the tangy, salty scent of teeming throngs of humanity around him. He'd feed tonight, perhaps a plump young woman. Paris nightclubs were always fruitful for just such.

The Arc de Triomphe stood before him. He'd last seen it in 1944, when the German hordes had been driven from Paris. He'd fought alongside the Resistance, not out of any sense of duty or justice but simply reveling in the license to kill, the opportunity to glut himself on those who would be his prey in any case. Ios had then been known as LeBeau the Black, the *Stalker de nuit*, the Night Stalker. He'd killed German officers and, more delightfully, their traitorous French mistresses, spreading terror in the occupying army.

But that was the mechanized wars of the twentieth century, massed armies marching across entire continents. This evening was in the early years of the "civilized" twenty-first, when cowards waged wars against the innocent.

A crowd gathered around the Arc this evening to listen to a troupe of musicians who played for coins at the base of the monument. Ios walked past, breathing in deeply the scents of humanity, letting his hunger grow. A young Parisian woman in a silk dress smiled drunkenly at him, and a gaggle of loud, garish American tourists passed in the opposite direction, camera flashes strobing as they went.

Ios' senses, ever attuned to that which went unnoticed by the ordinary, suddenly sharpened. A small, hunched figure hurried towards the Arc. Ios' eyes narrowed as he studied the small man. His hair was black, his face bearded, his body swathed in a large coat even in the warm summer air. Ios breathed deeply as the man passed a few meters away, his practiced sense of smell cataloging the little man: an Arab. Many such as he infested Europe now, drawn in by the Continent's insanely tolerant immigration policies. A tang of chemicals mixed with the acid sweat of fear accompanied the man as he hurried past.

Alarmed now, Ios turned to walk quickly away, but too late. The small, gnome-like figure walked to the base of the Arc and detonated the bomb he carried.

The blast picked Ios up, stripped the clothing from his body, seared his skin, and threw him hundreds of meters away. He landed against a building, tried to rise, fell again. His legs were useless, his left leg in particular shredded; one lung was full of holes. He coughed and spat blood he could not afford to be without. He tried to gather his strength, but his ancient body failed him. He would need several hours to heal himself.

Around him sirens blared, lights flashed. An emergency medical worker noticed him, gave him plasma, had him loaded into one of the busses commandeered as ambulances and taken to hospital.

Revived by the plasma and by a modest feeding he'd taken from a young nurses' assistant at the hospital, he'd walked out into a shocked and bloodied Paris again the following evening. He walked into an Internet café, rented a computer terminal, and read the news. An Arab terror group claimed responsibility. The Islamic State was based now in the Christian—and the Muslim—Holy Land, in Iraq, and in Syria.

Ios bought passage on a plane to Cairo that night. With his ability to force his will over his flesh to a certain degree, he'd forced his hair to grow thick and black, his skin to grow swarthy, his features to change somewhat. In the Saharan night the Night Stalker was born again. This time he set himself to hunt the authors of the latest indignity to his immortal body. He infiltrated the groups and enthralled their leaders. He killed when it suited him, sent them on stupid errands when he found it amusing to let the English and the Americans kill them for him. In the end the Americans and the English had won what history labeled the Third World War, the Arab kings and dictators had fallen by the wayside, and elected parliaments had taken their places. A lasting peace was the final irony of Ios' latest quest for revenge. It was indeed a fine joke to play on the foul, bloody-minded cowards who masterminded terror campaigns that were a thing of disgust to even the ancient, legendary predator of mankind.

Ios sat up suddenly in the bed, startled into wakefulness by the flash from his chief thrall. *My master*, the woman reported, *they've found out about Chin. He resists you. The captain has ordered you to be detained. I must send Marines to find you.*

Do so, child. Do not let yourself come under suspicion. I will deal with the Marines if I must.

So, somewhere in this Captain's mind, the ancient fears still live. Ios chuckled inwardly. At some primal level he was actually gratified, even though this necessitated a quick escape and a new identity.

So, they've found the boy from the blood storage facility, he thought. His mind reached out to the two thralls in his yacht. He touched the girl's mind.

Your craft is spaceworthy, Master, but with only one drive tunnel. Your navigation and environmental systems are repaired. There is still cosmetic damage.

No matter, he told the girl. *Do what you can do to make the ship ready. I will leave this place soon.*

In the meantime, Ios was sure that there would be Marines knocking on his door at any moment. It was time to make himself scarce, and from his wanderings on the ship he thought he knew just where to go. Flowing to his feet, he strode out the door, turned right, and blended into the lunchtime crowd that was beginning to flood the corridors. As he walked, he pulled a small, black electronic device from an inside pocket of the black cloak he wore. He pressed a stud, and a small red light began blinking. *There,* he thought, *if they would hunt me, then let them come hunt me at a time and place of my choosing. And what better place than the one place they'd least suspect?*

Let them come there, then, and find out just what it is they are truly facing.

Chapter Eleven

The hangar bay

"You there, come on out." Ophell and Guerra looked up from their work to see Gunnery Sergeant Anthony and two Marines, all armed with M65 rifles. "Report to your section chief. There won't be any more work here for a while." Both engineer's mates nodded and left. Anthony walked to the comm panel and punched a code from memory.

"They're gone, Master Chief. I'm putting two Marines on guard inside, and the rest outside. I'll be hanging around somewhere in the bay myself. He ain't going anywhere in this yacht, sir."

"Good deal, Gunny. Let me know if anything comes up."

ER One

"There you are, Captain. I got Marines all around the yacht." Gillespie had his back turned to the main ER as he stood in the office, murmuring the words in a low voice. Lieutenant Colonel Sandelescu was interviewing Lieutenant Jones out in the ER. "And, I've got my two former Marines looking around again too. They'll dig around wherever Ios has been seen before and call in as soon as they can pick him up. Any particular reason you don't want the colonel in the loop on that last, sir?"

"Let's just say I want this bit of the op compartmentalized, Master Chief."

"Aye aye, sir. Anyway, ain't any way he's getting on that yacht."

"Now that you mention it, did your former Marines turn anything up on Ios?"

"Sir, one of them sat in the Deck Four lounge and watched Ios check out every unattached female crewmember that walked in. He left by himself, but my boy talked to the barkeep, and Ios was in the night before. I guess he left with a radiology-first that had drunk a little too much. Barkeep knew the lady, and I've already talked to her section chief. She's going to be checked out by the chief surgeon personally."

"Good. Good work by your man, too, Master Chief. We'll make sure to write him up for something when this is all over." Gellar got up and walked out into the ER. "Well, Colonel?"

"Sir, Chin was on duty alone last night. That has to be when the nine units went missing. There's no official record of anyone coming in, sir, no requests filed, or anything. The security readouts show the main door opened once during the shift, but the video stream was corrupted. There's no way to know who came in or what they did."

"Who would know how to do that, Colonel?"

"Anyone who's had the Security Advanced Course and the Sec-Tec School, sir."

"And who on this ship would have had both of those courses?"

"Only me as far as I know, sir."

"Is there any way the data-stream could have been corrupted accidentally?"

"Yes, sir, a power surge could have done it, or a radiation spike from some piece of equipment, even a gamma spike from outside the ship."

Behind Colonel Sandelescu, Master Chief Gillespie caught Gellar's eye. He was shaking his head slowly.

"Very well, Colonel, thank you, that will be all."

"Yes sir. I'll head on back to the Security office, sir, unless you need me somewhere else."

"No, Colonel, I'll call down there if I need you."

Sandelescu spun on her heel and left the room. Master Chief Gillespie motioned to Gellar. "Sir, we gotta talk about this."

"I agree, Master Chief. Doctor Moses, will you join us? Let's go in the office."

They went back into the little ER office. Master Chief Gillespie closed the door behind them before he spoke.

"Sir, I don't like to say this, but the colonel, she's lying."

"Why do you say that?"

"Those security readouts, sir, they're hardened against everything, radiation, physical damage, even particle beams up to a point. You can zorch the section with the whole output of a starship's signals system and not touch those readouts. Ain't no radiation spike gonna touch them, sir, you know what I'm saying? They had to be wiped manually."

"How do you know that, Master Chief?" Doctor Moses asked. "I thought you had to have special training on those systems?"

"Ma'am," Gillespie snorted, "I been in this Navy forty years. That's longer than three-fourths of this crew's been alive, including that colonel there. I was an engineer's mate on the old Dreadnought *Ranger* out on the Grugell border when you were still in high school, ma'am, no disrespect intended." The master chief cast a pointed look at Doctor Moses' graying hair, and amended, "Well, since you were in college maybe. But my point is, there ain't a system on these ships I don't know forwards and backwards."

"Including the security monitors?"

"Hell yes, sir."

Gellar turned to look at the computer terminal on the desk. "You think you could break in there and recover any data?"

"I didn't think you'd ever ask, sir. Let me have a minute at that terminal."

It took twenty minutes.

"See here, sir and ma'am, these here systems keep a data loop on the twelve-gig cache file. Now if someone who's just had some book learning on these systems wants to get rid of a few minutes of data, like, they'd just come in and drop a few lines of code into the main datastream file at the right time-code, and the system reads it like it's corrupted, right?" Gellar and Moses nodded.

"That's all fine and dandy, sir, but they don't tell these kids in their book learning to go in and look at the cache file. Now this cache stores an image of the datastream that goes back twenty-four hours, just in case you have a system crash on the front end. Then the system can go back and recover the stream. All you've got to know how to do is to uncompress the cache and pull it back into the main display. I got a little utility I picked up from an old shipmate that does that. And here, sir,"—he punched one final key—"is an image of the guests our PM2c Chin had last night."

The screen dissolved to show an overhead view of the front counter of the blood storage facility. On the screen, just entering through the main hatchway, was a fuzzy but unmistakable image of Colonel Sandelescu, and just behind her...

"Ios," Gellar snorted.

"And with the good colonel leading the way, sir."

"Master Chief, get hold of that gunnery sergeant. I want both of them found at once."

Conference Room One, two hours later

Assembled once more in the conference room nearest the bridge, Gellar, the chief surgeon, chief nurse, the exec, and Master Chief Gillespie waited for news from the Marines. After two hours, the handset on the conference table finally chimed.

"Conference One, Captain Gellar here."

"Sir, Gunnery Sergeant Anthony. We've got Colonel Sandelescu, sir. We found her unconscious in her quarters. Ios apparently hit her in the back of the head and stuffed her in a closet, sir. We're taking her to ER One now. She's under restraint, just in case."

"What about Ios?"

"No sign of him, sir. We're still looking."

"Very well. Keep me posted."

"You got it, sir."

Gellar replaced the handset. "Well, they found Colonel Sandelescu, stuffed into Ios' closet in her cabin."

Doctor Moses started up. "Is she alive?"

"Alive, under restraint, on the way to ER One. She took a hit on the back of the head."

The master chief slid his chair around and tapped away for a moment on the computer terminal set into the table, and then picked up the handset, punching a four-digit code. The rest of the group stared at him as he spoke rapidly into the handset.

"Yeah, this is Master Chief Gillespie. Get me Senior Chief Hooker."

He held a hand over the mouthpiece and mouthed, *Main Scanner Control.*

"Pete? Andy. Hey, can you give me main scanner control up here at terminal number," he slid over and read a serial code off the terminal, "six-four-three? Yeah. No, I got a trick or two up my sleeve, I'm helping the Old Man find something. Yeah. Yeah, I'm in for poker Saturday. You bet, bring your money. How much? All of it, boy!" Gillespie laughed at a comment from the other end, said, "OK, Pete, see you then. I'll kick it out on this end when I'm done. Thanks."

He replaced the handset and looked up into the stares of the rest of the group.

"Hey, you all should know by now, it's the chief petty officers who really run this Navy."

He pulled his chair up to the terminal where, for the last two hours, he had been coordinating the ship wide search. He tapped away as Gellar and Hoff moved to stare over his shoulder.

Hoff couldn't contain himself any longer. "Master Chief, what are you trying to do with the main scanner? You can't scan internally."

"No, sir, the damn Book just says you can't scan internally. Forget the Book—I'll show you how the chiefs on this barge get things done. Ma'am," he addressed Doctor Moses, "can you give me any bio readings on this Ios?"

"Yes, Master Chief," the chief surgeon replied, a new note of respect in her voice. "Can you bring up a main data frame, and I'll cross-link you over to his med-scan file?"

Moses and Gillespie put their heads together for a moment over the terminal. "Oh, yeah, that's the stuff," Gillespie noted. He tapped away for another moment.

"Now, see, what you have to do is send a subspace pulse out, and sort of reflect the scanner beam back off it into the ship. You have to set it up like this," he pointed at the program readout, "so that it alternates between the pulse and the scanning beam. Got a pulse interval of a hundredth of a second, gives you a nice even picture, pulses less than the interval your eye can detect, so you can't even tell it's a reflected scan beam. Neat little trick—an old engineering senior chief on the escort carrier *Merlin* showed it to me when I was a bosun's mate first. OK, folks, this is going to scan for a bio-signature with the hemoglobin numbers that the doc here gave me. If this is what it looks like, we won't get any false positives—if it trips, it'll be our boy. Should just take a minute."

It took just over forty seconds. The results displayed plainly on the screen. Gillespie had set the search to run and display over a schematic of the *Charity*, and the schematic was blank. A legend at the bottom of the screen flashed: NO MATCHES FOUND IN PROGRAMMED RADIUS.

"Crap. Doc, give me another reading I can use."

"Try basal metabolism. Here." She pointed. "This is the figure."

More tapping, and another forty seconds went by. This time a bright dot flashed on the screen, and the legend scrolled out: ONE MATCH FOUND IN PROGRAMMED RADIUS. A scrolled list of co-ordinates followed.

Gillespie looked up from the screen. "Sir, he's in the greenhouse."

"What? Are you sure?"

"Sure as I can be, sir."

Gellar grabbed the handset.

The greenhouse

Four Marines preceded Gellar and Master Chief Gillespie into the bright light of the now-evacuated greenhouse, their M65 rifles held at the ready. While the captain and the master chief waited just inside, the Marines fanned out and quickly searched the compartment. After that was done, one of them looked back at Captain Gellar and flashed a thumbs-up.

"Come on in," Gellar called to the chief surgeon and chief nurse. "Be careful." Doctor Moses and Chief Nurse Cartwright went into the greenhouse, each carrying a portable med-scan unit borrowed from the nearby Ward Four.

"Over here," Cartwright called. The Marines fanned out, rifles trained on the spot Cartwright indicated, under a hatch in the floor. It looked to be an irrigation system access panel, near the center of the vast greenhouse space.

"Careful, boys," Gillespie breathed as one of the Marines opened the hatch, with his rifle held one-handed at the opening. He trained the rifle's light into the open hatch. A curious look crossed his face, and he bent in to retrieve a small black box, with a dial, two studs, and a blinking red light.

"Damn him!" Gillespie shouted. "It's a damned decoy! We've been set up!"

There was an explosion and a shower of sparks from the high ceiling, and the artificial sunlight failed. The greenhouse fell instantly dark.

"Oh, shit."

A sepulchral voice echoed from somewhere out in the darkness.

"Ah, yes, my Captain, it is indeed a bad situation for you, yes?"

The voice seemed to ooze out of the very darkness itself. The four lights on the Marine's M65's stabbed out into the darkness, but nothing appeared save the waving fronds of ferns and palms, of a large ginkgo tree from Earth, and a flowering Heaven bush from Caledonia.

"Stand ready, Marines," Master Chief Gillespie breathed. "Shoot on sight."

The Marines fanned out, forming a protective cordon around the officers and the master chief. "Let's get back to the door. Slowly, people." Gellar was nervous now, certain that Ios was not only unstable, but dangerous as well.

The voice bubbled again out of the darkness. "Oh, but you can't see so well now, can you?" A dark, evil chuckle bubbled out of the darkness. "But I can see very well, Captain. Very well, indeed."

"Why not come out and talk to us, Ios? Why are you hiding?" Gellar called.

"Oh, my Captain, I should just walk up to your young Marines, who are so obviously anxious to shoot me? I've only just healed from what those foul, alien Grugell did to me, my dear Captain. I'm not quite ready to let your Marines punch holes in me just yet."

"They won't shoot unless I order it, Ios."

From behind them now, making the group jump and turn as one. "I don't believe you, my Captain."

A faint, dark form flashed across a light beam. Two M65 rifles spoke as one, stabbing polymer slugs into the darkness. Gellar bellowed, "CEASE FIRE! CEASE FIRE, DAMMIT!"

"Ahh, yes, Captain, not without your orders?" The deep, chuckling laugh came again, like bubbles of tar bursting on the surface of some subterranean oil pool. "I see. I see. Well, since you're so anxious to do me an injury, Captain…"

A scuttling sound came from somewhere out in the dark. "Aim low!" one of the Marines shouted. They played their beams on the floor, and a dark form moved low against an off-white planter. A stream of polymer slugs lanced through the form, to the chattering roar of the M65. Two of the Marines darted forward.

"Oh shit." One of the Marines turned, holding up a dark cloak attached to a length of wire.

"Back to the door, people," Gellar reminded them. As one, they moved slowly towards the hatch, the Marines' lights playing out ahead and behind.

"Oh, no, you're not leaving already?"

They stopped. Light beams played into the darkness, revealing nothing but plants. The voice came from somewhere overhead now.

"Have I perhaps been a poor guest, my Captain?" Ios' voice came thick, glottal now, as though his throat were full of phlegm. "Are my manners that bad, my Captain? And yet, perhaps I may be excused. I have not yet had my evening meal, after all."

The lights lanced overhead now, into the branches of what Gellar dimly remembered was called a banyan tree. Nothing.

"Close in, everybody," Master Chief Gillespie whispered. "Don't let him get to you."

A scream shattered the darkness, rising swiftly out of the middle of the group. A Marine brought his light around to bear on the form of Chief Nurse Cartwright as she was dragged, screaming, straight up into the tree by some unknown force. The scream was cut suddenly, horribly short as she disappeared from view.

"Julia!" Doctor Moses shouted. "Julia!" She grabbed an M65 from the nearest Marine, playing the light into the tree. "Julia! Are you there? JULIAAA!"

Silence.

"OK, everybody, out of here now."

They ran to the entry hatch, the Marines lighting the way. Gillespie hit the release, and the group fell as one into the corridor, gasping in exertion and fear.

"What the hell happened?" one of the Marines asked.

"Master Chief," Gellar gasped, "See if you can get some lights back on."

"I'll have to figure out why the emergencies didn't come on, sir. Might take a few minutes."

"Fast as you can, Master Chief, we've still got someone in there. Everyone else all right?" A chorus of nods, except from the chief surgeon, who crouching on the floor, hands still on the carbine. "Doc? Doctor Moses! Are you hurt?"

One of the Marines bent down and touched the chief surgeon's arm. "Ma'am?" he asked gently. "Ma'am, you hurt?"

"That thing has my best friend," the Chief Nurse said. Her voice was a low growl that startled Gellar. "Find it. Kill it!"

"Ma'am," the Marine said softly, "Suppose you give me that carbine?" He reached down and gently eased the carbine away.

Captain Gellar looked over to his second-in-command. The Chief Surgeon was close to losing control; however good a doctor she was, a possible combat situation was no place for her. "OK, Exec, I can't spare the Marines right now. Will you go with Doctor Moses back down to ER?"

"Yes, sir!"

"And then, go back up to the bridge and try to dig up some more data on our friend in there. Whatever he is, we know damn well now that he isn't human. Cross-link everything you can dig up, starting from the very beginning, see if you can find something we can use."

"You got it, sir." Hoff bent down, helped Doctor Moses to her feet, and guided her off down the corridor towards the lift.

"Master Chief?"

"Sir?" Gillespie had an overhead panel pulled out and was shining a penlight up into the access space.

"Where can he go from in there without coming out this door?"

Gillespie reached into the overhead, opened a box, and began flipping switches. "Good thing they put the emergencies right outside the door. Space Systems finally got something right. Sir, I ain't got good news for you. There's a huge return in there for the main ventilation recirc units. See, sir, they pull in fresh air from the greenhouse, and run it through four Environmental suites, and then out to the ship. The vents decrease in size as they go to keep pressure up, but he should be able to go quite a ways. Call it maybe three decks down or up, and maybe a third of the way fore and aft from the intake, which is dead center in the top of the Greenhouse. And it's the biggest compartment on the ship, sir, he can hide right in there."

"Not for long, he can't. He knows we're on to him now. And you know, Master Chief, where he'll try to go."

"Aye aye, sir." Gillespie looked at the Captain. "He'll be tryin' to get to that ship of his." He was silent for a moment, still engaged in whatever he was doing inside the panel. "Surprised to see Doc Moses come unglued like that. A Navy doc—she should have seen people get hurt before."

"We all have our breaking points, Master Chief," Gellar pointed out. "We can disassociate ourselves from a lot, but seeing your best friend taken like that, that's rough. And from the chief's record, she's never been in combat, and isn't really trained for it; she'd a damn good trauma surgeon, but we've been at peace for quite a while now."

"I suppose so." The master chief finished what he was doing and reached up to bang a panel door shut before sealing the overhead back in place. "Emergencies should be back on, sir."

Gellar opened the door and leaned to look inside. A dim but usable light filled the space now from the emergency lights. The four Marines preceded Gellar and Gillespie inside.

"OK, stay within sight, everyone. Let's see if we can find Nurse Cartwright."

They found her, a few meters from the banyan tree. Her body was lying curled against a large polymer planter, uniform shredded, and when a Marine tipped her head back, her throat was torn out as though by an animal.

"Sir, this don't make sense," the Marine said, recoiling. "Look at that—there ain't no blood?"

Gellar knelt by the corpse. "And there won't be. Look at her color—no post mortem lividity, no pooling, no bleeding from the wounds, just a little capillary seepage." He looked up at the Marines and the master chief. "There's no blood in the body."

"So, we've got a murderer on the ship. You, Marine, you got a comm-link?" The Marine lance corporal in charge of the detail nodded at Gillespie. "Good, get Gunnery Sergeant Anthony on the horn." He turned to the captain, shaking his head. "Don't know why I didn't think of that earlier, the Marines all carry comm-links. Sir, I think we need at least a squad of Marines around that yacht right now."

"Agreed. See to it, Master Chief. Let's get out of here," Gellar ordered. "You and you"he pointed at two Marine privates"pick up Nurse Cartwright and get her out of here. Take her to the examiner's office for now. I'm ordering a ship-wide Code Red alert. The greenhouse is closed until we find Ios."

Chapter Twelve

ER One

Andrea Moses sat on an office chair in the ER office, overcome with grief at the news of the chief nurse's death. A young ER doctor had looked her over and advised a small sedative, which she refused.

A parade of memories of a twenty-five-year friendship cascaded through her mind. They had celebrated marriages and commiserated over divorces together, rejoiced over promotions, plotted for joint assignments, and traveled the length and breadth of the Confederacy together.

And now Julia's gone, and I have to go on alone. My best friend killed by some kind of monster after we rescued him, after we saved his life!

A thought struck her. *His exam data and blood samples,* she thought. *Commander Hoff's up on the bridge right now, going through data records looking for information on Ios. I wonder what I can turn up in the lab?*

She stood up suddenly, barking at the young doctor on watch in the ER. "Lieutenant! I'll be in the main lab. If the captain calls, send it down there." Suddenly revitalized, she strode out of the ER, turning left and disappearing into the corridor.

The bridge

Commander Hoff found himself at the terminal again, staring at the main data search feature.

How do I go about this? He wasn't sure where to begin, so he brought up his saved search on Belos Ionescu. *Might as well begin at the beginning.* He tapped away at the keyboard.

FROM RESULTS FIND ALL MATCHING DATA REFERENCE GYPSY*

There were two links:

> SZGANY SANDU
>
> SZGANY METALSMITHING

The second one didn't seem like it would be too useful, so Hoff selected the first.

> The Szgany Sandu were a tribe of Romanian Rom, or Gypsy, who inhabited the Wallachian region from the early eighth century until the early twenty-first. Their oral histories were unusual in their inclusion of legends of an Old One who would one day deliver the tribe. The Old One, referred to as Old Belos or the Old Master, was rumored to appear from time to time in the region of the Carpathian Mountains dominated by the ancient Castle Ionescu, a typical fifteenth-century stone fortress in the region bordering Transylvania.

Old Belos, eh? Hoff almost smiled at the remark. *It seems Old Belos is still around. There's one question answered.*

He tapped away again.

FROM RESULTS FIND ALL MATCHING DATA REFERENCES
PROPER NAMES.

SANDELAS

SANDELASCU

SANDELESCU

SANDOS

SANDUS

SENDELESCU

SENDOS

Sandelescu? Hoff tapped away again, bringing up the main search screen. He sat thinking, fingers drumming idly on the panel as he did so.

So, our security chief is descended from a Gypsy family that was tied in with our immortal friend in fifteenth century Earth? What are the odds of that?

I wonder about his weird blood numbers, and the stealing from blood storage? What about that?

He tapped away at the main data search again.

FIND ALL DATA INCLUDE ALL KEY WORDS BLOOD, HEMO-GLOBIN, WALLACHIA, SZGANY.

One entry included all the search terms with one hundred percent relevance: WAMPIR.

Hoff stared at the entry. The term was vaguely familiar. He brought up the data link:

> A blood-sucking ghost, or the soul of a dead person
> superstitiously believed to come from the grave and
> wander about by night sucking the blood of persons
> asleep, thus causing their death. This superstition was
> prevalent in parts of Eastern Europe as late as the

twentieth century, and was especially prevalent in Hungary about the year 1730.

There were several links for further data. Hoff spent the next three hours reading, and growing more chilled by the moment.

The main med-lab, 1745 hours

"Get the captain down here." An orderly scurried to obey the chief surgeon's barked command.

Andrea Moses stared down into the e-beam microscope for the thousandth time, unwilling to really believe what she'd found in Ios/Ionescu's blood. But, as a scientist, she was unable to deny the evidence that lay before her.

Captain Gellar walked into the lab no more than five minutes later. "What is it, Andrea?"

"Take a look at this." She motioned him towards the eyepieces.

"What the hell? That's a virus."

"It's not just a virus," Moses pointed out. "It's a retrovirus, and one of the most complex I've ever seen. It's a gene-splicing retro, to be exact. If I didn't know better, I'd almost say this little bastard was engineered."

"This was in Ios' blood, wasn't it?"

"You bet it was. I think this is the source of Ios' weird abilities. Take a look at this." A computer terminal stood on the desktop a meter away, and she motioned Gellar towards the screen where a genetic analysis screen stood on display.

"That's not human DNA."

"No, it's human DNA, but it's been extensively modified. There's roughly thirty percent more genetic information than in a typical human, and several lengths of non-coding DNA seem to have been co-opted for some other purpose. Now exactly *what* this does, I'm not sure of. But I'm willing to bet that longevity and uncharted regenerative abilities are a couple of effects."

"So, Ios is infected with this retrovirus? Can you come up with a hunter-killer antivirus for it?"

"I could, but it wouldn't matter. There's no reversing the genetic changes, or the morphological changes that are associated. Ios was human once, before he was infected with whatever this bug is, but he'll never be human again."

"And, I suppose, this must also be the cause of his low hemoglobin count. Could that have something to do with the Blood Storage theft? Or with, well, Julia Cartwright's death?"

"Only if his system is extensively modified to extract hemoglobin directly from his digestive tract. It wouldn't work in an anemic human, but with Ios, who knows? We didn't get the chance to run that many systemic tests—we mostly did work related to his burns, and some of the standard blood and tissue screens. That's how we discovered the low hemo count."

"And the scanners didn't find him on the hemo count scan," Gellar mused. "Because he'd brought his hemo count back up with the blood he'd taken!"

"Maybe—but remember, we didn't really find him on the basal metabolism scan, either. He anticipated us and used a pretty sophisticated little metabolic simulator. Chief Whooton down in Physical Systems told me he'd never seen anything like it. He may have a way to shield himself from scans."

"I suppose, if his physical readings are that far off normal, he would want to find some way. OK, now what do we do with this information?"

"There's more, Captain." Both doctors turned to see Commander Hoff in the hatchway. He looked stricken.

"What is it, Exec?"

Hoff walked into the room, speaking in a low voice. "I can bring up all my searches and let you read them, sir, but it'd be quicker to give you a thumbnail."

"Very well, go ahead."

"Sir, we should go somewhere else." Hoff inclined his head towards the two techs working a few meters away.

"My office is just up the corridor," Moses said, and they headed that way.

The hangar bay

A ten-man squad of Marines was now stationed in the hangar around the *Black Dragon*, with no two closer together than three meters. "Just like The Book says," Gunnery Sergeant Anthony muttered with a satisfied grin. His own platoon of Marines was, he maintained, the best on the ship, if not the best in the Fleet. If Ios popped in here, he'd be in for a rough go.

Overhead, a pair of glowing red eyes peered through a vent duct grate. Ios hissed in rage at the sight. Ten Marines all spaced at intervals, all well-armed. He'd never make it to his ship without being chopped apart.

The vent duct here was only sixty centimeters across, but Ios' body flowed, crackled, reversed back on itself. His head elongated and flowed backwards under his stomach, his shoulders dislocated and pulled through afterwards, and he flowed back up the vent shaft like a weird, primal serpent, sliding up towards the enlisted crew's dormitories.

The chief surgeon's office

"OK, Exec, what have you got?"

There was a small, round conference table in the chief surgeon's office, and the three officers seated themselves there. Commander Hoff was sweating.

"Sir, does the word 'Wampir' ring any bells?"

"No, not really. Andrea?" The chief surgeon shook her head once.

"Well, that's what I think our Ios is." He shook his head and continued.

"There's an old eastern European legend, sir, about the Wampir, or Vampire. In the old stories, the Wampir was a supernatural being, a walking undead demon that attacked living people and drank their blood." He went on for another ten minutes.

"Of course! That old nineteenth century novel, *Dracula*! I've seen dramatizations of it."

"The virus," Moses said, a speculative tone in her voice. "The retrovirus could cause enough genetic reprogramming to cause the kind of morphological changes to make a primitive culture see the result as a supernatural being."

"Yes, ma'am. But there's more. I ran a search on associated records in fifteenth century Romania, and found a Gypsy tribe that was supposed to serve an almost godlike master, named 'The Old One,' or—get this—'Old Belos.' They were called the Szgany Sandu, and they frequented an area in the Carpathian Mountains near an old fortress known as the Castle Ionescu."

"Go on."

"Captain, the Szgany Sandu stayed in the area into the twentieth century and split into several smaller family groups. One of the offshoot family names, sir, is Sandelescu."

"Oh, shit."

"You said it, sir."

"We need to talk to Colonel Sandelescu right now."

"She's in the security ward now," Moses pointed out. "Let's go down there."

Main Engineering, 1830 hours

"Well, good evening, Master Chief."

"How you doing, Orlando?"

Senior Chief Petty Officer Orlando Neff was in charge of environmental controls, and he represented Gillespie's best hope of tracking Ios through the various ducts and crawl spaces in the *Charity*.

"We got a problem, Orlando. I need to know how far a man could get in the ventilation system, starting from the greenhouse."

"Shit, Master Chief, which direction? Look here," he motioned towards a huge ship's schematic that covered the better part of the office wall. "You know the main air intake in the greenhouse branches out four directions in to environmental controls, then from there it branches out to the rest of the ship, right? The ducts get smaller with each outlet, and then there are about sixty returns that run back into the greenhouse. That's the whole point, Master Chief—we get about sixty percent of ship's oxygen from those plants. OK, the greenhouse is on Deck Four, right? And the open area goes up another four decks, up to Eight. Biggest compartment on this bucket, that room. Well, the ducts leaving the greenhouse are over a meter wide, and they reduce a little bit at each vent to keep flow up—how much depends on the flow rate and the size of the compartment you're venting into, but figure you can get up to Ten—the top deck—and down to Two, or One, if you're kind of skinny. You can get port and starboard almost all the way, fore and aft about a third of the way back, almost all the way forward. Hell, Master Chief, if a guy wanted he could get almost anywhere."

"How about the main hangar bay?"

"I don't think so." Neff leaned in to look hard at the aft portion of the ship's schematic. "No, I don't think so, Master Chief. The main hangar's almost all the way aft—remember the bay doors are just above the drive tunnel outlet. These here three ducts are only sixty centimeters across. A little kid, maybe, but anyone grown up's going to get himself stuck in there, you know?"

"Well, that's good, at least."

"So, what's up, Master Chief? We got someone loose in the ducts?"

"Keep this quiet, Orlando, I'm not kidding, but yeah. There's a character loose in there, we figure he got into the system in the greenhouse. We've got to find the son of a bitch."

"Why didn't you say so? Look here," Neff motioned Gillespie towards a large electronic display in the main workshop. "This here is the newest environmental gizmo in the Fleet. We got it installed right before we left dock a few weeks ago. It uses a graphic display to model the airflow rates through the whole ship. Tells you if there's a problem somewhere, a blockage, a bent duct, whatever."

"So, what's it telling you now?"

Chief Neff examined the plot closely. "Well, Master Chief, it's telling me your guy ain't in the ductworks."

"Any way to backtrack, run a history on this?"

"No, Master Chief, it don't work like that. You can only see what's going on right now, there's no recording feature. Wouldn't be a bad idea, though."

"Crap. Orlando, I want you to keep a man on this, twenty-four-seven, until I say different. If he goes back in the air system, I want to know about it. As in I want to know immediately, any hour of day or night. Page me."

"Aye aye, Master Chief. What's this guy done, anyway?"

"Need-to-know, Orlando."

"I hear ya, Master Chief."

Master Chief Gillespie left the compartment in a hurry, heading for the Goat Locker at first, but half-way there he found himself heading for the hangar instead. He stopped outside the dimly lit bay, staring in at the *Black Dragon*, seemingly deserted.

What was it that this ship reminded him of?

Why do I keep thinking about the Ranger? he wondered. "What is it about this guy's ship," he asked himself aloud, "that bugs you, Andy? Why do you keep thinking about the *Ranger*?"

He thought back again to that time, thirty-six years ago. Hadn't a yacht come on board the *Ranger* then, too, just a few days before the murders began? It had only been aboard for a day, two at the most. It had been a square, boxy little thing, charcoal gray like this one instead of the usual white or light gray of space-going craft, but not sleek and streamlined. That yacht had been older, square-bodied, with only one Gellar drive mounted squarely atop the passenger cabin.

What had it been called?

Gillespie spun on his heel and headed for his quarters. His late supper could wait.

Security ward, Room Two

"Colonel? Can you hear me?"

Doctor Moses leaned over Sandelescu's bed, cajoling her to full consciousness. She took one of Sandelescu's hands, rubbed it, turned it over and patted the underside of her wrist.

"Christine?"

Sandelescu's eyes fluttered open for a moment, immediately closing tightly against the light. A groan escaped her as though torn from her body.

"Christine, wake up," Doctor Moses cajoled. "Wake up, please."

The Marine's eyes fluttered open again, focusing finally on Captain Gellar where he stood at the side of her bed.

"Sir," she groaned. "Sir, I'm so sorry..."

"Sorry? For what?"

"Sir, he injected me with something. It was like I was sleep-walking, sir. I don't know how he got to me."

"Injected you? With what? Doc, is there any trace of anything in her blood work?"

"No, we haven't found anything abnormal."

"Christine," Gellar prodded, "how did he do it? What did he use?"

Sandelescu tipped her head to the side, pointing to four small marks on the back of her neck, over the spine. "He hit me with something here, sir." A few centimeters above the four marks, a large swelling showed where Ios had clipped her into uncon-sciousness.

"A neural toxin?"

"Could be," Moses allowed, "but it would have to be pretty sophisticated to keep us from finding it."

"Either that or it metabolizes quickly, and Ios stuffed her in that closet when it started to wear off."

"I don't think so, Jared." Moses looked skeptical.

Gellar pulled a chair to the side of Sandelescu's bed. "Colonel," he said in a conversational tone, "I want you to tell me all about Ios, how he got to you and what he had you do."

"Sir, it started when I went into his room that first time. He must have had some kind of autoinjector hidden somewhere. I remember a sting, like some kind of insect bite, and then everything just faded out. The rest is like a nightmare. I know I took him to Blood Storage, and I know I spent some time in his guest quarters... Oh, God, I do remember that part."

"What part?" Gellar asked, afraid he knew the answer.

"Sir, he had me drugged, I just couldn't resist him." The normally stern, seemingly emotionless Marine began to sob. "I couldn't even lift a hand to stop him, he just took me..."

Gellar began to feel an ice-cold rage building.

A maintenance crawlspace

Ios had found a good hiding place for the moment, in a service crawlway of some sort near the hangar bay, but he knew he'd have to be moving again soon. Before he made his next move, he sent his thoughts out to his chief thrall, lying now in a hospital bed. Her thoughts came through tangled, confused, but the ship's captain was with her, and his thoughts stood out. A cold wall of rage filled the captain's mind, a barely controlled rage.

Good, Ios thought. *As I planned—he is protective. He will not think as clearly now.*

He slid back into the air duct and began a serpentine slither forward towards the enlisted crew's dormitories. He had to draw the Marines away from his ship, and he had a plan on just how that could be achieved. It was time to set up his diversion. The fact that he would be able to feast in the bargain was an added bonus.

Chiefs' quarters, Stateroom One

Gillespie sat staring at his personal terminal's screen. He still had an extensive personal log from every ship he'd served on, all the way back to the repair ship *Orwell*, his first assignment out of Engineering Basic School. Back then he'd had the habit of snapping pictures of anything interesting or unusual that came along, a habit that persisted to the present. He'd even snapped a couple of pictures of the shot-up *Black Dragon*, surreptitiously in case Mr. Ios would object.

On his screen now was a thirty-six-year-old image of another rich man's toy, the yacht that had landed on the *Ranger* two days—he had the dates now as well—before the murders started. A square, boxy, dark gray yacht with a single Gellar tunnel, its name clearly visible on the bow.

The *Black Dragon*.

"You son of a bitch," Gillespie breathed.

He brought up an info browser and thought hard for a moment about an old book he'd read when he was a teenager. A very old book, a book from nineteenth century Earth. He'd always thought it was the work of a vivid imagination, no more. Now, he thought he might know better. The title came to mind after a moment, and he found the text in the computer's data storage.

Dracula, by Bram Stoker.

The master chief scrolled down the text and began to read. There was a way to kill this thing, and this book would remind him what that was.

Chapter Thirteen

Crew's dormitory, Bay Two, Room Four, 2045 hours

A fifty-centimeter air vent led to the back wall of every junior enlisted crew dormitory room. Less than a meter away on each side stood a clothing closet for the use of the four occupants.

A rattle sounded in the empty confines of Room Four. The air vent grate dropped to the floor, and a dark shape flowed out of the vent, dropping to the floor and congealing into the tall, dark shape of Bel Ios. On regaining his full shape, he dropped into a defensive crouch, but the room was empty.

Ios hissed at the empty room. The vent grate lay on the floor behind him. He bent and picked it up, snapping it back into place before he flowed into the right-hand closet. His overtaxed system required sustenance again. The hunt was on, and in this place, all he had to do was await the prey. He pulled the door shut behind him.

In the closet, he settled himself comfortably before reaching out with his senses, with his mind, to touch his chief thrall.

Master, she reported, *they are hunting you.*

I know, my child. I have been hunted before. Reveal nothing; tell only what I instructed you to tell them. No more.

Three hours later

"Hell of a day," Lance Corporal Miles Messner commented as he strode down the corridor with his three roommates, heading for their quarters after an hour's worth of attitude adjustment in the Deck Four lounge.

"You said it, bro." Private First Class Petros rubbed his forehead. "Man, I've got the worst headache from staring into ventilation ducts all day." The other two Marines, Private First Class Ingram and Private Moss, chimed in with their own accounts of security alert duty.

"It's gonna be rough until they find whoever this clown is we're looking for," Messner predicted. He slapped his hand on the panel to open the door to the four-man dorm room the young Marines shared, and the four trooped in, as they did most evenings.

"Is it cold in here?" Ingram asked. "Someone check the enviro settings."

A thump and a shuffle behind him made him turn his head and look. A tall, weird figure was unfolding itself from one of the wall closets. "Ahh," it hissed, revealing, long, interlocked teeth. "Just what I was hoping for."

Security office, Deck Six, 0800 the next morning

"Sarge, you seen Messner and Ingram this morning?"

Staff Sergeant Jules Tipp looked up from his terminal, squinting at Corporal Ozakanian briefly. "Why, weren't they at muster this morning?"

"No, Sarge, neither of them."

"That's not like them. They're good troops. They're roomies, aren't they? Call down to their dorm room, see if they overslept."

Ozakanian consulted his duty roster before lifting a handset and tapping in a code.

"No answer, Sarge."

"OK, well, go on down there and find them."

The bridge, 0848 hours

"Captain, call for you from Security."

Gellar rubbed his eyes—he'd only managed about thirty minutes of sleep—and picked up the handset recessed into an arm of his bridge chair. "Captain speaking."

"Sir, this is Gunnery Sergeant Anthony. We've found four of my Marines murdered, sir, Bay Two, Room Four in the junior enlisted dorm. Master Chief Gillespie and Doc Moses are already on the way down, sir, but the Master Chief, he said I ought to call you too."

"Yes, Gunny, he's right. Thank you. I'm on my way down."

"Aye aye, sir. It ain't pretty sir."

"Great." Gellar laid the handset down and got up slowly to leave the bridge. "Exec, you've got the conn. I'll be down in the junior enlisted crew's dormitory. Page me if you need me."

Master Chief Gillespie met Gellar at the entryway to Room Four.

"Morning, sir. All due respect, sir, you look like shit."

"Gosh, thanks, Master Chief. You should see it from my side. How much sleep did you manage?"

"About an hour, I think," Gillespie replied with a wry look. "I did some database research for a while, and then spent most of the night in Engineering trying to re-rig the scanners to find this bastard. I napped an hour in Chief Neff's office."

"You've got me by a half-hour, then."

"You're still a young man, sir. How's your stomach? Strong? You'll need it to be when you go in there."

"Really? I've been a Navy doc for a while, Master Chief. I've seen nasty stuff before."

"Sir, you ever seen four Marines that have been *eaten* in their own quarters?"

Gellar winced, but he went inside to find a furious Gunnery Sergeant Anthony watching Doctor Moses conduct an examination of the remains.

And of those remains there were precious little. Moses looked up from where she knelt on the floor to take a DNA sample from a severed arm. "I've got remnants of four Marines here, Captain."

"Ios?"

"Good bet, don't you think?"

"How did he get in here?"

Gunnery Sergeant Anthony spoke up. "Right here, sir. See how the air vent panel is popped loose?"

"But that's only fifty centimeters wide!"

"Ain't no other way in but the door, sir, and this door's coded. All the crew dorm doors are coded. Unless Ios can fake someone's palm print, he didn't come in that way."

Gellar stepped to the air panel. He squinted hard at the opening, and then pulled the panel cover off all the way. A few strands of hair were caught in a junction between two sections of air duct, about a meter down the shaft. Gellar retrieved them, handing them to Doctor Moses.

"Run these through your DNA scanner, Andrea, and see what it looks like."

Moses dropped the hair strands in her scanner and pushed a contact. The analysis took only a few seconds.

"I'd have to run a full spectrum analysis in the lab for it to be admissible, but right now, I'd say that this is from our friend Ios."

"Sir," Anthony ground out through gritted teeth, "what kind of man is this? I mean, these were *Marines*, sir, ain't no one man going to come in here and take four Marines by himself. Lance Corporal Messner, he maxed his last three Physical Standards tests; he was selected for NCO and Force Recon schools. He was a tough damn kid, sir!"

"I know, Gunny. Where's Colonel Sandelescu?"

"Still in the Sec Ward, sir. Are we going after this guy?"

"Yes, but we've got to find him first. He's got some way to hide from our scans."

"Sir." Gillespie leaned in the open hatchway and motioned to the captain. Gellar took the three steps to the entryway, inclining his head to listen to the master chief's softly spoken comment. "Sir, think about this some. What's this Gomer going to want to do eventually?"

"Get back to his yacht?"

"Roger that, sir. Now let's think about this here. We know now he can get through the smaller ducts somehow, so I reckon he's been to the hangar bay. We've got a squad of Marines around that yacht, sir. 'Wampir' or not, he can't get past those boys. They've all got loaded rifles while they're in the hangar—they'd cut him to pieces."

"Go on."

"Sir, figure our boy saw those Marines around his yacht. You gave him a tour and told him about the ship, right? He might know we only have a short company of Marines on board, right?" Gellar nodded. "So, sir, he gets up into the crew dorms and raises a little merry hell to make us pull some of the jarheads out of the hangar bay to look for him. So, sir, if we do that—pull all but, say four Marines out—and put those four inside his ship instead of out in the bay…"

"I follow you, Master Chief. The regs about private ships don't apply when you're looking for a suspected criminal, so we can board his ship and put Marines inside."

"That's what I'm thinking, Captain." His look was bordering on murderous.

"What's up, Master Chief? You look like you could chew through a bulkhead."

"Sir, you read about the *Ranger* Incident, right?"

"You bet, it was required reading at the Academy."

"Well, sir, there was a private yacht docked on the old *Ranger* two days before those weird murders began. I looked it up last night. Guess what that yacht was called."

"I think I see where you're going. It was the *Black Dragon*, right?"

"You got it, sir. Not this *Black Dragon*, but another one, an older ship by the same name. Our boy was on the *Ranger*, sir. I've got several scores to settle with this guy, sir, and best of all, I think I might know how to go about it now."

"But first we've got to catch him, right?"

"Right, sir. And we know right where to do it."

"OK, Master Chief. Take Gunny Anthony down there and see to it. Get his four best Marines in there, with squad paralyzers and side arms."

"Aye aye, sir." Gillespie motioned to Anthony, and the two non-commissioned officers left swiftly as Gellar bent to help Doctor Moses with her unpleasant task.

The greenhouse

At the top of the Greenhouse, inside the main ventilation intake, there was a tight bend in the main duct. On the inside of that bend, a small piece of sheet metal had come slightly loose, and now that piece of metal was looser, held in place by only a single rivet. Under the loose piece of sheet metal was a small dead space, and in that dead space, undetectable by the ship's scanners, hid Bel Ios.

His recent feast, of blood and flesh both, filled his ancient body with strength. His vampire senses were at their peak, his mind sharp, and his awareness acute to a fault. Minds and warm, salty bodies scurried through the ship, and his senses reached out through the ventilation system to every corner of the ship, tracking the movements of the crew.

Sharp as his awareness was, though, he was limited. Except at very short ranges, he could track general movements of bodies, but not individuals.

His body lay in the dead space, curled deceptively into a fetal curl. A fine, spider-web-thin material had slowly spread from his body into the air duct system. The webbing brought information back to his brain along the tiny filaments. A body of troops had just left the hangar space where his ship remained.

He focused on the large hangar bay, tuning his senses a little finer. There were still some warm bodies in the hangar space, but fewer than before, no more than one or two, it seemed.

His long jaws cracked into a jagged grin. Reaching out with his telepathy, he contacted his chief thrall where she lay in the ship's hospital area.

My child, how can I get my yacht out of the hangar spaces?

Master, she replied, *the force field at the opening will only drop if the pre-set cycle is initiated from the control booth. I can give you the codes, Master, but the booth will be manned.*

Leave that to me, Ios hissed in his thrall's mind. *I will deal with anyone in the hangar when I prepare to leave. I must leave you here, child.*

Yes, Master.

You have served me well, child. You will remember Old Belos, Lord Ionescu. You will tell your children—make sure they remember as well. It is the duty of the Szgany Sandu to serve me, child. Rememberrrr!

He withdrew his probe. It was still early in the day, and the ship's company was active. *Wait until late in the night,* he told himself. *How fortunate for me that humans still cleave to their sleeping schedules, that night is still night. Even in space, the night is my time. On this night, I will take my ship and leave this place.*

The hangar bay, 1900 hours

Gunnery Sergeant Anthony had been asleep the better part of the day. Like the hardened campaigner he was, he had the uncanny ability to sleep almost on command, and now he was awake, refreshed, and ready to take one of the four guard posts inside the *Black Dragon* herself. A full squad of Marines waited in the sealed warehouse space next to the hangar, and were prepared to charge through the cargo bay door at the press of a panic button on any of the four guard's armored battle vests.

Three other Marines waited inside the *Black Dragon* in full battle dress, including armored vests, leggings, and helmets with low-light vision systems. All the lights were out inside the ship, and only a faint emergency light glowed outside.

Anthony and one Marine waited in the cockpit, and the other two in the tiny engineering space at the rear. Anthony shifted slightly where he sat on the floor, back against a panel. He adjusted his grip on the squad paralyzer he held in both hands. While the one-handed, holstered neural paralyzers that were standard issue to Marines in the ship's crew decks would knock a strong man flat, the squad paralyzers, built to be fired like a carbine, would project a wide band of neural disruption force that would stun a dozen rioters. The Marines' vests projected a light force field around them that would protect them against the neural blast, but not against a physical impact. The vests' power packs didn't carry enough energy for a physical shield.

Anthony looked down at the tiny comm-link he wore on his wrist. Passive scanners were placed all around the hangar bay. If anything moved, a red light would blink on his comm-link. And, since the only Marines on the twelve-hour night guard watch inside the bay were his four inside the ship, any movement could only be Ios.

And Anthony had a score to settle.

Main Engineering, 2310 hours

"Page Master Chief Gillespie."

"Excuse me, Senior Chief?" Engineer's Mate Second Class Kilgore was aghast. "It's almost midnight!"

Senior Chief Petty Officer Orlando Neff turned away from the air-system panel, glaring with fatigue-reddened eyes at the third watch NCO. "You heard me, Kilgore, page the Master Chief, and do it *right now!*"

The handset at Chief Neff's elbow chimed exactly three minutes later.

"Main Engineering, Environmental."

A familiar, although exhausted, voice came from the handset. "That you, Orlando? What are you doing down there at this hour?"

"I couldn't sleep, so I figured I'd come on down and have a look at the air system watch."

Behind him, EM2c Kilgore snorted to another EM2c, "Come down, my ass, he's been here for almost twenty-four hours non-stop staring at that panel."

"Master Chief, I think we got a track on your guy," Neff continued, ignoring the comment. "I'm following a flow rate disruption in the air system, in the works leading from the green-house aft. I don't understand something, though."

"What's that?"

"Well shit, Master Chief, if this is supposed to be a guy in the system, he's gotta be a skinny bastard. He's almost back to the hangar bay, and the ductworks he's in are narrowing down awfully tight—maybe fifty, sixty centimeters. And there's still some airflow—he's not even completely blocking the duct."

"That's our boy, Orlando. Good work! Listen, I'll fill you in after this is over. Right now, I've got stuff to do. Stay on that panel, let us know if he heads off anywhere else."

"Aye aye, Master Chief."

Chapter Fourteen

The hanger bay

A tiny red light flashed three times on Gunnery Sergeant Anthony's wrist comm-link, and a tiny tone sounded in his ear. The tinny but recognizable voice of Master Chief Gillespie came through the earpiece.

"Heads up, Gunny, you got company coming, through the air ducts overhead."

"Roger that, Master Chief," Anthony breathed. He hissed orders at the Marines hidden in the ship. There was a faint rustling of cloth, the snapping of power switches turned on, and the clicking of the joints in polymer armor, and then all was silent. The Marines were prepared for action.

High overhead, in the ceiling of the cavernous hangar, two glowing blobs of red appeared in the grate of an air vent. Ios scanned the hangar carefully. The huge bay appeared to be empty but for a stack of crates, a maintenance cart, and the *Black Dragon*, still scarred but spaceworthy.

Gingerly he reached out, loosening the grate covering the air duct. He worked the grate loose, slowly, quietly, finally bending the tough steel into a tight roll to pull it inside the duct. Relaxing his guard for a moment, he flowed slowly out of the duct and hung, suspended from the ceiling like some weird, primal bat.

Still nothing moved in the hangar. He remained where he was for the moment, listening carefully. A heart was beating somewhere below him, perhaps several, but he couldn't pinpoint the location. A faint scent of blood came to his large, beaked nose, but with the air vent just above him, the scents were confused.

Ios knew his time was limited. His strength was at its peak now, after his feast of the previous night. He had to make his play now.

Releasing his hold on the edge of the air duct, he fell for a few meters before extending his arms. Muscle and bone crackled and popped as his flesh flowed, flattened, spread, until at last he floated down to the hangar floor like a huge, black autumn leaf.

Landing, he shuddered once, yawned hugely, and regained his normal shape. The *Black Dragon* was just there, a few meters away. He made for the hatch, grinning.

The hatch swung open from the inside before he could reach the yacht. An armored Marine stood in the hatchway, a grim look on his face. "Got you, you bastard," he said, leveling his energy weapon and firing.

Ios leaped for the cover of the nearby maintenance cart, but the energy bolt grazed his ribs, sending a searing bolt of shock down his side. His left side went numb from the chest down.

He landed hard, hearing behind him the thundering footsteps of several Marines pouring out of his—*his*—ship. Shouted orders echoed through the hangar bay as Ios felt sensation flow back into his leg. He rose to face the troops.

"So, you would fight with me, would you?" he taunted them. "Ah, but I was a warrior long before your grandparents were born. Come, then, and fight!"

Anthony was taken by surprise, but only for a moment. A squad paralyzer should knock down any ten men, and he'd hit Ios, but here he stood before them. "Fire! Fire!" he shouted, and all four Marines unleashed fans of shimmering fury at the tall, thin figure.

Ios leaped over the spray of neural energy with an almost liquid motion. He rolled in midair, reaching down one impossibly long arm to seize the Marine on Anthony's right. A quick twist and a pop of bone, and the Marine slumped to the deck, his neck broken. Anthony and the remaining two swung their weapons, fanning energy after the retreating Ios, who clung to the deck now, seeming almost to flow like a sentient liquid towards the warehouse bay door...

...which rolled open, disgorging a full squad of ten Marines in combat armor. A squad paralyzer bracketed Ios squarely, slamming him against the deck. He hissed and rolled, trying frantically now to escape, but in doing so he forgot the three Marines behind him.

Gunnery Sergeant Anthony ran forward, roaring his anger and training a sustained burst of neural energy on Ios' prone form. "Keep it on him! Keep it on him!" Four more squad paralyzers and eight hand paralyzers slammed their beams into the ancient vampire, pinning him writhing to the deck.

Ios gagged, screeched, and fought. Under the scathing energy beams, he felt as though a thousand tons of rock had fallen on his ancient body, but his strength had not completely left him yet. Agony shot through him as he forced himself up, up, finally managing to stand.

"Shit! Hold him!" Anthony shouted. "Keep the beams on him! Full power!"

Every fiber of Ios' being raged; his vampire spirit was screaming at him to kill, *kill, KILL*! He was dimly aware of more humans pouring into the hangar as he fought, finally forcing his body to obey, stumbling forward. The energy spray increased as he got closer, and he battled against it as though he swam against a mighty current. He was forced down again, dropping to one knee, reaching for one of the Marines bearing a larger weapon. The youth backed away, but Ios' arm stretched out impossibly, three, four meters. His hand elongated, his nails flowed into chisel-tipped chitin claws, finally breaking out of the blast and seizing the Marine's throat, tearing it out in a red welter. One of the five squad paralyzers dropped to the deck.

Ios stood again, recovering slightly under the weakened assault. He reached and grabbed again, making the Marines dance away from his grappling-hook hands. The paralyzer beams wavered, weakened, and the ancient vampire broke loose.

He flowed forward, batting energy weapons aside, pausing to snap one neck as the Marines fell back before him. The leader of the troops stood before him, still directing a blast of neural energy that washed over Ios like water as his body adapted to the assault. He reached for the grim-eyed figure, grabbing him by the neck, drawing him close to stare into his ice-blue eyes.

"So, you thought to kill me? Better than you have tried." He drew his free hand back to strike.

This time, though, Ios' arrogance was ill founded. He'd never fought a trained Recon Marine before, and Gunnery Sergeant Anthony was far from beaten. He dropped the useless paralyzer and waved his left hand impotently in Ios' face. As the weird, glowing eyes flickered towards the moving hand for an instant, Anthony reached his other hand to the small of his back, retrieving a half-meter long, serrated fighting knife. Summoning every bit of strength he had, he slammed the titanium blade into the center of Ios' chest, twisting the knife as it struck home.

"*RECON!*" Anthony screamed a victory cry as Ios dropped him and staggered away, coughing a spray of black blood. Anthony hit the deck hard, scuttling backwards on all fours away from the wounded vampire.

Ios dragged the blade from his chest and dropped it to the deck, still trailing a stream of black liquid as he staggered towards the open hatch of his yacht. Another Marine appeared before him, this one sinking his fighting knife home in Ios' shoulder. A third knife sank into his back, skewering a kidney. He shrieked in agony anew, turning to grab at the Marine behind him, catching him, slamming him to the deck, striking with chitin claws to snap his spine.

Anthony strode forward, bending to retrieve his fighting knife, stepping in behind Ios. He slammed the knife home again, aiming for the spine, feeling the blade slide between the vertebrae. He twisted the blade again, forcing the bones apart, feeling the spinal cord sever. Ios dropped to his knees, hissing, turning his upper body towards Anthony. Anthony watched as Ios' jaws gaped open, wider and wider, revealing a jagged row of fangs, behind which a black, pointed tongue writhed like a snake. His jaws crackled and snapped, elongating into a wolf's muzzle as needle-pointed fangs sprang from his gums.

Anthony unholstered his personal hand paralyzer, stuck the discharge point in Ios' gaping maw and fired, slamming the horrible figure to the deck.

Running footsteps came from behind him as he looked down at the bloody, writhing form. Impossibly, Ios was moving again, attempting to stand, regaining his balance. The Marines backed away, openmouthed in amazement. Ios made it as far as one knee when Gunnery Sergeant Anthony was suddenly knocked to the side.

It was Master Chief Gillespie who pushed past, rushing at Ios with an object made of—*wood?* Anthony told himself in stunned amazement. *What has he got?*

Gillespie sprang at the vampire before he could completely recover, slamming his sharpened wooden stake home dead center in the weird figure's chest. Ios fell to the deck and lay still at last. A snarl disfigured his already ugly face, but only his eyes moved, darting back and forth at the growing crowd that gathered around.

The master chief bent forward, placing both hands on his knees and breathing heavily. "I really am getting too old for this shit," he muttered. "Sir, I expect the Navy to reimburse me for one Earth League genuine oak baseball bat," he announced in a louder voice as Captain Gellar and Commander Hoff hurried up to the grisly scene.

"A baseball bat, Master Chief?"

"Don't you ever read books, Commander?" Gillespie straightened up to grin at the executive officer. "Only way to bring down a Wampir is a wooden stake through the chest. I think I probably had the only damn piece of wood on this ship. I borrowed a carving knife from one of the kitchens, been whittling down that handle for the last few hours."

Behind them, Gunnery Sergeant Anthony shouted for medics. Two teams rushed out of the cargo hold. Anthony tapped a contact on his wrist comm-link to call for more medics and litters.

"He's not dead," Gellar observed. He bent over Ios, taking care not to get too close. The sulphurous eyes glared up at him. "He doesn't seem to be breathing, but he's not dead."

"No, sir, you got to cut his head off," Gillespie informed his Captain. "And burn him. Or just burn him. Hell, we could probably blast him out an airlock—that'd probably do the trick."

"No, Master Chief, monster or no monster, the law says he's got rights. But we've seen how fast Ios, or whatever his name really is, can recover." Gellar straightened up. "Let's get a litter team over here. No, belay that. Take care of our Marines first. I want Mr. Ios taken to a holding cell in the brig. Two Marines go with them. They can pull that stake out in the cell, then the force field goes on and he stays in the cell."

"Sir, you just gonna slap him in a cell after all he's done?" Gunnery Sergeant Anthony was nearly beside himself with rage, but his years as a Force Recon Marine had left him highly disciplined.

"No choice, Gunny," Gellar replied. "We'll document all the evidence, turn him over to the judge advocate on New Wichita after we report to TF947. That's all we can do. Excuse me, we've got hurt people here—I've got work to do." He turned away, shouting instructions at the medics still running into the hangar bay.

As the captain ran to help the wounded, Master Chief Gillespie went back to the ancient vampire, still pinned by the whittled oak bat. He leaned over Ios/Ionescu, looked into the raging, sulphurous blobs that were his eyes, and spoke in a calm, conversational tone.

"You remember the *Ranger*, don't you, you son of a bitch?" The blazing eyes focused on him, and the heat in them doubled. "You turned someone on that ship into something like you, didn't you, you worthless bastard?" Gillespie dropped to one knee. "Well, I'm sure you read about what happened after you left, didn't you? Remember the name Gillespie, monster? It was on all the news reports."

The vampire's eyes locked on the master chief's. There was a faint look of, what, recognition?

"That's right, monster. That was me. I'm the Gillespie that saved a hundred and four lives on the *Ranger*, and I've still got scars to show for it. And now, you bastard, so do you." He reached down, took hold of wooden bat where it projected from Ios' chest, and yanked it back and forth savagely once, twice. A froth of blood bubbled from Ios' mouth, and his great hound's teeth were bared, just for a moment, reflexively. "But you're worse than dead now, you son of a bitch." Gillespie wrenched the bat once more, twisting it until the vampire's face warped in agony. "You're caught. And you're going to spend one hell of a long time in prison." The master chief stood up, folded his arms across his chest, and looked down dispassionately at the prone form.

"Payback's a bitch, ain't it?"

He turned and strode from the hangar bay. Some of the ghosts from his past would rest a little more easily now.

Chapter Fifteen

Main med lab, 1000 the next day

"Good morning, Andrea. Any news on Colonel Sandelescu?"

Looking up from a terminal, Doctor Moses wasn't surprised to see Captain Gellar standing in the entryway to the main lab. She smiled at the captain. "You look a lot better, Jared."

"Eight hours of sleep. Having Ios in the brig behind a force field did wonders for my personal stress level."

"Yours and mine both, I expect. I only just got up an hour ago myself." She smiled broadly. The relief she felt at Ios' capture was mirrored tenfold on Gellar's face. "As for our good colonel, she's recovering nicely. Fit and ready to go and get back to duty, in fact. She's going to have a nasty headache for a few days from that knock on the head, but she's strong. She'll deal with it." Moses turned back to the terminal, tapping a couple of keys. "In fact, I was just updating her chart. I'm going to release her back to duty after the noon meal."

"How was her blood work?"

Moses knew precisely what Gellar was getting at. "No sign of Ios' virus. She's clean."

"Good. Is she up to a visitor?"

"As long as it's not Ios. She'd like to rip his face off right at the moment."

"Can't fault her for that." Gellar frowned. "Last night, Master Chief Gillespie suggested blowing him out of an airlock. I wouldn't mind, personally. I've got two Marines in the morgue, and another with a broken spine."

"I know, Jared. I saw the injured one last night. He's undergoing stem-cell neural regeneration therapy with Doctor Upstead; he'll be fine in a few weeks."

"Well, that's a bit of good news, at least. Good thing we've got a good neurologist on board."

"That's our *Charity*, Jared. Best of the best."

"Is the colonel still in the security ward?"

"Yes, I didn't see the point in moving her. Not when she'll be back to duty today."

"All right. I'm heading down there now."

The security ward

Gellar found Lieutenant Colonel Sandelescu frowning at the remnants of her breakfast tray.

"Come on, Colonel, don't look at it like that. The cooks try hard."

"I know, sir, I'm just not sure what it is they're trying to do." She pushed the tray table away and ran long fingers through her thick, black hair. "Sir, when can I get out of here? I've got a department to run."

"Relax, Colonel. That's up to Doctor Moses, and she's decided that you can go back to duty sometime today, as long as she's satisfied you're recovering."

"I'll be fine. I've got an incredible headache, but I'll be fine."

Gellar pulled a chair up to Sandelescu's bedside. "Christine," he began, startling the Marine, "how much do you remember?"

"Being under Ios' control, you mean?"

"Yes."

"Not much, sir." A haunted look crept into her eyes. "It was like, I don't know, a bad dream. Like I was sleepwalking. I can only remember flashes here and there—I remember something about Blood Storage, and I remember showing him around the berthing areas."

"We've found a lot out about Ios. One thing in particular, Colonel, affects you."

Sandelescu looked at the captain expectantly.

"Did your family have any old stories, Christine, about an old Belos, or a Lord Ionescu? Anything like that?"

"Not really. My grandfather used to tell stories about Earth, and how we were descended from a Gypsy tribe." She smiled. "He used to claim he came from a line of Gypsy kings."

"Christine, Commander Hoff has been combing over our computer records. He's found out a lot about Bel Ios.

"His real name, or his original name, impossible as that seems, is Belos Ionescu. He was born on Earth, in old Romania. One of the links we found has an image of him, taken around the time he was wounded in the Arc de Triomphe bombing in Paris, just before World War Three began."

"What? Sir, that was a couple hundred years ago!"

"It gets better," Gellar continued. "There's a record of him as a landowner and feudal lord of some kind in Wallachia, back in the fifteenth century. He had a tribe of Gypsies that served him, the Szgany Sandu."

"Sandu?"

"Yes. And Sandelescu..."

"Is an offshoot of the old Szgany Sandu?" A look of shock settled over the Marine's features.

"That's what the computer says. Christine, Ios, or Ionescu, or whatever he is, is hundreds of years old."

"How?"

"He's apparently what was known in the old days as a 'Wampir.' Back in the old days, they thought that he was some kind of demon, a supernatural monster of some kind. Doctor Moses has found a virus in Ios' blood."

He filled Sandelescu in on what the crew had found out about Ios/Ionescu to date, as the look of horror on her face grew.

Chapter Sixteen

The brig

Ios sat cross-legged on the cell's narrow cot, eyes closed. His wounds had healed, even the chest wound where the wooden stake had pierced him, coming close to skewering his heart. But his rage was still growing, and his hunger was almost out of control.

A Marine was seated at the end of the corridor, positioned where he could easily see the force-field door on the cell. Another Marine sat at the office desk near the brig entryway. Both were clad in polymer body armor, and both were armed with M65 rifles loaded with high-explosive slugs. Spaceship or no spaceship, the Marines weren't taking any chances. Ios had surreptitiously looked into both minds, finding hard, disciplined, and determined psyches. Both Marines were filled with anger, and the anger was directed at him. He'd felt the like before. *They'd happily blow me into space, if the captain would let them*, he thought.

But I will not be the one taught the final lesson in this adventure. As his body remained motionless, Ios' vampire consciousness crept out into the ship. His chief thrall, the Marine's commander, was visiting with the captain. Well and good. He left her alone.

He'd lost control of the boy who worked in Blood Storage. The mind wasn't attuned to his, and the young man was strong— too strong, given the brief chance Ios had been given to recruit him. There were two other minds still in thrall to him, though, young, easily influenced minds, accustomed to taking orders. He reached out to those two now and began feeding them instructions even as they continued their work in Main Engineering.

The sweet, salty tang of blood filled his senses. Senses grown more acute than ever in his need hammered the scent of blood into Ios' brain, driving his vampire being almost mad with lust.

Soon, he told himself. *Soon. After the endless centuries, another few hours are as nothing. Wait. Wait.*

The bridge, 1300 hours

"Commander Hoff, you want to go visiting?"

Hoff looked up from his station panel to see Captain Gellar and Colonel Sandelescu standing behind him.

"Sir, you're not thinking what I think you're thinking, are you?"

"It's only fair, Wils. You were the one that did all the research work. Wouldn't you like to get a better look at the ancient marvel you've uncovered?"

"You're going to try to question him, sir?"

"I'm planning to ask him a few questions, yes, but I doubt he'll be too cooperative. And I'm only talking to him through a force field."

"And I've got a thing or two to ask him myself," Sandelescu added, her face set in a grim mask.

Hoff stood up. "All right. All right. I guess I'm as ready as I'll ever be."

The brig

Ios' eyes popped open, startling the Marine sergeant who stood looking at him from the corridor. He brought his rifle to bear quickly, but the force field shimmered unbroken between them. Ios merely cracked his long jaws open in an evil grin.

"You are about to have visitors," he informed the Marine. "Your captain, the second in command, and the Marine commander, if I'm not mistaken."

"How do you know?"

"I know." Ios closed his eyes again.

A moment later the hatch to the brig slid open, and the three predicted people walked in.

"Sergeant?" Sandelescu called out. "The captain wants to talk to the prisoner. Is he awake?"

"Yes, ma'am," the sergeant called, staring at Ios through the shimmering haze of the force field. "He's awake."

Gellar turned to Colonel Sandelescu. "Are you sure you want to do this? Nobody will blame you if you don't."

"I'm sure, sir."

The three walked down the corridor to the brig's only occupied cell.

Ios' eyes snapped open, and a weird smile played across his face.

"Good afternoon, Captain, Commander. My dear Colonel Sandelescu." Ios nodded, his smile broadening.

Gellar laid a hand on Sandelescu's arm.

Ios laughed once, a short, hard laugh, almost like the bark of a large dog. "Ah, how little humanity has changed through the ages. Captain, this young woman could break you in half, and still you feel the need to protect her."

"No more games, eh Ios? Or should I say, Ionescu? Through the ages, indeed—you were there to see them, weren't you?"

"Indeed, Captain, you know that very well yourself now, don't you?"

"Thanks to my exec, yes, we do."

The ancient vampire stood up, turning his back on the trio and speaking at the blank, white wall at the rear of the cell.

"What a lot of trouble you've caused me, Captain. You've exposed me. You've brought humanity's buried memories to light again. People have long ago stopped fearing the unknowable horrors that stalk the night, the predators, the Wampir. Now, thanks to you, they will know those old fears again. This will make my life all the more difficult, my dear captain."

"I wouldn't worry about that," Gellar said in a conversational tone. "Things won't be nearly that difficult in your prison cell on New Wichita."

"You would put me in prison, Captain?"

"A court will put you there."

"And how long will they hold me?" He laid a long-fingered, clawed hand on the rear wall, splaying the fingers out. "A life sentence?" His baying-hound's laugh boomed out again. "You think you can put me in a cage forever, Captain?"

Ios' voice grew deeper, more glottal, as though he spoke through a mouthful of phlegm. "You think you can hold the Old One, the hunter of men, in a cage forever? For, Captain, that is what you must do. For one day the cell will fall away, the door will rust away, or the power will fail, and the Old One will walk the night again."

He turned around, and three mouths dropped open in shock.

Ios had transformed into something beyond belief.

His eyes glowed like red-hot coals. His nose flattened against his face, and had grown whorls like a bat's, while his ears elongated until they came to points near the top of his head, ending finally in brushes of stiff black hair. And his jaws were worst of all, elongated into a wolf's muzzle full of ivory knives. He stood leaning slightly forward, and his long arms hung to his sides. As they watched, his fingers stretched with small cracking and popping noises, his nails growing into chitin chisels, until his hands grew to resemble deadly grapples.

"You—you *are* a Wampir!" Gellar gasped. "What kind of monster..."

Ios hissed his anger from behind the cell's force field. His long, angular jaw flexed, revealing dagger-like teeth. Gellar took an involuntary step back.

"Yesss, Captain," Ios hissed, his tongue writhing like a snake in his gaping jaws. "I'm not quite what you first thought, am I?"

"Who—what—are you?" Commander Hoff demanded.

"She knows," Ios hissed, pointing at Lieutenant Colonel Sandelescu. "Ssshhe, is one of my own. Sshhe, is one of the Rom, one of mine, one of the Followers. Her blood speaks to me, and it speaksss, to her."

Gellar and Hoff gaped. Colonel Sandelescu's eyes were glazed, her mouth slightly open, her breath coming in shallow gasps.

"You sssee?" Ios hissed.

"Let me tell you a tale, Captain," the creature in the cell continued. "Let me tell you of a young man sent off to fight the Turk in the Great Crusade, sent off to fight under the banner of the Dracul warlord Vladimir Tepes. Thisss young man, Captain, was wounded unto death in battle that fateful summer of 1453."

Ios grinned, his teeth gleaming whitely, his fangs interlocking. "I'm speaking of myself, of course, Captain. My birth name is not Bel Ios, as you have discovered, but Belos Ionescu. I was born in the ancient Earth province of Wallachia, in the year 1438 on the calendar of the Christians."

"In that fearful siege, in that fateful year of 1453, I was wounded in the chest by a Turkish lance. I lay dying in the field, but as the sun set, I was visited by an attendant to Vlad, a German leecher called Hess. He was Wampir, this Hess, and when he left me, I was Wampir as well. My wounds healed, and I walked away into the night. I have hunted as one of the Wampir since that night; I am now, by Earth calendar reckoning, over nine hundred years old. No other has lived so long, Captain; no other of the Wampir survives to this day.

"I am the last of my kind," he concluded, folding his impossibly long fingers together.

"For nine centuries and more since that night, I have lived and hunted. The old Vlad Tepes was demonized by history for deeds that were largely mine. When mankind grew sophisticated, so did I. When mankind went to war, so did I. What paradise a world war was to one such as me! The battle, the frenzy, the blood, ah yes!" He laughed again, lost for a moment in rapturous memory. He shook himself like a great dog and continued.

"And then the day came when humanity conquered the very stars themselves. When my prey went beyond the sky, so too must I follow. Over the centuries, I had amassed a fortune indeed, and I used it to commission a private yacht. Not the one you hold in your hangar now, but the first *Black Dragon*, a crude affair by comparison. Still, it served my for many decades, until ten years ago I commissioned the ship I call home today."

"And that ship took you over the Grugell frontier?"

"No, Commander, the ship took me nowhere by itself. Over the years I heard many stories of the Grugell, and in the end my curiosity consumed me. When you've known the ennui of a millennium, the thought of anything new—some new tidbit, some tasty morsel you've not yet sampled—becomes irresistible. So, I approached a Grugell mining colony, under the pretext of trading for some of their wines. Such trade goes on, surely you know, outlawed as it is on both sides."

"I've heard that," Hoff admitted.

"You have indeed. I wager you've a bottle or two tucked away in your quarters, do you not, Commander?" Hoff looked away in embarrassment.

"But I digress. I did indeed visit that colony, and stayed there for some days, and in that time, I sought to feed. But these aliens, foul beings that they are, they were no gastronomic pleasure at all—and the effects of that feeding, the transfer of the curse I carry, the effects were, shall I say, rather violent?"

"I know," Gellar admitted. "I've seen it."

"And that, Captain, is how I came to be your guest. I fled the colony, but two units of their Navy were in the vicinity, and I was pursued, fired upon, damaged grievously.

"And now I find myself here, in your cell, awaiting the pleasure of your mortal law." He shook himself, choked, gagged, and shuddered back into a semblance of normal form.

"You son of a bitch," Sandelescu breathed.

Ios cocked one hairy eyebrow at the Marine. "My dear, to talk so, after what we've shared together!"

"Let's get out of here," Gellar suggested. They left the brig quickly, accompanied to the corridor by Ios' booming laugh. They regrouped in the corridor, all of them rather badly shaken.

"Exec, do me a favor. Call up to the bridge; tell the signals watch officer that I'm going to want to talk to the judge advocate on New Wichita as soon as possible. Colonel Sandelescu, you and I have to talk. Can you come up to the bridge conference room?"

"Yes, sir. Let me call down to the security office first, all right? I should let the duty NCO know where I'm going to be."

"Of course."

Thirty kilometers aft of the *Charity*

Group Commander Tottalastrik had been waiting for the message from the Imperial Navy, but he wasn't looking forward to seeing Admiral Grigoratchik IX's wrinkled visage appear on the monitor.

"You will continue to follow the Confederate ship," the admiral's image ordered. "Give the monster one more standard day to attempt an escape. If his ship leaves the Confederate Navy ship's hangar, you will destroy it. If it does not... We must not wait until the ship reaches the Task Group. You have a clampon lander on your ship. One standard day from now, you will use it. Close on the Confederate ship and send in one of your best in the clampon lander. He will board the Confederate ship, track down and destroy the monster."

"Yes, Lord," Tottalastrik responded automatically, knowing even so that the beamed subspace recording couldn't hear him. He wasn't optimistic about the chances of one Grugell operating alone in the heavy gravity of a Confederate ship, but the admiral wasn't finished yet.

"I'm beaming you a technical readout of the Confederate Navy's medical cruiser class. The information contained in this file should enable your commando to enter the ship's main computer records, locate Ios, and find a way to destroy him. It will also, of course, provide a location he can attach his clampon lander to best avoid detection. It seems our brethren in the Intelligence Services aren't completely incompetent, after all."

Tottalastrik tapped a stud on the panel with one black claw, opening a link to his command center. "Order the helm to close in on the Confederate ship, bring us five kilos off their stern. Leave Commander Diforastid's frigate ten kilos back to cover us. Send SubLieutenant Vickatatrick in to see me."

"Yes sir," the speaker buzzed.

Main Engineering

"Hey, Commander!" Senior Chief Petty Officer Dub Eddlestone called up through the cavernous space to the *Charity*'s engineering officer, Lieutenant Commander Fred Hoskins, who hung over the catwalk two decks above to answer.

"What's up, Chief?"

"I got a bubble in the drive tunnel. Picked it up right after we popped back into subspace. Are we in clear space to do a blow-through?"

"Hang on a second, let me call up to the bridge."

Hoskins picked up a handset, tapped the code for the navigation station on the bridge, and spoke for a few seconds.

"Yeah, go ahead, Senior Chief," he called down.

"Aye aye, sir." Eddlestone turned to his panel and began setting up the blow-through.

The Gellar drive had developed a "bubble," a zone of quantum flux in the energy conversion stream in the kilometer-and-a-half-long drive tunnel. Since a bubble would reduce the efficiency of the drive, and could possibly start a harmonic flutter that would damage the ship, the Navy's standard practice was to do a "blow-through." A hefty dose of anti-matter was injected into the drive tunnel at the leading edge, resulting in a flash conversion, a controlled matter-anti-matter explosion that the Gellar's initial field conversion drove through and out the rear of the tunnel, clearing any irregularities and restoring the smooth flow of energy through the progression of conversion fields.

Another result was a blast of concussive force a good ten kilometers to the rear of the drive tunnel outlet, a phenomenon that was described with a variety of crude names having to do with excessive intestinal gas production in humans, but was described in the Navy's engineering schools as "backblast." Regulations required the clearing of space aft of the ship before a blow-through was carried out, a formality in this case as the *Charity* was traveling unescorted.

Or so they thought.

It took Eddlestone a minute to program the sequence, adjusting the injection to account for the size of the bubble. He opened a view window on the computer screen to the small aft navigation scanner as well—regulations required it, and he just liked watching the big energy flare. "It's going to be a big one." He chuckled to himself. The workstation sat against a curved bulkhead. Behind the bulkhead was the machinery and huge tunnel of the star drive. Eddlestone patted the curving bulkhead affectionately and told the ship, "OK, honey, we're gonna get rid of that gas ball for you." He picked up the handset on the workstation and punched the button to Page. "All hands, stand by for blow-through, say again, stand by for blow-through." The surge of energy would cause a noticeable lurch, and anyone caught off balance could be tossed to the deck. "Blow-through will commence in three, two, one, *mark!*" He stabbed the final key.

The *Charity* took a lunge forward, then settled back to normal.

"I hate to think what that was like before we had good inertial dampers," Eddlestone called up towards the catwalk. Lieutenant Commander Hoskins' voice came back down, "I'd hate to think what it's like getting caught behind a drive fart."

Three kilometers aft

Tottalastrik was dozing in his command chair when his helmsman let out a startled squawk. "Sir, energy surge from the Confederate ship!" He yanked the control yoke to the side and jammed the ship's drive power control all the way forward.

Tottalastrik looked up at the main viewer, where the Confederate hospital ship hung in space as before—except now a flare of white-hot gas was streaming out of the drive tunnel, directly at the Grugell frigate.

"It's going to hit us," Tottalastrik commented, strangely calm. "Full shields, please, Tactical."

Barely in time, the tactical officer raised the ship's force field defenses. The wake of energy crashed into the frigate, catching it on the front quarter as the helmsman tried in vain to turn out of the oncoming blast. The ship slammed to the side, driven broadside to the blast, rolling three times before the Helm got a semblance of control. They rode the energy wave out at an angle, finally emerging from the stream far to the rear of the Confederate ship.

"Is the cloaking device still functioning?" Tottalastrik called out over the piercing shriek of an alarm.

The tactical officer shouted a reply. "Yes, Group Commander. We have shock damage on levels four and five, but the engines are on line, and weapons are on line. Sir, shall I return fire?"

"No. That wasn't an attack."

"Sir?"

"That wasn't an attack. I've seen it before. Their engines use a mass tunnel. They occasionally fire a charge of anti-matter through the engines to clear any disturbances in the conversion matrix. I knew that, but I didn't take it into account—that was stupid of me. Take up station as before, but this time three kilos to the rear, and three kilos to one side. Stay clear of their mass tunnel outlet."

"As you command, Group Commander."

"Well, that was entertaining," Tottalastrik observed coolly. "Back to stations, everyone."

Bridge conference room

"I hate it when they do that."

Gellar chuckled, settling back in his chair. "Gets you in the stomach, doesn't it?" Colonel Sandelescu nodded, frowning.

"Are you feeling all right, Colonel? You look a little pale." Gellar's voice was concerned.

"I'm fine, sir, just a little tired. Hungry, too."

"Well, you've been through a lot. That's what I wanted to talk to you about, Colonel."

"Yes, sir, I thought as much."

"Commander Hoff showed you the results of his computer search, right? We're dealing with something none of us ever expected, Christine, and I'm certain that Ios has abilities we don't know about. What we *do* know about him is frightening enough. But in your case, in particular..."

"I know, sir. The Szgany Sandu. Sir, that was almost a thousand years ago."

"Yes, and you'd think those old bloodlines would be long gone by now. It's not like people live in tribes anymore. There are sixty-six settled planets in the Confederacy now, and three more opening up for colonization in the next year. But still, Ios recognized you, Christine. He picked you out as one of the Szgany Sandu at a glance. We can't afford to take chances with him—he's too dangerous."

Sandelescu stiffened suddenly. "Sir, are you relieving me of my duty?"

"No! No, Colonel, I wouldn't dream of doing that. You have a bright career yet ahead of you; I wouldn't do anything to jeopardize that. I expect to see general's stars on your uniform one of these days." He leaned forward. "But what I am asking you to do is to stay away from Ios. Don't go into the brig spaces at all.

Gunnery Sergeant Anthony can handle everything down there, can't he?"

"Yes, sir, he's my best man."

"Fine, then, it's settled. There's plenty for you to do as it is—the Marine contingent commander on a cruiser shouldn't have to play prison guard in any case. Now," Gellar continued, "tell me, how are you really feeling? You don't look well."

Sandelescu managed a weak smile. "I'm tired, sir, tired and starving. I feel like I could eat a whole Hecation renlawyer, raw."

"Very well, Colonel." Gellar grinned at the Marine. "This, then, *is* a direct order. You are to proceed from this conference room to the wardroom, where you will eat as much of a dinner as suits you, and from there you will go to your quarters for a minimum of twenty-four hours of sleep, rest, and recovery. I'll prescribe a sleep aid if you'd like one."

"No, sir, I don't think that will be necessary."

"Good! I won't expect to see you before this time tomorrow then, Colonel. Dismissed."

Main Engineering

"Hey, Commander, you want to come take a look at this."

"Still watching the flare replay?" Hoskins chuckled. The senior chief was known for his love of fireworks.

"Yeah, sir, but take a look at this." Senior Chief Eddlestone enlarged the frame with the recorded blow-through flare display, frozen now just at the start. "Watch, now, sir, I'll run it at half-speed."

The image on the screen slowly unfolded. The rear navigation scanner showed a small portion of the aft end of the ship, just above the drive tunnel outlet. As they watched, the flare grew brighter and brighter, growing into a tongue of yellow-white energy that streamed backwards from the ship. A slight flutter came into the display from the sudden lurch of power, and the energy stream flowed out further still. Eddlestone stopped the playback suddenly and pointed at a spot just to one side of the energy stream.

"See there, sir? That disruption in the stream, like it hit something?"

"Well, I'll be damned, I've never seen anything like that before. There wasn't anything on the scan back there a few seconds before. Navigation checked, just like the Book says."

"Sure looks like the stream hit something, though, don't it?"

"You're right, Senior Chief, it sure does." Hoskins leaned over the panel. "Can you magnify that section of the flare?"

"I think so, sir, just a moment." The NCO tapped a few keys and used the panels' touch-pen to line out the portion of the screen in question. "Here you go, sir." The disturbance shimmered and enlarged.

"Hell, Chief, you know what that is?"

"I think I do, sir." He pointed at the screen. "See that, that's a pylon with a drive pod, and follow along here, that's a portion of a hull. Sir, we got us a cloaked Grugell frigate in tow."

"Well, we did, anyway. That flare must have shaken them like a rat caught by a big dog."

"Sir, if they got their shields up in time, it should have only shaken them up some. They could still be back there."

"Sharp work, Chief. I've got to tell the captain about this. Any chance we could catch them again like that?"

"Not a chance, sir. They'll be staying clear of the tunnel outlet now. The Grugell, they may be mean but they sure ain't stupid."

Hoskins laughed. "You're right, Senior Chief, and when you're right, you're right. Good enough. I'm going to go call the bridge."

Chapter Seventeen

The bridge

Captain Gellar watched the slow-motion playback for the third time. Commander Hoff and Master Chief Gillespie each watched over his shoulders.

"Those bastards," Gillespie observed.

"Clever, aren't they?" Gellar chuckled. "All stop. Drop us into normal space. Signals," he called across the bridge, "send a hail on all guard frequencies. Tell the Grugell that we know they're back there."

A few moments passed by before the electronics mate first class at the signals station replied. "Sir, there's no reply."

"Zorch 'em," Gellar ordered.

"Sir?" The ElM1c spun her chair around, a questioning look on her face.

"You heard me. Zorch them!"

"Aye aye, sir."

"Sir," Commander Hoff pointed out, "there's a chance they were damaged by the blow-through. If they were knocked out of subspace, they might be half a light-year behind us now."

Gellar shook his head. "I bet they're not. They probably aren't in our wake anymore, but even if we knocked that one's star drive off line, there's bound to be another one. They're back there somewhere. Why hasn't some Space Systems genius figured out a way to track a cloaked ship yet?"

At the signals station, ElM1c Gennie Franklin was powering up the ship's long-range hyperphone pulse transmitter. She angled the transmitter to project a directed signal on a twenty-degree arc to the aft of the ship, punched up enough power to drive a hyperphone signal a hundred light-years, coded in a simple hailing signal, and punched TRANSMIT.

Several billion kilowatts of energy blasted back at the cloaked Grugell frigate.

"They're zorched, sir," ElM1c Franklin called out.

Master Chief Gillespie chuckled. "I always loved that trick. The signals watch over there is gonna have a headache for three days."

A moment later, a face Gellar recognized as Group Commander Tottalastrik swam into view on the main screen.

"You know, Captain, I'd probably be justified in returning fire on you after that." A haze of smoke drifted across the bridge of the Grugell ship behind the group commander, and two Grugell crewmembers stood well back from what was presumably their primary signals station, which still emitted a few sparks.

Gellar smiled politely. "Well, Group Commander, we know that you were caught in the wake of our blow-through, and we were concerned for your safety. When you didn't answer hails, we thought that perhaps your star drive was knocked off line, and that may have left you light-years in our wake. So, we boosted signal power to see if we could pick you up. We're a medical ship, you know. We're required to render assistance wherever necessary. And besides," he continued, "you have now demonstrated that you can hack into our ship's main display through our signals station, so I'd say that's retaliation enough for the moment. Please extend my compliments to your signals staff. Now, Group Commander, may I ask why you are still following us, almost ten parsecs into Confederate space?"

"I think you already know that answer to that question, Captain."

"Of course. You're after our guest."

"You belabor the obvious, Captain."

"And you, Group Commander, just don't get it. Bel Ios is a Confederate citizen. He's safely in our brig, and he will be taken to our Fleet headquarters to stand trial. If the Grugell have charges against him, then you may pursue extradition through the normal diplomatic channels."

Tottalastrik smiled suddenly, and spread both long-fingered, clawed hands out in an appeal to reason. "Captain, we are soldiers, not diplomats. Surely you can see the reason behind dealing with a monster such as this out here, among the stars, rather than go through the tedium of a formal trial?"

"That, Group Commander," Gellar replied coldly, "is why the Confederacy is a republic, not a dictatorship. Our people have rights."

The smile evaporated from Tottalastrik's narrow, bone-white face. "Very well, Captain. I leave you to your contemplation of your captive demon's 'rights,' then." The main screen went blank.

The Grugell frigate

"Did the clampon lander get away clean?"

"Yes, Group Commander. It should dock on the hull of the Confederate ship in ten minutes."

"Good. Obliging of that Confederate captain to tell us where the monster is being held, is it not?" Tottalastrik sat back in his command chair. "Have SubLieutenant Vickatatrick report to me immediately upon his return."

"Yes, Group Commander."

The *Charity*, on the bridge

Master Chief Gillespie finally broke the silence. "Uppity bastards, ain't they sir?"

Gellar had to laugh. "Yes, but I swear, it's hard to hold your temper sometimes dealing with them. I don't know how anyone could live in a dictatorship like that."

"Well, sir, they ain't human, they don't think like us, and for that matter, Earth has had more than its share of dictatorships if you read your history books."

"That's true." Gellar swung around to face Signals again. "Take a message to the Commander in Chief-Task Force 947, please."

"Recording—go ahead, sir."

"CINC-TF947, this is the *Charity*, inbound from Tarbos." Gellar gave a quick synopsis of their encounter with Ios, his history and abilities, their casualties, and the Grugell involvement. "Due to these events, we are re-routing directly to New Wichita, to hand Ios over to the civilian authorities there. We will then depart New Wichita immediately for rendezvous with TF947. Please advise if you have other orders. *Charity* out."

"Send that immediately please, Signals."

"Aye aye, sir. It will take about sixteen hours for the Fleet to get the message, based on their last known location."

"Very well," Gellar replied. "Helm, Astrogation, new course, best possible speed for New Wichita. All ahead full."

The *Charity*'s hull, just outside the security section

SubLieutenant Vickatatrick floated his tiny, claustrophobic clampon lander to a feather-light contact on the Confederate ship's hull, where ceramic super-conducting magnets activated to hold it firmly in place – moments before the cruiser leaped back into subspace.

A tiny scanner showed him precisely where to burn through the hull to avoid cutting any cables or tripping any sensors. It was the work of moments with a tiny laser torch to cut a portion of hull out to enable him to wriggle through into a maintenance crawlway. He placed the section of hull to the side, to be carefully welded back into place before he left.

He glanced at his tiny illuminated navipad strapped to his wrist. He was only a short ways from the detention area. The crawlway would take him most of the way there.

The heavy gravity of the Confederate ship was oppressive, but he had a mission to carry out. Vickatatrick pulled a tiny light from his armored vest, clenched it between his sharp, serrated front teeth, and started crawling.

A few minutes crawling down the dusty maintenance space found him looking down through a grate at an empty corridor. Another glance at his navipad told him that the detention area would be just around a corner to his right front. The grate pulled open easily, and Vickatatrick dropped into the corridor.

He drew his weapon immediately. Slowly, carefully, he crept up to the hatchway to the detention area. His target would be just inside, through a small office area, down a corridor.

A moment's quick glance around the corner revealed one Confederate seated at a desk, leafing through a paper pamphlet of some kind. Another Confederate sat with his back to the hatchway, watching some display on a viewscreen set into the wall.

Careless, Vickatatrick told himself. *Careless indeed, but that makes my mission all the easier.*

Dialing the power setting on his weapon to a heavy stun setting, to allow for the massive musculature of the Confederates, he stepped quickly around the corner and fired. Two bolts of jade shot into the tiny office, dropping both targets to the deck, twitching.

Good, Vickatatrick congratulated himself. *Good. Now on to the primary target, and then I can get out of here.*

He strode down the corridor, looking into the cells. Only one cell had a force field active. When he reached the cell, he recognized the monster immediately; the thing lay on its back on the narrow cot, eyes closed, seemingly asleep. It matched his briefing images perfectly. This was the monster Ios.

A tiny device from his vest pocket attached to the force field controls, and in a moment a white light began to blink. Vickatatrick turned his weapon up to full power, and tapped the tiny blinking light, aiming at the prone form on the cot. As soon as the shimmering field dropped, he fired.

Green lightning slammed into the cell, but struck only the empty cot. *Empty?* Vickatatrick thought in alarm. *How could he have moved so fast?*

He leaned into the cell, cautiously, weapon held ready, but it did him no good. A taloned hand shot down from the ceiling to seize him by the throat, dragging him upwards to where Ios clung to the top of the cell. Vickatatrick found himself staring into Ios' glowing red eyes.

"You are persistent creatures, aren't you?" the monster hissed. Vickatatrick shook his head, gasping in a fight for breath; he didn't speak any of the Confederate's language. "You came to kill me, then?" Ios continued, in Grugell. "How unfortunate for you. You came here in a ship?" The Grugell SubLieutenant nodded, black eyes wide. "Then, you must take me to it. Distasteful as this is going to be, I will have to compel you to see me to this ship of yours."

The monster's head dropped to Vickatatrick's neck.

The wardroom, 1755 hours

Gellar was still picking idly at the remains of his supper when the page came through.

"Captain Gellar, please call 9642, Captain Gellar, call 9642 please."

That was the code for the brig! Gellar jumped to his feet and walked quickly to the handset that hung on the wall at the rear of the wardroom. All the conversation in the compartment had ceased at the call.

"Captain here," he said quickly as soon as the call was answered. "What's going on?"

"Sir, Master Chief Gillespie here. Sir, Ios is loose. He's gone, sir. The brig watch was stunned, but they don't know who did it. He had help from outside, sir."

"Run the security monitor files, Master Chief. I'm on my way."

"Already running the security stream, sir. Got a video replay now. Uh, sir, you ain't gonna like this. It was a Grugell commando let him out. He came in, stunned the watch—yeah, wow, knocked 'em both down just like that. There he goes into the cell bay—wait one, sir, let me fast forward a bit—yeah, there they go, Cap'n, Ios strolling out right behind the Grugell boy nice as you please."

"Oh, great. I think our friend Tottalastrik was lying to us, Master Chief."

"That ain't no shit, sir. You coming down here?"

"No, I'm sure you've got things under control down there. I'll be up on the bridge. I think I'm going to have another chat with Tottalastrik. I have a feeling we won't have to zorch him this time."

"Roger that, sir. I'm going to get a couple more Marines down here to take the watch, and get these two up to ER to get checked out."

"Good idea. Call me if anything else comes up."

The look on Gellar's face as he left the wardroom made the two ensigns seated near the door cringe. "Sheesh," one of the said in a low voice, "you ever seen the Old Man that pissed off?"

When Gellar got to the Bridge, much to his surprise, a call from the Grugell Group Commander was already waiting. Gellar sat in his command chair and picked up the handset.

"No hacking through to our main display this time, Group Commander?" he barked into the mouthpiece.

"Captain," Tottalastrik's voice sounded strangely subdued, "we seem to have a common problem, you and I. Would it be possible for us to meet in person? I ask you to drop into normal space so we can meet. I can personally pilot a shuttle to your ship, if you'll allow it into your landing bay."

"Sir," the tactical officer called out, "Grugell frigate decloaking off the starboard bow!" He adjusted the main display to show the silver orb floating in space, trailing its twin drive pods.

Gellar looked up at the display, and then spoke quickly. "The only problem I have at the moment, Group Commander, is a video stream of a Grugell commando breaking into *my* brig and releasing a prisoner. What did you use, a clampon lander? Group Commander, you've illegally boarded a Confederate ship, and—"

Tottalastrik cut him off. "Captain, yes, I freely admit to sending an officer to board your ship, and once this crisis has passed I will surrender myself to your custody if you choose to press charges, but right now you must listen to me. I did not sent my officer to release Ios, but to kill him. Now this officer's clampon lander has been found in our landing bay, with the officer unconscious inside—and he's been *changed*, Captain, changed to one of the monsters the like of which I've already shown you. I will most likely be forced to destroy him, Captain, and he comes from an important family—the Emperor Himself will be demanding an explanation. Now, Captain, I really must speak with you in person!"

Gellar was taken aback. "You really are willing to come over here unaccompanied?"

"You have my word as an officer of the Grugell Empire."

I wonder if that's really any good, Gellar wondered, but kept the thought to himself. "Very well, Group Commander. Bring your ship alongside mine, I think it best that we both stop right here until Ios is found. Bring your shuttle around to our hangar bay, and I'll see that you're assigned a landing clearance."

"I thank you, Captain." A click, and the message terminated.

"Oh, shit," Gellar breathed. He stood up and walked to the helm station. "All stop," he ordered. "Hold your position. Tactical, the Grugell frigate will be moving alongside. Signals, send a message down to the hangar bay to allow one Grugell shuttle to land. I'm going to go receive the Grugell commander."

The Exec, Gellar knew, was sleeping in his cabin after an all-night research session on the legends of the Wampir. There was, however, one other person he wanted involved in this meeting. As he walked out the bridge hatch, he called over his shoulder to the signals watch: "Oh, and page Master Chief Gillespie, have him meet me in the hangar bay."

Chapter Eighteen

The hangar bay, five minutes later

Master Chief Gillespie was waiting for Gellar in the hangar bay's control tower.

"Never thought I'd see it, sir, I gotta admit," he observed as the silver cylinder of the Grugell shuttle floated to a landing in the hangar, a few meters from Ios' yacht. As it settled to the deck, spidery landing gear unfolded, and the tiny ship came to rest.

It took a few moments for the atmosphere in the hangar to be restored. Gellar and Gillespie were waiting at the hatch when that was done. Gellar was surprised to see six young crewmen lined up outside the entrance as well.

"Got to have all the dog and pony show, eh sir?" Gillespie winked at his captain and waved the crewmen inside, where they formed two ranks of three on each side of the Grugell shuttle's hatch. As the hatch opened and the stick-figure form of the Grugell group commander stepped out, Gillespie took an ancient bosun's whistle from his vest pocket and blew a long, three-note blast.

Gellar stepped forward, looking up at the Grugell officer. "Group Commander, welcome to the *Charity*."

"Thank you, Captain. I assume that was a display of military courtesy?"

"Yes, a very, very old one, dating to the days when men sailed on Earth's oceans in wooden ships with canvas sails."

"Interesting. You Confederates, how you cling to ancient traditions, even out here among the stars."

"The modern world moves so fast, Group Commander, that we sometimes find comfort in reminders of simpler times."

Tottalastrik looked puzzled but let the matter drop. He folded his black cloak around his thin form, and looked once around the hangar. "Do you have a place where we could speak in private, Captain?"

"Yes, we have a conference room near our bridge. If you don't mind, I'd like Master Chief Gillespie to sit in. He's the one that figured out how to capture Ios in the first place."

Tottalastrik looked Gillespie over carefully, noting his rank insignia. "You are not an officer," he noted.

"No, *sir*, I work for a living," Gillespie bristled. "I don't know what things are like in your Navy, but over here it's the chiefs that keep the damn ducks all in a row."

To the Confederates' surprise, Tottalastrik threw back his head and laughed—a thin, weird sound. "Very well—'Master Chief,' is it? If your Captain has such faith in you, then so will I."

"That's all we ask, Group Commander. If you'll come this way, please?"

"Of course, Captain. Is it very far? The gravity on your ship is positively oppressive."

A maintenance crawlspace a hundred meters forward

Once again Ios had gone into a semi-dormant state, sending out his fine tendrils of webbing through the ship's crawlspaces and ventilation ducts to extend his senses.

So, the Grugell commander himself has come to parlay, has he? They don't know where I am, which ship I am hiding on. In the darkness of the crawlspace, his wolf-like jaws cracked open in a grin. *This will work out exactly as I planned.*

He drifted off into the dreamtime again while he waited, and unbidden came memories of the old days, of his own transformation.

A haze of smoke still hung over the battlefield. Shrieks and screams echoed in the red evening light; the smell of blood and emptied bowels filled the air. Vlad had won this battle against the heathen Turk, but at what cost?

Belos lay on the hillside where he had fallen, skewered through the belly by a Turkish lance. He coughed and tasted blood. Belly wounds were almost always fatal but never quick. A torturous, pain-filled horror would precede his final rest, unless a sympathetic passer-by could be cajoled to swiftly end his pain with a sword or a spear. He was only a boy, only fifteen summers, but he knew he would not see another sunrise.

He didn't know how true that thought was to prove.

A dark figure flitted by in the edge of Belos' pain-hazed vision. "Please!" he called. "Help me!"

The tall, thin figure stopped, turned, strode to bend beside the boy.

"Help you? You are beyond help, lad." The voice was thick, the accent guttural. A Teuton—Prussian, perhaps a Saxon.

"Help me to a clean death," Belos pleaded. "The pain is unbearable. I beg you, use your sword, and take my head. I cannot heal from this wound."

"Let me be the judge of that, boy. I am Hess, leecher and sawbones to the Impaler himself." Hess took a curved knife from his belt, slit open young Belos' tunic.

"Ahh," Hess hissed like a great snake. "A vicious wound indeed. Lad, you will not recover, not by any normal means. But you will walk again, and you will seek revenge on the Turk for this injury to your person."

"I had not thought to see another sunrise," Belos gasped.

"Oh, and you shall not," Hess replied. "Indeed, lad, you shall not." He leaned over Belos, and his jaws gaped. His face elongated to the cracking and popping of bones and muscles as a hound's teeth sprouted through his gums. Hot, stinking saliva splashed on Belo's chest. Panicking, he found strength somehow to scuttle back-wards, away from the beast, but one great, chisel-tipped hand slammed down on his chest and held him still as the great fangs sank into his neck.

He awoke sometime later, to find it fully dark. The flickering red lights of fires still danced here and there on the field. A groan escaped his torn lips, bringing the weird figure of the leecher Hess back to stare down at him.

"The thing grows fast in you, lad. You were born to be one of the Wampir. Look!" He pointed down at Belos' stomach.

It took Belos a moment to realize that the pain of his stomach wound was all but gone. He struggled to sit up, looked down at himself. Only a slight scabbing remained of the wound, and even as he watched, the scabs dropped away to reveal pink new tissue beneath.

"How..." he began, pausing in confusion.

"The essence," Hess hissed. "The very stuff of life to such as me, lad. To such as you now as well. Now attend! There are things you must know before I leave you to walk into the night."

"Wampir?" Belos said, finally realizing what Hess had said. "My grandfather spoke of them, monsters who live in mountain passes and steal children in the night to suck the blood from their bodies and the marrow from their bones."

"The weakest among us are of that sort, boy. I sense a greater strength in you. You, boy, will be a father of Wampir. Now listen!"

Belos stood up, stretched his arms experimentally. He felt not just healed, he felt strong as a lion!

"You have been given a great gift, boy," Hess went on. "You have also been given several great weaknesses. Are you hungry, lad?"

"Never more so than now," Belos admitted. "I feel I could eat an entire bullock."

"The bullock will suffice you not, lad. Meaner fare will sustain you for a time, but as the sunlight and the flesh of beasts is to the common men, so starlight and the blood of men—ah, and women!—so that is to the Wampir."

"So, I must kill men for their blood?"

"Kill, no, not always. You can take without killing, and you can feed without changing your prey as I have changed you to save your life. Your instincts will guide you as your change progresses."

"And the others? You said weaknesses."

"There are three. Wood and silver will act as a poison in your blood, should you be stabbed or impaled.

Fire will burn you, destroy you if you are burned badly enough. Finally, you will look on the sun no more. Sunlight will burn you as acid. A few moments in the sunlight, and you will die."

Belos took a moment to digest this information. Finally, he had one more thing to ask. "Why?" Hess looked at the boy, raising one bushy eyebrow. "Why change me, save my life, tell me these things?"

"I had a wife once, and children," Hess spat into the night. "I came to the land of the Wallachs to brew and sell the beer of my homeland. Then, one morning, a band of Turkish warriors fell on our village out of the darkness. We were not soldiers, only innocent villagers, but the path of war fell over us. My family was butchered."

"I'm sorry," Belos replied, even though the human feeling of sympathy was fading in him already.

"I wandered into the forest, injured and helpless. One of the Wampir, one of the poor ones you described, found me, fed on me, but not enough to kill me. The morning was coming on, and he was forced to withdraw. However, I was changed after that night, and now, I seek my revenge. That is why I came to Vlad, boy, and that is why you will walk now as my son, as one of the Wampir, because you have cause for seeking revenge even as do I. The Turk warlord you seek is the leader of a great army, and Suleiman Bulut is his name. He brought war to this land, and it is against him you—and I—must seek our revenge."

"And so I shall," Belos vowed.

Bridge conference room

In all his time in service, Gellar never would have expected having a Grugell officer, a group commander no less—the equivalent of a rear admiral in the Confederate Navy—staring across the conference room table at him. Master Chief Gillespie took a seat rather nearer the door and sat glaring at the Grugell officer.

Tottalastrik simply took his seat as gracefully as his build allowed, folding his long, sticklike legs carefully under him. He adjusted the folds of his long black cloak around his thin frame, folded his long, white hands in front of him, and finally spoke.

"Captain. Master Chief. Our problem is simple—there is a monster on the loose. We do not know on which ship he hides. Our internal monitoring systems show no sign of him, but that is, of course, inconclusive."

"More than you think," Gellar said. "He's found some way to shield himself from our scanning systems. Probably yours as well."

"I wondered if that might not be the case."

"So," Gellar continued, "what do we do about it? Obviously, Ios has to be found."

Master Chief Gillespie spoke up at last, still glowering at the Grugell officer. "Sir," he growled, "it's the same thing as before, right? We know what he is going to want to do, right? We have one spot on our ship where we know he's going to try to get to, sooner or later."

Tottalastrik leaned forward. "The answer is obvious, is it not? Ios may be a monster, but he's not a soldier. To win any battle, you must present your enemy with a situation he hopes for, and expects. When he takes the bait you've carefully presented, you strike."

"We know what he hopes to do."

"Then we must find a way to make it easier for him, without arousing his suspicions."

Three hours later

The Grugell shuttle left in a hurry. Tottalastrik had the craft aloft even before the force field dropped, and shot out of the hangar as fast as safety allowed, looping up over the top of the Confederate ship to return to his own flagship, a kilometer to the *Charity*'s starboard. Captain Gellar and Master Chief Gillespie had accompanied him to the hangar bay, saying nothing to the Marine guard around Ios' yacht except to warn them out of the space before it depressurized.

Gunnery Sergeant Anthony appeared in the hangar bay's control tower a moment after the Grugell ship left, before the hangar was re-pressurized. "What's going on now? Why's he leaving in such a rush?"

"Because there's a monster loose, and it might be over there on his ship. This whole thing might be worse than we thought," Master Chief Gillespie blurted out.

"Master Chief!" Gellar barked. "Don't!"

"Aye aye, sir! Sorry, Gunny," Gillespie apologized. "I can't tell you anything much. The captain will fill you in on what we need your Marines to do."

Anthony looked at the Captain, eyes wide. "Sir?"

"Gunny, I need you to get every Marine you have awake and hunting. We need to scour every maintenance crawlspace on the ship, every air duct we can get into, look in every closet, every storage cabinet. I'm going to have engineering work up some UV searchlights for your M65's, they'll hurt Ios worse than bullets."

"We leaving the guard on his ship, sir?"

"No, Gunny, pull 'em out. We'll need them worse elsewhere, and even if he gets back to his ship, he can't get out without someone in the tower to depressurize and drop the force field. I'm not worried about that."

"I'm worried about him trying what he tried on that Grugell passenger liner," Gillespie muttered.

"Keep that to yourself, Master Chief!" Gellar's voice was uncharacteristically harsh, prompting a stare from the Marine.

'Passenger liner? I didn't know they even had..."

"You don't need to know that, Gunny," Gellar snapped. "We don't have time to explain things to everyone right now. All in due time, Gunny, all right? Let's find that murdering monster first."

"Yes, sir," the Marine replied, more than a little concerned now. "Sir, I should let Colonel Sandelescu know about this."

"Yes, Gunny, of course. She should be in her quarters, but you can go coordinate with her. If she feels up to it, I'd like her to direct the search."

"You got it, sir. I'll head up there now."

After the Marine saluted and left, Master Gillespie looked sideways at Gellar. "You think this will work, sir?"

"For all our sakes, I sure hope so."

The maintenance crawlspace

Ios moved slightly, cracking the webbing cocoon he'd allowed to grow over himself. He flexed his limbs. His strength wasn't at its peak, but it would have to do. His sensory tendrils had relayed events in the hangar bay; the Grugell ship leaving in a rush, a Marine sergeant shouting at the troops guarding his ship to leave, to prepare to search the maintenance and air supply spaces.

Time to go, Ios told himself. His vampire consciousness reached out to one of the two he still held in thrall. *You, child, will help me.* He fed her the codes that the Gypsy girl had given him, the codes to open the hangar and allow his ship out of the bay. *You will come now to the hangar bay, to my ship. It is unguarded. You will meet me there, and then you will turn the force field off so that I may leave.*

He entertained the thought briefly of taking the girl with him, but dismissed it. She would only become a nuisance in short order, unless he converted her, which he had no intention of doing. Worse, taking her would make the Navy pursue him to much greater length. No, simpler to wipe the memories of his control from her young mind, and leave her here.

Of course, there would be time for one more feeding before he left. He still had to chase away the taste of the foul, alien Grugell, who for some reason converted all too easily, whether he wished it or not.

The Grugell flagship

Tottalastrik landed in his own flagship's landing bay with a bump. The space was barely re-pressurized when he leaped from the shuttle, shouting orders at his personal aide who waited, as per standing order, in the landing bay awaiting the group commander's return. "Call the flagship commander and the security officer, and have them meet me in my office immediately. Signal the other two ships, order them to remain cloaked and keep at least thirty kilos distance. Any unidentified small craft they see are to be engaged and destroyed." He jogged towards the landing bay entrance, forcing his aide to jump to catch up. "I'm going to my office now. Get up there as soon as you get those calls made."

Once the search was well under way, Tottalastrik closeted himself with the flagship's commander and security officer. "Before we proceed," he announced, "I want to know the condition of SubLieutenant Vickatatrick."

"Worse than before, Group Commander," the security officer replied. "His skeletal structure seems to have gone almost completely plastic. I've had to close off almost all ventilation to his detention cell, for fear he'd escape through the grates. I've got two security troops watching him with blasters set to full power. He keeps throwing himself at the force field, even though it is turned up to full power."

"Has the ship's surgeon examined him?"

"As best as he can from outside the cell, Group Commander. We don't dare allow him to go in. We'd have two of them on our hands then."

"His diagnosis?"

The frigate's commander spoke up. "I spoke with him myself, Group Commander. Apparently, the monster Ios infected him with some kind of disease-causing agent, a very sophisticated agent indeed, a polymorphic virus that rewrote the sublieutenant's body chemistry completely. The surgeon fears the disease is likely to be highly contagious, Group Commander. He recommends disintegration and sterilization of the cell."

"Very well, see to it yourself, Commander."

Tottalastrik spun his stool around, turning his back on his two subordinates for a moment. "I doubt that Ios is on our ship. I suspect that his sending the sublieutenant back here infected was a ruse. His own private yacht is still on the Confederate ship, and that is where he will want to go. There's no advantage to his stealing a Grugell shuttle."

"Of course, Group Commander."

"So, while our search of our own ship will continue, I suspect he will find a way to get to his own ship. The Confederates only know of this one frigate. Now I've ordered the other two to take stations thirty kilos angled off the Confederates' stern. If and when Ios appears, the Confederates will try to take him in a tractor beam to tow him to their authorities. We, on the other hand, won't allow that. We will destroy him. Commander, have your weapons division ready two anti-ship homing torpedoes."

"As you command, Group Commander."

"We will have revenge for what the monster did on the mining colony."

Chapter Nineteen

The *Charity*'s hangar bay

The *Black Dragon* sat quietly, unattended, alone in the hangar bay. With the Marine guards gone, and even the control tower watch enlisted in the ship-wide search, there was nobody to notice EM1c Audrey Ophell slip into the yacht.

A moment later, a sinister black form detached from the hangar's ceiling to float to the floor in front of the ship. Ios recovered his human form and stood for a moment, searching with all his supernaturally acute senses. The scent of young, hot, salty blood and feminine essence from inside his ship was overpowering, but other than that, he detected nothing, nobody.

This is suspicious, he thought, *suspicious indeed. It is a trifle too fortuitous, that this captain should obligingly draw off his guards and leave my ship unattended. He leaves rich bait in the trap, almost too rich.*

If I can get the Black Dragon *out of this bay, can I out-maneuver him? This hospital ship has no arms, but the Grugell ships do, and I know there is at least one in the area.*

He entered his yacht slowly, silently. The young girl awaited him, seated on the small couch in the main living area. Her eyes were wide; her breaths came in shallow gasps. Ios put a tendril of thought into her mind, calming her. *Be still for a moment, child.*

His chief thrall, his Gypsy woman—she was awake and active. Ios could sense her mind, could sense the bit of himself that lived in her. *Child, my loyal one, what are they doing, leaving my ship unguarded?*

The reply came almost at once. *Master,* her thoughts came, guarded and swift. *I believe they leave your ship unguarded on purpose. It makes no sense.*

What are they planning?

I don't know, Master, but I suspect they hope for you to take the Dragon *out of the hangar bay. They will then take you in a tractor beam, and tow you to the Fleet base on New Wichita. This ship's engine is much more powerful than yours, Master.*

Ios stood for a moment, thinking. *Can you disable the tractor beam mechanism, child?*

I can, Master. It will take an hour or more.

Do so, then. I have a task I must carry out before I leave in any case.

The Grugell would present a different problem. *Child, advise me. I must evade the Grugell. How best can I do so?*

They will not fire on you this deep in Confederate space, Master. There are treaties. Their Commander would be disintegrated.

Good, child, good. Ios withdrew from his thrall's mind.

In her quarters, Lieutenant Commander Sandelescu smiled to herself. *So, you believe they will not fire on you, old dragon? You underestimated me, 'Master,' and I will see you destroyed for what you've done. For what you've done to my ship, my crewmates, and to me.*

She got up off her narrow bunk and began to get dressed. She had a visit to pay to the tractor beam generator control suite.

Bridge conference room

"Sir, the motion detector's gone off. There's some movement in the yacht," Master Chief Gillespie announced. He was staring into the terminal on the conference table again, watching the display intently. "Something's gone in, but it's stopped now—no, there's a little movement, not much—OK, now it's stopped again. I'm switching to the hangar bay monitor scanner, sir."

"Good work, Master Chief, just like you said, he was here. Looks like he's making his play."

"He's a cagey one, sir, but he ain't no Navy man. This is almost too easy."

"Like you said, Master Chief, he's no Navy man," Gellar replied. "He's not counting on the technology."

"You say so, sir."

Inside the *Black Dragon*

His hunger temporarily sated, Ios turned his attention to other matters.

The *Black Dragon* was functional. Not fully restored, but functional. The ship's computer told him, as he had been informed, that only one of the ship's drive tunnels was functional, but that would have to do. Environmental controls were functional. The cargo bay was untouched. The ship's reserve power cells were fully charged, and the one good drive tunnel's starting electrets were functional. Ios stopped in the entryway to the piloting cabin, frowning at the remaining scorch marks showing through the repair work. The Grugell blaster had done lasting damage.

No matter, he thought. *I will have to shed the* Black Dragon *now, and take a new identity. A lizard will shed its tail to evade a predator, and so must I, humanity's last great nightmare, shed an identity to save myself.*

Ios walked back into the main cabin. His mind ticked over accounts, locations, planets, and refuges. He had twenty caches of cash, valuables, and identity documents hidden all over the Confederacy, and two more on rogue planets that answered to neither the Confederacy nor the Grugell Empire. Adopting a new identity would be as easy as changing his cloak.

A groan brought his attention to the girl, who lay sprawled across his narrow couch. Her coveralls were ripped open, and a slight trickle of blood showed on her neck. Ios had sated both of his raging lusts on the young technician, and while he'd taken care not to infect her—a difficult task at best of times, all the harder when his appetites ran strong—he had left her seriously weakened.

"Girl!" he called. "Wake up!" He strode to the couch, and gently slapped her cheek with one sharp-nailed hand. "Wake up now!"

EM1c Ophell's eyes fluttered open, focusing blankly on the vampire.

"You will go to the tower now. In a short time, I will contact you to open the blast doors and the force field. Do you hear me, child?"

"Yes. I hear."

"Then go. Go now!"

Ophell got up slowly, staggered towards the hatch.

"Dress yourself! Close your garment, girl!"

She pulled her coverall closed, fastened the remnants of the closure, and left the ship slowly, walking in a drunken meander towards the tower.

Bridge conference room

"Sir, you'd better take a look at this."

Gellar stood up and stretched. "What's he up to now, Master Chief?"

"Not him, sir, he had someone in the ship. Give me a second, I think I know her…" He fiddled with the display, adjusting the scanner's magnification as Gellar came to look over his shoulder. "Yeah, that's her. She's one of the techs that was working on Ios' ship, a young petty officer, engineer's mate first class, uh, Ophell, that's it."

"What's she doing?"

"I don't know what she's been doing—she looks pretty messed up, see, her coverall's torn—but she's heading for the control tower. Ios is going to make his move, sir."

"Good! Call down to the tractor generator suite. Tell 'em to stand by. If you 'd keep an eye on that monitor, Master Chief, I'm going out to the bridge. Time to get the tactical watch officer on his toes."

"Aye aye, sir. Nail the bastard."

Gellar strode into the bridge, angling for the tactical station, where the watch officer was glaring suspiciously at a tactical plot showing the Grugell frigate off the *Charity*'s starboard. "Lieutenant Waxman!"

"Sir?"

"Pick up the aft scanners on your terminal. Angle them down on the hangar bay doors. Stand by." Gellar picked up the handset on the tactical station, punching in a code.

"Tractor control? This is the captain. I need tractor control at the bridge tactical station. Yes, right now. Thank you."

"No activity, sir. Are we expecting an inbound?"

"Outbound. You'll have tractor control here in a moment."

"Got it now, sir, just came on."

"Good. You've seen the private yacht we took in? Bel Ios' yacht?"

"Aye aye, sir."

"He's going to be coming out of the hangar bay in a few moments. When he does, nail the tractor beam on him, hold him no closer than a kilometer aft of the ship. Lock the beam in for towing." Gellar turned to the signals station. "Signals! Get me the Grugell flagship."

Settling in his bridge chair was a welcome relief. The handset buzzed almost immediately.

"Gellar," he said into the handset.

"You called, Captain?" Tottalastrik's voice sounded almost whimsical.

"He's here, Group Commander. I expect him to duck out of our hangar bay at any moment. We're standing by with a tractor beam."

"Very good, Captain. If you'll indulge me, I'd prefer to observe until you have him securely locked in your tractor beam and are under way. You are unarmed, after all, if he should break free."

"He won't. But you're welcome to observe, Group Commander."

"Thank you, Captain." The signal cut off abruptly.

The Grugell flagship

"Weapons, stand by torpedoes. Helm, stand by on the cloaking device, stand by for maneuvers. Communications, signal the other ships, tell them to stand by on weapons. All ships to fire on my order." Tottalastrik barked the orders out rapid-fire at his flagship's bridge crew, overriding the flagship's commander.

"We have you now, monster!"

Chapter Twenty

The *Black Dragon*

Ios sat at the controls, examining the scrolling start-up read-outs he'd never taken the time to really learn to understand. His hand poised over the button to fire maneuvering thrusters.

Child, he called out to his last Gypsy. *Is the tractor disabled?*

It is, Master.

Then I go. Wait one year, then seek me out, my child.

I will, Master.

Ios reached with his thoughts up to the control tower, where the girl slumped, barely conscious, against the control panels. *Now! Now, child, open the blast doors and drop the force field!*

A slap on the firing stud, and the *Black Dragon*'s underside maneuvering thrusters fired, lifting the yacht a meter off the hangar bay deck. The blast doors were sliding open, the shimmering force field dropped, and a blast of escaping air carried the yacht out into space.

The *Charity*'s bridge

"There he is, sir!" Lieutenant Waxman's voice raised an octave in excitement. "He's just pulled out!"

Gellar spun his chair around. "Send your scanner view to the main screen. Stand by on tractor beam!"

Grugell flagship

"Sir, the yacht, it's leaving the Confederate ship's landing bay!"

"Excellent." Tottalastrik's narrow face split in a vicious grin. "Wait for him to engage his main engines. I do not want a major incident now. We are in enough diplomatic trouble as it is. When he engages his main drives, I want all torpedoes set to his drive signature. I want no accidental hits on that hospital ship, do you hear?"

"As you command, Group Commander."

The *Black Dragon*

Ios fired his aft maneuvering thrusters, pushing his craft away from the Navy ship. His one functioning star drive's starters were charged. It would only take ten, perhaps twelve minutes to accelerate to the point where he could jump to subspace. His inertial dampers were functioning. Ios hit the starter switch, and the one Gellar tunnel sparked, spat, and sprang to life.

Charity's bridge

"Stand by tractor beam, Tactical. Be ready to slap it on him at one kilometer."

Lieutenant Waxman was glued to the display. "Sir, he's at six hundred meters. Seven hundred. Gaining speed. Eight hundred. Nine hundred. One kilometer."

"Engage tractor beam," Gellar barked.

"Engaging—*negative function on the tractor beam, sir,* I have a bad generator warning on the tractor beam!"

"Get me tractor control!" Gellar shouted at Signals. On the screen, the *Black Dragons'* one functioning Gellar drive flickered to life.

Grugell flagship

Tottalastrik almost leaped off the stool he'd appropriated from an engineering technician. "There! Weapons, get an analysis on that drive. Engage cloaking device! Helm, move to pursue!"

"Group Commander," the weapons officer called out. "I have a reading on his drive signature."

"Match generated readings and fire two torpedoes. Send the readings to the other two ships, order them to match and fire, two torpedoes each."

"As you command."

A moment later, two anti-ship torpedoes leaped from the Grugell frigate's forward launch tubes, followed in seconds by four more from the other two cloaked ships.

Charity's bridge

Master Chief Gillespie burst into the bridge. "What's going on? He's pulling away!"

"The tractor beam's down, Master Chief, Tractor Control says the generator's been disabled…" Gellar was interrupted by a shout from the Tactical station.

"*Grugell frigate cloaking off the starboard beam, sir!* Showing turn to port—he's gone sir, lost contact, he's gone into cloak." Lieutenant Waxman watched the screen intently, but before he could return to the yacht: "TORPEDOES LAUNCHED TO STAR-BOARD! Sir, I have two torpedoes launched to starboard," Waxman glanced at another indicator now beeping and flashing red. "Two more twenty kilometers to port, sir! Two more! Twelve klicks beneath the keel, sir! Sir, I'm tracking six Grugell torpedoes!"

"SOUND GENERAL QUARTERS," Gellar shouted. "Helm! All ahead flank! Evasive maneuvers, prepare to fire decoys." The *Charity* was unarmed and unarmored, so all they could do was run. The decoys were barrel-sized canisters with generators that mimicked the ship's Gellar drive signature. They weren't considered to be too reliable.

"Sir, I have bearing changes on all six birds—they're tracking Ios, sir."

"Belay that order, Helm. All ahead full, reverse your course, bring us around after that yacht."

The *Black Dragon*

Ios punched up full power on his one functioning drive. The normally graceful yacht wallowed like a hog with the asymmetric thrust but accelerated, all too slowly.

A beep on the panel sounded, strident. However ancient, Ios lacked the instincts that a trained Navy pilot would have had, and it took him a moment to look to see what was wrong.

Grugell flagship

"Group Commander, all torpedoes are in acquisition. The Confederate ship is moving to pursue, but he won't make the turn in time."

"Good. Continue to monitor, Weapons. Helm, you will continue your pursuit course. Communications, order the other ships to trailing formation."

The *Black Dragon*

Ios threw the yacht into a wild, corkscrewing pattern, feeling the ship respond sluggishly running on only one drive. The first torpedo shot past, barely missing. The homing weapon looped up to turn for another try.

Damn that lying wench, Ios thought bitterly. Another torpedo was coming in fast, growing huge on the aft scanner. Ios ducked the ship low, passing under the first weapon that, having completed its turn, raced in to the front. The torpedoes collided aft of the *Dragon*. The ship slammed forward, caught in a shock wave as the weapons' thermonuclear warheads went off. A shower of sparks shot out from the bulkhead behind the ancient vampire.

There are four more. The readout was as plain as the thought was bitter. He'd never accelerate to the subspace barrier in time.

But his instincts forced him to try.

His vampire senses availed him naught here. He was pursued not by men but by robots, by killer machines with a nose for his ship. The *Black Dragon* skipped, jinked, ducked, and dodged at Ios' command, but every evasive move cost him speed, and speed was what he needed. He needed speed, to break the subspace barrier, to break into subspace where the torpedoes couldn't follow

A vicious yank to port, followed by a rolling, porpoising move dodged one torpedo, and a sudden reversal of course in a hammerhead loop foiled the next, but both looped around to seek his energy signature.

After all these centuries, he thought bitterly, *to have it end thus, killed by mindless machines launched by ichor-filled, foul aliens. At least I know that one of my own lives on, and that something of me will continue into the future. What a fine, final joke to play on my tormentors!*

"Come on, then, machines, killer robots, test your mettle against mine!" Ios shouted his defiance. He yanked the ship hard to starboard, chopped power to the engine, let another torpedo flash past to his front, slammed the power on full again.

The power! The engine! The torpedoes are homing on my engine signature! He reached out one hand, slammed the emergency cutoff. His single working Gellar drive faded into silence, and the *Black Dragon* coasted on powerless. Ios cut all the cabin power, cut all but essential environmental.

Grugell flagship

"Group Commander, he's cut his engine power. His signature has dropped off the scope. The torpedoes have lost the target, they are circling."

"Switch to visual guidance. All ships to transfer torpedo guidance to individual controllers."

Charity's bridge

"Sir, he's cut engine power," Lieutenant Waxman announced. "He's drifting. All power seems to have been cut. The Grugell torpedoes have gone into seek mode. He's thrown them off, sir."

"Won't last," Master Chief Gillespie observed. "They'll switch to visual tracking. That dark ship of his isn't easy to see, but he hasn't got far enough away. They'll get him."

The *Charity* accelerated, diving after the drifting yacht, but the spaceborne hospital wasn't built for speed or pursuit. They didn't have any time to spare.

"Have we got tractor control back yet?" Gellar called out. "What the hell is wrong with our tractors?"

"No, sir," Waxman said. "Won't matter now, sir. They've got him again." On the main screen, the bridge watch looked on as, one after the other, all four remaining Grugell torpedoes swung about and raced after the yacht.

"*Hard to starboard!*" Gellar shouted. "Ahead flank, come to new course one eight eight by nine zero positive! They're going to hit him with four nukes..."

The *Charity* wallowed hard but responded, rising slowly to dodge the expected blasts, turning to starboard and arcing north to leave the area.

The *Black Dragon*

"And so, it comes to this," Ios repeated the thought out loud as the four Grugell torpedoes turned and sped towards him again.

At the last moment, a scene from the far past, almost eleven centuries before, came back to him.

It was the face of the old man, the old Turk Suleiman Bulut, baring his yellow teeth in his last act of defiance and snarling, "One day, monster, you will perish in the flames as I intended. One stronger and faster than I will kill you."

Ionescu had laughed, taunted the old man, "That day will never come, you old fool! I've destroyed all you hold dear, and I'll live for centuries after you and all yours are forgotten. Take that to the grave, Suleiman Bulut!" And then he'd struck with hands like great talons, striking the old Turk down.

And now his own death pricked up its mechanical ears and sped towards his coasting, powerless ship. It was too late to restart his one engine, too late to do anything but scream his last, impotent rage at the mindless machines. In the last seconds, he could almost hear the laughter of Suleiman Bulut before his millennia-long life was extinguished at last in a blaze of nuclear fusion.

Charity's bridge

"Well, *that's* a kill," Gillespie pointed out unnecessarily. On the main screen, a series of white-hot flashes betrayed the bursts of four thermonuclear warheads. The screen dimmed hurriedly to accommodate the flare of fusion, as a new star shone briefly in the depths of space, fading rapidly to an expanding cloud of hot gas and radiation that sent lines and sparkles of interference racing across the screen.

"All stop," Gellar breathed. The *Charity* shuddered briefly with reverse thrust as the ship slowed, stopped.

"Sir," Signals said, barely above a whisper, "the Grugell group commander is calling."

Tottalastrik's image shimmered into view, replacing the fading fusion fireballs on the main screen.

"You lied to me, Group Commander," Gellar snapped. "You had no intention of letting us take Ios to our authorities to face justice, did you?"

"Of course, Captain. Your intuition does you credit."

"Your integrity does you no credit, Group Commander. The word of a Grugell officer, indeed! What happened to your 'Grugell justice,' Group Commander?"

On the screen, Tottalastrik snarled, baring his serrated, predatory teeth. "You have just *witnessed* Grugell justice, Captain Gellar. Pray that you never witness it again." The image on the screen snapped out as the signal was cut off, returning the view to the last, fading remnants of the nuclear bursts.

"Sir, three Grugell frigates decloaking dead ahead." Lieutenant Waxman switched the main screen view, backing off the magnification to show three gleaming silver Grugell ships appearing out of the blackness of space. One by one, they peeled off, turning for the Grugell frontier and their home port. Their drive pods flared orange as the ships accelerated, broke into subspace, and were gone.

"Damn," Gellar muttered. He dropped back into his bridge chair with a sigh. "Secure from General Quarters. Helm, resume course for New Wichita, ahead full. We'll have to make a full report to the Fleet command."

"Aye aye, sir. Resuming previous course, engine room answers ahead full."

Master Chief Gillespie came forward to stand next to Gellar's chair. "Sir, you know, I'm not all that certain who the worst monster was in this deal. The one that was killed, or the one that just flew off for home."

"He made an alliance of convenience, Master Chief. We shouldn't count on the Grugell doing that very often."

"Roger that, sir."

Gellar turned to the signals watch again. "Call down to Records, have a yeoman come up to the bridge conference room with a recorder. Call down and ask Doctor Moses and Colonel Sandelescu to join us. And tell Engineering I want to know what the hell happened to our tractor suite. Master Chief, Exec, I'll want you both in on this too. We'll have to compile a report to send to Third Fleet. This is going to rattle cages all the way back to Tarbos."

Chapter Twenty-one

Next morning

Ten hours of sleep can work wonders, Gellar thought as he strode into the main med lab. Chief Surgeon Moses and Master Chief Gillespie had their heads together at one end of the lab, and at the other, Lieutenant Colonel Sandelescu sat impatiently on a bench.

"Good morning, Colonel," Gellar greeted his security chief. "Feeling better?"

"Yes, sir. Sir, could I speak with you a moment? In private?"

"Yes, of course," Gellar replied. "Let me talk with Doctor Moses first, I'll only be a second."

Gellar walked over, a smile growing to a broad grin on his face as he saw Doctor Moses smiling at Gillespie like a young girl. She was patting his hand affectionately as he leaned over the computer terminal she was using. *The master chief and Doctor Moses?* Gellar almost laughed out loud with the relief of normality reasserting itself. *I bet* nobody *saw that one coming.*

"Good morning!"

Doctor Moses looked up, snatching her hand back and blushing furiously. "Oh, good morning, Jared, I was just going to call you." Master Chief Gillespie muttered a quick, "Oh, uh, good morning, sir," before noticing something on the far wall that suddenly required his scrutiny.

"You look well this morning, Andrea." Gellar grinned.

Moses smiled, looking down at her desktop. "Well, I've got some good news."

"About Colonel Sandelescu, or is it something else?"

"It's about our young Marine, Jared, as you know perfectly well. Her tests came out clean. No trace of Ios' virus. She can go back to duty whenever she wants."

"Good! She said she'd like to speak with me in private for a moment, Andrea—can I borrow your lab's office for a moment?"

"Of course!"

Gellar walked back across the lab, motioning for Sandelescu to follow him into the tiny office. There was a small couch on one side of the office, and Gellar headed that way. Colonel Sandelescu assumed a strict position of attention in front of him, bringing a frown of confusion. "What is it, Christine?"

"Sir, I'll give it to you in writing later today, but I'd like to inform you of my intention to resign my commission immediately on our arrival at New Wichita."

"What? Why?"

"Failure to perform my primary duties, sir. I no longer consider myself fit to hold the position of command in the Corps."

The bridge, two hours later

"Sir," the signals watch officer called out, "incoming text message from Third Fleet."

"Acknowledge it, print it up, thank you," Gellar replied. Colonel Sandelescu's announcement still perturbed him.

The Signals ensign handed him a message a moment later.

TO: CSS CHARITY CAPT J GELLAR

SENDS: CINC3FLT

MESSAGE RECEIVED THIS HQ. REPORT TO CINC7FLT AT EARLIEST POSSIBLE ARRIVAL NEW WICHITA. YOU ARE TO EXPEDITE TRAVEL TO NEW WICHITA. COMTASKFOR947 WILL BE INFORMED OF YOUR DELAY.

Well, Gellar thought, *that was quick.* He turned to the helm station. "Lieutenant, maintain current course for New Wichita. All ahead flank."

Lieutenant Tomason's eyes went wide, but she dialed in the change quickly. "Engine room answers all ahead flank, sir."

"Very well."

New Wichita

Commander in Chief Third Fleet (CINC3FLT) Admiral Stefan August reclined in his rather expansive desk chair, the only symbol of his four-star rank visible in a fairly Spartan office.

"Captain, if you didn't have some video and the testimony of some very good officers—yourself included—I'd have a hard time believing all this."

"Sir, I have a hard time believing it myself." Gellar leaned forward in his chair and dropped an optical storage disk on the admiral's desk. "I had my exec compile all the records he found, and some more information he's uncovered since then on this disk, sir."

The admiral picked up the disk. He regarded it warily. "Is this going to give me more gray hair than I've already got, Captain?"

"It probably will, sir." Gellar leaned back, frowning. "It sure did for me. Sir, you know Ios by reputation, right?"

"Yes, I had my aide pull his biographical when you signaled in."

"Then you know the official, the trillionaire recluse wine dealer. Sir, that disk has the rest. His real name was Belos Ionescu. He was born, sir, believe it or not, in the fifteenth century on Earth. Ionescu fought in the Crusades, was wounded in battle and healed by some 'leecher,' a primitive healer."

"And that's when he picked up this disease?"

"Yes, sir. The most recent English term for what that healer and Ionescu were was 'vampire.' He had a really agile little retrovirus in his blood that seems to have been responsible for his morphological changes and for his abilities. The downside of that virus is that his bone marrow was no longer able to keep his blood count high enough to support a raging metabolic level, which was why he had to take blood directly."

"And you don't think he had the opportunity to pass that virus on before he died?"

"No, sir. We identified five crewmembers he had contact with, and they're all clean. We know that he converted several Grugell, but the Grugell, well, they've no doubt dealt with them in their own way."

"Disintegrated." The admiral snorted.

"Probably, sir."

"And Master Chief Gillespie, our hero of the *Ranger* incident, he spotted Ios as the one who was responsible for those murders as well?"

"Not exactly, sir, but we've confirmed that it was Ios that docked his first *Black Dragon* on the *Ranger* just before the murders took place. It's highly probable that he infected someone on the *Ranger*, and that whoever that person was, probably was your killer."

"And whoever it was, was probably killed in the explosion. Very convenient," the admiral noted. "Well, your master chief might just rate a second medal, Captain. I'm thinking several of your crewmembers will be rating awards for this incident."

"Yes, sir."

"And you personally as well—you handled the situation very well, Jared. I appreciate your bringing this directly to me. I don't think we should take Ios' word for it, though, about his being the last one. I think this information should go directly to the president."

"To the president, sir? That's not all that easy, is it?"

"Not for most people." The admiral chuckled. "But President Koga was once an ensign working the signals panel on the cruiser *Ticonderoga*. It was my first command. He was a bright kid, but I had to jack him up a few times. He had a problem with nerves. Seems to have gotten over it now, though. Hasn't been a bad president, and at least the Navy's getting properly funded these days."

Admiral August stood up, extending one gnarled hand across the desk to shake Gellar's. "Good work, Captain. Outstanding work. I'm going to keep your ship here in space dock for a few days so my Intel staff can interview everyone involved. I want them to have a good look through the data you've gathered before you leave port as well. Don't worry, Captain, I'll have you on your way to TF947 within the week. I've already talked to Admiral Crittendon; Horrible Horace can get along without his medical ship for a few more days. Thanks for coming in."

Gellar snapped to attention, saluted, and gratefully left. Commander Hoff was waiting for him outside.

"How'd it go, sir?"

"Better than I'd expected. Too many admirals like to breakfast on starship captains." He turned to leave Flag Country, as he called the admiral's headquarters section, pulling out his pocket watch as he went. "Eleven-fifteen. When will our shuttle be back at the skyhook?"

"Sixteen hundred, sir."

Gellar slapped Hoff on the back, grinning. "Good! Let's go off base and get some lunch. If there's one thing these farmers know how to do, it's put up a meal. I feel like a steak, and I hear they grow the best beef on this rock."

"Hey, you're the boss, sir, and as you know, I always follow my captain's direction."

"That's why you're a good exec, Wils. Come on, let's get out of this museum."

Elsewhere on the Navy base

Heartbeats, all around her, heartbeats, lungs noisily passing air in and out. Her senses were now acute to an almost unbearable degree, and former Colonel Sandelescu was having a hard time dealing with it.

She had considered reporting her infection. She had considered turning herself in for treatment, imprisonment if necessary, and the chance of a cure.

She had considered suicide.

However, the virus was changing her—mentally as well as physically. Her nature before Ionescu had previously been based on integrity, honor, and duty; now her emerging vampire nature tended towards self-preservation, anonymity, indulgence. The Marine colonel was being absorbed in a darker, more secretive being.

Her ride down in the crowded shuttle and the more crowded skyhook bus had been almost unbearable. The cacophony of voices, pounding hearts, blood rushing in veins all around her. And her hunger! Before leaving the ship, she'd ordered and eaten two large, rare steaks in the wardroom—stem cell clone steaks, to be sure, but meat all the same—and her hunger raged unabated. She was all too afraid she knew what to do about it, but that had to wait.

She had a half day to spend out-processing, turning over issue equipment, receiving her final pay statements, and undergoing a medical check. No problem with medical, though—her virus was dormant, lying low in her liver until it was safe to complete the transformation. Even in the infancy of her change, she had that much control.

Her uniforms had been left on the ship. She wore a simple gray coverall purchased in the ship's exchange, and an old cloak, long, black, and hooded, that she had received as a gift very recently. Peering out nervously from under the shading hood, she realized that even her vision had changed. Two young crewmen sitting across from her almost glowed, the blood-rich areas of their faces and heads standing out as though illuminated from within.

She ran her tongue over her eyeteeth. Both upper canines were beginning to lengthen, growing into needle-pointed fangs. She'd have to be careful until she got out-processed and off the Navy base. From there, she had whole Galaxy to hide in.

Finally, she was finished. She idled nervously in the lobby of the huge Navy headquarters building as the late afternoon light faded. At last, the sun went down—it was late autumn now on New Wichita, so sunset came around eighteen-thirty local time. As darkness fell, she slipped out the big double doors, walked down the stairs, and headed towards the gate.

The Main Gate

Just there, the main gate, and beyond it lay the rest of an un-knowable existence. Sandelescu hurried towards the gate, suffering the stares of the two petty officers on guard duty until a familiar voice out of the darkness stopped her.

"Are you sure you won't reconsider, Colonel?" She turned to see Captain Gellar stepping out of the gatehouse. She took two steps to face him.

"I sent the exec on back to the ship," Gellar explained, "but I had to ask you just one last time to reconsider. Your resignation is one hell of a loss to the Corps."

She stood still for a moment, thinking furiously. "I can't, sir. You don't understand how it is—I failed in my primary duty! I was *responsible* for security on your ship, sir, and I let that monster take control of me." Even in the dim light of the street she knew it would be obvious that she was close to tears. Her voice cracked as she went on.

"At least five people are dead because of me, and how many more were injured? Sir, I won't ever be able to trust myself again. You can't imagine what it was like, to be used that way, sir, you just can't."

"Well, it's your decision, of course. But we'll miss you on the *Charity*, Christine."

Sandelescu drew her cloak around her, hugging herself in the folds of cloth. "I'll miss the Corps, too, sir. It's been my life. But I've got to find a new life for myself now." She raised her head to look at Gellar from the darkness under the cloak's hood. Her eyes glinted oddly in the dim light.

"What will you do here on New Wichita? There's just not much here besides the Navy base. Mostly farms."

"I don't know, sir. I won't stay here. I think I'll wander a while, see what opportunities present themselves." Her eyes gleamed almost yellow now. *How odd—a trick of the light?* Gellar thought. He glanced over his shoulder at the large streetlight glinting yellow behind the gatehouse, but the thought left his mind almost as quickly as he formed it.

"I'm sure something will come up." Sandelescu turned away from the captain. "I've got plenty of time," she said. "Plenty of time."

She pulled her cloak's hood over her head and drifted off into the darkness, seeming almost to float in the dim light. Gellar shook his head and turned to head for the skyhook and his ship.

The night folded around her like a comforting shawl, wrapping her in darkness. She found a side street, an alley, and doubled back on her trail. Her new-fledged vampire instincts told her to make sure she was not followed. But the Navy base sent no Marines, no security troops after her. No one cared where she went. No one cared what she did.

She paused to watch up and down the street for a moment. In the evening, a few locals hurried about some business or other, but like most farming towns the settlement outside the Navy base rolled up the sidewalks early.

She watched a few more minutes before a voice bubbled out of the shadows behind her, startling her.

"And so, one more of the Elite have come to me at last," the voice crooned. Sandelescu snapped around to see a tall shape flow out of the shadows. Two glowing coals shone from where eyes should be. "I knew you would come here. I sensed my son's death some days ago." The shadowed form's head shook. "He never learned to stretch his awareness farther than a few meters. More's the pity; he never even knew I survived the Crusades. I suppose he thought me dead many hundreds of years ago." He looked up at the sky, where the stars were scattering into view. "My yacht is at the landing field a kilometer from here. We should go there now."

"Who are you?"

The man—if he was a man—stepped into the faint light of a street lamp, and laid back his hood. A wizened face peered at her from under a shock of white hair. "You may call me Grandfather, child. But in the company of mortal humans, you must call me Hess."

She considered this for a moment. "Yes, of course, Grandfather. Are we to leave New Wichita now, then?"

"Yes, child. A Galaxy awaits us."

Book Two
Pirate

Tarbos

The year 2376 saw the Confederacy's government and the Confederate Navy pulled in several directions at once.

The discovery of several marginally habitable planets outside the generally recognized boundaries of the Confederacy was directly responsible for the first problem, that of piracy in trade routes along the edge of the Galactic arm. While the three worlds were too poor in resources to attract any organized settlers or corporate interests, they were remote enough to appeal to other elements of Confederate society—namely, criminals seeking to avoid imprisonment.

Wilson, Last Chance, and Jinx, known as the Rim Worlds, quickly became known through the Confederacy's underground as a haven for every sort of criminal, and as the populations grew on the outcast worlds, industries slowly sprouted—including ship-building. The Confederate Congress outlawed trade with the Rim in 2355, but a brisk underground traffic nevertheless sprang up, not only with Confederate worlds but also with elements of the Grugell Empire.

It was in 2371 that the first incident of a pirate strike occurred. The *Wilson Lykes*, a freighter bound for Avalon from the agricultural colony of New Wichita, came under attack at a rally point. An unknown ship bearing obsolete but still effective Confederate particle beam emitters disabled the ship's star drive before sending boarders to strip the ship's crew of valuables and make off with grains, frozen meats, and other products of the rich farmlands of the new colony.

Pirate strikes increased rapidly, with two incidents in 2372, five in 2373, and six in 2375. Late in 2375, the Confederate president at last ordered the Navy to stop the attacks and in so doing discovered evidence that there existed other carriers of the viral infection first recorded in the well-known "Ionescu incident."

—Morris/Handel, A History of the First Galactic Confederacy, University Publications, 2804 CE

Chapter One

Nobody but myself and the devil knows where my treasure is hid, and the longer liver will take all!

—*Blackbeard*

The Rim Worlds, 2375 CE

Of all the habitable worlds yet discovered and settled, there were three that did not fall under the jurisdiction of the Confederated Free Planets or the competing, militaristic Grugell Empire. These three dry, barren, metal-poor worlds lay on the outer edge of the Galaxy, orbiting stars that were on the fine fringe of territory just before the vast, empty nothingness of intergalactic space.

The three worlds circled type-G stars, a trio of them. All three lay within a rough triangle forty light-years on a side, making commerce between the three cheap and easy, compared to the hundred and eighty light-year span to the nearest Confederate world. Only a hundred and ninety-five light-years separated the three from the Grugell Empire, and since the three were settled by humans but outside control of Confederate law, trade with the Grugell was as common as trade with the Confederacy. The three occupied a fortuitous position for such trade, lying as they did in an otherwise barren triangle of space in between and on one end of the border between the two interstellar civilizations.

Being on the fringe of the Galactic disk, all three worlds were poor in metals, poor in mineral resources, poor in life, water, and all the essentials to maintain a thriving human economy. That being so, the Rim Worlds had never attracted the normal sort of settlers that colonized friendlier planets; instead, the Rim attracted the desperate, the hopeless, criminals fleeing prosecution, thugs and brigands seeking a safe base of operations. Nobody went to the Rim unless they had nowhere else to go.

Government on the Rim Worlds, such as it was, was anarchy flavored with a touch of absolute dictatorship whenever a particular robber baron or strongman managed to grab hold of the controls for a few Standard months or years—it never lasted long.

Survival on the Rim was brutally Darwinian. On the three Rim Worlds of Jinx, Wilson, and Last Chance, settled by the fugitives, outlaws, bandits, and castoffs of both the Confederacy and the Empire, the very ruthlessness of life ensured that few of them lasted more than a year or two. The current 'ruler' of Jinx had been in place for ten years, which was a record as far as anyone knew.

The Rim Worlds were a regular thorn in the side of the Confederacy, though, as all three contained sufficient resources to support minor shipbuilding and supporting industries, which were put to use building pirate raiders for anyone who could afford them. These raiders would occasionally foray into Confederate space to strike a freighter, a yacht, an unsuspecting and undefended orbital station, to shatter holes in the hull and land boarding parties to make away with anything valuable that could be swiftly removed.

Due to the anarchic systems of governance in the Rim Worlds, though, the ships were generally poorly built and equipped. A routine patrol by a frigate or two of the Confederate Navy was generally all it took to keep the pirates on their own side of the unmarked line at the edge of Confederate space.

In August of the Confederate Standard Year 2375 CE, all of that was about to change.

Jinx, August 3rd

Jinx had no skyhook, no Jinx Ground Control to manage incoming spacecraft, no routine low-orbit-to-surface shuttle. If your ship was not equipped for surface landings or outfitted with a landing shuttle, Jinx wasn't on the list of places you could visit.

The private yacht *Red Witch* was equipped for surface landings. Only minutes after arrival at Jinx, the *Red Witch* left her Gellar drive tunnel in a parking orbit, marked it with a coded beacon and an anti-matter self-destruct switch, and floated gently down the planet's gravity well to the surface.

The yacht set down at sunset on a large concrete landing flat on the dusty outskirts of the planet's largest city, Eastside. It was a large, blood-red ship, big for a private yacht. It had the sleek lines of an atmospheric racer—manifestly a rich man's personal toy.

Rich men never came to the Rim.

A lazy, thin wind blew a few scraps of paper across the landing flat as the ship settled gently to the ground. A drift of such trash slumped on one side of the cracked, chipped concrete pad. The landing field gave the overall impression of sloth, rundown poverty, and careless maintenance.

A short, rotund man, as wide as he was tall and clad in a greasy gray coverall that he had apparently slept in for several months, walked slowly up to the yacht as the main hatch swung open. He had a personal datapad in one grubby fist. About one hundred meters away, two skinny, dirty men in equally greasy coveralls lounged against a run-down maintenance shed.

"Anyone in there?" he called.

"Yes," a voice called back. A tall, skinny old man with a shock of white hair emerged, glaring at the last remnants of red sunlight on the western horizon. He was oddly clad in a black coverall, black boots, and a long, black hooded cloak; the nights were chilly in Eastside this time of year. Glittering yellow eyes under shaggy white brows inspected the fat man carefully. "Are you the master of this landing field?"

"I work for 'im. What's your ship, and who are you?"

"My ship is the private yacht *Red Witch*. I am Joachim Hess, and this is my granddaughter, Christine." He motioned to a tall, statuesque woman with long, raven-black hair, dressed identically to the old man, as she stepped off the ship's ramp behind him. She looked down at the fat man, her eyes glinting strangely in the dim glow of the perimeter lights.

"Pleasedameetcha." The fat man yawned, tapped the information into his pad. "How long you figger on staying on Jinx?"

"Why?" Hess asked calmly.

"Port fees, you know? Rate goes down if you're here over a week. Drops again if you're here over a month."

"We'll be here more than a month. Shall I arrange payment with you?" Hess did not intend to pay any fees, but best not to let the fat, greasy little man know that yet.

"Yep. Monthly rate is two hundred. We take Confederate dollars, Grugell gnoks, or the equivalent in raw materials, electronics, or other supplies."

Hess grinned, displaying strong, oddly pointed yellow teeth. "Confederate currency, then."

"Wha's yer business on Jinx?"

"Trader."

"And the broad? She part of the business, or a sightseer?"

"I'm part of the business, you smelly little toad," the woman snapped.

The two men leaning against the maintenance shed cackled out a laugh. "Hey, Fatty," one of them called out. "I think she likes you!"

"Don't get all wound up, sister, the boss says I gotta ask, I ask. I would ask what you're trading, but the boss don't want to know that. Don't ask, don't tell—that's the rule here on Jinx. About the only rule, really." He turned to Hess. "See that line of ships over there? The empty berth second from the far right end, that's yours. Can you taxi your boat over there, or you need a tug? Costs forty bucks for the tug."

"I'll taxi the ship over, Grandfather." Christine shot a sulfurous glare at the fat man and walked back in the ship. A moment later, the hatch closed, and the ship backed away, pushed by puffs from the maneuvering thrusters, and turned to taxi to the parking ramp.

Overhead, the sky darkened to a deep, deep black. Only a few stars were visible here, on the very edge of the Galactic arm. Hess looked up at the sky and smiled; the night was his friend, and the nights on Jinx looked to be very, very dark indeed—Jinx didn't even have a moon to reflect a bit of light into the night sky. He looked at the fat man and smiled again, but there was no humor in his gaze. "Well, my oily friend, shall I come to your office to sign docking agreements? Or will you accept my word as a gentleman?"

"Neither, Pops. Tony and Freddy over there are going to put an electronic boot on your boat as soon as it's parked. If"n you don't pay, you don't leave. Signing papers, what?" The fat man barked out a laugh. "Ain't any lawyers or cops out here, Pops. Ain't no Navy, ain't no Confederate snoops. These here are the Rim Worlds." He gestured at the sky, pointing vaguely at the two bright stars that dominated. "Ain't any law out here. You don't like that, you best not stay."

"Oh, I like that fine." Hess chuckled. He extracted a small flask from a pocket inside his cloak. "Tell me, my rotund friend, have you ever sampled Grugell wine? No? Let us repair to your office, then, and I'll pour you a wee bit. Invite your friends, too, of course. My granddaughter will no doubt join us as soon as she has secured our ship."

Fatty frowned at the flask. "Sure, I guess." The old man's eyes had this odd trick of reflecting the red lights that illuminated the boundary of the field. "I *am* sort of thirsty."

"As are we," Hess agreed. "Christine and I. As are we."

He placed one skinny arm around the fat little man's shoulders and guided him to the landing fields' tiny office.

Elsewhere in Eastside

"Tak—hand me that circuit board."

Andrew Bates was probably the best quantum design technologist in the Galaxy, but a stiff prison sentence resulting from his weakness for strong drink and recreational drugs had driven him to jump bail on his home world of Caliban, taking passage on a tramp freighter for the Rim. Now he earned his drinks designing and building main computer banks, long-range scanners, and hyperphones for the pirate ships operating out of Jinx. He was unremarkable physically: medium in height and weight, with dusty brown, carelessly cut hair and the typical lack of muscle tone found in those who spend most of their lives at a computer.

His partner was Takatrattik VIII, whom Andrew called "Tak" for short; Andrew's frequent inebriation made the Grugell technician's full name too hard to pronounce. Tak was under a sentence of death for a botched assassination attempt on his superior, the chief tactical officer on the Grugell Navy battle cruiser X-22.

Neither of the two trusted the other. Neither even liked the other. But their skills complemented each other, and their technical savvy also kept them both safe from double-crosses through a network of non-lethal—and some lethal—booby-traps that formed a gauntlet around and in their tiny workshop in Eastside's crime-ridden warehouse district. They survived in the brutal society of the Rim by being useful, and by possessing knowledge that nobody else in the Rim could offer.

"Here. I'm not sure I can work out the programming, Andrew," Tak said in his abrasive, high-pitched voice. "I don't understand the physics well enough."

"Time for another trip to the library at Wilson?"

"No," Tak demurred. "I'll try again to get the information by hyperphone."

"All right."

"The key is going to be in the decryption algorithms," Tak said. "It may take years just to work out the translation details."

"So take years, then. It's not like we can hire any help."

"I suppose so." Tak frowned at his computer screen, mentally translating the English text into Grugell in his head. "Still..."

"What?"

"I wonder what would happen if you digitalized the data and ran it through a reverse k'tackk filter?"

"Huh?"

"I'm not sure how to say it in English," Tak replied. He cackled out something in chittering Grugell. Bates looked irritated; he knew only a few words of his partner's native language. Like most humans, he found the combination of squeaks, trills, rattles, and clicks that made up the Grugell tongue almost impossible to reproduce.

"I have a copy of a quantum filter I used in the Navy—the Grugell Navy, obviously—but I'm not sure how to make it work in Confederate computer systems," Tak went on. Confederate computing technology was at least a generation ahead of Grugell systems; a robust free-market economy saw to that.

"What kind of storage?"

Tak rummaged in a desk drawer, extracting at last a small chip of plastic. "I converted it some time ago. It's on a standard phoebe data chip, forty-eight terabytes."

"Let me see it." Bates took the chip from his partner's thin, clawed hand. He plugged the chip into a port on his desktop terminal.

"This is in Grugell, then?" Within ten seconds, Bates had found the Directions for Use (DFU) file that typically accompanied Grugell software.

"Yes, obviously."

"Can you translate this?"

"Print a copy," Tak squeaked. "I'll get to it."

"This week?"

"Perhaps."

"We don't make any money just sitting around on our asses," Bates reminded his partner.

"I'm well aware of that. I'll start translating tomorrow, does that suit you?"

The human half of Bates-Tak Technologies just shrugged.

The CSS *Dallas*, August 16th

Task Force 947 traditionally patrolled Alpha Station, a million-cubic-light-year section of the Confederate-Grugell border in an area where settled worlds of both civilizations lay relatively close by.

In July 2375, attacks on three freighters by pirate ships operating out of the outlaw worlds of Last Chance, Wilson, and

Jinx forced Rear Admiral Gennifer Wilson, COMTASKFOR947, to detach two light cruisers and three destroyers to deal with the threat. Formed as Task Group 947.3, the cruisers *Glengarry* and *Dallas* followed the destroyers *Isaac Gauss*, *Reuben James*, and *Roland Pierce* to the section of ill-defined "border" nearest the Rim Worlds.

Captain Antonio Silvestri assumed command of the Task Group on July 28, 2375, and plotted a patrol pattern intended to allow deep space scanning of suspected jump points. A tall, spare man, forty-six years old, Silvestri had close-cropped gray hair, pale blue eyes, and a sharply hooked nose that gave him an almost hawk-like appearance.

He was also ambitious to a fault. Using his own ancient *Dallas* as the flagship, he intended to gain his own promotion to rear admiral by halting the increasing raids from the Rim Worlds into Confederate space.

They had been at their patrol station for three weeks.

The *Dallas'* Combat Information Center was well equipped, even if the ship itself dated back to the Grugell War. A slight shudder went through the flagship as she dropped out of subspace at a scanning point. Reports began coming in quickly.

"No transit tracks detected." The *Dallas'* newly updated sensor suite could track subspace transits up to ten Standard Days after a ship passed.

"What's the nearest settled system?" Captain Silvestri asked.

"New Wichita is a hundred and eight light-years from here, sir," the tactical officer reported, "and we're eighty light-years from the nearest of the Rim Worlds; Jinx is eighty light-years at oh-five-oh by six, Wilson is ninety-six at oh-eight-oh by negative nine, and Last Chance is a hundred and two at oh-one-oh by one."

Silvestri thought a moment. Admiral Wilson's orders had been clear: *intercept pirate traffic out of the Rim Worlds*. Silvestri could only see one way to do that.

"Signal all ships, new course oh-three-oh by one. Standard pyramid formation, flagship at the base rear. All ships are to proceed at standard drive. We'll rally when we drop out of subspace; make it a seventy-nine-light-year jump. Designate exit point as Rally Point India."

"New course oh-three-oh by one, sir, standard pyramid, standard drive," Tactical repeated, and began passing the new orders out to the task group.

The new course took them technically out of space recognized as belonging to the Confederacy, which caused the navigator's eyebrows to rise; but Silvestri was not a commander you argued with. The space around the Rim was technically open for travel, anyway, claimed by neither Confederacy nor Grugell. The petty officer at the navigation console shrugged, plotted the course, and sent the vector to Helm.

"We'll park right on those pirates' front doors," Silvestri said to no one in particular as the *Dallas'* star drive rumbled into life, "and see if they want to come out and play."

Eastside, August 18th, evening

Lobo was one of Eastside's most notorious watering holes; presided over by a convicted murderer escaped from the New Albion Penitentiary and three of his former prison henchmen, the Lobo offered a wide range of liquid refreshments and other, more addictive commodities from both sides of the Confederate/ Grugell border.

Certain other 'entertainments' could be had there as well. However, Christine Hess was not seeking a doxy. The liquid refreshments stored behind the bar weren't her goal, either. Her hunger, and some of her other, baser lusts, had gone unsatisfied long enough.

Over the years, the virus had changed Christine, physically and mentally. All of her passions and emotions were magnified. Her lusts, her hungers were, at times uncontrollable. The hard, professional Marine officer had at this point almost submerged into a darker, more self-centered being: a predator, a vampire.

Hess, however, held to an odd code of ethics that seemed to be the real, underlying force behind what the old man said he wanted to do at any given moment. While she had heard him rationalize nearly any course of action, he shied away from preying on the innocent and virtuous. Criminals and thugs of any stripe, on the other hand, were fair game.

Jinx was populated entirely with criminals and thugs. For the first time in quite a while, Christine felt free to indulge herself.

A rummage through her small stock of clothing unearthed a black synthleather bodysuit she had not worn for some time. Combined with knee-high black boots, the outfit showed off her Amazonian physique to good advantage; she smiled in the bathroom mirror in the cheap flat old Hess had leased for them both. Her sharply pointed canine teeth interlocked as she grinned.

I'll have to watch that, she reminded herself. *I hope it's dark. But not too dark.* She flipped off the light switch and looked into the mirror for another moment, where her eyes gleamed back at her, tiny dots of red in the darkness.

On her way out of the apartment, she picked up her black cloak, swirling it over her shoulders as she walked out the door. Hess looked up from his book pad, frowning, as she left, but said nothing—this time, at least. The old man disapproved of her solitary forays, of course. His disapproval just made the urge all the stronger. She knew he had 'adopted' her out of concern for her well-being, or so he claimed; "there are so few of us," he once pointed out, "that I could hardly let one of my own bloodline go untutored, unassisted into the galaxy all alone, now could I?" He claimed also that he had spent enough time alone. Moreover, Christine had to admit as she walked through the darkness, the old man had taught her a great deal, and perhaps, given his age, a bit of condescension was understandable. However, it infuriated her all the same. Tonight, the urge to defy him in some small way was uncontrollable.

Lobo was only a block away from the flat. She covered the distance in a few minutes.

The bar was loud, smoky, and dark. That, of course, was just what Christine preferred. Only a handful of people were in the bar, all of them clustered in little groups, drinking steadily, conversing in hushed tones. Jinx was not a place where one drew attention to one's self. Eastside was even less so, and the Lobo least of all.

She evaluated the bar's patrons carefully. Three hard-looking women in low-cut blouses and short skirts sat at a table against the back wall. *Professionals,* Christine assessed accurately. Several small groups of men and a few—very few—women sat around tables and on barstools, murmuring in low conversation. No music played in the dim barroom; the one small vidscreen behind the bar was showing a rerun of a comedy show that had been popular in the Confederacy six decades earlier.

One man sat alone at the bar, a tall, skinny man in a dirty gray coverall. He was nursing a mug of beer and staring down into the bar's scratched surface.

Perfect. She walked over to the bar and took the barstool next to the skinny man, who didn't even glance her way.

"All alone?" she asked, her voice carefully pitched an octave higher than her normal contralto.

The skinny man looked up quickly, blearily focusing on her long black hair before making eye contact. "Ymm," he slurred. "M' alone. Wan' stay tha' way, too. Don' need no doxy 'night."

"I'm not a professional, friend," Christine told him.

"Y' looks like one."

"Please." Christine waved at the bartender. "I'm a pilot. I just got in yesterday." She looked up at the bartender, who was wiping his hands on a dirty apron that had been white at some point in the distant past. "Red wine, if you would," she told him.

Bates' eyebrows shot up. "Wha' kinda pilot? Pirate? Freighter?"

"No, I'm just a private yacht pilot."

"Oh." The skinny man regarded her for a moment. He seemed to sober up a bit suddenly. "Private yacht, you say?"

"Yes. The *Red Witch*, out of Corinthia," she replied, selecting a planet at random. "Why?"

"Jus' wondering." He looked down at his drink for a moment, his brow furrowed. Finally he sat up straight, looked Christine in the eye, and stuck out his hand. "Andy Bates, Bates-Tak Technologies," he slurred.

Christine took the hand, smiling. "Christine Hess, pilot, private yacht *Red Witch*."

"Cool." Bates chuckled. "I been hopin' to meet a pilot. What's your cap'n like?"

"He's my grandfather, in fact," Christine replied. "A trader."

"Trader, eh?" Bates winked at her.

"Yes," she replied, coolly. "A trader."

"Of course." Bates chuckled. "Both sides?"

"Of the border? Yes, of course. Why else touch base here for supplies?"

"Good point."

"You have something in mind, don't you?"

Bates threw back his head and laughed. "Besides th' obvious, eh?" He looked at Christine's breasts for a moment, licked his lips, his earlier disinterest instantly forgotten. "Yeah, I got a deal you might be interested in. M' partner and I got a new gadget we want to try out. We don't trus' any of the pirates that fly off this rock; they'd kill us and keep it to themselves. We wan'a sell it."

"Of course you do," Christine said, laying her hand on Bates' skinny fingers. "Let me get you another drink."

"Sure," Bates agreed, not realizing he had just bargained away his free will for the price of a glass of cheap local ale.

Two hours later

Bates' home was a tiny hole of a flat above the Bates-Tak workshop. A stairway led from the littered, stinking street to the heavily shielded door. Bates was in a flurry of nervousness during the short walk home with the tall, black-haired woman hanging on his arm. He was all too aware of the eyes that followed their path, not knowing that he could not have been any safer in the company of a platoon of Confederate Marines in full combat armor.

Christine clung to the skinny technician's arm, laughing, feigning a mild drunkenness she had not been capable of achieving in years. Leaning on him as he led her up the narrow stairs, she threw her arms around him at the landing and kissed him once, hard.

"Y' gon' take advantage of me, since I'm a little drunk," she said, giggling.

"Me? Not me, I'd never do such a thing." Bates hiccupped, more than a little under the influence himself.

"Oh?" Christine looked disappointed. "Why not?"

Bates grinned. "Let's get indoors. Ain't safe outside at night 'round here."

He stared blearily at the doorframe, tapped three times at three different places, and said, "Andrew Bates. Gorilla. Toffee. Sandbox."

The door clicked open.

"Handy," Christine breathed, genuinely impressed.

"It's good to be careful 'round here. If anyone tries to force that door, the electrical charge I've got rigged would blow 'im halfway to the landing field. Code changes every day, an' it's keyed to my voice. Let's go inside, have 'nother drink."

"I've got a better idea," the tall, raven-haired woman announced. Her eyes seemed to catch an odd glint of light from the dull yellow tube over Bates' door...

"Let me guess," Bates said, leading her inside.

The apartment was tiny, dark, and chilly, but it had been many years since the cold had bothered Christine. "Let me get some heat on," her host told her, turning away to a wall panel.

"That won't be necessary." She reached around him, placed her hands in a sensitive area, and kneaded gently. "We can warm ourselves, can't we?"

"Sure," Bates gasped.

"Where's your bed?" Christine's hunger was aroused, and not just for sustenance.

"This way."

He led her through a narrow doorway into a tiny room occupied mostly by a narrow, unkempt bed. Before he could turn, she shoved him hard, down on the bed.

"Hey," he began, before the woman fell on him, kissing him hard, roughly, tearing at his shirt. She stood briefly, dropped her hooded cape on the floor, kicked off her boots, wriggled out of her body suit, and fell on him again.

"You're anxious." He laughed as she tore at his belt buckle.

"You have no idea," she husked, opening his trousers. She climbed to straddle him, guiding him into her.

"Whoa," Bates breathed. "You *are* anxious."

"It's been too long," she said, "for many things." She looked down at him with eyes that suddenly flared red.

"What the hell..." Before Bates could finish the thought, Christine grinned, baring fangs like those of a great cat. He tried to roll away, but her hands slammed down on his shoulders with irresistible strength.

"Not so fast," she said, her crimson eyes burning into his watery blue ones. "You have knowledge that we can use, little man, and there's only one way to make sure we get it—we, and no one else."

"What do you mean?"

"You're about to find out." With that she bit him, sinking her fangs into his neck, drawing off blood from his pulsing carotid artery even as she jerked on his body, drawing off fluid from another source. She carefully held back the virus that teemed in her system, only draining him enough to gain a tight control over his weak, undisciplined mind.

Whatever his secret was, it now belonged to Christine Hess.

Chapter Two

Rally Point India, August 19th

Three weeks at the rally point, and all Captain Silvestri had to show for it was a whole lot of nothing.

The four ships of Task Group 947.3 were spread out on a half-light-year front; each was running continual scans from their long-range sensor suites.

The *Dallas'* Combat Information Center had become a tense, unhappy place, presided over by a tense, unhappy Captain Antonio Silvestri. On the morning of August 19th, he was seated in the CIC, glowering at the big scanner tank showing the disposition of his ships, when the petty officer at the scanning station spoke up.

"New contact, designate Papa-One."

Silvestri was in the scanning station in one long jump. "What is it?"

Chief Electronics Mate Jan Udell answered without turning, her attention focused on her console. "Something small, sir. Private yacht, maybe. It just dropped out of subspace about sixteen thousand klicks out."

"What's he doing?"

"Just hanging there, sir. I only caught him by luck; I was calibrating our long-range electronic signature scan. We've only really been scanning for subspace tracks."

"Have you got a proxy out that way?"

"Yes, sir," Udell answered. "About fifteen hundred klicks from this guy; I've already got it headed his way." She switched the view on her main screen to show the ship, a small, private freighter from the looks of things, but there was a small domed structure atop the pilothouse.

"Particle beam emitter," Captain Silvestri observed.

"Yes, sir. And those ports on the sides, just aft of the drive tunnel intake—those look like missile bays."

"Armed ship. A pirate. Tactical Action, get the *Reuben James* headed that way. They're to intercept and board, by force if necessary."

Silvestri leaned over Chief Udell's shoulder to examine her readings. "Why the hell would he drop out clear the hell out here?"

"I got a bearing change, sir; yeah, he's turning. No ID transponder, but engine signature looks like a Gellar drive. There he goes, accelerating; going, going, and he's gone, back to subspace. That was quick."

"Find out where he went," Silvestri ordered.

"Scanning now. There's his track coming in," Udell pointed at a gray line, superimposed over the display, "and there he goes, back along the same bearing." She tapped a few contacts, superimposing the scanning display over a chart of the area. "Jinx, sir; looks like he was out of Jinx, and that's where he scooted back to."

"He saw us sitting out here and ran for home?"

"I suppose it's possible, sir."

"OK, good enough. If we can scare them into staying in their own little cesspools, then so much the better. If they want to come out and fool around, then we'll be ready for them."

"You say so, sir." Udell looked once more at the screen before switching to another scanning mode. "But we're way too far off for the navigational scanners on any private trash-hauler. He shouldn't have detected us. What warned him off?"

She looked up to see why the task group commander had not answered, but Captain Silvestri had already left the compartment.

Sixteen kilometers away: the Grugell frigate *K-510*

"The renegade received our warning, Commander. He's gone back into subspace."

"Very well," Commander Tikkitraskell IV replied. "Keep our cloaking field active. Continue to monitor the Confederate ships."

"As you command."

The *K-510*'s orders were simple: Liase with and provide aid and reconnaissance to human pirate ships operating out of the Rim Worlds.

It wasn't satisfying, but it was better than guarding convoy routes inside the Empire—even the Grugell suffered the occasional renegade.

The Emperor's intent was to disrupt trade in the systems near the frontier, draw the Confederate fleet to that area, and in so doing prepare for the Empire's move to annex several as yet uninhabited systems claimed now by the Confederacy. The *K-510*'s newly redesigned long-range subspace scanning suite and improved cloaking device made it the perfect ship for the job.

If only I were allowed to engage the Confederate ships, Tikkitraskell thought. *With surprise on our side... It would be glorious.*

Jinx

"Grandfather."

'Joachim' Hess looked up from where he sat, cross-legged, on the floor of the rented flat. "I am meditating, child," he snapped. "Are you blind? You know I do not like to be disturbed while —"

"This is important," Christine interjected.

Hess frowned at his granddaughter before scrutinizing the man with her. "What is it? Who is this boy?"

"Tell him."

"Umm. My name is Andrew Bates. I'm part owner of Bates-Tak Technologies. We develop and build scanners and signals systems for starships."

"Yes? And this is important? Some grubby technician?"

"Tell him all of it," Christine urged. "Tell him of the signals system you're inventing."

"Well, it's complicated," Bates began, his face pale and sweaty. Christine motioned him towards the couch; he almost staggered as he moved to sit down.

"It has to do with quantum physics. You see, there's a property of what we call entangled pairs of quantum particles, leptons and muons, specifically," Bates began, "that they retain their bond when separated—according to our study, even if they're separated by as far as forty light-years. That's the farthest we've tried it, but in theory it should work no matter how far away they are."

"And?"

"We think we can build a binary-coded signals system based on that principle. Using particles of identical quantum characteristics, entangled in a collider of our own design, we think we can make..."

Hess was ancient, but his knowledge of current technology was well above average. "You think you can build a signals system that will function over interstellar distances?"

"Instantaneously," Bates agreed.

Hess's glittering yellow eyes opened wide in surprise for the first time in hundreds of years. "Gods of all the stars." He turned to his raven-haired granddaughter, who stood impassively watching. "Child, do you understand the effect this will have on interstellar culture? On banking, investment, commerce? On… everything!" Hess stood up, almost dancing in excitement. He bent to examine Bates' pale, sweating face. "The exchange of information alone… This is a revolution! I remember when the first planetary computer Internet came into being on Earth, how it changed everything. Almost overnight, commerce, communications, education, everything changed!"

"I've read of that," Christine agreed. It was ancient history to her, and in spite of all she'd seen and learned from the old man, it still amazed her that he had actually seen it firsthand. "It did occur to me that this might have a similar impact."

"And you took control of this man? You have not changed him, have you?"

"No, Grandfather. There is no virus in him. I merely weakened him enough to control him. It was not difficult—he is a weak man in any case."

"Excellent. Well done."

Hess walked to the flat's door, then back, thinking. "We must retain this for our own use, our own advantage."

"He can't be the only one that is working on such a device, Grandfather. Information such as this can't be held exclusively for long, if at all."

"No, of course not. One of the lessons of time, child: every advantage is but temporary to such as we. But we must *use* this advantage while we have it."

"Use it? How?"

Hess grinned, revealing yellow, needle-pointed teeth. "These *pirates*, child," he chuckled, "offshoots of—descendants of—the privateers I operated alongside during the Grugell War, over a hundred years ago. They are disorganized, undisciplined. But with signals systems like this to coordinate their operations, and a strong hand in control, we could accomplish much in a brief time."

"Grandfather," Christine said, "this one tells me they already have a leader."

Two pairs of eyes—one jet-black, one glittering yellow—fixed on the technician.

On the couch, Andrew Bates sat, pale, weak, waiting. Hess walked over to him, smiling, and bent to look into his eyes.

"Tell me," the old man ordered, "about this leader."

Elsewhere in Eastside

"Message from the *Ophelia*, Boss."

Robert "Green-eye" Hogmanay looked up from his dinner, his unaccountably jade-green eyes—the source of his somewhat obvious nickname—glittering at his chief aide, Patrick Toombs. "What is it? You read it?"

"No, Boss, you said anything from the *Ophelia*, you wanted to see right away. Just came in, so figure it was sent two, three days ago."

Hogmanay reached for the message pad, scanned it quickly. "Well, that Grugell captain was telling the truth. There is a Navy task group camped out there. They're probably doing long-range scans, looking for our transit tracks."

Hogmanay was a heavy, florid man with thick, red-brown hair falling over the collar of his tailored shirt. The ruddiness of his cheeks and the protruding red nose above the tangle of thick, red beard gave away Hogmanay's one weakness, a fondness for locally brewed whiskey that sometimes left him incommunicado for days at a time. That had not stopped him from seizing control of Jinx within three years of his arrival. He was a twelve-year veteran of the Confederate Navy, a former tactical action officer who last served on the dreadnought *Arcadia* before an attempted mutiny charge led to his flight to the Rim.

Now, ten years later, Hogmanay was in sole and undisputed control of the planet, and the leader of its population of outcasts.

"You think they'd try to intercept? Tricky, that," Toombs observed.

A former Navy man like his boss, Patrick "Paddy" Toombs had fled not a mutiny charge but merely a charge of misappropriation of Confederate property. Six years earlier, Toombs had been charged with diverting a percentage of the materials shipments going into the construction of the New Wichita orbital dock and pocketing the proceeds. The Confederate prison at Tarbos was less appealing than a flight to the Rim, so Toombs used a fake identification disk to book passage on a tramp freighter bound for Jinx the day after the Navy Magistrate filed charges. Something of a born second fiddle, Toombs survived by making himself valuable, and his value lay in a unique ability to gather and analyze information.

Hogmanay leaned back in his chair. "Not too tricky. Shipping lanes are pretty well set, and it's not that hard to project where a transit trajectory will hit one. I'm sure all their ships are running full proxy spreads, and that enables them to cover the lanes pretty well. They've probably got escorts with most of the convoys, and if they can just alert them..."

"Our ships aren't armed well enough to go head-to-head, not even with a destroyer."

"No." Hogmanay looked down at what was left of his steak. His appetite was suddenly gone.

"Boss," Toombs ventured.

"Yeah?"

"We still got those mines, right? The ten-kiloton fission mines?"

"Yeah." Hogmanay smiled. A lucky hit on a freighter the year before had yielded four ten-kiloton magnetic mines intended for the Fleet replenishment group off New Albion.

"We were planning to try to find a buyer, right? But they've been sitting around in the warehouse, because nobody out here in the Rim is too anxious to mess around with a nuke, and it's nothing new to the Grugell—they've got plenty nukes of their own already. Maybe, Boss, instead o' selling them, we should use them, like they was intended for, eh?"

"How?"

"We've still got a few old Lancer missile bodies lying around," Toombs said. "I've had a couple of guys at the shipyard looking into modifying them to use as satellite boosters—since we've got no skyhook, we have to launch satellites from the dirt, and remember when we were talking about trying to get comsats up for the phone and vid systems here?"

Hogmanay nodded. "Yeah. I decided it wasn't worth the trouble."

"Well, Boss, the missile bodies are still sitting over there. Half a dozen of them, at least. They're old MkI types, with regular high-explosive warheads, but we should be able to retrofit those mines, strip the casing off them, and turn them into missile warheads."

"Just might work at that," Hogmanay mused. "The implosion device in those mines is pretty much the same as the nuke warhead option on a Lancer, right?"

"Except that it's twice as big," Toombs agreed. "Standard Lancer MkI nuke was a five-kiloton warhead."

"But the ten-k warhead will work?"

"I'm no expert, Boss, but I seem to remember the only real difference was a small amount of fissile material and a deuterium booster. We've got a former ordnance petty officer that should know how to do it."

"Paddy," Hogmanay said with a grin, "you've got something there. As soon as the *Ophelia* gets back, you tell Homer Gibson that I want to see him. Then get over to the shipyard, get those Lancer bodies loaded up on a cargo skimmer and on their way back over to my warehouse over on Gills Avenue. We've got plenty of tools and such there to refit those missiles." He picked up his glass of local ale and held it up to the light, and for a moment watched the bubbles rising slowly through the amber liquid. "It will take some time, but I bet the Navy won't be going anywhere. If they do, the Grugell will tell us."

"That's how I see it," Toombs agreed.

"Maybe we can give the Navy a little something to think about, eh?"

Paddy's face split open in a huge, gap-toothed grin. "You betcha, Boss."

Chapter Three

Task Force 947.3, September 21st

"Nothing on the scans, sir," Chief Udell replied to Captain Silvestri, for the fifth time that day. The flagship's Combat Information Center now operated in an air of constant tension, which emanated from the frustrated captain.

"I don't get it," Silvestri grouched. He resumed his pacing back and forth across the CIC. "They've been hitting the shipping lanes once or twice a week for two years now. Why have they gone quiet all of a sudden? Here we are almost at the end of September, and nothing since, when?"

"Last contact was August 19th, sir," Chief Udell replied.

"Sir." Silvestri turned to see Commander Joan Lipinsky, the *Dallas'* executive officer. "They're getting some intelligence from somewhere. That scout—it had to be a scout, sir—that popped through a few weeks ago? They knew right where to look for us."

"No reports of any pirate strikes on shipping since then, either," Silvestri mused.

"No, sir."

"Well, they sure aren't going to give up."

"No, sir."

"Well, you know what the obvious answer is. They know we're out here. How they know isn't all that important, but they *do* know, and they're waiting for us to leave."

"Well, sir, we could move in closer to the Rim. The three Rim Worlds are only separated by about forty light-years. I'm sure Navigation could come up with a patrol pattern that would allow us to follow a checkerboard scanning pattern, say jumps of a half light-year each followed by a global transit and normal space scan."

"Go on," Silvestri ordered.

"If they're waiting for us to leave, sir, then they'll have to send a scout out once in a while. Best case, we'll be able to intercept. Worst case, we'll be able to pick up a transit track and see where they're headed."

"We could cover the grid the first time fairly quickly, and leave proxies at each scan point, and then just send one ship—maybe the *Reuben James*, Dick Anderson is tugging at the leash over there—to pick up the datastream at regular intervals."

"Sounds like a plan, sir."

"Good." Silvestri grinned and jabbed a lean forefinger at his exec. "You can be in charge of planning it out. You have twenty-four hours. Get with Tactical Action, Navigation, and Scanning, and don't go cheap on the proxies; we came out with a bit more than the standard load. We can always send a destroyer back to TF947 for more if we need them."

"I'll get right on it, sir."

"Jinx seems to be the hotspot. Plan forty percent concentration of the grid where it can cover the lanes out of Jinx, thirty percent each for Wilson and Last Chance."

"Aye aye, sir." Commander Lipinsky smiled evilly. "I'll find you some pirates."

Eastside, a warehouse, September 21st

"Nobody said this was going to be easy, Boss," Paddy Toombs reminded Green-eye.

"I know."

After leaving the Gellar drive tunnel in low orbit, the navigation and freight section of the *Ophelia* barely fit in the largest of Hogmanay's warehouses, but the dictator was more than a little concerned about the possibility of someone seeing the refit of the pirate ship from space. Hogmanay stood now in the doorway of the cavernous building's small office, scowling up at the hulk of the old converted freighter as technicians swarmed over it. One of their number approached the boss, datapad in hand.

"Boss," he said deferentially, "the particle beam projector's upgraded; it's probably half again as powerful as it was. We're getting that Grugell anti-proton projector slaved to the targeting computer now. We set it into the hull just at the outlet to the drive tunnel, so it will get a good field of fire."

"The missile refits?" Hogmanay demanded. "How are those coming along?"

The grubby technician looked at his pad, stabbed a contact. "We had some trouble coming up with enough titanium to machine new nose cones," he admitted, "but we finally stripped some plating off that ship that crashed on landing over at the Livermore field last year. We've got nose cones made, and two men are working now on refitting the nukes to fit in them."

"Fusing?"

"Two modes, proximity and command-detonate. You can change mode after the missile's launched, as long as you're within range of standard radio."

"How about range? Can you enhance the range any?"

"Not really," the techie said. "Sorry, Boss, but we just don't have the stuff to upgrade an ion drive like that. I'd have to fabricate a whole new drive, probably a whole new body to put it in—which means basically building you a whole new missile. Give me a Standard Year and I could probably do it, but in the time you gave me..."

"I know. Never mind."

The technician nodded. "I better get back to work, Boss."

"Go ahead."

Paddy Toombs watched as the tech walked away. "You still want to try this with a standard MkI body, Boss?"

"I'd rather have a little more speed and range," Hogmanay admitted. "When I left the Navy, the MkIII Lancer was almost half again as fast as the MkI ever was, and had power for twice as much maneuvered flight. The MkIV was in the works then, and I figure it's in the Fleet by now. For sure it's better than the MkIII."

"Still, we have particle beam and anti-proton projectors to back it up."

Hogmanay shook his head. "Won't matter. We're only going to get one shot at this. You know as well as I do, Paddy, there's no way the *Ophelia* can even afford to hang around once she's spotted. Even a frigate has the advantage in every way, speed, maneuverability, firepower—especially firepower. No, the *Ophelia* has to sneak in from behind, launch, and run, unless we want to lose her. I don't intend to lose her. We can't afford to spare a ship."

"True," Toombs agreed.

"Besides," Hogmanay smiled suddenly, "I intend to be on her."

"Boss?"

"You heard me. I still owe the Navy for a few things."

"Yeah, the mutiny charge, right?"

"Captain James was *incompetent*." Hogmanay exploded in rage. "He didn't listen to the navigator, he wouldn't listen to *anyone*, and there we were about to blunder across the border. How long would any ship last alone over there, Paddy? *You* tell me. Even a dreadnought."

"Not long, Boss," Toombs said quickly. He'd long since learned that you didn't disagree with Hogmanay—especially when he was angry.

"So I try to take control, try to save the ship—hell, I *did* save the ship—and what happens? I'm under arrest."

Hogmanay fought back his rage, forced himself to calm down. He glared up at the hulk of the pirate ship. "So, yeah," he ground out through clenched teeth. "I owe the Navy for a few things. And I'm going to be there to see when they get some of their own back."

"I understand, Boss." Toombs didn't, but that wasn't something he could admit and survive.

"Come on," Green-eye said, motioning towards the main bay door. "Let's get out of here. I need a drink."

Eastside landing field

In the fading light of an Eastside evening, four figures walked across the dismal landing field to a row of parked yachts. The four figures—one human, one Grugell, and two human in appearance only—stopped in front of the second ship from the right-hand end of the row.

"This is our ship," Christine Hess said, a certain tone of pride in her voice. "The *Red Witch*."

"Very opulent," Tak observed. "An expensive ship, yes?"

"Does that matter?" Christine snapped. Her dislike for the Grugell renegade was apparent.

Hess placed his hand on Christine's arm, looked at her for a moment: *Calm yourself.* "It is only a modest ship," he said, "compared to the original *Red Witch*—that was a considerable craft, with a crew of fifty. That ship would have made a pirate vessel indeed! But times change, and needs with them—so now we travel in a much more modest private yacht."

Tak looked skeptical as they filed into the yacht. Private Gellar drive yachts were never cheap or modest, and the *Red Witch* was undeniably luxurious in its appointments.

"Signals console in the main control station?" Bates asked.

"Yes." Hess nodded. Both technicians headed that way.

"We're only concerned with one thing," Christine said, following them. "Will your device work in our ship?"

"Let's have a look. Standard console," Bates said, examining the pilot's station. "Chandler & Wright shipyards, Earth, right? Monoblock interface. Microfusion backup power system—yeah, this will work just fine. Just need one thing." He extracted a small penlight from his coverall pocket, bent to look underneath the console. "Yeah, you have an open serial bus port here—three, in fact. We can plug right into that, place the system here under the dash, and run it to the channel options switch on the top. You won't even be able to see any difference until you power the system up."

"The installation will not be difficult, then?"

"No," Andrew Bates answered. "We designed the interface to work with a standard, Dietz-compatible console. It will work in any ship designed and built in the Confederacy, any ship built in the last fifty years, anyway. Our transmitter doesn't draw all that much power, only a few hundred milliwatts."

"Proceed, then," old Hess ordered. "As soon as you are finished, we will test your device. If it works, plan on building more."

"All right."

Chapter Four

The *Ophelia*, October 9th

"Three, two, one, normal space!" The *Ophelia* dropped out of subspace with a slight rattle. After a moment, Captain Homer Gibson pointed into his small, rather primitive scanner tank. "OK, Boss, see there? There's the Navy. Right where the Grugell said they'd be."

"Yeah," Green-eye agreed. "And looking the other way, too."

"They're scanning out towards the Rim," Gibson said. He pointed at the tiny green dots in the tank. "This big one in the center—looks like a cruiser. I bet that's the flagship."

"Figure he'll have a spread of six or eight proxies out," Green-eye mused. "Too small for us to scan, but if he's doing a standard pattern, they'll be on a hemisphere formation about a hundred thousand klicks across, centered on that ship."

"So we should we hit him from behind?"

"He'll have at least half the proxies set to scan globally at intervals," Hogmanay continued. "That's SOP for the Navy. Lesson from the Grugell War."

"Is the gadget ready?" Gibson asked his weapons tech.

Two decks below, one of the two refitted Lancers lay waiting in the starboard missile bay.

"Ready, Cap'n," the former Navy chief gunner's mate answered. His conviction in absentia of fraud and embezzlement on

New Albion had not affected his technical skills. "Weapon's green across the board."

"Get me a target solution on this mark," Gibson said, indicating the green dot that represented the cruiser *Dallas*.

"One minute."

"That long?' Hogmanay demanded.

"This isn't a real targeting computer," Gibson said. "It's not that easy to adapt a navigation console into a targeting system, especially with the talent we've got out here. A minute's the best we can do."

"All right, then."

Gibson and Hogmanay watched the time display on the bottom of the scanner tank tick slowly. After forty-eight seconds:

"Solution computed and locked in. Flight time will be about sixteen minutes. Weapon checked and ready in all respects."

"Let 'er go," Hogmanay ordered, not caring at all about usurping Gibson's authority on his own ship.

The old Lancer body leaped from the pirate ship's missile bay, leaping into space on a spear of blue from its ion drive.

The *Dallas*

The sudden shout from the tactical action officer in the *Dallas'* Combat Information Center made everyone jump a half-meter off the deck: "MISSILE LAUNCH AT SIX O'CLOCK!"

Captain Silvestri was at the scanner tank in one long step. "What is it? Grugell?"

"No, sir, it's an old Lancer, a Mark I. Look at that drive signature. A Mark I, shit—damn thing must be eighty years old."

Silvestri grabbed a handset. "Bridge, CIC, incoming missile. All ahead emergency, evasive pattern three. Launch countermeasures."

Under their feet, the old cruiser rumbled as her Gellar drive came up to full power.

"Picked it up on a proxy, sir," the petty officer on the scanner breathed.

"Sharp work. Stay calm, everyone," the captain ordered. "Weapons, get a fix on whoever launched on us. Target with particle beams."

The *Ophelia*

"She ain't gonna make it, Boss," Gibson observed. "The cruiser just kicked her main drive in. She'll outrun the missile."

"How close?"

"About ten klicks short, maybe," Gibson replied.

"Can you retarget on one of the smaller ships?"

"No way, Boss. Not with this old kludge we've got for targeting."

"Switch to command detonation. Get it as close to the cruiser as you can, then torch off the nuke. Should get some EMP damage." Hogmanay's voice betrayed his disappointment.

"Got some incoming particle beam fire," the scanning tech called out.

"We'll evade those. We're pretty far out for particle beams," Gibson said. "Get our shields up."

"Get ready to run for it as soon as you hit the button," Hogmanay advised. "They'll turn in to launch on us as soon as that warhead goes off. They'll be carrying current hardware, too.

We can't outrun a Mark III or a IV, not if they launch inside their envelope. They can hit us faster than we can get to subspace."

"They'll have to turn and acquire first," Gibson snapped. "Helm! As soon as that nuke bursts, ahead emergency, new course one-ten by fifty, get us to transit as fast as you can."

The *Dallas*

"Talk to me, Scanning," Captain Silvestri ordered.

"It's homing on us, sir, but it's going to come eleven, twelve klicks short of us at our current acceleration."

"Goddamn pirates," Silvestri said to no one. "Launching on a Navy ship. We'll show them a thing or two."

"Warhead detonation! Sir, we have warhead detonation on the missile. Looks like a ten-kiloton fission warhead."

"Damage report," Silvestri snapped. "Where the hell did they get a ten-k nuke?"

"Minor EMP damage to long-range scanners; I'm switching to alternates. We'll be back online in fifteen seconds. It'll be a minute or two for the decks to report, sir."

"Turn back in. Get me a firing solution."

"No good, sir," the tactical action officer reported. "They've gunned the engine. They'll be able to jump before we could get them inside our launch envelope, and they're a bit too far out for particle beams."

"All right. Watch for their jump. Get me a track."

"Pulling away, sir. They'll be gone into subspace in a minute or less. Fast little ship."

Silvestri dropped back into his chair with a disgusted grunt.

One of the lessons from the long-ago Grugell War had been that engagements between starships fell into two categories, due to the speeds and distances involved. Battles were either carefully planned and executed hit-and-run affairs, where the speeds and intervals made computer fire-control a necessity, or they were hull-to-hull slugfests, with ships battering away at each other at point-blank range and depending on redundant systems, hull strength, and shielding to survive.

These pirates, they'll never be able to go head-to-head with us, Silvestri assumed, correctly as it happened. *They'll have to try to hit-and-run us, try to keep us running from place to place, and try to keep us off balance.*

It was a good tactic, Silvestri knew. But the Navy had practiced it, too.

Those sons of bitches, Silvestri thought, bitterly. *They want to play, do they? Firing on my flagship, even. I'll teach them what it means to play in the bigs. Their fire control isn't up to par, and their hardware is fifty years or so out of date. We can take them; we just have to catch them first.*

"Signals, send to all ships," he announced. "Prepare for new course and speed orders. We're going to pay these pirates a visit. Oh, and call Commander Lipinsky to the CIC. Her patrol and scanning plan goes into effect now—I hope she's got it ready."

Jinx, October 12th

Word of the aborted attack spread rapidly through the anarchic information channels of the Rim. Within hours of the *Ophelia's* return to Jinx, the details reached Hess' leased flat in Eastside.

"Stupid, stupid, *stupid!*" Hess was angrier than he had been in a hundred years. For an hour since receiving the news, he had paced angrily, back and forth across the main room of the little flat.

"He could hardly have done anything worse," Christine observed from her seat at the tiny dining table. She leaned forward, her chin propped on one hand, thinking. "The Navy was no more than a nuisance before now. After he fired a nuclear-tipped missile at a Navy ship—and the flagship of a task group, at that…"

"They'll be hunting pirates with abandon," Hess raged. "They may even move on Jinx itself. That fool, that wretched, base fool…"

"He's made things harder for us."

Hess stopped his pacing. His wizened face turned thoughtful for a moment. He turned to face Christine, frowning. "You know, child, we may be able to turn this to our advantage."

Christine sat up very straight, her eyes wide. "What do you mean?"

"We may be able to use the Navy's involvement to our advantage. If we can aggravate them further, cause them to draw into Jinx itself and away from the periphery of the Rim, we may be able to use that."

"To our advantage, Grandfather? How will drawing the Navy into Jinx be to our advantage?"

Hess explained, briefly. "It would of course be necessary to first send several ships to Wilson and Last Chance, there to await further orders."

"What about Hogmanay?" Christine demanded. "Do you plan on including him in your plan, and in the profit? You won't have control of the ships otherwise."

Hess sighed. "I had assumed we would have to… remove… Green-eye and his cabal in time," he admitted. "It is perhaps a level of involvement that some would think unwise —"

"*I* would," Christine interjected.

"It is necessary, at times, to act decisively," Hess snapped. "The isolation of the Rim will help us maintain our anonymity." The old man moved to the fold-down couch, sat down, scratched his head.

"You underestimate the Navy, Grandfather. Especially their Intelligence apparatus. They have capabilities far beyond anything we can match—I *know* how they operate, I was a field-grade officer in the Marines, I saw and evaluated intelligence reports. They are the cutting edge. These pirates, they're not only untrained scum, they are untrained scum with equipment that is fifty years out of date."

"We need only remain undiscovered for a few months," Hess replied. "Enough profit in that to carry us to our next venture."

"And when we are discovered? If they discover our true nature?"

Hess looked thoughtful. "Christine, for almost a thousand years I have manipulated the hearts and minds of men to achieve my goals. You have yet to live even your first century, so you must allow me my sense of scale. There are times when it is not only necessary, but also desirable to gamble greatly. I have done so before. Once in my infancy, during the Crusades, I engineered the downfall of the would-be Turkish conqueror Suleiman Bulut. He was a rare leader of men—had he succeeded in his goals, all of Europe may well have been a Muslim caliphate for centuries to come. During the Second World War, I admit, I gambled and failed—I was very nearly the power behind the German dictator Hitler, but I miscalculated, was outmaneuvered, and fell from favor..."

Christine's eyebrows shot up as she remembered her early Earth history. "Hess? Rudolf Hess, Grandfather? That was *you*?"

"Indeed." Hess leaned back on the couch, looking smug. "There is much about my past I have not told you—much that I have told no one. I have used many names. I was born Johann.

Now, I use the name Joachim. I have used Sebastian, Maximilian, Reinhold, Gregor, Heinrich, and many more. In those years, I did use the name Rudolf."

"But Rudolf Hess committed suicide in a prison cell. There must have been a body."

"I had been a prisoner for some time. Years, in fact. I grew weary of it. Death is an easy thing to fake for such as we, and even necessary—one must not be seen to live too long. Another lesson I must one day teach you, child."

Christine took a moment to digest this new information. There was far more to the old man than she had thought.

"But I digress from my point," Hess continued. He raised one thin, bony finger for emphasis. "There are times when it is necessary to act decisively. This is one such. We have an opportunity here, child. There are risks, but the rewards are commensurate. We need only three months here, perhaps four, time enough to launch one series of raids from Last Chance and Wilson and land the take here on Jinx. Then we will move on. We will make the profit. The pirates will pay the price."

"As you wish," Christine conceded.

But, she thought, *I will make my own plans, in case you fail again. There will be no war crimes trial for me.*

Chapter Five

Bates-Tak Technologies, October 18th

"Andrew!"

Bates looked up through bleary eyes as Christine Hess swept into the workshop, followed by the old man. "What is it?"

"Your timetable has been changed," old Hess announced. "We require your prototype to be ready for testing within ten days."

"That's not possible," Tak objected from his high stool at his own high, narrow workbench. "We have other contracts to fulfill as well, and you said that you didn't want us to deny our other clients—you didn't want Green-eye to know we were working on this signals system. *You* said that, old man."

"I've changed my mind," Hess snapped.

"We're already working almost eighteen hours a day," Bates complained. "How much more are we supposed to do? There are only twenty-six hours in a day. Here, anyway."

Christine walked over, laid a hand on Bates' cheek. "Hess just told you, give up your other contracts," she said, her voice deceptively, seductively gentle. "How many other projects are you working on now anyway?"

"Two," Bates breathed. "One for Green-eye's man Gibson, we're building a long-range transit scanner for the *Ophelia*. The other, a security shield for Owens Container's warehouse."

Hess smiled, baring yellow fangs. "Subcontract the Owens job. Inside Tech will be glad of the work, and they can handle it. Forget the *Ophelia*. Green-eye and his cabal are about to become... irrelevant."

"If you insist," Tak snarled. "You're paying the bills, old man, but take care—whatever you are planning, plan well. The price for failure is likely to be higher than any of us are willing to pay."

"Allow me to worry about that," Hess told the displaced Grugell officer.

Andrew Bates held up a ten-centimeter-square titanium casing containing a few circuit boards and a shining, whirling magnetic bubble. "All right," he said. "Tak can arrange the subcontract. Can't you, Tak?" The Grugell nodded slowly. "Then I'll keep working on this."

"Call us when you're ready, Andrew." Christine smiled. "We'll run a test in ten days. Sooner if you can."

"What about Green-eye?" Tak asked.

"We will... *speak* with Green-eye." Hess chuckled. "Trouble yourself with his work no longer."

Hess turned and strode from the tight, confined workshop into the clear, starless Jinx evening. Christine followed, pulling her cloak tight about her as she strode behind the old man.

"And when will we move on Green-eye, Grandfather?"

"Tomorrow night."

"That soon?"

"If t'were to be done, 'tis best done quickly," Hess quoted. "There is nothing to be gained by waiting."

"Then for once," Christine said, "we agree."

The *K-510*

Commander Tikkitraskell IV was contemplating a rather drastic act, one that would form a complete violation of his confirmed orders from the Imperium. If successful, group commander rank was within his grasp. If unsuccessful, a quick tribunal followed by disintegration would be his lot.

But Tikkitraskell never had been one to shy away from risks.

"Signals Officer," he snapped. He spun his bridge chair to face the communications station. "Prepare to send a message to that human renegade Hogmanay." He pronounced the human name with some difficulty. "I will have the message coded for you shortly."

"By your command, Commander."

"What do you wish to tell him, my Commander?" Tikkitraskell's subcommander, Kestekratell XI, spoke up from his station. He was an ambitious young officer; Tikkitraskell was in the habit of watching his back with his second-in-command around. He was a fawning, polite sort—that would gladly shove a superior in front of an anti-proton projector to further his own career.

"This situation grows stagnant," the commander snapped. "I grow tired of waiting. We cannot engage the Confederates on our own—the *diplomatic* repercussions would be severe." Sarcasm dripped from his voice at the mention of diplomacy; Tikkitraskell was a Grugell of the old school. "But we can supply improved scanning equipment and arms to the human renegades."

"A violation of our orders, Commander," Kestekratell noted. "Is it not?"

"One might see it as a, shall we say, 'liberal interpretation' of our orders. Even so, we must be circumspect. I will contact Hogmanay, and you will be responsible for the actual equipment transfer. Some scanning equipment, an anti-proton emitter,

Sky of Diamonds

and two or four torpedoes won't make much of a dent in our inventory. We'll find some way to account for them. Keep it quiet. Pick yourself one or two assistants and see to it personally." That, conveniently, would allow Tikkitraskell to frame the incident as the act of an overly ambitious inferior, in the event of failure.

That fact was not lost on Kestekratell, but he had little choice but to carry out his commander's orders. Still, in every danger there was an opportunity. Kestekratell thought he might already see one in the unsavory task he'd been handed.

"By your command," he answered, a slight smile on his narrow face.

Eastside, Hogmanay's compound

"Visitor, Boss," Patrick Toombs called from just outside the door to Green-eye's private office.

"Who is it? What do they want? I'm busy." Hogmanay looked up from his old terminal, where he had been casually watching a locally made video featuring several women performing acts of unspeakable obscenity.

Toombs stuck his head in the door. "It's that Grugell from Bates-Tak," he said in a lower voice. "That outfit over in the warehouse district that's been building scanners and signals equipment for us. Says he needs to talk to you direct, Boss. Won't tell me anything."

"Oh, hell, why not. Send him in." The thug-dictator of Jinx swiveled his desk chair around to face the door, looking up as the tall, spare form of the Grugell technician strode in.

"So, what do you want?"

"I do not enjoy coming to you with this, sir," Takatrattik VIII began. "I do not enjoy disturbing the routine of your day. Events require me to do so."

"Events? What events?"

"Events that involve my partner, a woman with whom he is involved, and the woman's companion, who claims to be her grandfather. I suspect there is something strange about these people. I suspect they have taken my partner under control."

"I see."

"Further, sir, and I am speaking as a former officer in a Navy where advancement by assassination is usual—I suspect that the woman and the man intend to attempt a coup."

"You think so?"

"I do." Tak's face was set in a hard, snow-white mask.

"And by coming to me with it, you hope to stay in good with the winning side, is that right?"

"The thought had occurred to me," Tak admitted. "Sole ownership of Bates-Tak had occurred to me as a possible reward."

"You'd better sit down." Hogmanay indicated a chair across from his desk. "Paddy," he called, "bring in that bottle of whiskey and a couple of glasses. Send out for some sandwiches, and then come on in yourself." He looked at Tak, who was seating his tall, spare frame awkwardly in a chair made for humans. "We've got some planning to do."

"Indeed," Tak agreed, "and time may well be of the essence."

"You think you know what they'll do?"

"They will strike you here, of course, where you feel safest. What could be more obvious?"

"We can make that pretty hard for them," Hogmanay said. "Oh, yeah—we can make that *really* hard."

Hess' flat, October 19th

While Hess regarded his 'granddaughter' as a mere child, and generally treated her as such, he did admire her military training and abilities. He drew on those abilities now to reconnoiter and plan the assault on Green-eye Hogmanay's compound.

"My recon droid has returned, Grandfather," Christine announced as she swept in on the afternoon before their planned attack. She held up a flat, black disk, ten centimeters across. "I have images of Green-eye's compound."

"Indeed," Hess answered. "And?"

Christine took her personal pad out of her coverall pocket and laid it on the small dining table. Old Hess walked across the kitchen and looked over her shoulder as she brought the images up on the pad's tiny screen.

"It will not be difficult. There is a force-field fence," she pointed, "and some sort of weapon on the roof of the house. There are no towers, no guard posts, and no roving patrols. There are two guards at the gate, none on the grounds. The weapon on the roof was unmanned during the entire three hours the reconnaissance droid was in the area."

"You look satisfied with this news, child." Hess grinned. "You think this will go easily?"

"I expected more. Hogmanay was in the Confederate Navy. He should know how to establish a secure area. Still," she held up the droid, "there may be measures on the grounds that this did not recognize. An old-fashioned percussion mine or a sonic grenade tripline might not show up on the droid's scan."

"You have a plan to deal with that eventuality?"

"I have a white-noise generator. That will deal with any sonic grenade line. As for explosive mines, I recommend we minimize our time on the grounds as much as possible. The house is not centrally located in the compound; it is set back from the street. There is a place where the force-field fence is only twenty meters from the house."

"A mere hop," Hess observed.

"Yes."

"Very well. I suspect that Hogmanay will not have placed any such passive defenses; he feels secure in his grip on this world. Still, we may not be too cautious this night."

"I agree," Christine answered.

"Rest now," Hess ordered. "I go to take my rest as well. We move one hour after midnight."

Later

"They're expecting us." After pausing a hundred meters from Hogmanay's compound, Christine had sent her recon droid once more over the buildings to scan with infrared and high-resolution radar. She watched now on her personal pad as the 'take' from the droid scrolled across the tiny screen.

"You think so?" Hess' white, furry eyebrows went up a notch. He leaned closer to watch the video stream.

"Fifteen guards, Grandfather. Four guards stationed at the gate, four patrolling the grounds, and two at the front door of the house. Two more are guarding the back door. There are three on the roof; two of them are operating the crew-served weapon. It's an energy weapon of some kind I don't recognize. It may be Grugell. I cannot tell how many may be inside, besides Green-eye."

Hess pursed his thin mouth, thinking. "The roof, then. We'll take the weapon first."

"Of course. I recommend moving inside from the roof and drawing the outside guards in; we should dispose of them before going for Green-eye." After all the years flown between, Christine Hess still talked, still planned, like a Marine.

"Yes," the old man agreed. "But you will dispose of them. I will go to where Green-eye sleeps." He reached out, taking Christine's shoulder in a claw-like hand. "Now attend! You may take from the men when you kill, but give nothing back. Do you understand?"

She shook the old man's hand off. "I understand," she snapped.

"Very well."

The force-field fence around the compound reached three meters into the air and opened only at the gate, but that did not hamper the two invaders. First old Hess, then Christine, slipped to a dark corner at the back of the compound and leaped, floating over the shimmering force screen like a deer bounding a fence. A second leap took the pair lightly, so lightly, to the flat roof of the large, blocky house.

Rupert Guntz was one of Green-eye's most trusted henchmen. His post on the roof, overseeing the operation of the Grugell anti-proton projector, was proof of that; he had a comfortable seat, a stationary post, and a safe perch from which to watch for any invaders.

Or so he thought.

A slight scrape on the roof tiles gave Christine and old Hess away. Guntz and his gun crew turned to see two figures flowing towards them. Guntz grabbed for his sidearm—in vain, as the white-haired figure grabbed his arm with one hand, his throat in the other.

"Oh, no," the weird figure gurgled, glaring at Guntz with eyes like coals. "I'm afraid not." Behind him, Guntz heard only one startled squawk from the gun crew, then two sharp thuds. A moment later, the last thing he heard was the cracking of bone, his own bone, as Hess crushed his neck.

"Well done, child," Hess breathed. "Leave these three. We go in now."

Christine nodded, and her eyes flared in the darkness; her anticipation, her hunger was almost out of control now. The door to the lower level was set into the flat roof; Hess pulled it open and dropped lightly inside. Christine followed.

It was dark inside, but that mattered not at all to Christine and Hess. Hess pointed and raised his eyebrows; the message was clear: *You, child, take the guards.* He inclined his head in the other direction, up the narrow corridor. *Green-eye's room is this way. I will deal with him. You may... indulge yourself.*

Christine nodded and grinned. She glided away down the corridor. Hess moved in the other direction, rounding a corner to see a large, husky man—a bodyguard—standing watch outside Green-eye's door. Hess slid down the corridor, against the wall, flowing like smoke on a breeze. He was within a meter before the bodyguard sensed his presence—too late. Hess struck the man with a hand bearing chisel-tipped nails, striking through his rib cage to find his fluttering heart and crush it. The bodyguard slid to the floor, an astonished look on his face. Hess took his ident-card, slid it in the lock panel beside the door, and moved quietly into the darkened room.

A floor below, five men were seated at a round table where a card game was in progress. While still on the upper level, Christine sensed them even through the closed door at the bottom of the staircase, their heartbeats, the blood rushing in their veins, all of it loud as shouting to her now. She smiled in the darkness. One hand moved to slide the closure of her black overall open several centimeters, revealing the upper curves of her breasts.

How easy men are to distract. In her hunger, it took her a moment's effort to quench the fire of her eyes, damp them to their normal black. Once that was done, she opened the door, stepped through.

"Hello, boys," she greeted them as five heads turned as one in her direction.

"Who are you?" one of them demanded.

"Green-eye thought you boys could use some entertainment," she said.

"Well, he did, eh?" Five chairs pushed back, five sets of hot eyes focused on Christine's cleavage as she strolled forward.

"Of course," she informed them, "all entertainment comes with a price, yes?" The largest of the thugs was at her side; she caressed his cheek with one finger.

"A price?" The henchman smiled, stared down the front of Christine's open coverall. "What sorta price?"

The other four men were crowding in now; just what Christine wanted—all of them within easy reach at once. She continued her stroking, running one finger down the big thug's neck to rest just over his carotid artery.

"Nothing much," she said, her smile seductive, her voice sweet. "Just your lives—and your blood." She struck then, slamming her hand sideways into the thug's neck, stunning him. Spinning, she turned sideways to another as he reached for a projectile pistol at his waist, kicked the gun from his hand, spun again and sent her other foot crashing into his throat. The other three started to back away slowly, even as Christine let the fire back into her eyes, let her teeth show as she grinned at them. "Oh, no," she chided them, "I'm afraid I can't allow you to leave just yet. I have needs, and you are going to fulfill them."

Fangs bared, she advanced on them.

Moments later, the outside guards heard a voice, the voice of the largest of the bodyguards, calling to them. "You guys, get in here now! We've got an intruder! Get inside, now now now!" The outside guards, even to the two at the gate, ran as one to obey the senior man's voice, imitated to perfection by Christine Hess, who waited for them just inside.

Green-eye Hogmanay, thug-dictator of Jinx, awoke to a sudden chill. He had fallen asleep in his big leather chair, a bottle of whiskey at his side. His room was dark. He knew his bodyguard was just outside the door; there was nothing to worry about.

But two glowing red orbs a few feet away betrayed an intruder.

"What the..." he croaked. The orbs flowed closer.

"What, indeed," a voice bubbled out of the darkness. "By all means, Green-eye, turn on your light. Look on the face of your fate."

"Light," Green-eye mumbled, terrified. A yellow light tube on the ceiling flickered on. He gasped as the figure behind the glowing red eyes sprang into view.

"What the hell..."

Hess's hunger had at last driven him beyond control. He opened his jaws wide to show Green-eye his fangs, and his eyes blazed. "You," he gurgled, "you, Green-eye, look on one of the Elite. I grant you this rare and priceless gift, to see what most men never shall, to have the chance to understand—for a moment— what most men can and should not. Ah, but I see what you are thinking! I see your fear, all too easily. Rest your mind, Green-eye. You will not become one such as me. I can prevent that, all too easily. You will merely become—dead."

Hogmanay lay, frozen, panicked, as the weird figure moved closer—and closer. Hess displayed his fangs again. His hot, charnel house breath washed over Hogmanay. "Dead, indeed," Hess gurgled, "and I'm afraid the time for that has come." With that the old man struck, pinning Hogmanay to the chair and sinking fangs deep into his neck.

Five minutes later, Hess met Christine back on the roof. "It is done," he announced. "The others?"

"Dead." Christine smiled. She wiped her mouth with the back of her hand, which came away scarlet. "None will change."

"Well done."

"Grandfather," Christine said, "there's more." She held out a personal datapad. "I searched Hogmanay's office. This was on his desk."

Hess took the pad, examined it, scanned quickly through the various files and messages. "Well," he admitted, "it seems perhaps Green-eye was a tad more clever than I'd thought. I wonder how he chanced to make contact with the Grugell?"

"Their interest in this is obvious," Christine replied. "They wish to put pressure on the Navy, to move ships into this sector. They may use the diversion to launch an action elsewhere along the frontier."

"You think so?" Hess examined Christine with glittering yellow eyes. "Yes, you might be right. Foul creatures, those Grugell."

"Does this change our course of action?"

"Not to begin with," Hess mused. "Not to begin with. Indeed, on the short term it works very much to our advantage. We will of course accept the weapons this Grugell commander offers. We will proceed as planned for now. Later... Later, I think we will find a way to turn this Grugell commander's plans back on him. It simply would not do to have him survive this. Were word of Grugell involvement to spread, it might enable some to, as they say, put two and two together. No, we will use him—and then dispose of him."

"How?"

"That I do not know yet," Hess replied. "Events will unfold, and I am confident an opportunity will present itself. If necessary, we will betray him to his own command structure." He tapped the message pad. "I suspect that his orders do not extend to this."

Christine smiled again. "I would enjoy that."

"We do not do this for enjoyment, but for profit," Hess chided her. Then he smiled. "But, since our course is set, you may consider the enjoyment as an added bonus."

"I will, Grandfather. I will. There's more, though," Christine added. She took the pad back, quickly brought up another file, handed it back to Hess.

"Ah—so *that's* how they knew."

"We should have suspected as much. We don't have the option of controlling him as we do Andrew, and he's been suspicious of us from the start."

"So, we have another loose end that will eventually have to be tied up." Hess thought for a moment. "I think I may know how to do it. Have you set the incendiary devices?"

"I have," Christine replied. She looked at the slim black time-band she wore on her wrist. "The first of them are set to go off in two minutes, forty seconds."

"Good. Let us go now."

They left the compound through the now-unguarded front gate. Behind them, the first glow of a fire began to show through the windows of Green-eye's residence.

The only roadblock to Hess' undisputed control of the fledg-ling pirate fleet was now removed.

Chapter Six

Task Group 947.3, October 27th

"The rest of the task group has come out of subspace, sir." The electronics mate third class at the scanning console looked up. "Maneuvering into standard pyramid formation now. We hit the transit target almost perfectly, sir—we are just inside the orbit of the gas giant." The Jinx system had only one gas giant, a Neptune-sized planet forty astronomical units outside the orbit of the inhabited world. "Permission to launch proxies, sir?"

"Granted," Captain Silvestri answered. "Full spread, standard dispersion. Signals, send to all ships: 'Maintain standard formation, launch full spread of proxies.' Signal *Reuben James* to begin their patrol pattern."

"Sending now, sir."

"No subspace tracks, no traffic in the area," Scanning called out.

"Sir, we're in position as planned, about two hundred million kilometers out from Jinx's sun, about ten degrees in front of the planet, ten degrees north of the ecliptic."

"Very well. Helm, hold position here. Scanning, send two extra proxies to Jinx. Program them for high-orbital scanning pattern. Targets include landing fields and major industrial sites, like shipyards."

"Sir, it will take several days to get proxies to the planet from here."

"Get me an ETA for the proxies. I don't want to move the Task Group in too close. I don't want them to know we're out here just yet."

"Programming now, sir," Scanning answered. "Sir, ETA on the proxies at Jinx is four days, six hours, twenty-seven minutes."

"Launch as soon as you're ready."

"Five minutes, sir," the electronics mate second class answered.

"Very well." *I wonder what we'll find. What could there be on a backwater like Jinx?*

Eastside

The word for the meeting went out through Jinx's underground channels, along the back alleys, over the subterranean pathways of the planet's Internet, through words whispered in taverns, warehouses, and back offices. On a Friday evening they gathered at a leased warehouse co-opted to serve as a conference room.

They were leaders of local operations. The owner—by assassination—of Jinx's one operating shipbuilder was there. The leader of the gang that controlled the planet's three landing fields was present. The Commodore—a title that was plainly self-appointed—of an eleven-ship pirate fleet was present, as were a dozen or more lesser lights, all aspirants to Green-eye Hogmanay's position. The usual retinue of assistants, bodyguards, and *consigliore* accompanied each, as they filed in, curious to see who their mysterious host was, wondering meantime why there had been no word from Green-eye since the burning of his compound.

There was no sign of Hogmanay's former assistant Toombs; he also had been unaccounted for since the burning of Green-eye's compound.

As they came in, they were each surprised to see at the head of the conference table only a skinny old man clad in an old black coverall and an even older, badly worn black Navy pea jacket. The old man's narrow face was lined by time, his hair a white brush standing straight up on his head, his hands skinny white claws where they lay clasped together on the table. Strangest of all were his eyes, glittering yellow where they peered out from under bushy, tangled white brows.

Behind the old man stood a stunning, Amazonian woman with jet-black hair tied tightly back. She was dressed in a severe black business suit; mirrored sunglasses hid her eyes. Her face was pale but stern, her mouth set in a hard line. The men present, hard cases all, had the impression she would be a tough customer even among their company—exactly the image Christine Hess intended to project.

The old man stood up. "Welcome," he said. "And thank you all for coming. Please, help yourselves to drinks," he indicated a small bar set to the side of the area, "and seat yourselves around my table."

With a murmur of conversation, they did so, the principals seating themselves while assistants and bodyguards took up positions behind their employers.

"You are all curious as to the nature of this meeting, yes?" Hess looked around the table, his glittering yellow eyes resting briefly on those of each attendee.

Heads nodded.

"I have several things to tell you all," Hess began, "information about recent events about which you are all no doubt curious. I will then tell you all various other things, and I then I have a proposition to place before you all. My proposition involves some risks, of course, to you and to the various enterprises that you control. The rewards will be commensurate with the risks. I will ask only that you place yourselves and your enterprises under my direction."

"*Your* direction?" The 'Commodore' snorted derisively. "And who the hell are you? And what about Green-eye?"

"Who am I? A complicated question, that, but you are required only to know this: I am called Hess." The old man's eyes flashed, showing a brief, startling flash of red. "Green-eye is... no longer a factor."

"Hess?"

"You heard him," Christine snapped.

"What happened to Green-eye?" the leader of the landing field cabal wanted to know.

Hess grinned, showing long, oddly pointed yellow teeth. He reached in a pocket of the pea jacket. He tossed something on the table in front of the landing-field man, something that flashed in the light and jangled on the table.

The man picked up a length of silver chain, read the small titanium tag attached to it: "Richard Farmer Hogmanay, Oh-six-five-four-three-nine-oh-five-five-six-nine. AB positive. Atheist." He looked up. "What the hell? These are Navy dog tags."

"Yes," Hess replied.

"Green-eye's tags," someone else said. "He always wore them. Said it was a reminder of how much he owed the Navy."

"And the only way you could have got them," the 'Commodore' observed, "is if Green-eye is..."

"Dead," Hess answered in a companionable tone.

"You killed him?" This came from the shipbuilder. Hess just looked at him and smiled. "So, what's to stop one o' us from wastin' you?"

"Is that your chief bodyguard? That large man behind you?" Hess asked.

"Yeah. So what?"

"Christine?"

Christine looked over at the man, who towered a good half a meter over her, and probably had double her mass. "Yes, Grandfather?"

"A small demonstration is in order."

"As you wish." She smiled at the bodyguard. "Such a big man. Quite a fighter, are you?"

"Huh. Would I be a bodyguard if I wasn't?"

"Could you fight me, then?" Christine asked.

"Are you kidding?" The thug looked at her and leered. "Are you offerin' me something, sister? Be careful what you wish for, honey."

"You think so?" Christine stepped from behind Hess' chair. "I'm challenging you, big man. Would you like to concede now? Or shall I break a few of your long bones first?"

"What the *hell*, sister," the man blustered. He strode swiftly towards the sweetly smiling Christine. "Nobody talks to me that way—for sure no *broad* does..."

He reached for her throat as he drew near, but she was no longer there. His extended arms were seized in a grip of iron, his own momentum turned against him as he crashed face-first into a steel support beam.

"Somuvabish," he slurred through a mouth suddenly filled with blood. He staggered, regained his balance, and turned to face the still smiling woman. He threw a punch, only to find his fist stopped cold, clenched in a fine, crimson-nailed hand. The hand squeezed, driving the bodyguard to his knees to the sounds of small bones crackling.

"Do you yield?" Christine asked, still smiling sweetly. "Or shall I break your arm?"

"Yeah," the bodyguard muttered, voice strained with agony. "I give."

"I can't hear you," Christine said.

"I said *I give*," he snapped, loud enough for the room to hear.

"That's better." She released his hand, turning to face a ring of staring eyes and open mouths.

One of the bodyguards near Hess had picked up a length of centimeter-thick steel bar. Hess stood up, took it gently from the man's unresisting hand, and neatly tied it in an overhand knot.

He dropped the bar on the table with a loud *clang*. "I presume we now have your undivided attention?"

Heads nodded.

"Good. Now, shall we get down to business?"

"And what business is that?"

"We," Hess looked directly at the 'Commodore,'" are going to engage the Confederate Navy."

Behind the shipbuilder, one of the bodyguards stared at Hess, then at Christine, then back to the old man. His eyes met Hess's for a moment, just enough for recognition to flash between them. He did not recognize the woman, but he knew the old man, and more important, he recognized the power they yielded. After the meeting, he would speak with his employer about it.

Or perhaps not. The thought came to him unbidden. *It may be better to handle this myself, to avoid any complex explanations.*

Yes. I'll handle this myself.

In low orbit over Jinx, November 1st

Navy proxies were one-meter titanium footballs, powered by an egg-sized microfusion reactor. An ion drive served for sub-light propulsion. The forward two-thirds were crammed with a wide range of miniaturized sensor platforms. A high-resolution radar, ground-penetrating radar, microwave, ultraviolet, infrared, and visible light scanners filled the body of the devices, along with a tiny hyperphone burst transmitter to relay information back to the proxy's mother ship.

Normally, the Navy deployed proxies in a screen around individual ships and task groups at rally points, or anytime the ships were traveling at sub-light speeds. Their purpose was to provide early warning of the approach of any other objects in normal space.

In recent years, the technical arm of the Navy, Space Systems Command, had enhanced proxies with additional automated capacities to enable commanders to use them as stealthy, unob-trusive scouts. They could be programmed to infiltrate an enemy formation, or to conduct planetary surveillance.

Two such proxies were now in low orbit over the Rim World Jinx. On command from the *Dallas*, they fired tiny maneuvering thrusters and turned their sensors downward towards the planet's surface.

Both devices immediately began cataloging sites that fit their preprogrammed parameters. One proxy's path took it over Eastside on its first orbit. The locations of Jinx's sole shipbuilding facility and the Eastside landing field were recorded in the proxy's flat metallic brain. At the top of the hour, as programmed, the proxy extended a small rod antenna and shot a thousandth-of-a-second burst hyperphone transmission back to the *Dallas*.

Unnoticed and unknown, the two proxies continued their orbital sweeps, recording and reporting their findings back to the task group commander.

The *Dallas*, November 6th

"It's starting to take shape, sir," Commander Lipinsky commented.

"It is."

Captain Silvestri and his executive officer, along with the group tactical action officer, were reviewing the take from the orbiting proxies, both of which were now on their way back to the *Dallas*.

"Look here, sir." Commander Lipinsky pointed at a symbol on the rotating tri-di globe rotating slowly in the scanner tank. "That's a landing field. Not a very big one, but none of these pirate ships are very big. See the row of ships parked over along the side? And this" she pointed at another blip on the opposite edge of what looked to be a medium-sized city "this is a shipyard. Nothing much bigger than a middling-size private yacht—whatever they build there has to go up the gravity well. No orbital facility here at all. That means even a ship the size of one of our *McKee*-class corvettes is more than they can put up."

"Just as well," Silvestri snorted.

"No skyhook, either," Tactical commented.

"Did you expect one? That's a pretty sophisticated piece of technology, even now—growing nanotube fibers in the quantity you need for a skyhook is tricky."

"True enough, sir," the young lieutenant commander answered. "Just makes it easier."

"If we get approval," Captain Silvestri pointed out. "Granted we are just proposing to send a friendly reminder—but the admiral's going to have to sign off on it. I don't doubt she'll hyperphone back to Tarbos first. She'll want to pass that buck."

Commander Lipinsky made a sour face. "So, figure three, four weeks to get approval?"

"If they're fast," Silvestri said. "While we sit out here and wait." He thought for a moment, and then looked up at the exec. "Plan it out anyway. Use one projectile, no more. Make that shipyard the target. If the lace-panty section does give us approval to go ahead, all I want to have to do is say 'Go.'"

"Aye aye, sir," Commander Lipinsky answered. She wore an evil grin on her face.

"Make up a list of targets, too," Silvestri added. "Medicine balls are cheap, and I have a funny feeling it won't end with just one."

"Already in the works, sir."

"Good job."

Silvestri turned to walk away, only to be stopped by a comment from Commander Lipinsky: "Holy shit."

"What is it?"

"Look here, sir," Lipinsky said. She had the display focused on Eastside, and increased the magnification now to display a series of rooftops and empty streets. "Look at this building here."

"Well, I'll be damned." Someone had used white paint to place a message on the rooftop:

NAVY

OPTIMAL CONDOR

"OK," Silvestri ordered, "get the intelligence section to look up that code *right now*."

"Naval Intelligence has someone on *Jinx*?"

"So it would seem," Silvestri said. "Now we just have to find out what it is they want."

Jinx, Eastside Shipbuilding, November 7th

E.M. "Mike" Rosen had held the reins of Jinx's infant shipping industry for almost twenty Standard Years. Rosen had for the last three years considered himself to be Green-eye Hogmanay's logical successor to the "ownership" of Jinx, and was less than pleased about the succession of the old man Hess to that spot.

He was even less pleased to see the old man himself walk into his office late one afternoon as the sun was setting outside his office window. Uninvited and unannounced, Hess walked in and seated himself in the larger of two chairs across the desk from Rosen himself.

"I require use of a ship," the old man said without preamble.

"Izzat so?" Rosen leaned back in his chair and regarded the old man cautiously.

"Yes. I require a small ship, a fast ship, as soon as possible. Within the hour, preferably. I will require the use of the ship for no more than a day or two."

"Can I ask what for?"

"You may *ask*," Hess calmly replied. He smiled, and said nothing more.

"Well, then." Rosen scowled, but held his patience. He turned to his small desktop terminal and tapped a few contacts. "I have the *Queen of Eden* out on the landing field, she was prepping to leave on a run into the Empire to trade. I suppose they could spare a couple days, if you're willing to cover his expenses, plus the owner's charter fee."

"Gladly," Hess agreed. "Will you contact the ship's master now? I would like to see him immediately."

Rosen looked at the old man for a moment, eyes narrowed. His first instinct was to refuse, but there was something about the old fart's bearing, his demeanor... "I'll call him now."

Bate-Tak Technologies, November 9th

"Tak," Andrew Bates said in a low voice. "I think it's ready. I think it is going to work."

The Grugell renegade unfolded his tall, spare frame from his workshop stool and walked over to his partner's table.

In front of Bates, on the worktable, a ten-centimeter square of titanium sheeting enclosed several million muon switches, a tiny microfusion power supply, and a whirling magnetic container enclosing, like a genie in a bottle, a single quark, linked by quantum entanglement to an identical unit in the *Red Witch*.

"Christine is at the ship, seeing to a repair," Tak remembered. "Try calling her. The unit over there isn't set into the panel yet, but it has power—it should work."

Bates plugged a headset into a standard data port on the side of the unit. "*Red Witch*," he said into the headset's boom mike, "this is Bates-Tak. How do you copy?"

There was silence for a few moments before the reply came back, reproduced with perfect, digital clarity: "This is the *Red Witch*. Hello, boys—I see it's working."

"So it seems," Bates agreed. "At least here—we're only a few kilometers away, but theoretically, if it works here, it should work anywhere."

"*Theoretically*," Christine's voice came back, tinged with irony. "But a more comprehensive test is in order, don't you think? I'm sure my grandfather will agree."

"You could take your ship a few light-years away, somewhere in open space," Bates offered, "and try from there."

"Better to go farther abroad—to Wilson, I think. That's... " Bates heard in his headset the sound of tapping on the yacht's navigation console," forty-two light-years. That should be an adequate test. I'll speak to Grandfather about it when he gets back—tomorrow, or the next day."

"All right. Where is the old man, anyway?"

"That," Christine said, chiding Andrew, "does not concern you."

The *Dallas*

"So, there *is* a Naval Intelligence officer down there."

"Yes, sir," the ensign from Intelligence agreed. The young man was more than a little nervous, with the task group commander and several other senior officers reading over his shoulder as he sat at the intel terminal in CIC. "The code led us to this file: Marine Lieutenant Colonel Robert Patrick, Fleet Intelligence Special Operations. The second part of the code is a request for extraction."

"Extraction?" Silvestri asked.

"Yes sir."

"We can't extract him without a carrier," Commander Lipinsky pointed out. "None of the ships here have any tactical landing craft, just regular shuttles. If we can get a carrier sprung loose from TF947, maybe we can get him out."

"He wouldn't be calling for extraction unless there was something going on down there that he thinks we need to know about right away," Silvestri mused.

"Sir," the intelligence ensign said, "If he's down there on a covert operation, he should have a tight-beam neutrino transmitter. We may be able to contact him."

"We're too far out," Lipinsky objected. "We can't pick up a TBN from Jinx way out here."

"True enough, and the proxies don't have that capacity." Silvestri looked up from the terminal, from the file image of the

Marine officer who was stuck, all alone, down there on a world full of thugs and killers. "I'll send a hyperphone message to COM-TASKFOR947, and see if she can spring a carrier loose long enough to get this guy off the surface."

The other officers in the CIC thought that he didn't sound too optimistic. He was not.

Chapter Seven

The *Queen of Eden*, **November 10th**

The *Queen of Eden* had one tiny stateroom for a passenger, which Hess had claimed as a matter of course. There was little to do on the tiny ship until they reached the destination Hess had ordered, so he took the time to sleep; as he slept, the past came swimming back to his unconscious mind:

Night was falling over the battlefield, the wonderful darkness coming down at last. Hess took his slouch hat off and turned his face up to see the stars. The broad-brimmed hat, jacket, and cape were hot, but protected him from the killing sun—still, it was a relief when night came down. While the Union Army did not yet know it, the Battle of Gettysburg had ended with the disastrous charge of Confederate infantry up Cemetery Ridge; now Major "Abraham" Hess was overseeing the gathering of wounded and the disposition of Confederate prisoners. He relished this chore. Wherever wounded and dead lay in rows on a battlefield, the opportunities to feed abounded. The hunger for blood had led Hess to one red field after another for hundreds of years. This war, this American Civil War, had been one of the most fruitful.

The afternoon had been breathtaking. The Confederate general, Pickett, had marched his entire division up an open hillside, where they had fallen to the Union guns like wheat to the scythe. Hess had fed marvelously the nights before, taking from Confederate wounded on the wooded hills and ridges. He never took enough to kill, never left anything of himself to change those he fed from. This evening promised another feast, and Hess was eager.

"Major Hess," a voice called. He turned to see Captain Alexander Craig, the adjutant of the 72nd Pennsylvania Infantry Regiment. "Colonel Baxter sends his compliments. He wishes to see you at the regimental command post as soon as possible."

"My compliments to the colonel," Hess told the earnest young officer. "I shall be back up the hill momentarily." He returned the captain's salute, watched as the young officer turned and went back up Cemetery Ridge.

He looked around. The hillside was too open; too many lanterns moved about the battlefield. His hunger would have to wait.

"Old man," a voice called near him. A familiar voice.

Nearby, a beckoning hand rose from a patch of weeds. Hess walked over to see a Confederate Army captain lying in a fencerow.

"Stefan," he greeted the Southern officer. "How is it that I come to find you here?"

"I am brought here by the same hunger that brings you, old man," the Confederate said, "the same hunger that leads us from war to war." He coughed blood; several fragments from a Union cannon's canister charge had struck through his chest and stomach and shattered his legs.

Hess looked him over quickly. "You are badly hurt," he said, "but you will heal. Within a day, perhaps two, you will recover."

"Would that this had been you instead of me." Stefan grimaced.

"And why would you wish that on one who has been as a father to you?"

"Because I would kill you where you lay, 'Father,'" the wounded figure rasped, his eyes bright with hate. "For what you have made of me—for the curse you have laid on me."

Hess drew his revolver, cocked it, aimed between Stefan's eyes. "You wish to be free of this life? I can easily destroy what I have made—if the ball does not kill you, a stake and the morning sun surely will."

Stefan shook his head. "No. It is the pain." He had no real wish to die; not while the object of his hatred, his intended vengeance, stood before him as a reminder of the goals he still had for his life.

Hess uncocked the Army Colt and returned it to its holster. "As you wish, my son." He smiled. "I must take my leave of you now—my commander summons me, and afterwards, as you know, there is the hunger."

"Pray I do not find you on some other field, Father, with these circumstances reversed," Stefan hissed.

Hess smiled, gave the figure in the Confederate uniform a mocking salute, turned and walked away.

He awoke suddenly, startled for a moment to find the *Queen of Eden*'s stateroom around him, instead of the canvas walls of a Civil War Sibley tent. "Stefan, my son," he breathed, "after all the centuries, why is it that you come to haunt my dreams now?" He sat up, shook his head to clear it. A face, a form, swung into his memory—the bodyguard from the meeting. *Stefan? Could it be?*

There was no way to be sure. *Events will play out as they will,* he reminded himself, *and if that bodyguard is indeed Stefan, after all these years—well, then I will deal with him as I must.* He got up, washed and dressed, and picked up his datapad to read a while.

Ten hours after the ship had climbed out of Jinx's gravity well and linked up with its orbiting Gellar drive, there was a tapping, and the door to the stateroom swung open. Hess looked up from his pad to see the ship's master, one "Bob" Kingsley.

"All right, Mr. Hess," the converted freighter's captain announced. "We are at the coordinate-set you specified, just inside the gas giant's orbit. The Navy's about ten degrees ahead of us in the ecliptic, but they don't seem to have picked us up yet. Do *not* count on that to last. What now?"

Hess stood up. "We will not be here long, Captain. Is your signals tech at his station?"

"Of course," Kingsley replied, mildly offended at the question.

"Good. If I may accompany you to your bridge, I have a message to send."

The walk to the bridge took only a minute, down one corridor and up a narrow ladder to the top of the ship's navigation module. Hess looked around the claustrophobic compartment, and walked to the signals console.

"Send this," he ordered the signals tech, showing him the screen of his datapad.

"You want me to send a broad-wave radio hailing message? Out here? To who?"

"Send the message, please," Hess snapped.

"Captain?"

"Go ahead," Kingsley ordered, curious in spite of himself.

It was the work of moments to transmit the message. Hess pulled out his watch, watched the seconds tick by. Thirty-eight seconds later, a blinking red light on the signals console indicated a reply.

"They're asking for a visual channel," the signals tech said.

"Do so, then."

"On that terminal." The tech pointed to a screen on the left-hand side of the console. Hess stepped to the side, looking into the screen as the pinched, white face of a Grugell commander swam into view.

"*You're not Hogmanay,*" the Grugell said in his own language, his black eyes widened in surprise.

"*No,*" Hess agreed, in the same chittering, high-pitched tongue. "*Hogmanay is... no longer in the picture. I am his successor. You may call me Hess.*"

There was a delay of a few seconds; the Grugell ship was still at some considerable distance. The *Queen of Eden*'s captain and her signals tech traded a look; neither had understood a word other than 'Hogmanay' and 'Hess.'

"Very well," the Grugell continued in fluent English. "Hess, then. Why have you called me?"

"*Commander Tikkitraskell* IV," Hess continued in Grugell, startling the commander with the use of his name as much as with his effortless command of a language most humans could speak only with great difficulty. "*First, I wish to thank you for the superb weapons with which you have supplied Hogmanay's—now my—fledgling fleet.*"

"Are you going to ask for more?"

"No," Hess replied. "The materiel you have already supplied will more than meet my needs. A serious violation of your orders, Commander, is it not, to pass weapons to human renegades?"

"Perhaps. Perhaps not. Unusual circumstances call for unusual measures." Tikkitraskell lied easily, but Hess had a thousand years' experience in duplicity.

"Indeed," Hess answered smoothly. "Indeed they do. Since you are so confident, Commander, I am sure you won't mind if I verify your orders with your immediate superior, Group Commander Appatchik IX, Imperium contact code six-nine-zero-one-tzek-ki'sk, currently on the *T-100*?"

How does he know that? Tikkitraskell's face showed his surprise and anger for a moment before he regained his composure. "What makes you think the Group Commander would be interested?" he replied.

"So, you *are* in violation of orders." Hess smiled at the screen.

"If that were so," Tikkitraskell snapped, "it would not concern me to compound that violation by blowing you out of space."

"Oh, I'm certain of that," Hess agreed. "This is why I have left a complete inventory of the weapons you delivered to the pirate Hogmanay, with all codes and manufacturing serials, at my facility on Jinx. That information will be transmitted to your group commander in three Standard Days, if I do not return to Jinx safely."

"You *are* clever," Tikkitraskell admitted.

"In affairs such as these, it is prudent to trust no one. Have not you, Commander, also found that to be the case?"

Tikkitraskell chewed that over for a few moments. "What is it you want?" he asked at last.

It occurred to Hess that the Grugell had one thing that might prove even more valuable than weapons. It was far from certain that Tikkitraskell would release the information needed, but there was always the chance.

Hess thought furiously, while keeping his expression carefully neutral. *Could it be that I have this commander in that tight of a corner? He may well decide to destroy us, and we would be helpless to stop him. If I succeed, the rewards could be incalculable.*

Taking the chance, Hess told him what he wanted.

"I cannot give you that!"

"Then my message must go to your group commander," Hess told him. "I'm so sorry." He reached for the console, as though to switch off.

"Wait!" Tikkitraskell looked around him. "Clear the bridge!" he barked at his command crew. "Everyone out!"

He looked back at the screen, frowning back at Hess' grinning, ancient visage. "Is there not *anything* else you will accept?"

"There is not," Hess said.

At least he did not ask for the command override codes, not that I could have provided them. The radio codes that allowed an Imperium vessel to take remote control of any Grugell ship were closely held. Only a group commander or higher had access to those.

If he even knew those existed, I would have to destroy him—and the consequences be damned.

Tikkitraskell closed his eyes for a moment, thinking, but there was nothing else to do, and anyway, a Grugell could only die once. *A traitor to the Empire is what they will call me. If anyone learns of this, that is.*

Therefore, I must ensure that no one does.

"Agreed, then," he conceded. "Prepare to receive data transmission."

Eastside, November 11th

A day later, Christine Hess stood at the Eastside landing field an hour after sunset, watching as the navigation/freight section of the *Queen of Eden* settled slowly to the chipped, cracked concrete pad. Moments after the ship's maneuvering thrusters sputtered to a stop, the lower hatch opened, a ramp dropped, and the familiar tall, thin figure of old Hess emerged.

"Grandfather." Christine greeted him as he walked towards her, smiling. "I assume you found what you were looking for?"

"I did indeed," Hess said. "More than I was looking for, in fact."

Christine looked sideways at the old man as they turned to walk to the skimmer she had waiting to take them back to the flat. "More?"

"Much more. However, until I can ensure that the data I was given was complete and accurate, I believe I will keep it to myself."

"If you say so." Christine frowned. "I think you play your cards too close sometimes, but if that's how you want it..."

"You needn't worry—you will know everything in good time, if all works out. If it doesn't, it won't matter."

She thought about that for a moment, finally deciding to drop the subject. "Andrew and Tak are ready to test their device over an interstellar distance."

"So soon?"

"You did tell him ten days," Christine pointed out.

"I did. Have they finished installing the system in the *Red Witch*?"

"Of course, just as you ordered. I can have the ship under way yet today, if you want to test the device immediately. I recommend taking the ship to Wilson or Last Chance for the test; the Navy seems to be ignoring traffic within the Rim."

Hess stopped in mid-stride. "How do you know this?"

"I sent the *Ophelia* to Last Chance. She arrived back only this morning."

"You sent a ship to another system without my knowledge?"

"Yes, obviously," Christine replied, her annoyance obvious in her voice. "You were off on the *Queen of Eden*, successfully as it happens, and even a hyperphone message would not have reached you much before your return. I knew we would have to travel some distance for a proper test of the new signals system, so I thought it prudent to make sure the Navy wasn't intercepting local traffic. It would seem they are not, for the time being at least. I suggest we take advantage." She met his angry gaze evenly, not backing down an inch. "That figures into your plan, does it not?"

Hess glared at her for a moment. "Very well." He turned to walk towards the skimmer. "I never expected the Navy to interfere with local traffic. Their concern is only with traffic leaving the Rim. But you are right; my plan does depend on that."

"Best to be sure," Christine snapped. "That's how I see it, and I acted accordingly. I'm not a child, Grandfather; I'm fully capable of making these decisions on my own, you know."

"What's done is done, at any rate. When can you be ready to leave for the test?"

"Within the hour, if you like."

"Good."

Chapter Eight

Hess stomped across the tiny workshop, first one way, then the other. Andrew Bates sat staring sullenly at the communicator. Tak, as usual, perched on a high stool at his workbench, ignoring the other two.

A crackle came from the makeshift signals panel Bates had built into his workstation. Hess leaped to Bates' side. Even Tak looked up, expectantly.

The panel's main screen suddenly sprang to life. A pattern of interference raced across the screen; sparkles and lines danced for a moment before the image shimmered, stabilized, into Christine's face.

Her voice came through with crystalline clarity: "Grandfather? Are you there?"

"I am, child." Hess clapped his hands together in delight. "Where are you?"

"In high orbit over Wilson, Grandfather. Forty-two light-years from where you sit. I can see you." There was a note of wonder in her voice.

"It works," Bates breathed.

"Amazing. Simply amazing. Christine, can you tie your scanners into the signal, as Andrew showed you? Show us an image of the planet's surface."

The unmistakable blue-brown-rust surface of Wilson swam into view for a moment, replaced quickly by Christine's face. "It works, Grandfather, as he said it would."

"Wonderful." Hess laid a gnarled hand on Bates' shoulder, making him flinch. "Andrew, you and your partner here have changed things greatly to our advantage."

"I thought it would work... I mean, you never quite believe it until you see it. Instantaneous communications over forty light-years..."

"Distance should be irrelevant," Tak added in a reverent tone. "The entangled particles should still act in unison. And an infinite number of possible channels to use will make signals security almost unbreakable."

"And yet you do not know exactly *how* it works," Hess marveled. "We accomplish so much, and know so little..."

"True enough," Bates said. "But it *does* work. That's the main thing."

"We are almost ready," Hess announced. "Andrew, how long will you require to build eleven more devices?"

"If I can get the materials, two, three weeks."

"I will see that you get the materials. Tak, I'm certain we may rely on your assistance?"

The Grugell renegade frowned. "I do not like to do this. But I will help Andrew on one condition."

"And that would be?"

"Simply this, old man: That once the twelve systems are all in place, I be allowed to go on one of the pirate ships as crew. I was a warrior once. I've had enough of squatting on this rock, taking orders from humans."

Hess laughed a strange, bubbling laugh. "Ah, yes. Of course. Very well, Tak, it shall be as you wish. You will of course still be taking orders from a *human*. But warrior you shall be again, my Grugell friend."

A warrior that will perish in battle, Hess thought. *I shall make sure of that, my un-trustworthy friend. The knowledge you possess may even allow you to go back to the Grugell and keep your head. That, I cannot allow.*

Treachery was a staple among the Grugell, Hess knew. However, he had a thousand years of experience at treachery; the Grugell were mere amateurs by comparison.

Hess smirked at Tak as the Grugell turned back to his workbench. *I shall make sure that you tell no one outside the Rim of this device you have helped create.*

"Now what?" Christine asked, from her seat forty light-years away.

"Now, we plan," Hess answered. "Return to Jinx at once, child. As soon as you arrive, call the various ship masters and arrange a meeting for a week from tonight."

"What you are planning to do, Grandfather, will bring the Navy down hard on Jinx, on the planet itself."

"Indeed it will," Hess replied. "I'm counting on it."

The *Dallas*, November 17th

"Transit track detected, designate Papa-Nine," Scanning called across the flagship's CIC. "Track is inbound from Wilson."

"Put it in the main tank," Commander Lipinsky ordered. She consulted her timeband—0340, ship time. *It's probably nothing worth waking up the captain.*

"This is odd," the electronics mate first class at Scanning said as the track appeared in the main tank. "This track has a break in it—looks like they did a quick deceleration, dropped out of subspace for a moment, then scooted right on towards Jinx. Pretty good little bit of piloting."

Commander Lipinsky looked into the main scanner tank. "Put our positions up on this gadget," she ordered.

After a moment: "Done, ma'am."

"Oh, bloody hell," Lipinsky muttered. "Whoever it was, they did that little drop-out maneuver only a hundred and ninety klicks north of us. If they were on the ball at all with their navigational scanners, they know we're out here now."

That was the piloting equivalent of hitting a needle with a projectile gun from twenty kilometers away. "That's a *damn fine* bit of piloting," Scanning affirmed.

"Well, that complicates things some."

Jinx

Hess was waiting at the landing field when the *Red Witch* settled gently to the battered concrete. He walked forward as the main hatch swung open and Christine stepped down.

"Success, then." He greeted her with a grin. "Our plan can go ahead as we hoped."

"It is amazing," Christine agreed.

"And the other task? Did you carry that out as well?"

"It wasn't easy, but I managed a quick in-and-out deceleration and scan. The Navy is indeed out there, right where the Grugell said they would be. They have moved to a scanning position just inside the orbit of the gas giant. I have a listing of ship numbers and types."

"Well done," Hess said. "Everything is going according to plan."

As they turned to walk away, a figure watched them from the darkness of an open hangar door—a figure whose eyes flashed briefly red as he turned to slip away.

Hess' flat, November 18th

Even before her transformation, Christine Hess had been a light sleeper; a career in the Marines had seen to that. In the time since her change, she had learned to screen out most of the routine sounds of her surroundings.

Therefore, when a slight scrape awoke her two hours before sunset, her instincts kicked in with a vengeance.

Someone is outside.

She lay still in the darkness, listening. Old Hess was in his room, on the other side of the flat, his breathing low and even.

Slowly, quietly, she slipped out of bed. The sound had come from the flat's entrance door. Christine moved with all the skill of an experienced Marine combined with the talents and enhanced senses given her by the virus that teemed in her blood, drifting across the flat as if she were a waft of smoke on an eddy of air, but it did her no good. The intruder knew exactly where she was.

He came not through the door but the window, startling Christine as he punched through the polymer sheet with a loud crash. She struck out with a spinning kick as the figure darted to-wards her, gasping in surprise as her bare foot struck his forearm; she felt as though she had kicked a steel beam. Before she could react, the intruder lashed out, catching her in the shoulder with a rock-hard fist, sending her across the room. She hit the wall and slumped to the floor, stunned.

Before either combatant could move, the flat's lights blazed on, and there stood old Hess in an ancient dressing robe. His face was a mask of fury that cooled as he looked at the intruder—and looked again.

"As I live and breathe," he muttered. "Stefan—it *is* you?"

Christine gasped as the stranger looked at Hess and then back at her where she crouched, naked, on the floor—looked at her with eyes that flared red, red as her own, and bared fangs to match!

"Aye, old man, it's me," the stranger answered. "Are you surprised to see me, after all these years?"

"Stefan Niculescu," Hess said. He took a step forward. "Surprised? No, no—I saw you with your employer. I know you recognized me. What is it you want, my son?"

"Only what I've wanted for all of a thousand years, old man—your head."

Hess appeared to ignore the remark. "How is it that I find you attacking your brother's daughter?"

Niculescu glared at Christine, who was easing herself slowly to her feet. "She is Belos' child?"

"She is the child of a man and a woman, but Belos made her what she is today."

"Even as you made Belos and me what we are," Niculescu snapped.

"Ah, my son, after all this time, you have not yet learned to accept that? You still prefer death on that long-ago battlefield to the thousand years of life I've given you?"

"I was a man," Niculescu answered. "You made me other than that. Still, I did not come here to rehash old enmities, Father. On behalf of my employer, I am here to kill you."

Hess crouched, his eyes flared, and he opened his mouth—wider, wider still—as teeth like ivory knives sprouted from dripping gums, and his hands turned into talons. "Come, then, boy, and try."

Niculescu threw himself at Hess, who neatly sidestepped his 'son's' reaching, taloned hands, striking at his exposed side as he passed, shearing through jacket and shirt to strike flesh beneath. The intruder rolled, came lithely to his feet, pressed a hand to his side—it came away red.

"Damn, but you're fast as ever," Niculescu hissed.

"You have no idea," Hess agreed.

They circled each other, slowly.

After the initial attack, Niculescu ignored Christine—a mistake. Most of her personal effects were in her room with her clothing, but one item lay close to hand, in the drawer of a small table along the wall she'd been thrown against—she reached the table now as Niculescu and old Hess were locked face-to-face, retrieved it.

Niculescu lunged again, seizing Hess by one arm, and drew back a taloned hand to strike—but Christine fired the small, personal neural paralyzer first.

The weapon washed over Niculescu with little effect, but it disoriented him for a moment—all Hess needed. Wrenching his left arm free from the attacker's grasp, he spun, using the momentum of the move to slam his right hand against—and *into*—Niculescu's chest.

Niculescu stood, staring dumbly, as Hess withdrew his hand … dropped something on the floor, something that plopped to the tile, fluttered briefly, and lay still—Niculescu's heart. The intruder puffed up, gasped, and slumped to the floor.

Christine looked at the fallen form of Niculescu, realizing that his eyes were still open and moving.

"He is not dead," Hess told her, "at least not completely." His face and hands were back to normal now, except for the blood that dripped from his fingers.

"Who is he?"

"Upon a time, he was a soldier of the army of Vladimir Tepes," Hess said. "The last I saw him, he was serving as an officer in General James Longstreet's corps in the American Civil War. Since then, who knows? Unlike your father, he quickly learned to shield his thoughts from me. A strong lad, indeed."

"I thought..."

"You thought you and I were the only ones? That we were the only bearers of the Elite virus?"

"Yes," Christine admitted.

"With good reason," Hess said. "I have often thought as much myself. This one, I had not heard of in five hundred years or more."

"He said his employer sent him—do you think that his... condition... was known?"

"I think not," Hess said. "We will know soon enough if it was—and if not, he could hardly give away our own status without betraying his own. A close call, though. All too close."

"What do we do with him now?"

"We must destroy him. Go to the warehouse, start the incinerator. He must be burned—yes, to ashes. I will wrap him in something, and join you presently."

"Of course." Christine was only too glad to agree.

"And, Granddaughter?"

"Yes?"

Hess grinned at her. "Clothe yourself first."

Christine looked down, seeming to see her nakedness for the first time, and laughed.

Eastside, November 19th

The familiar Eastside warehouse had once more been pressed into service as a conference room.

Hess welcomed the masters of eleven armed pirate ships with drinks and a light buffet. The eleven ships represented by their captains made up roughly half of Jinx's pirate fleet. Ten other ships had already left the system, leaving no word of their destinations or of their intended course of action—as Hess had ordered.

The eleven captains accepted drinks from a smiling Christine and selected a few favored tidbits from the buffet before seating themselves.

Hess sat at the head of the table. There was no plate at his place; only a glass of red wine stood on the table in front of him. Once the eleven pirate ship captains were seated, Hess stood and waited for the mutter of conversation to die down before speaking.

"I thank you all for attending," he began. All eleven captains knew that their continued existence had depended on their attendance, but Hess let that pass, and so did the captains.

"We face an interesting opportunity. The eleven of you command eleven armed ships. You have to date been operating on your own, or in conjunction with one other ship at best. Of late you have not been operating at all."

"Thanks to the Confederate Navy." One of the captains snorted. "Laying out there by the gas giant."

"Nobody can jump out of here without the Navy picking up the track," another complained.

"Indeed," Hess agreed. "The Navy has become a quite effective barrier to your operations, all the more so because your ships are no match for even the smallest Navy warships, using current tactics."

There was a chorus of nods and muttered agreement.

"Using current tactics, that is," Hess continued. "I propose adoption of new tactics, tactics made possible by a new communications device."

Eleven sets of eyebrows went up, but none of the captains offered a comment.

"In the past, coordination of attack has been limited by communications. Victory in battle is to the units that can coordinate their maneuvers, to adapt to a changing situation, to take advantage of the enemy's movement.

"Until now, the difficulty has lain in the nature of space-borne combat, in the distances and speeds involved. Reserve forces must be located far enough from the initial engagement to avoid detection, yet close enough to move quickly into action. Optimum placement is five to ten AU from the prospective engagement."

"Yeah, we know all this," one of the captains objected. "Even with hyperphones, it's hard to get a message across fast enough to react."

"And we don't all have hyperphones," another added. "That's expensive hardware."

"Indeed." Hess smiled. "Indeed. But imagine, if you will, the advantages you would gain from a signals system that communicates instantly, over any distance, even one of light-years."

Laughter. "There ain't no such thing." Someone chuckled. "It's not possible."

"Oh, but it is, my friend. It is not only possible, it has already been built. I would be more than happy to arrange a demonstration."

"Well, old man, if it's true..."

"It is, I assure you. I do not expect you to take me at my word; you are more than welcome to see for yourselves."

"If it's true," the pirate continued, "we could sure throw the Navy a few surprises."

"And if I added several Grugell torpedoes and a few new anti-proton projectors into the bargain?" Hess asked.

"In that case, we might just be able to make a pretty good fight out of it. Maybe chase the Navy out of here."

"Exactly my thoughts," Hess lied.

Another of the pirate captains raised his glass to salute Hess. "Well, then," he said, "let's make some plans!"

The *Dallas*, November 20th

"There goes another one," reported Senior Chief Petty Officer Georges Villiers, the duty NCO at the CIC scanning station. "Transit track, just popped up, designate Tango-Tango Nine."

Captain Silvestri rubbed his eyes—it was 0216 ship time. "Where to?"

"He pulled out of Jinx, sir. Looks like he's headed for Last Chance."

"Very well."

Lieutenant Commander Andrea Connors, the overnight watch tactical action officer, spoke up. "Sir, we could have one of the destroyers go after them. The *Isaac Gauss* is positioned to follow the track and try an intercept."

Silvestri thought for a moment. His standing order was to avoid interference with traffic within the Rim.

"No," he said after a few moments. "No, let them go."

"Sir," Connors protested, "in the last five Standard Days, traffic between the three Rim Worlds has increased by a factor of three. Shouldn't we assume that something is going on?"

"What could be going on, Commander?" Silvestri stood up, stretched. "So, the traffic has picked up. So what? They can trade back and forth among themselves until Hell freezes for all we care."

"We've left Wilson and Last Chance uncovered by moving in so close to Jinx," Connors pointed out.

"She's right, sir," Senior Chief Villiers pointed out. "We've focused almost all of our scanning capacity on one world. Granted that this is the main one we're concerned about, but right now, sir, a pirate could jump to one of the other Rim Worlds and transit from there to the Confederacy with only a twenty to forty percent chance of us picking them up on a proxy."

They were right. "All right, Commander, what do you recommend?"

"Sir, I recommend placing one destroyer at a good scanning location to cover the lanes out of Wilson and Last Chance. They can run an enhanced proxy spread, and at least give us warning of any large movement out of the Rim."

"That leaves us with only one destroyer and the two cruisers here at Jinx," Silvestri said.

"Unless we move back to our initial rally point," Chief Villiers added.

"No, I don't want to do that. Jinx is the largest of the Rim Worlds; it has the most shipbuilding and landing capacity, the most people, and the most everything else—and most of the traffic we've seen is coming out of Jinx."

"We could still move the destroyers," Connors said, pushing her captain as much as she felt possible. "They don't have anything that can go head-to-head with us, sir—it's not like they're going to come out and attack two cruisers."

"Very well," Silvestri agreed, stifling a yawn. He looked at his watch. "I'm going to sleep on it for a couple of hours—send a messenger to wake me at 0500."

"Aye aye, sir."

Silvestri didn't know it, but ships already climbing out of Jinx's gravity well would focus his attention tightly on that world, to the exclusion of the others.

Chapter Nine

Forty AU off Jinx, November 22nd

It was an old trick. It dated to the closing days of the Grugell War, but it was a trick that the Navy still had no effective counter for—no one did. Three pirate ships, trajectories plotted by Andrew Bates' updated scanning and navigation hardware, dropped out of subspace in the middle of Task Group 947.3's formation and launched a spread of Grugell torpedoes.

Their arrival was heralded by a shout across the *Dallas'* Combat Information Center. "TORPEDO LAUNCH TO STAR-BOARD," the petty officer on the scanning console shouted. "Three unknown ships in the formation, sir, designate Raid-One—sir, they're Gellar drive signatures, but those are Grugell torpedoes."

"The hell," Silvestri breathed. "Details," he snapped at the scanning tech.

"Tracking six torpedoes. Two targeted on the *Dallas*, two on the *Reuben James*, one on the *Glengarry*—one seems to have gone bad, sir—it's gone wild, moving north out of the formation."

"Target those inbounds," Silvestri ordered.

Weapons chimed in. "Targeting with particle beams. One hit—second hit, sir. Both inbounds destroyed."

"Good." He stabbed a button on his CIC chair console. "Bridge, CIC—bring us about, head into the attack. Engage with particle beams and Lancers as soon as we unmask batteries."

The reply came swiftly; the executive officer's voice came back almost at once: "CIC, Bridge, we are engaging now." Below the CIC deck, the ship's massive Gellar drive began to thrum with increased power.

"Very well," Silvestri replied.

"*Reuben James* is showing turn to starboard," Scanning called out. "One of her inbounds is gone." According to Fleet S.O.P, the individual ship captains had begun evasive maneuvers and returned fire on their own. "There goes the other."

"What about the *Glengarry*?"

"She's turned into the attack, sir," Scanning replied. "Two missiles launched from the Glengarry."

"Put it into the main scanner tank," Silvestri said. He got up, feeling the familiar rumble under his feet as the old ship accelerated, and walked across the CIC.

The Red Witch

"Damn," Christine Hess muttered. She had parked the yacht inconspicuously a hundred thousand kilometers south of the main Navy formation to watch and coordinate the attack.

The initial attack was not going at all well. The vaunted Grugell torpedoes were exploding all over the sky like Avalonian fireflies in the mating season.

"Calm yourself, child," Hess's voice came over the quantum signals device. The old man watched now, in real-time, from the safety of the Bates-Tak facility on Jinx. "It is all to plan—I never expected the initial attack to succeed."

"The Grugell downgraded the torpedoes they sold us," Christine complained. "They shouldn't be that easy to hit."

"Did you expect anything different? They are a treacherous race."

"No, Grandfather, but I expected at least one or two hits."

"It doesn't matter," Hess replied. "These pirates are nothing but pawns." The Navy ships had as a group turned into the ambush and were engaging the pirate ships; Christine watched one of the pirates blossom into a white-hot thermonuclear fireball.

"Order the second group in now," Hess snapped.

Christine stabbed the panel, sending a code out over the quantum system to the second group of three pirate ships waiting a tenth of a light-year away. All three ships, receiving the order instantly over the Bates-Tak quantum signals device, immediately jumped to subspace.

The carefully planned and calculated jump only took the pirate ships a few moments.

The *Dallas*

Captain Silvestri was forced to grab the scanner tank for support as the *Dallas* shook suddenly. He looked down to see three more red blips suddenly appear in the tank, to the rear of the formation, and the thin green lines of Grugell anti-proton emitters tracing from them towards his ships.

"Scanning," he barked, "get me an ID on those three new contacts."

"New contact, designate Raid-Two—they aren't Grugell, sir, Gellar drives again."

"Son of a bitch," Silvestri muttered. "This is going to make a stink back on Tarbos."

Signals called out: "*Reuben James* reports three hits, sir. Her shield strength is down twenty percent."

Scanning added, "Raid-One is turning back in—one ship is hit and drifting, the other two are firing particle beams."

Task Group 947.3 was bracketed, with enemies fore and aft.

"These are just damned pirates," Silvestri roared. "How can they be this well coordinated? And where the bloody hell did they get Grugell weapons?"

Silvestri sent maneuvering orders to the Task Group, but it took several moments for the messages to be received and acted upon, while the pirates seemed to move as one.

"Raid-Two has cut off the *Glengarry*," Scanning reported. Silvestri looked in the main scanner tank. The light cruiser had been left momentarily out of the Task Group's protective envelope, ushered to the south of the formation by an awkward turn. The three pirate ships from Raid-Two closed in, peppering the cruiser with anti-proton fire. The cruiser responded with particle beam emitters, catching one pirate ship and slicing its hull open as the other two dodged north and turned back in to resume the attack.

"Get the *Reuben James* and the *Gauss* headed that way," Silvestri ordered.

"Sir, that only leaves the *Roland Pierce* with the flagship," Tactical called out.

"Very well," Silvestri snapped. He was dangerously close to losing control of himself. Moments later, the two destroyers peeled off the main formation, Gellar drives glowing orange as they arced south to join the *Glengarry*.

"Order the *Pierce* to take station five kilometers to our starboard bow." Silvestri looked into the scanner tank again. The two remaining ships of Raid-One were turning, showing acceleration as they tried to break off the fight. "Pursuit course. Pursue and engage."

In the tank, the bright yellow vector lines of Lancer missiles bloomed as the *Roland Pierce* launched on the nearest pirate ship.

Jinx

Hess watched in the tri-di display as the battle unfolded. His long, skinny frame unfolded out of the chair where he was perched; a pattern was developing. *Yes*, he told himself, and picked up the handset on the quantum signals console.

"Third group, engage now—split the middle," he ordered.

Two hundred million kilometers, almost nine light-minutes away, five more pirate ships—the balance of Hess' makeshift fleet—copied the orders instantly and programmed their jump.

The *Dallas*

"Sir, new contact, designate Raid-Three," Scanning called out.

"What the hell?"

"Five ships, sir, all Gellar drives. They just popped out, sir, exactly in the middle of the formation, between us and the *Glengarry* group."

"What? How?"

"They're launching—some old Lancers, some Grugell torpedoes. Got some anti-proton fire coming in."

The *Dallas* shuddered again, and then once more, as the green bolts of Grugell anti-proton projectors slammed into the flagship's shields. The five pirates had dropped in between the two groups of Navy ships headed in opposite directions, perfectly positioned to take each group from aft. Two pirates peeled off after the *Dallas*, while the other three engaged the *Glengarry* and the two destroyers speeding to her aid.

"Update," Silvestri ordered. The main scanner tank was a hash of lines, vectors, and red and blue ship designators.

"Raid-One has lost two ships, the third is dead in space. Raid-Two has lost one ship. The other two are running for the C barrier under full drive with the *Pierce* and the *Reuben James* in pursuit. Raid-Three-Alpha is engaging the *Glengarry*, and Raid-Three-Beta is one hundred kilometers aft of us, engaging us with anti-proton fire."

The way ahead was open, then. Silvestri stabbed a contact.

"Bridge, CIC, ahead two-thirds, new course one-ten by five," he said.

"CIC, Bridge, copy that, ahead two-thirds, one-ten by five." Almost immediately, the ship's Gellar drive responded.

"Come on, big D, let's go," Silvestri breathed. He turned towards the signals panel. "Send to the *Pierce* to maintain station. All aft emitters are to engage Raid-Three-Beta. Send to *Glengarry*, turn north, and rejoin main formation as quickly as possible."

Jinx

"That will be enough, I think," Hess said aloud. He stabbed a clawed finger at the signals console. "Recall all ships."

Of the initial eleven ships in the pirate fleet, six replied and acknowledged the order. On the *Red Witch*, Christine heard the order and engaged full drive, setting her course for Jinx.

The *Dallas*

"What the hell?" Silvestri leaned over to examine the scanner tank. Three pirate ships were destroyed and two crippled, but the remaining six turned as one and arced south, leaving the Navy ships to their rear, facing the wrong way. Within three minutes, all six were gone into subspace.

"I don't get it," Scanning said to no one in particular. "They were way too well coordinated. I doubt we could plan a raid that well, even if we had the courses and speeds all plotted in advance. In this kind of engagement, plots go to hell the moment your enemy starts to maneuver."

"They were well coordinated, weren't they?" Captain Silvestri walked to the signals station. "Order all ships back into standard formation. Send to the *Pierce* to pull in those two crippled pirate ships, board and look for survivors."

"Sending."

"I want to know how those ships coordinated an attack like that," the captain said. "Prepare also to send a hyperphone message to COMTASKFOR947. The admiral is going to want to hear about this."

Chapter Ten

The *Dallas*

"Survivors coming aboard now, sir," a voice crackled out of the speaker on Silvestri's CIC chair. "And, sir..."

Silvestri's patience was long since exhausted. "What? What is it?"

"One of them is a Grugell, sir," the voice replied.

"Really? Well, now there's an interesting twist," the captain mused. "Hold them there in the hangar. I'll be right down."

Five minutes later, Silvestri strode into the *Dallas*'s commodious hangar to see a gaggle of Marines holding roughly twenty prisoners under guard. The gunnery sergeant in charge of the detail walked up to the captain, saluted. "The prisoners, sir," he reported, "all civilians. There's that one Grugell, over to the left by himself." The non-commissioned officer pointed to where a characteristically tall, thin, pale Grugell stood alone; a Marine lance corporal held a carbine on the alien from three meters away. Silvestri walked over. He stood in front of the tall, thin alien, looking up at the nearly three-meter high, stick-thin Grugell.

Clasping his hands behind his back, he addressed the alien brusquely. "Do you speak English?"

"I do," the Grugell snapped. He wasn't wearing a uniform, just a rather scorched, stained, ill-fitting blue coverall. In spite of his circumstances, he seemed faintly defiant, upbeat, almost chipper.

"Who are you?" Silvestri demanded.

"Takatrattik VIII."

"Very well, Takatrattik Eight. What are you doing out here? Who sent you?"

"I signed on with a pirate ship, the *Aurora*," Tak replied.

"Are you telling me you were not sent here by the Grugell Navy? Not by the Imperium?"

"I was not." Tak knew now the pirate fleet had abandoned him; he saw no reason not to cooperate. "I left the Grugell Navy some years ago. I was—shall we say—evading the unpleasant consequences of an act I attempted."

"He's a fugitive," the Marine gunnery sergeant laughed. "The Imperium probably has a healthy price on his head. The Rim attracts all sorts like that from our side. No surprise that some Grugell end up there, too."

"Maybe we should turn him in," Captain Silvestri quipped.

"I think you will not," Tak chirped, bouncing up and down as he spoke, "once I tell you what I know."

"What's that?"

"I know how the pirates coordinated their maneuvers. If I am not mistaken, Captain, you are wondering even now how the pirates were able to react so quickly to your deployments. Are you not?"

"I suspect you already know the answer," Silvestri allowed. "Why? What do you know about it?"

"I know a great deal. About the signals system the pirates used, that works instantly over great distances—even interstellar distances. I know how it works. I know how to build more." He held his head up proudly. "I helped design it."

Silvestri and the "gunny" traded a look. "Is that so?" Silvestri said. "And what would you like in return for this information? I presume you have a quid pro quo in mind?"

Tak was not familiar with the human expression but took the meaning from its context. "In return for the information, I will not be executed or imprisoned. I will be allowed to work for the Confederacy, doing what I have been doing on Jinx."

Silvestri turned to the Marine. "See to it that the other prisoners are fed and checked out in Medical, then toss 'em in Detention. This one, feed him, see if you can find him something better to wear, and then bring him up to my office in an hour." *I have to call this one in. We'll have to get someone out to look through the wreckage of those ships, too. If he is telling the truth...*

"Aye aye, sir," the Marine agreed.

Jinx, November 23rd

"They did as well as could be expected," Christine noted. She, Hess, and Andrew Bates were in the small office space of Bates-Tak Technologies, reviewing the telemetry of the pirate battle.

"The *Aurora*?" Hess asked.

"Lost in the battle," Christine replied. "It was in the forefront of the initial attack, after all, and exposed longer than any of the other ships."

Exactly as I intended. "Ah, well." The old man sighed, but he was smiling. "They were outclassed and outgunned, and yet they inflicted damage on the Navy ships. Better still, they left the Navy with a mystery." Hess was well satisfied. "They know that this attack was coordinated in a way that they don't understand."

"The Navy will move more ships to this area now," Christine pointed out. "We have to assume there were some survivors—I expect they will know by now where the ships came from, and so they will likely move on Jinx itself."

"Exactly so."

Christine looked at the old man, a puzzled expression on her face. "They no doubt know who sent the ships, too, Grandfather. When they come, they will be looking for you."

Hess stood up and grinned at her. "Never mind—I have no plans to be here when they arrive. Are all the surviving ships dispersed as I ordered?"

"Yes, Grandfather. None of them are at the landing field. We have them refueled and scattered in empty warehouses around Eastside."

"Excellent," Hess replied. "I expect the Navy to respond quickly. Their first response will be a reasoned one, but enough to send a message. The landing field will be one of their targets." He turned to Andrew Bates, who slumped in a chair nearby.

"Andrew," he said, "you have my condolences on the loss of your partner."

"He wanted to go out to fight," Bates muttered. "He wanted to be a warrior again."

"Indeed. Moreover, he met his end in a fashion suited to a warrior. Now, you must turn your attention back to your work."

Bates got up, slowly, and walked out of the room, towards the workshop.

Hess turned back to his granddaughter. "You are keeping a tight grip on him, child?"

"He is brilliant," Christine answered, "but weak. His mind is a fine one. He could have achieved almost anything, but he cares for almost nothing now but his next drink. I am pushing him to work faster, but I don't know how much more we can expect of him."

"You will help him stay focused," Hess ordered her. "Keep him away from the drink until his tasks are complete. I know you have other—charms—that you can use to help him stay motivated. Oh, yes, don't attempt to evade the issue, Christine—I too have my baser appetites. We all do. The changes in us brought on by the

Elite virus only strengthen those urges. Amuse yourself with him as you please; your favors only serve to strengthen your hold over the boy."

She smiled suddenly. "I will."

Hess pulled his watch out of a pocket, looked at it. "Sunset is in one hour. I go now to meditate, and then I believe I will go into the Eades district for an hour or two." The Eades district was best known for a large and prosperous brothel, the Mills House. "My own needs have been neglected long enough."

Christine nodded as the old man left the room. Deep inside, somewhere in Christine's almost forgotten human psyche, she felt a small pang of sympathy for whatever unfortunate doxy Hess selected. She suspected the experience would not be a pleasant one.

Chapter Eleven

The *Dallas*, November 30th

For decades before the advent of space flight, fiction writers had postulated that an enemy in orbit, at the top of a planet's gravity well, could wreak havoc on a planet simply by "throwing rocks." In the case of the Navy's newest orbital bombardment system, the 'rock' was nothing more than a five-thousand-kilogram iron ball coated with a ceramic compound to help it resist atmospheric heating and erosion.

Space Systems Command called the iron ball an "orbital kinetic energy projectile," or "OKEP," but Navy crews called the weapon a "medicine ball."

Following the pirate attack on Task Group 947.3, Captain Silvestri's plan to use an OKEP on Jinx had suddenly broken free of its bureaucratic quagmire and sped to the Fleet admiral's desk, where it was approved and hyperphoned back to the *Dallas*.

The OKEP launched from a specially adapted missile bay on the underside of the cruiser, which was now parked in a low orbit with a clear view of Eastside. Following three runs of the target acquisition program, Silvestri ordered the OKEP launched at 0645 on a Friday morning.

Breaking cleanly away from the cruiser, the iron ball dropped towards the rust-brown surface of the planet below. Millimeter-band radar from the *Dallas* tracked the projectile; tiny attitude thrusters that fired and then dropped away from the weapon made a minor course adjustment a minute and a half into the flight.

The ceramic coating protected the simple iron of the medicine ball from burning off in the atmosphere as it gained speed, streaking through the early-morning sky like the meteor that it effectively was. Few people were out and about in Eastside at that hour. The few that saw the ball at impact saw nothing else after that.

The OKEP struck the planet's surface forty-eight meters south and west of its intended impact point, in the dead center of the Jinx Shipbuilding yard. Traveling at orbital velocity slowed only slightly by the atmosphere, the enormous kinetic energy instantly translated the matter of the ball into white-hot plasma, creating a blast that approximated that of a medium-sized fission warhead. The blast destroyed the shipyard, as well as a good portion of the industrial sector of the city surrounding it; windows were broken as far away as the Okomo District, eight kilometers away.

Jinx

The shipyard itself was deserted; Hess had anticipated the move. However, Jinx had lost the only shipbuilding capacity on the planet at a stroke. Ten minutes after the rolling boom of the OKEP's impact rolled across Eastside, the news reached Hess at his flat.

"No matter," was Hess' only comment on learning of the catastrophe. "We have enough ships to last for the purpose at hand."

Christine was less than pleased. "How many were killed, injured?" Somewhere down deep in her psyche, the Marine officer—the human Marine officer—still lived and felt some small concern for the 'troops' in her charge.

"What does that matter?" Hess asked.

"Sometimes I think you have no feelings at all," Christine said in a low voice.

Hess had been standing at the flat's one small window, gazing out on the night; now he spun around to face his 'granddaughter,' and his eyes flared like coals under a bellow's blast.

"You... dare... imply I care for nothing?" he hissed. "I have known the love of a family. I still know daily the pain of their deaths at the hands of raiders, of scum exactly like these pirates that infest this barren rock. You think that I do not feel that loss to this day? You think that I do not feel a thousand times the sense of loss a child like you could understand?"

"Grandfather..." Christine began. Her voice trailed off, weakly, as Hess held up one bony, clawed hand and bared his long yellow teeth.

"No. It is time you knew. Let me tell you, child, of what losses a man can know. In that long-ago time, I had a family, yes. I had a wife, Anna, and children, Felix and Elsa. I took them far to the south of our home in Bavaria, south and east to the Carpathians, there to build a hostel, an inn, to brew and sell the beer of my homeland. And it was there that war came to us, raiders led by a Turk, Suleiman Bulut."

The old man was calming somewhat now, his anger fading— but only a little. His eyes still flared red as fire.

"My children—all of our village's children—were put to the sword. My Anna was taken by force by two, three, four of the raiders—taken, as were many of the other village wives and daughters, as their men were forced to watch. The fourth raider murdered her even as I broke loose from two Turks that held me and sprang for his throat, only to be clubbed senseless. They threw Anna and me into our inn and torched it. Ah, but what did they know? I had a bolt-hole, a cellar with a door opening into the alley behind the inn. The flames woke me, and I crawled through the cellar, past the barrels of my beer, into the alley's shadows."

"Burnt and dizzy from the knock to the head, I fled into the gathering night, fled into the hills, as my family, my life burned behind me." Pacing now, back and forth across the narrow living room, the old man seemed more agitated than angry.

"I made it as far as a small pass in the hills. Then, as the first gray light of morning found me sobbing my losses in the rocks, then he came to me."

"Who? Who came to you?"

"I know not who he had been, or what became of him afterwards," Hess said. "He was the poorest of our sort, a scrabbler in the forests and mountains, who lived on the blood and flesh of beasts. I was weak, indeed half-dead. He fed on me, briefly, and gave me something of himself in return. I learned centuries later that what he gave me was not a curse, as the village stories claimed, but a disease, a virus, one that does not sicken and kill but that makes its host strong!"

"By then the sun was rising, and the poor one fled. I crawled into a narrow cave, a merest cleft in the rocks, there I thought to die." He was silent then, for a moment.

"But you did not," Christine prompted him to continue.

"No," Hess agreed. "Indeed, I awoke as evening came on, and I felt strong! I had been a healthy, even a hearty man before, age forty but well built. However, that evening I felt I had the strength of ten! I would go forth from the cave immediately, to pursue the raiders that had taken my family, but when I emerged the lowering sun hit me like scalding water, so that I must retreat into the darkness of the cave."

"There I considered my next move. I remembered vaguely the old wives tales of the village, when the local Wallachs would gossip of the wampir that lurked in the hills and lived on the blood of men. 'So,' I thought, 'it seems the tales were true. Wampir, now am I, with the strength of ten, and the urge to live on the blood of men? Ahh, but it is not just any man whose blood I want!'"

"Once the evening fell, I went forth from the cave and proceeded, not hot on the trail of the Turks but instead to the army of the Wallachian princeling Vladimir Tepes. There I attached myself as a leecher and sawbones to the army. Eventually my 'skill' at healing grew as I practiced my arts, which brought me to the attention of the Vlad himself, until I served at his very side."

"I was less cautious then than now. After each battle I would recruit, always young, strong men who would have died of their injuries but not for the 'healing' abilities of the Elite virus. I recruited them to the ranks of the Elite, charging each with making war on the Turks, most especially on the soldiers of Suleiman Bulut. One such was your 'father,' who took vengeance on Suleiman Bulut in my stead and made me proud. Indeed, your father's cleverness and tenacity were second only to my own, until at last, in the early years of Man's expansion into space, there were only the three of us left among those that fought in the Crusade, and the two others knew not that I survived."

"But you quickly made yourself known to me," Christine observed.

"You needed me," Hess replied, "and, I admit, I was weary of being alone. Your father taught you nothing before his death; you would not have long survived on your own, with no one to guide and teach you. A century, perhaps two—what lifespan is that, when I have lived a millennium! And you can too, and should."

"I plan to," Christine agreed easily.

"I still feel the losses of those early days," Hess went on. "More, I grieve for the loss of my home. Earth is too heavily peopled, now, too many live there, too many for such as we to live in anonymity, and anonymity is what we require if we intend to survive the centuries. But oh! How I miss the deep, dark forests of Bavaria, the crags of my adopted home in Wallachia, the woods, the hills, the rivers! To hear once more the calls of night birds, the howling of wolves in the hills! I fear that never again will I know those joys, and I long for them every night."

"I was born and raised on Mars," Christine said. "I don't miss my home. There is nothing there but dirty mining domes, dust, lichens, and rocks."

"Earth is your home," Hess corrected, "the home of all Mankind. Do not forget that. Perhaps, one day, even such as we will be able to return..." His voice trailed off, sadly, and his eyes dimmed. He shook himself to throw off the sudden pang of melancholy.

"So, you see, I do feel, child, I feel all the losses, all the weight of a thousand years of remembering those sweet days of love and bright sunshine, days that I will never regain. For all that I have gained in the centuries I have lived, walking always in darkness, has never—can never erase that loss."

Christine could offer no reply.

"In any case, child, the loss of these pirates, these scum, these raiders, bothers me not at all. They are as one of a kind with the raiders than killed my family, and I waste not a moment's worry on their health or their heads. They serve our purposes for the moment, and so we will use them; when the time comes, we will move on, and leave them behind."

"Yes, of course."

Hess was not yet finished lecturing. "It is not only for profit that we move and feed only among the dregs of this society. We are predators, child, but we are not mindless beasts. Were we to prey on the innocent, the virtuous, we would be no better than the scum that killed my family so long ago, no better than the scum that live here on the Rim. All of a thousand years ago I swore to prey on their kind alone, and for a millennium I have kept my oath. Moreover, these pirates, they are not men of honor as were the Marines you commanded. They are raiders, thieves, murderers, and any fate they meet is no worse—can be no worse—than they deserve."

"They are all of that," Christine had to agree, "and no doubt much worse, in many cases."

"Let us speak no more of this now," Hess ordered. "Please, child, leave me alone for a while. I have ghosts with whom I must speak..."

Christine got up, silently, and made to leave the flat.

"Granddaughter." The old man's voice stopped her at the doorway. "Send signals to the men and ships on Wilson and Last Chance. They are to proceed on their forays, as planned."

She did not turn, but only answered, "Of course, Grandfather," and went out into the night.

Wilson, December 1st

Wilson alone of the Rim Worlds had a small orbital station and graving dock. On receipt of a message from Jinx, a message received at the same instant of transmission, three pirate ships left their orbital berths and jumped into subspace.

Last Chance

The four ships leaving Last Chance, the least of the Rim Worlds, had to climb out of the planet's gravity well and link up with their orbiting Gellar drive tunnels before making their preplanned jumps.

All seven ships proceeded to their prearranged rally points and dropped out of subspace to await their targets.

Chapter Twelve

New Wichita, December 4th

"New Wichita ground, this is *Cripple Creek*; we are in our assigned orbit."

"Copy, *Cripple Creek*. Stand by for skyhook assignments for transfer shuttles."

"Roger that," Captain Richard Blair answered. He laid his handset down on the console at the freighter's tiny signals station. Shorthanded as Universal Freight's ships normally were, the *Cripple Creek* had come on the Tarbos-Avalon-New Wichita run with no signals technician, requiring the captain to make clearance calls himself.

The *Cripple Creek* was an old ship with an old design history. A small navigation module and the modest tunnel of the ship's somewhat underpowered Gellar drive surmounted a kilometer-wide, dull-gray cargo disk.

Like the others of its class, the *Cripple Creek* was neither fast nor agile. Its owners and operators required neither speed nor maneuverability, only capacity and reliability. Carrying a crew of ten, the minimal amount required for navigation and maintenance, the ship was only one of the many freighters that carried out commerce throughout the Confederacy, including to relatively new worlds like New Wichita.

Captain Blair walked slowly back to his bridge chair. Only two other crewmembers were on the bridge, now or at any other time. The helm was always manned, as was Navigation. The signals, scanning, and damage control stations were vacant unless the ship was in an alert status, which it had not been since Blair assumed command, two years previously. If not for the helmsman's habit of tying the main forward scanner's readouts into his secondary panel, there would have been no warning at all—not that it did the aging freighter any good.

"Cap'n," the Helmsman said, "there's a small ship coming in to our front—kind of fast, sir."

Blair stood up, frowning. He had taken just one step towards the helm station when the emerald-green bolt of a Grugell anti-proton blaster crashed through the hull just above the bridge, sending spears of fundamental particles ripping back and down through the ship. The *Cripple Creek*'s bridge crew had no time to even notice the flash of green before they and their duty stations were obliterated.

Two other bolts struck the ship, one lancing through the Gellar drive and destroying several of the conversion field generators, the other slicing through the ship's engineering section at the rear of the navigation module. In moments, the *Cripple Creek* was wallowing helplessly in space.

Eight minutes later, the pirate ship pulled alongside and ran a specially adapted docking umbilical across to the *Cripple Creek*'s hull. Two men wielding a crudely adapted mining laser torch cut a two-meter hole in the freighter's hull even as two others were still securing the umbilical's seal against the hull. There was a smell of burning paint and ozone for a moment, before the detached section of hull was kicked into the freighter with a loud clang.

"Let's go," called out T. P. Burr, the boarding party's leader. A refugee from a mining colony on a moon of the big gas giant in the Hecate system, Burr had long shown a knack for brawling, as well as a good knowledge of what sorts of high-tech equipment could be readily converted for cash. Seven men moved aboard the crippled freighter, projectile pistols at the ready.

What remained of the *Cripple Creek*'s crew was in no position to resist the well-armed and practiced raiders. Burr ordered three survivors locked into the freighter's escape pod and jettisoned, knowing that they might make it safely to the planet's surface or not; the raider chief cared not at all. Within the space of three hours, the freighter was stripped of instruments, valuable cargo, favored foodstuffs, and anything else of value that could easily be carried away. Even as a shuttle loaded with security troops from New Albion launched from the skyhook to investigate the cargo ship's sudden silence, the pirate ship cast loose from the wrecked freighter and leaped into subspace.

At a rally point on the New Albion-Zed run, it was two freighters and four pirate ships. The helpless freighters, dead in space exchanging cargos going in different directions, were boarded and ransacked. The raiders left both ships drifting and helpless, their star drives holed by repeated particle beam hits.

In high orbit over Zed, pirate raiders from two ships burned their way into the *Star of Tarbos*, a passenger liner. The ship's captain and most of her minimal security complement were killed in a ten-minute running battle through the ship's passageways. The raiders herded all passengers *en masse* into the ship's huge Promenade section, where the pirates robbed them of cash, credit and cash cards, jewelry, personal electronics, and anything else of value; two men who tried to resist were badly beaten. The *Star of Tarbos* signals watch officer managed to send a distress message before his console was wrecked, but Zed lacked a skyhook, and before any forces from the surface could react, the pirates withdrew into their ships and disappeared into subspace.

All in all, five ships were hit within one Standard Day. Hyperphone messages flew from Zed, New Albion, New Wichita, and Avalon to Tarbos, but the messages took from six to eight days to arrive, even with the newest wave-phase boosting signals systems available.

Tarbos, December 16th

In spite of strong term-limit provisions set into the Confederate Constitution, a small class of professional politicians had managed to arise. By skipping continually from one elected position to another, some at the Confederate level, some locally on Tarbos, President Thomas Hanson had managed to stay in one elected office or another since just after his twenty-sixth birthday, crowning his career by parlaying his trouble-free term as governor of Tarbos into the presidency.

Hanson had managed to stay balanced on the crest of the wave of events mostly by taking as few risks as possible, and he followed that cautious practice as president. Caution was foremost on his mind when he convened a meeting with his secretary of state, secretary of defense, and Confederate security advisor to discuss the message from the commander of Task Force 947.

There was no doubt where Secretary of Defense Anna Muniz stood. "We should have annexed the Rim Worlds years ago," she insisted. "The longer we wait, the longer it will take to uproot those damned pirates that infest the place."

"I'm not convinced that's necessary," the secretary of state said. Unlike Secretary Muniz, Nick Tupikov had been an integral part of President Hanson's staff since the beginning in Mountain View city politics. "There is a threat from the Rim, certainly, but I think we can deal with it in the short term for now."

"I'd prefer that," the President admitted. "I don't want to get embroiled in a four- or five-year-long battle to pacify three planets full of outcasts."

"We'll have to deal with this sooner or later," Muniz objected.

"This administration won't," Tupikov pointed out. "We have an election in eighteen months for the president's second term. In all candor, Anna, we only have to reduce the threat from the Rim for five or six more years, then it will be someone else's headache."

"You're saying we should pass the buck, then?" The expression on Secretary Muniz's face clearly stated her opinion of that notion.

Hiroshi Katoh, the President's Confederate security advisor, was one of the few in the room with any practical experience outside of politics; a retired Navy captain, he had actually commanded a heavy cruiser in Task Force 947, and was familiar with the planets under discussion. Nevertheless, three years of service with President Hanson had managed to infect him with the caution virus as well: "I'm not sure I would want to commit troops to an occupation of several years. That's what it would take; at least a short division of Marines for each planet, several supporting ships

in orbit, probably for two or three years. It's not a modest under-
taking. And what would we gain?" He tapped at his personal pad
for a moment. "Three Type III worlds, all three poor in resources.
They're low in water, metals, everything. Last Chance in particular
is only marginally large enough to hold an adequate atmosphere.
In fact, the shipbuilding industry on Jinx has to import metals
to manage to put together even small ships—I've got a note here
that they managed to import a freighter full of iron, titanium and
aluminum scrap from Corinthia last year."

The president looked up. "How? There's been a moratorium on
trade with the Rim for years now."

"There are ways," Katoh said. "No doubt the ship's registration
is somewhere else, probably forged at that—but the metal ended
up on Jinx, at any rate."

"We'll have to look into that," President Hanson said.

"So, Mister President, what orders are we to send to the task
group commander?"

The president looked at the ceiling for a moment. "We can't
get involved in an occupation. The risks, military and political, are
too great. We can destroy the shipbuilding and landing facilities
on all three planets, and that will easily shut them down for ten
or twelve Standard Years, maybe longer. How would the Navy go
about that?"

Secretary of Defense Muniz spoke up, still angry over the
course events were taking. "We've got the *Nolan* here at the Fleet
Dock, finishing a refit of her Gellar drive. She has the 345th
Marine Regiment embarked. Figure they can be ready to leave
dock in four or five days, then it will take her about two weeks
to get to the Rim under full drive. We'll want to detach a carrier
from Task Force 947 to support landing operations..."

"Are landing operations really necessary?" the president asked. "Can't we just use an orbital bombardment to take out shipyards and the like?"

"We can, but that's not much good if the pirates are set up in underground bases or dispersed hangars. We'll want to land Marines and take control long enough to make sure we've destroyed all of the shipping facilities."

"All right. Go on."

"Tactical operations we'll leave to the commander at the scene, but figure three, four weeks for the Marines on the surface to do their jobs. Then we can pull the task group back and return to normal patrolling operations in the area."

"I'm more worried about the Grugell than the pirates," the president admitted. "What if they try to take advantage of this to make a move somewhere else along that part of the border?"

"If they do, we'll clean their clocks," Muniz said with great assurance. "The dreadnoughts *Arcadia* and *Borealis* are both with Task Force 947, and we've just shipped our newest fleet carrier, the *Kiev*, out to join them. The Grugell don't have that kind of strength. No, I don't expect they'll try anything."

"All right, are we all in agreement?" Heads nodded around the room; Secretary Muniz sat still, staring at the president with a faint challenge in her eyes, but said nothing.

"Very well," the president said. "Secretary Muniz, start cutting orders to the Fleet. Thanks for coming in on such short notice, everyone. That will be all."

Six weeks to the day after the attacks, Captain Silvestri received one terse order from COMTASKFOR947:

TO: COMTASKGRP947.3

SENDS: COMTASKFOR947

REINFORCEMENTS ON THEIR WAY TO YOUR
LOCATION. DETAILS OF TASKED SHIPS TO FOLLOW.
ON THEIR ARRIVAL, YOUR TASK GROUP TO PROCEED
AT BEST POSSIBLE SPEED TO JINX AND DESTROY BY
ORBITAL BOMBARDMENT ALL SHIPPING FACILITIES,
LANDING FIELDS, AND SHIPBUILDING FACILITIES,
AND ALL ASSOCIATED INDUSTRIES. LANDING
OPERATIONS TO COMMENCE UPON COMPLETION OF
BOMBARDMENT.

YOUR OBJECTIVE IS TO DESTROY ALL SHIPPING
AND SHIPBUILDING FACILITIES AND WITHDRAW TO
AWAIT FURTHER ORDERS.

"Well, well," Silvestri commented on receiving the message.
"Someone at Fleet has finally grown a pair."

Commander Joan Lipinsky was less enthusiastic. "What's this
mean, 'destroy all shipping and shipbuilding facilities and withdraw'? We're going to send strike craft and Marines down there
to knock things over, and then just go away to let these pirates
rebuild?"

"Apparently so," Silvestri said. "It seems they only grew a small
pair," he quipped.

"We're just buying time, then," Lipinsky complained.

"You know how a politician's mind works, Commander. And
this" Silvestri tapped the screen of the message pad, "has politics
all over it. President Hanson has only a year and half until the next
election, the Rim Worlds aren't good for anything, and he doesn't
want to spend any political capital on a long, drawn-out battle to
bring them into the Confederacy by force. Can you imagine the
cost of just rounding up all the criminals, thugs, and hooligans we
know are down there? Even just on Jinx alone, never mind Wilson

and Last Chance? Here we are eighteen months from an election, and the president isn't going to subject the taxpayer to a soaking in the name of annexing three worlds that are poor in metals, poor in water, poor in everything."

"So, we're going to kick that can down the road for him, at least until the election."

"That's right." Silvestri grinned sardonically. "You're learning, Joan. You're learning."

Lipinsky looked at the next message, a listing of additional ships ordered to the Task Group. "At least we're getting a carrier—the escort carrier *Seattle*."

"Half a carrier is better no carrier," Silvestri observed.

"We'll be able to get that Marine intel-type off the surface."

"That's true. I wonder what he is so anxious to tell us?"

Chapter Thirteen

Jinx, Hess' flat, December 24th

Christine looked up as the flat door banged open. She was not surprised at the sudden entry; her enhanced awareness rarely let her down, and her grandfather's aura was well known. "One more week, then we leave," Hess announced as he swept into the flat. "Our goals are met. We have our profit, the pirates have suffered for it, and the Navy is moving on the planet. It is time we moved on."

"Andrew?" Christine asked from her seat on the fold-down couch.

"He stays here," the old man ordered. "Let the Navy find him, if they can. Now that this venture is behind us, it is in our interest to let this technology be widely accepted. It will yield untold economic benefits, and we will profit along with the rest."

"Very well." Christine picked up her personal datapad, tapped two contacts. "We have converted as much of the larger material to cash as this planet's economy will absorb. Some of the smaller, more valuable electronics, a few kilos of rare pharmaceuticals, fifty kilos of gold, and a hundred kilos of metallic germanium are already stowed in the *Red Witch*. One more week should allow me to liquidate the rest of our holdings here."

"Good work, child. I have a few loose ends to tie up as well. This has been a very profitable stop; less than a year, and our gains are considerable."

"Net profit looks to be on the order of sixteen million Confederate dollars," Christine confirmed. "That's the current figure. After liquidating our assets here, we may gain yet another million."

"That is more than enough to carry us to our next venture."

"And what is our next venture, Grandfather? Where do we go from here? There is the colony on New Wichita; it is close by, but there is also a Navy base there."

"I think that may be too close quarters to the Navy for us after this," Hess said. "In truth? I have not yet decided. I think it prudent we avoid the Rim Worlds for a few years. I have heard rumors of two or three worlds opening for colonization as private corporations, theoretically outside the Confederacy's control. Perhaps one of them; I would prefer to go somewhere where we can stay for some time."

Christine nodded her agreement. "There is the other problem, Grandfather."

"The Navy? It will take them some time to act. I anticipate a week, perhaps ten days."

Christine looked the old man in the eye. "You know something."

"No more than common sense, child, and knowledge of history. The weapons of war change with the centuries, but one thing remains the same—you cannot win a battle until you have men with personal weapons standing on the ground. There are no troopships in orbit. When the troopship arrives, then they will act."

"Well," Christine agreed, "last I knew, that was the usual practice on landing exercises. You know, one thing I'm curious about, Grandfather..."

Hess looked at her. "Yes?"

"You mentioned that you last saw Stephan Niculescu in the American Civil War."

"Yes. I was serving in a Pennsylvania volunteer infantry unit in the Union Army. One of many wars I've seen in a millennium of life."

"How many wars have you fought in? And why? When we can live as long as we can, why risk it all in a war?"

"An excellent question, child. Of course, all men crave what they cannot have—maybe it is partly that. War brings a chance to dance with the death that the Elite virus denies me. Perhaps it is that which has driven me so many times to war. Or is it the blood? Oh, you but can you imagine the feast that awaited one of us after one of the huge battles on old Earth?"

"I see," Christine said. "Still, I'll be content to avoid the battle that's going to take place here in a few days."

Hess looked thoughtful for a moment. "Child," he said, "is our ship prepared for departure?"

"It's hidden in a warehouse at the moment, Grandfather. I could have it ready to clear the planet on short notice."

"Do so, then, tonight. I think we should be ready to leave this place on short notice, in the event the Navy reacts more quickly than we anticipate."

"I'll take care of it right now. Grandfather, it could be difficult to leave, since the Navy already has ships in orbit."

"You need not worry about that." Hess smiled. "I have plans for just such a contingency." He didn't elaborate.

Christine considered that for a moment, decided not to pursue the matter. "I'll be on my way, then."

"Good, child, good. Do you know where young Andrew is?"

"In his workshop at Bates-Tak, as of an hour ago. He should still be there."

"Good. I will be going there myself—I have one last project that requires Andrew's skill."

Jinx, high orbit, December 28th

Captain Silvestri retained command of the newly expanded Task Group 947.3, which had grown to include the destroyers *Tiberius Pope* and *Ivan Kopolksy*, and the escort carrier *Seattle*.

In the *Dallas'* Combat Information Center, Silvestri monitored the deployment of his ships into a standard orbital formation. "What's the status on the *Nolan*?" he demanded of the signals watch.

"Still en route from Tarbos, sir," the electronics mate third class at the signals console answered. "Last signals have her arriving in five Standard Days."

"With the 345th Marines on board." Commander Joan Lipinsky grinned at the Captain from her station at the main scanner tank.

"Once the Marines get here, we'll be ready to move."

"You know, sir, they must know we're up here. I'm surprised they haven't tried anything—all these ships must be setting off every detector on the planet."

"What can they do?" Silvestri demanded. "Anything they have has to come up the gravity well, with us blazing away at it the whole way. They know that. They're probably doing just what we'd do in their shoes—hunkering down to try to ride this thing out. But once our bombardment stops, and they come crawling out of their hidey-holes..."

"...Then the Marines will be dropping in on them."

"That's right." Silvestri grinned. "And no sign of any Grugell in the area; it looks like our friend was telling the truth about that much, anyway."

"And he's singing like a bird to the Intel people," the exec agreed. "Be interesting to see what they get out of him."

"Message from the *Seattle*, sir," Signals called out. "Captain Walkerton requests permission to begin strike operations."

"Granted," Silvestri said. "Tell Linda to let 'em have it. Send also to *Seattle*, to execute special operation Safe Haven."

"Sending now, sir." The signals watch NCO grinned.

The Seattle, low orbit

"Signal from the *Dallas*, Captain—we are cleared to launch strike missions. Also, 'Execute Safe Haven.'"

"Thank you, Signals. All hands, prepare for launching operations," Captain Linda Walkerton announced into the wand mike on her bridge chair. "Helm, bring her about."

The escort carrier pulled north and hard to port, bringing her out of the main formation to clear the entrance to her massive hangar. Two flights of A-71 strike fighters leaped from their berths, ion drives flaring blue as they dove for the planet's surface.

"Signals, send to *Dallas*, VF-62 and VF-90 launched, on mission profile," Captain Walkerton ordered.

"Sending now, ma'am."

Moments later, a smaller ship, painted dull gray and mounting no weapons, exited the carrier's hangar. Once in open space, the pilot tuned his short-range TBN receiver in to a beacon on the surface and headed towards the location that showed on his navigational scanner.

The *K-510*

"Move the ship in closer," Commander Tikkitraskell IV ordered. The Grugell frigate, cloaked, was already dangerously close to the deploying Confederate battle group, which was sending small craft—undoubtedly strike fighters—to the surface. "I want to observe this."

"Commander," Kestekratell XI protested, "we are within ten thousand kilos of the Confederate flagship. To move closer, even with the cloaking device active, risks discovery."

Tikkitraskell drew his personal blaster, coolly aimed, and fired. Subcommander Kestekratell fell, charred and smoking, to the deck.

"Does anyone else care to question my command?" he demanded of the frigate's bridge watch. A dread silence filled the chamber.

"Very well. Helm, move us in to five thousand kilos of the Confederate carrier."

"By your command!" the Helmsman answered quickly, his voice a note higher than normal.

"Scanning, monitor and record all launching and recovery operations. I want full data on the Confederate strike fighters." Tikkitraskell walked over to the smoldering corpse of his former subcommander, nudged it with an impeccably polished boot. "Someone remove this rubbish from my bridge," he snapped.

Jinx

Bates-Tak Technologies—Hess supposed that now it was only Bates Technologies—was as cluttered as usual. Also as usual,

Andrew Bates seemed to possess an uncanny facility for finding exactly what he needed.

"Here we are," he announced after a brief browse through his former partner's terminal. "He annotated the labels in English. All the override codes, frequencies, everything. I knew Tak kept a copy."

"Excellent, my boy, excellent," Hess hissed. He leaned over the technician's shoulder to read the translated Grugell characters. "And this will allow you into a Grugell ship's computer?"

"Within limits," Bates agreed. "I don't have a hyperphone transmitter, so it would have to be a ship in orbit, or pretty close to it. I've got a pretty powerful radio transmitter for testing short-range signals systems, but we could never afford a hyperphone transmitter."

"If my suspicions are correct, you won't need one. How do you find such a ship, assuming one is in the area, running cloaked?"

"There's a brief interrogatory routine," Bates said. "And I have a utility Tak wrote that should translate any transmission into Grugell, in a format that the Grugell computer systems will recognize. Tak explained that much of it to me. Why?"

"Run it."

It took a moment for Bates to key in the routine and power up the big transmitter on the roof of the workshop. When that was done, he looked up at Hess, who merely nodded.

A prompt on the terminal screen glowed: TRANSMIT. Bates selected it.

Thirty seconds later, a stream of Grugell characters scrolled across the screen. "I can't read this garbage," Bates complained. "That damn translation utility only works one way."

"I can read it," Hess said. "The frigate *K-510*, cloaked, forty thousand eight hundred kilos—that's roughly high orbit." He read off the bearing figures, translating in his head to standard coordinates.

"What do I do now?"

Hess pointed at the screen. "Enter that. That's the command override code."

A brief burst of Grugell. "Accepted," Hess translated.

The *K-510*

"Commander," came the shout from the frigate's signals station, "someone has entered command override codes into our main computer!"

"Shut them down," Tikkitraskell barked.

"We can't, Commander! They are using Imperial command overrides. There's no way to cancel them."

"The Imperium? Here?" Tikkitraskell's question was rhetorical; nobody but an Imperial flagship could possibly have those codes.

But who else from the Imperial Navy would be out here, and why?

"Switch to manual control."

"Rerouting. It will take a few minutes, Commander."

Tikkitraskell and his crew did not know it yet, but they were fast running out of minutes.

Bates-Tak Technologies

"Excellent." Hess walked to another terminal, punched up a display of the Confederate Navy ship locations. "It seems luck is with us tonight. He is practically in the middle of their formation."

"What should I do?"

Hess returned to read over Andrew's shoulder. He pointed a clawed finger at one line of Grugell characters, beside which glowed a prompt. "That one. Select that one."

Bates moved the terminal cursor over the prompt and clicked.

The *Dallas*

"Grugell frigate decloaking off the port bow!"

Captain Silvestri leaped from his CIC chair and was at the main scanner tank in less than a second. "What the hell?" In the tank, the unmistakable signature of a Grugell frigate appeared, roughly eight kilometers from the flagship—point-blank range. "Particle beam emitters. Get me a firing solution!"

Bates-Tak Technologies

"This line now, Andrew. Ah, yes." Another small window opened on the terminal screen, showing…

"That looks like a tactical display," Bates breathed.

"It is, of course," Hess agreed. "Select, oh, this one." Hess pointed. "Now, boy, this prompt."

The *Dallas*

In the main scanner tank, another symbol appeared, originating on the Grugell frigate and accelerating rapidly away. "Torpedo launch! Sir, I'm tracking one Grugell torpedo, looks like it's heading for the *Reuben James*."

That was all Silvestri needed. "Forward emitters, match bearings and fire!"

The *K-510*

"Commander," the tactical officer began, but Tikkitraskell held up a hand to silence him. Their cloaking device had deactivated, and now there was the unmistakable shudder of a torpedo launch.

Someone has betrayed us. Who? And why?

Hess. The thought was bitter in Tikkitraskell's mind.

"That, base treacherous scum... Signals, send a hailing call to the Confederates."

Too late.

The *Dallas*

"That's a hit, sir," the tactical action officer called out. "The *Reuben James* has hit the torpedo, scratch the torpedo—there's another hit on the frigate," he announced as the particle beam swept back across the target.

"Can we get a tractor beam on that Grugell..." Silvestri began, as a white blossom opened suddenly in the scanner tank.

"Must have been their main reactor," Tactical commented. "Too bad."

"Yes," Silvestri agreed. "Would have been nice to find out who they were, and what they were doing out here."

Bates-Tak Technologies

"Run the interrogation routine again," Hess ordered.

Andrew Bates tapped several keys. "No reply. What happened?"

A loose end has been tied up. "I suppose they are no longer in the area," Hess said, his voice calm, his pose neutral.

"Hmm." Bates looked at the Grugell characters on the screen one more time, and closed the program.

"The other project I ordered—have you completed it?"

"Yes, last night," Bates replied. "I still don't know how you got those plans ... they'd be worth—"

"Andrew." The old man interrupted him. "Look at me."

Bates turned to face Hess, to face the old man's awful red eyes that seemed to burn into his very brain. "You will download the schematics for the device, those Grugell override codes, and the translation utility onto a data chip," Hess directed him, "and erase them completely from your system."

Bates, his will tightly controlled, turned and complied.

"Good, boy. Now, give me the chip."

Moving slowly, as though half-asleep, Bates removed a five-hundred-terabyte data chip from his terminal and handed it to Hess.

The Grugell ship and its commander were safely out of the picture. A key piece of secret Grugell technology was in Hess' grasp, along with a set of vital command codes. Only one person remained, other than the old man himself, who knew of his possession of Grugell secrets. Time now to take care of that, as well.

"Now, look at me, boy," the old man hissed. "We must be sure you remember none of this, when you go to the Confederates. I need no Navy frigates chasing me when I leave this system."

Bates could only stare, helplessly. Hess held him, trapped like a bird in a cobra's gaze. Helpless, he watched as the old man's eyes flared and bored like a drill into his mind.

Eastside

Two locations on Eastside had to be guarded, no matter how impossible the odds. The first was the headquarters of the Eastside Trust, where the planet's stocks of hard currency were stored in what passed for a 'bank.' The second was Singular Hydroponics, which grew most of the desert world's food in several massive, deep-tank algae farms.

Hess, in a show of defense, ordered three portable particle beam emitters and two emplaced Grugell anti-proton projectors set up on the Eastside Trust site. Two more particle beam emitters and two portable Javelin missile launchers covered the farms.

Acting on their own initiative, several groups of thugs with projectile rifles and neural paralyzers took up positions around Eastside Trust and the hydroponics farms. Several of their leaders were ex-Marine or ex-Navy, and did their best to deploy their 'troops' as well as possible.

VF-62, Hawk Flight

"Hawk Flight, this is Hawk Lead. Arm all weapons and proceed on attack profiles. Call your targets. Watch for anti-air. Good hunting."

The twelve A-71 strike fighters broke into pairs and, jinking and weaving, shot through Jinx's atmosphere to their targets.

Two pairs shot over the Eastside Trust. One particle beam emitter opened fire as they came into view; it was shattered seconds later by 30mm cannon fire from one of the fighters.

"Hobby, you and Tiger go right. Look for emitters and launchers. Snake, follow me, breaking left now."

Bolts of green fire shot skyward from the north edge of the Trust property, catching one fighter a glancing blow on the weapons wing. The damaged fighter rolled clear as his wingman obliterated the emitter and its crew with a Shrike missile. All four fighters passed low over the area, dodging fire from the remaining emitters. Pulling clear, they reformed, circled and shot low over the site a second time, sprinkling bomblets over the area. The Grugell anti-proton emitter took three hits and fireballed into the sky, while the two particle beam emitters were both damaged, their crews injured or killed.

"Hawk Lead, this is Hawk Two, anti-air at Site One neutralized. We have one bird with minor damage." 'Hawk Two,' Lieutenant Janice Moon, banked her fighter and peered at the ground through her polymer canopy. "Lead, there are some people on the ground. I have some ground fire coming up. Small arms fire only, nothing to worry about."

"Roger that, Hawk Two. Orbit and stand by."

Meanwhile, the other six fighters of VF-62 shot over the farms of Singular Hydroponics, launching anti-radiation missiles and dropping bomblet canisters all over the area. One of the Javelin vehicles managed to launch one missile, which went wild when a Shrike obliterated its controlling launcher. The other three air-defense emplacements were destroyed without firing a shot.

"Hawk Base, this is Hawk Lead, evaluate all anti-air at sites Alpha and Bravo as neutralized. Be advised, we have small arms fire on the ground at Site One."

"Roger that, Hawk Lead. Good shooting."

Ten klicks north of Eastside

The gray landing shuttle approached the beacon cautiously, taking care to stay well off the courses used by the strike fighters. The small ship's hull was made of radar-transparent polymers. Its scanning console was a masterpiece of passive sensor technology. The low detection profile and cutting-edge scanning systems made it the perfect ship for covert insertion and retrieval missions— such as it was performing now.

"There we are," the pilot, Lieutenant Roger Thomas, muttered to himself. The beacon's location was less than a kilometer ahead. He put his ship into a hover and flipped a switch to interrogate the area with an ultraviolet laser. A glowing purple spot in a patch of sand ahead marked the pickup point.

He switched off the laser and dove for the patch of sand, bringing the shuttle to hover again less than a meter above the sand.

A figure appeared suddenly from behind a patch of boulders, sprinting for the ship. Thomas touched a contact to open the passenger hatch and almost immediately felt his shuttle rock slightly with the added weight of his passenger.

"Go go go!" the man shouted. Thomas closed the hatch, turned the shuttle on its tail, and engaged full power, heading for orbital height as fast as his ion drive would carry him.

"Thanks for the lift," the passenger called from the back.

"My pleasure, sir," Thomas replied. He looked at the cabin monitor display, where his passenger was buckling himself into a seat. The man was tall, thin, wiry, dressed in rather badly worn civilian clothes. He looked as though he had been on the run for some time.

The object of special operation Safe Haven looked up at the monitor and smiled. "I'm sure glad to be off that rock," said

Marine Lieutenant Colonel Robert Patrick, Naval Intelligence—until recently known on Jinx as Patrick "Paddy" Toombs, Green-eye Hogmanay's right-hand man.

VF-90, Panther Flight

Four fighters of VF-90 flashed over the Eastside landing field as smoke was still rising from the impact of the OKEP, engaging anything that looked like a spacecraft or aircraft with cannon fire and cluster bombs. High-explosive bombs flattened the hangars. A giant, smoking crater from the OKEP strike marked the landing field itself. Reporting no resistance, the fighters returned to their assigned loitering station above the city.

Other fighters from VF-90 verified the destruction of the hyperphone transmission tower and scoured the city for any anti-air capability or any obvious defense strongpoints. Anything that looked dangerous was attacked with cannon, cluster bombs, and Shrike air-to-surface missiles.

Chapter Fourteen

Lieutenant Colonel Patrick sat at a table in the flagship's wardroom, hands cradled around his third cup of rich, black Forestian coffee. He took a long, grateful drink and leaned back in his chair with a contented sigh.

"You wouldn't believe the crap that passes for coffee down there," he told Captain Silvestri, motioning downward at the deck. "Some local brew they came up with—involves roasting the root of some native plant and brewing it up. That was the worst damn part of this assignment."

Silvestri was not interested in coffee. "You've had a chance to look over all our telemetry of the engagement with that Grugell frigate?" By the captain's order, the wardroom was deserted except for the two officers.

"I have," Patrick said. "I have no way of knowing if that was the same frigate that Hogmanay was communicating with, of course, but I would bet a year's salary that it was. They had already passed us several Grugell torpedoes and anti-proton projectors. I had the bright idea that we should take a torpedo and a projector apart and reverse-engineer them. Green-eye thought it was a good idea, too, so we did. Best look we've had at current Grugell hardware in a year." He extracted a twenty-terabyte data chip out of his shirt pocket and dropped it on the table. "Fleet intel will love this stuff."

Silvestri picked up the chip, looked at it thoughtfully. "I think they had downgraded the hardware some. The torpedoes in particular did not perform very well in battle, at least not when the pirates tried using them. Still, Space Systems Command should be able to unravel some of the technical bugs."

"I should think so," Patrick agreed. He took another long, blissful drink of coffee.

"Can you tell me what happened to Green-eye?"

"I'm not sure I know myself. I was lucky enough to be away from the compound the night it burned. Whatever happened there, it wasn't any accident—Hogmanay was no fool, he had a great system of guards and active defenses, and he was expecting trouble. Whoever got in there and took him out was damn good."

"What about the man that took over?"

"Hess? Weird old guy. I heard stories about the meeting he called right after Green-eye was killed, and I'm pretty certain he was the one responsible. I was keeping a pretty low profile by that time, figuring that Hess would probably want me out of the way too. I still heard things. I thought a lot of it was exaggerated, so I asked around a little. Turns out he—and his granddaughter—are a lot weirder than I thought. A *lot* weirder. As in 'Ionescu' kind of weird. When the Marines go down, they will want to be looking for that guy."

"Shit. Just what we need. I'll pass that on to the Marine regimental commander," Silvestri said. "The *Nolan* just dropped out of subspace. She'll be in the formation within the hour."

"It's going to be a pushover," Patrick chuckled. "Confederate Marines against a bunch of thugs with fifty-year-old hardware? No problem."

"Let's hope you're right."

Jinx, December 31st

Most of the outlaw world's population knew what was coming; word of the orbiting Navy ships had spread quickly. The leaders of syndicates and cabals, their associates, bodyguards, and assorted henchmen filled the planet's few underground shelters. The ordinary citizens of Jinx had scattered into the desert to await the outcome.

At 0600 local Eastside time, the final assault on Jinx began, as three OKEPs launched from the *Dallas* hit the main landing field, the headquarters of Jinx Shipping, and the world's only hyper-phone transmitter.

The *Dallas*

"I'm amazed at how smoothly this is going," Captain Silvestri commented as he watched events unfold in the main scanner tank. "Fleet exercises are harder than this."

"Yes, sir," Commander Lipinsky agreed, "but these aren't trained troops down there—just thugs with guns and a few antique anti-air weapons. This isn't a battle, sir, it's a pushover."

"True enough," Silvestri said.

"Message from the *Seattle*," Signals called out. "Evaluate all anti-air neutralized. All targets on profiles Alpha, Bravo, and Charlie hit and evaluated as destroyed."

"That's fast work," Silvestri said. "Signal the *Nolan* to begin landing operations now."

The CSS *Nolan*, low orbit

"Drop zone in thirty seconds," the *Nolan*'s helmsman called out.

"Drop Master, it's your ship," Captain Martin Gomez ordered. "Drop zone procedures—you may release when ready."

"Yes sir, Drop Master has the ship," Senior Chief Petty Officer Alexander Frost acknowledged. "Hold present course and speed. First drop boats away in five, four, three, two, one."

Two flattened lifting-body drop boats detached from the side of the troopship. Maneuvering thrusters fired to brake the craft into their drop trajectories, as the platoon of Marines in each boat braced for the rough ride to the surface.

Each Marine wore the M1A Personal Combat Armor system, a personal protection apparatus new to the Corps. Constructed of a high-impact carbon-fiber polymer, the armor's surface was coated with microchromatophores that allowed color changes to match a variety of backgrounds, while the armor itself contained a network of smart fiber ligaments attached to the articulations that effectively quadrupled the strength of the individual Marine.

In the bowels of the *Nolan* was the Marine Tactical Operations Center. There, several non-commissioned officers, overseen by a master gunnery sergeant, watched a series of telemetry readouts, as the M1A armor systems reported each Marine's respiration, heart rate, blood pressure, location, and a variety of other data.

On the *Nolan*'s Bridge, Senior Chief Frost continued the procedure: "Second pair of drop boats are away. Next drop point in twelve seconds."

Bates-Tak Technologies

A hastily cobbled-together radar station allowed Hess to watch proceedings from the relatively safe environs of the warehouse district, but he knew it wouldn't last.

"Grandfather." Christine was genuinely alarmed now as she pointed at the screen, "Those are drop boats. Each one will be carrying a platoon of Marines."

"Yes," Hess agreed. "Of course."

"There are still fighters orbiting over the city. It is only a matter of time before they detect our radar and try to attack it."

"You are right, child, of course. It is time to go."

The old man turned towards Andrew Bates, who sat shivering on his workbench stool. "Andrew," he said in a calm, smooth voice, "we will be leaving you now. I suggest you seek a place of shelter. The Marines will no doubt be sweeping through this area. It is well-known that you worked for us, Andrew, and I think you would be better served to surrender to the Marines and 'face the music,' as it were, for your past crimes, rather than to face the wrath of the pirates that survive the battle."

"Yes, I suppose you're right," Bate agreed, his face pale.

"Go now. Find shelter. You are released from our service," Christine told him. She touched his cheek, just a brush of her fingers against his skin—and watched as Bates' face suddenly cleared. With a startled look—the look of a man just awakened from a nightmare—he sprinted for the door.

"Time for us to go as well," Hess said.

"Our ship is only a few blocks away."

"Lead on, child."

Elsewhere in Eastside

The first drop boat of Marines landed five hundred meters from Eastside Trust, followed by another that landed long, almost a kilometer past their assigned point but well within sight of the 'bank.'

Explosive bolts blew the disembarking door off the first drop boat. First out the door was Gunnery Sergeant Ian Taylor, who quickly assembled his platoon of Marines in the dust of a deserted street.

"There's our objective," he shouted, pointing at the 'bank.' "What falls from the sky?" he demanded of his Marines in a full-throated bellow.

"Trouble!" First Platoon, A Company, 345th Marine Regiment roared back.

"Visors down and locked!"

There was a clatter as the Marines dropped the transparent plasteel visors on their helmets. With the visors sealed, the armor protected the Marines against most small arms as well as chemical and biological attack.

"Follow meee!" Gunny Taylor raised his M9 carbine over his head.

"Urrrraaahhh!" Giving voice to the ancient battle cry, the platoon fanned out and raced for the Eastside Trust building.

Gunny Taylor was the first man to the main doors. A burst of fire from his M9 shattered the door locks, and Taylor ran through the door shoulder-first, shattering the cheap aluminum frame and clear plastic panels. He entered the main lobby, followed closely by four more Marines. Tiny sensors on their armor accepted incoming visible light and translated it to the microchromatophores on the 'visually opposite' side of the suit, rendering the Marines almost invisible as the onboard microprocessors continually adjusted the display. Each Marine's helmet heads-up display constantly fed them locations of their fellow Marines, any other moving bodies, thermal and UV scans of the area, and targeting data for their M9 carbines.

The lobby was suspiciously quiet. "Hines, you and Diggs go right. Boone, cover that door to the left. Mendez, cover me, I'm going to check that stairway."

He crept up the stairway cautiously. His helmet scanner looked for infrared signatures—and found two.

"Mendez," he whispered into his throat mike, "Come up here, slow. I've got two guys just behind this door."

Before Mendez could move, the door burst open, disgorging two men with old projectile rifles. One of them fired, striking Taylor in the chest—where the carbon fiber of his armor reacted by solidifying into an impenetrable plate. While the bullet didn't go through, the impact still hit Taylor like a hammer blow, knocking him back down the stairs. He lost his grip on his rifle in the fall, but that did not stop him from retaliating. Rising to his feet in spite of the pain of a cracked rib, he picked up a large steel desk—his strength augmented several times over by the new smart-fiber armor—and threw it, knocking down both attackers.

"Mendez!"

Corporal Porfirio Mendez leaped up the stairway in a single bound, covering the fallen thugs while Taylor retrieved his rifle.

"All right," the gunnery sergeant muttered behind his visor. He tapped a contact on his wrist plate; when he spoke next, his voice boomed out from the armor, filling the building.

"Attention, everyone in the building, attention. This is the Confederate Marines. We have a platoon of infantry in full armor in and around the building. Come out and lay down your weapons, and you won't be hurt."

He listened for a moment. "You're only going to get one chance," he boomed.

It took a half-second for the helmet's audio system to re-tune after the speaker announcement. Taylor heard a voice, amplified by the receptors in his helmet, calling down from the next floor.

"Don't shoot," the plaintive voice called. "We're coming down."

"No weapons," Taylor called. "Come down with your hands on your heads."

Four men and one woman appeared at the top of the stairs, hands on their heads.

Elsewhere in Eastside

More drop boats landed across Eastside within a space of no more than ten minutes. A tactical command post was set up in the ruins of the Eastside landing field, and from there the officer in charge began coordination of operations on the ground even as the Marines overcame light resistance to seize the Singular Hydroponics farms, the ruins of the hyperphone station, and other key points in the city.

Within the space of one hour, the 345th Marine Regiment had completed landing operations and was in undisputed control of the city.

The Red Witch

Avoiding the fighters orbiting over Eastside was not easy, but old Hess surprised Christine by taking the controls himself. He proved to be a competent pilot, using the broken cover of the city itself by flying low to a section of slum-like suburbs before climbing into orbit.

The yacht's orbiting Gellar tunnel was undisturbed. Hess brought the *Red Witch* neatly into position while Christine handled the docking procedures. Immediately on completion, Hess started the star drive and headed for open space as Christine took a moment to activate the short-range scanners to clear their path.

"Grandfather," Christine called out in alarm. "The screen destroyers—there is one right ahead of us!"

"I know, child, I know."

The signals panel, open as usual to the universal 'guard' frequencies, crackled suddenly into life: "Unidentified spacecraft, this is the Confederate Navy destroyer *Polena Tesch*. You are in a declared orbital exclusion zone. Heave to and prepare to be boarded."

"They're moving to intercept. Let me take the ship, I can evade them—I hope."

"It's not necessary." Hess reached to the new panel Christine had seen Andrew Bates installing a few days earlier; she had not thought to ask its purpose. The old man stabbed a contact point.

"Now, watch, child, in the scanner."

Christine turned her attention back to the Confederate destroyer that had been moving to intercept them. Hess changed course, and the destroyer did not move to follow; instead, she saw on the screen as it hit braking thrusters and slowed to a stop.

It was almost as if... No. He couldn't possibly have...

In the pilot's seat, Hess was looking over at her, grinning.

"How?" Christine left the scanner tank, moved to stand beside the old man's bucket seat. "How? That destroyer should have had us."

"Indeed. Do you think that weapons were the only thing I was able to pry from that Grugell Commander?"

"A cloaking device? Grandfather, the Grugell would never let that technology out of their grasp."

"Never underestimate what a man—or a Grugell—would do to save his skin." Hess chuckled. "And besides, he didn't give me an actual device, just the plans and schematics. Your friend, our lost associate young Andrew, did the rest."

"But now he knows how to build one."

"No longer," Hess replied. "A talent of mine, which few even of the Elite possesses. He built the device, but he remembers none of it."

Christine sat down in the co-pilot's chair, shaking her head. "You never cease to amaze me, old man."

Hess looked at Christine, grinning widely, but offered no comment.

"All right. Where are we going?"

"I've heard of a new world, a private world, open now for colonization. A private corporation has claimed the planet. That intrigues me. I have the coordinates already loaded into our navigation console. Look for 'Roman Holiday.'"

Christine looked at the console. "I have it. I'm programming our course now."

"They should not be able to follow our track," Hess said, "if the data that Grugell gave us is correct."

It was not, but Hess had no way of knowing that.

Behind them, a Navy destroyer scanned space in a futile attempt to detect a pirate ship that had unaccountably disappeared, while the balance of the Task Group moved to invest Jinx. None of that concerned Hess and Christine now, bound as they were for whatever opportunity would arise next.

The *Polena Tesch* might have lost the yacht, but one other platform did not. As the *Red Witch* jumped, leaving the Rim instantly light-years behind, the dull gray form of a Navy proxy turned in space, recalibrated its sensors, and recorded their transit track.

Chapter Fifteen

The *Dallas*, January 4th

"CIC, Bridge, *Seattle* requests docking at the flagship for one of their landing shuttles."

Captain Silvestri, still flushed and grinning in victory, tapped a contact on the arm of his chair. "Bridge, CIC. Why?"

"They claim they have a prisoner from the surface that you'll want to talk to, sir," the voice came back.

"From the surface? Why not take him to the carrier with the others?" Silvestri wondered.

"They say he's claiming to be that Grugell technician's partner."

Silvestri's eyes opened wide. He stabbed the contact again. "Very well, contact the docking NCOIC for assignment."

Ten minutes later, a pale and shaken Andrew Bates walked aboard the *Dallas*. A medical team met him in the hangar and whisked him away to the ship's infirmary.

Ten minutes after a nurse had drawn blood and carried the sample away, the door to the exam room whisked open and Captain Silvestri walked in.

"It seems you're clean," he said without preamble.

"Clean of what?"

Ah, ha. "Just a standard medical screening we do when anyone is brought on board. You're clear of any communicable diseases."

"Oh. I guess that's good."

Silvestri seated himself in the chair next to where Bates perched on the edge of an exam table. "On the planet down there," he said, "you were working for a woman, is that right?"

Bates frowned, thinking hard. Something had clouded his memory of recent weeks. "Yes," he said at last. "A woman and a man."

"Tell me about them," Silvestri ordered. He took his personal datapad out of a jacket pocket, turned on the record function.

"His name is Hess," Bates began. "Joachim Hess. The woman... she is his granddaughter, Christine."

"Did you notice anything unusual about them?"

Bates smiled weakly. "I didn't notice much of anything that wasn't unusual about them."

"Go on."

Bates talked for just over an hour, as Silvestri recorded every word, to forward later to Fleet Intelligence.

The *Reuben James*

Grugell Imperium engineers and quantum technicians had re-engineered the latest mark of the Grugell cloaking device to minimize the signature of subspace transits, but in the three Standard years since then, Confederate Space Systems Command had handily managed to upgrade their transit scanners to compensate.

Commander Raphael Timmerman had parked his frigate sixty kilometers from the escort carrier *Seattle*. He was seated in his bridge chair idly watching the carrier recover strike fighters when the electronics mate second class at the signals station called out, "Sir, message from the task group commander. He's requesting visual."

"Put him through," Timmerman ordered. He flipped up the display screen on the arm of his bridge chair.

"Timmerman," he said as Captain Silvestri's face appeared on the screen.

"Raphael," Silvestri said. "Have you been monitoring transit tracks?"

"Yes, sir—I've got a half-dozen proxies watching our sector," Timmerman answered.

"Watching for cloaked ships?"

"No, sir," Timmerman said. "I wasn't aware that we were watching for any Grugell."

"We're not," Silvestri said. "I'm sending you the trace coordinates of a transit track we picked up leaving the Jinx system. I want you to follow that ship as best you can. You are to stop them, board by force if necessary and take ship and crew to the Fleet base at Tarbos. Can you do that?"

"I'll sure give it a shot, sir," Timmerman said, knowing the difficulties involved in following a ship through subspace transits. "I take it this isn't just a normal pirate we're going to all this trouble to catch?"

"Remember your Fleet Intelligence briefing on the Ionescu incident, Commander?"

Timmerman's stomach lurched. "I do, sir."

"Review all data on that incident carefully. According to Colonel Patrick, this might be a repeat. There are a man and a woman on the yacht you are looking for. If you manage to catch them, exercise all due caution in apprehending them. Do you understand, Commander?"

"I do, sir," Timmerman answered, wondering what all due caution meant in this instance.

"Also—there's a shuttle on its way to you now with a passenger who can identify both the man and the woman. He's a Marine

Fleet Intelligence officer; he will brief you in on all the details of who these two are and what they were up to on Jinx. Keep the specifics to yourself and your exec, clear?"

"Clear, sir."

"Very well. I am having the data transmitted to your signals section on a secure channel now. The shuttle will be to you in fifteen minutes or so. How soon can you be under way?"

"Give us ten minutes after we receive our passenger, sir, and we'll be hot on their tails."

"Good job. *Dallas* out." The screen went blank.

Well, Timmerman thought. *I'll be a son of a bitch.*

"Helm, prepare for new course and speed," he barked. "Signals, call down and tell the hangar to prepare to receive a shuttle. I'm going down there to receive our guest."

Epilogue

Jinx, January 10th

The Marines left Jinx within the week. They left a shattered world behind, with no interstellar communications, no shipbuilding capacity, no central control, and only minimal agricultural capacity. While several ships remained undamaged in hidden locations around the planet, there was no central organization to control their activity. Within the day, all but one of the pirate ships' masters had left Jinx for greener pastures.

Even as they were breaking down the regimental tactical command post, the Marine commander, Colonel Paul Sakinvosky, received word that OKEP strikes on Wilson and Last Chance had put those world's shipbuilding industries and landing fields out of business as well.

For the time being, the Rim Worlds were out of the pirate business.

The *Dallas*, January 12th

Andrew Bates and his erstwhile partner, Takatrattik VIII, faced each other across the narrow table in the flagship's Conference Room One. The dislike that flowed between them was almost palpable, and what Captain Silvestri had to say next was not going to help any.

"So, here's the deal," he offered the two technicians. "Andrew Bates, you skipped out on a twenty-two-year sentence for drug possession with intent to distribute. Takatrattik Eight, former officer in the Grugell Imperial Navy, the Grugell ambassador informs us that you are under a sentence of death by disintegration for the attempted assassination of your former commander."

"We both know all of that," the Grugell snapped. "What is it that you want?"

"Just to offer you boys a deal." Silvestri grinned. "Bates, your sentence will be suspended. Takatrattik Eight, the president will agree to grant you political asylum in the Confederacy. The Confederate president asks only one thing in return."

"And that is?" Bates wanted to know.

"You will both accept an exclusive twenty-year contract with the Navy's Space Systems Command on Tarbos. You will work there developing signals systems. You will help retrofit our ships with the new quantum signals device you have invented, and assist in producing training documentation and implementing the new system in fleet service. And, I don't think I need to add that you will be being watched closely—very closely."

"We will be working together again?" Bates looked over at Tak with distaste.

"Take it or leave it," Silvestri said.

"What are our alternatives?" Tak asked rhetorically.

"You have none worth considering, boys," Silvestri told him. "Personally, I suggest you sign. You already know what the alternatives are."

"Yes—death or imprisonment," Tak said sadly.

"At least," Bates agreed.

The two technicians looked at each other, and then turned defeated faces back towards Silvestri.

"Well, I guess I'm in," Bates said in a low, passive voice.

"And you?"

"I agree to your terms," Takatrattik conceded.

"A wise decision," Captain Silvestri assured them. He stood up. "We'll be leaving orbit within the hour. I'll send Petty Officer Oreza in; she'll show you two to your cabin."

"Our cabin?" Andrew Bates' eyes opened wide.

"Yes, your cabin," Silvestri said. "You two may as well learn to get along. You're partners now—again—and you're going to be partners for a good long time." He stood up and walked to the compartment's door as the two techs looked at each other in surprise and undisguised displeasure. "Yes," the captain said as the door slid open, "you're going to be working, and living, very closely."

Forty-two minutes later, the *Dallas* left orbit and jumped for the Fleet base at Tarbos, bearing the revolution of interstellar communications unhappily in its belly.

Book Three
Games

Roman Holiday, 2390 CE

While the Rim Worlds were settled by castoffs, renegades, and escaped criminals from both the Confederacy and the Grugell Empire, the unaffiliated world Roman Holiday was founded deliberately by one man with a specific vision.

The man called himself Vincent Giovenco and claimed to have come to Roman Holiday from Parma, Sicily, Earth, by way of Zed. Earlier in his career he had claimed to be a Zeddan native. His actual origins are unknown, but what is known is that he was a man of considerable wealth, able to personally finance not only transport to an unaffiliated, unsettled desert world outside the Confederacy's borders, but also to completely finance the beginning of what would become a considerable colony.

The new colony was dubbed Roman Holiday. From the very start, "Don" Giovenco based the new world's economy on gambling and prostitution, with a healthy leavening of alcohol and recreational drugs thrown in. As might be expected, Roman Holiday attracted undesirable elements of Confederate society, but it was allowed to operate without interference by the Confederate government. Several administrations during this period favored allowing Roman Holiday and other colonies like it to serve as safety valves, to keep criminal elements out of the Confederacy itself.

In 2386, following the investment of the Rim Worlds by the Confederate Navy, it became apparent that this policy would have to be reviewed. The pursuit of a particular wanted criminal from the Rim to Roman Holiday by the Confederate frigate *Reuben James*, and the subsequent engagement by the *Reuben James* of several armed pirate ships, would force an adjustment in the way the Confederate government viewed the unaffiliated worlds.

—*Morris/Handel, A History of the First Galactic Confederacy, University Publications, 2804* CE

Prologue

Augsburg, Bavaria, 1454 CE

The house was small but snug, built low and stout against
the chill of Black Forest winters. A small kitchen and sitting
area occupied the front of the house, with a bedroom in the rear
for adults and a loft overhead for children. A fire crackled in the
fireplace, warming the house against the December cold. Outside,
the moon glinted against a fresh fall of wet snow. The couple who
lived in the house sat now in that front room, listening to the
crackling of the fire.

The husband stood up suddenly and walked to the room's only
window. He stood looking out at the snow. "Anna," Johann Hess
said, "do you know I've been at the brewery for ten years now?"

Anna Hess smiled at her husband. "Ten years, is that a fact?
It seems only yesterday we were married. You were at the brewery
only a month then."

"I know. I'm wondering, though, if I'd be better off somewhere
else."

Anna looked at her husband of ten years with affection.
Johann was a tall, thin man with pale blue eyes and a shock
of dark blonde hair that tended to burst out in all directions
from his narrow, high-templed skull, no matter how he tried to
brush it down. Anna was as petite as Johann was tall, a small,
round-figured woman with brown hair and gray eyes. Johann was

thirty-five, four years older than Anna. Their marriage was joyful, content, in all respects but one: Johann chafed at being a minor employee in Augsburg's brewery.

Anna laid aside the shirt she was mending. "Somewhere else? You mean, at some other place in Augsburg?"

"No," Johann said. He turned to look at his wife; the low ceiling required him to stoop slightly. "I was thinking of Hungary."

"Hungary?" Anna's jaw dropped. "Why Hungary? Johann, it's so far away!"

"Yesterday, in the marketplace, there were two travelers that had come from the border area, where Hungary meets the lands of the Ottomans. There, in the mountains of the Wallachs, they said that many people are moving—as the Ottomans push into new territories, there are thousands of people moving on the roads. Many of them are wealthy people, Anna. I asked the travelers— they said inns are few there, and good German beer is almost unknown."

"And?"

Johann turned to face his wife. He knelt in front of her chair, took her hands in his. "Imagine it, Anna—an inn in a village in one of the passes, an inn that serves your good food and good Bavarian beer, which I know all too well how to brew. Here, in Augsburg, I'll never be more than a minor brewmeister's assistant in Herr Blucher's brewery; in Wallachia, we could grow wealthy!"

Johann looked into his wife's pale gray eyes, seeking approval. By the standards of his time, his culture, the decision was his—but he loved Anna very much and would make no such decision without her consent.

"What about the children?" Anna said in a low voice. "They won't grow up German, there in the land of the Wallachs. Johann, it's not even part of the Holy Roman Empire."

"Felix and Elsa will grow up good church members and good Germans," Johann assured her, "with us as their parents. And one day, perhaps a dozen years hence, with our fortunes made, we can return to Augsburg and live quietly here for the rest of our days."

Anna smiled. She ran one hand thoughtfully though her husband's unruly hair. "You've thought about this a great deal, haven't you?"

"Indeed, I have," Johann said. He clasped her hands in his. "I think this is best—I can be my own man, as I never will be in Augsburg—no portion in starting a new brewery here, with the Grosse brothers already in place. Where in all of Bavaria could I go and begin with no competition, with no Brewmeister already in residence? In the land of the Wallachs, I can start free and on my own, with no one to compete with me. I know brewing well enough, and with your cooking, and maybe a few rooms to let, we could do very well indeed!"

"I trust you, you know," Anna said. "If you think it best we go to Wallachia, then we shall go."

Johann sighed in relief. "I'll start saving pay towards an ox and cart," he said. "I thought we'd leave in the spring, when the snows are off the passes."

"As you wish," Anna said.

Johann stood up and walked to the fireplace, extended his long, narrow hands towards the blaze. "I'll be glad of it," he said. "I'm always glad to see the sun return with spring, anyway."

Sky of Diamonds

Chapter One

If you must play, decide upon three things at the start:
the rules of the game, the stakes, and the quitting time.
–Chinese Proverb

Earth, 2367 CE

Virgilio Garcia was a hacker.

He was not just any ordinary computer hacker. To call Virgilio Garcia an ordinary hacker would be to call Leonardo da Vinci an ordinary inventor, or Van Gogh an average painter, or Stephen Hawking a run-of-the-mill scientist.

No, Garcia was more than an ordinary hacker. Working from his tiny apartment in the old Earth city of Tijuana, crouched over his hand-built terminal, Garcia had managed to worm his way into secure systems the world over. Government systems, banking systems, and corporate networks—all had fallen before Garcia's skill.

Known on the planetary Internet as *El Machete*, Garcia had accumulated almost four million Confederate dollars in his hidden bank account—transferred and recovered from accounts of corrupt politicians, weaseled from would-be philanderers, worked painstakingly out of the private accounts of known gang leaders.

In November 2367, Garcia was setting up his biggest coup.

He looked up as his common-law wife, Constance, walked into the tiny cubbyhole that served as his office.

It wasn't easy for her to even walk into the room. Computer hardware crowded the tiny chamber; a dozen whirring, blinking servers occupied a rack on one wall, while twice that many monitors blinked and buzzed on and above the tiny desk where Garcia sat, tapping on his battered keyboard with his left hand, his right moving his thumb-dot to select and move data about the various screens.

"Good morning," the tiny, red-haired, almost birdlike girl sang as she walked in. "Still busy with the Tamburo family thing?"

"*Si*," Garcia replied, lapsing into his childhood Spanish for a moment. English had been the standard language of Tijuana since Mexico's annexation by the United States in 2212, but most residents of the former Mexico still spoke Spanish as a first language. Garcia had met Constance O'Hara in Chicago before persuading her to follow him to "TJ." She was a small, slim, red-haired, pleasantly mammalian girl, ardent but not an intellectual giant—which bothered Garcia not at all. He was more interested in Constance's physical assets and abilities, even though she had a propensity for biting in the heat of passion—the thought prompted Garcia to rub his chest where the girl had nipped him hard the night before.

Constance was carrying an aluminum tumbler. She sat the tumbler, beaded with condensation, in front of Garcia. He noted the smell of his favored breakfast, a blended concoction of milk, chocolate syrup, malt powder, and bananas.

"*Gracias, querida.*"

"I'm not sure I like you messing around with a Mafia family, VeeGee," Constance said as she took the room's only other chair. Garcia smiled at the nickname the girl had given him on their first meeting in Chicago, years before. It may have been unimaginative—Virgilio Garcia, 'V.G.', 'VeeGee'—it was obvious, but the hacker liked the way she said it.

"It's perfectly safe, Connie," Garcia answered her. "I'm behind three software firewalls, and I'm using four cutouts in the stream—one in New Mexico, one in Belize, one in Beijing, and one in Moscow. No one can follow me back through all of that."

"You hope."

"I know, *querida*. This is what I do, *entienda*? Besides, they're gangsters. Crooks. They think they are untouchable, but they have not yet reckoned with El Machete." He took a pull of the cold drink, wiped his mouth, and grinned. "And this morning I have made a breakthrough. See?" He pointed at the main monitor on the office wall above his desk. "My worm program has at last found the passwords to the Family's main accounts: two banks in Colombia, and two more in the Bahamas. I managed to attach a keytrace program to a private email to Emil Tamburo himself, an email in fact from his son Paolo—and now I have recorded every word and every symbol he entered into his personal datapad and main computer for three weeks now. Only last night, he accessed the accounts to transfer money—and I have his passwords."

"I'm not sure I understand all that, VeeGee," Constance said, her eyes wide. "How much money is it?"

"Almost thirty billion Confederate dollars! Would you believe it?"

Constance goggled. "What are you going to do?"

"Steal it, of course," Garcia burst out. "I already have three sham accounts set up in banks in Belfast, Macao, and San Paolo. Once that is done, *querida*, we will convert the cash in those accounts to certified transfer chips that we can take anywhere."

"What do you mean, anywhere?"

"Off Earth," Garcia said. "How would you, *mi querida*, like to live in a palace on Corinthia? Perhaps an estate on Tarbos? A beachfront estate on Caliban?"

Constance laughed delightedly. "All right, VeeGee," she agreed. "When do you plan on doing all this?"

"*Don* Tamburo is expecting a transfer of another twenty million dollars in three days," Garcia said. "I plan to wait for that—then, El Machete will strike."

Constance stood up, kissed the hacker on the bald spot in his thinning black hair. "You are the best, dear. Now the whole planet—maybe the whole Confederacy will know."

"But they will not know who El Machete is," Garcia laughed back, "or what became of him—only you and I will know that." He held up two liner tickets for a flight to Tarbos, departing the day after the transfer. "Only you and I will know where we've gone."

He was wrong in that assessment—exactly how wrong, he would find out all too quickly.

Parma, Italy, a week later

Emil Tamburo was many things, but patient was not one of them. Tension in the Tamburo compound outside Parma had been running extremely high since a little over thirty billion Confederate dollars had evaporated from his accounts only days ago.

The Tamburo compound was deceptively modest; there was only a large house surrounded by gardens on the Strada Argini Parma south of the city, overlooking the Torrente Parma. Only a careful observer would note the passive sensors, the automatic e-beam cutters in tiny turrets on the fence towers, the security droids that patrolled their programmed routes on paths carefully concealed by shrubbery. From his massive oak desk in the hardened basement of the house, Emil Tamburo ran an organized crime network that spanned a dozen worlds—and someone, some damned hacker, had just neatly robbed the family of a fortune that outstripped the annual Gross Planetary Product of several of the newer Confederate worlds.

Emil looked up from the polished wood of the desk as his sons, Paolo and Mario, suddenly entered the room.

"*Che?*" Emil demanded.

"*Padre.*" The older boy, Paolo, spoke first. "The hacker, *Padre*—we think we have found him."

Emil's eyes opened wide. "So?"

Mario held his personal datapad in front of his father's face. "Our technicians were able to back-trace the key-trace he put on your machine, Father. He is a clever hacker, this El Machete—he used a series of cutouts through co-opted servers in—"

Emil held up a hand, silencing his son. "Never mind about that. I do not care about any of that. All I want to know is, *where is he?*"

"Tijuana." Paolo grinned. "We have his name, his address, through our American contacts. He has purchased liner passage on the *Natchez Queen* to Tarbos in three days' time, but until then—"

"Can we recover our money?"

"He has already moved it," Mario answered. "To where, we do not yet know."

"Contact our people in America for support. No details—I want you two to handle this personally. Nobody else must know that this *insetto*, this hacker, took advantage of us to this degree."

"Of course, *Padre*."

"He will tell us where our money is, given proper motivation. See to it," Emil ordered his sons.

"Personally, *Padre*," Paolo assured him. "Mario and I leave on the 1900 semi-ballistic to Los Angeles tonight."

"He will talk," Mario added. "Then, we were thinking, perhaps, he would take a long swim a few miles offshore."

"*Molto bene.*" The elder Tamburo sat silently for a moment, drumming his fingers on the desk. "You will be discreet, of course?"

"Of course, *Padre.*"

"We don't need the Americans looking into our operations."

"No, *Padre.*"

"It's been too hard to gain good contacts in America," Tamburo mused. "The few we have are valuable. It has been even more difficult to gain good contacts on Tarbos. We should have better information sources inside the Confederate government. Once the matter of this hacker is concluded and we have our money back, that will be our next order of business."

The Tamburo sons nodded and took their leave.

Wallachia, 1455 CE

"It is a long way from Augsburg," Johann told his wife. The small Wallachian village of Svato, in the foothills of the Carpathian Mountains, lay before them.

"It's a long way," she agreed, "but it's a pretty town, here in the shadow of the mountains. We'll do well here."

"No other villages along this road from some miles," Johann agreed. "No inn in this town. With a well-built *gasthaus* and good German beer, we should do well indeed. Aside from the mountains, it's not really so different than the Black Forest, is it?"

He turned. The young couple's children sat atop the pile of bedding and furniture in the ox-drawn cart; Felix was ten, Elsa eight. "*Vater,*" Felix piped up, "is this our new home?"

"Indeed it is, my son."

"Why are we stopped here, then?" Elsa asked.

"Why indeed? Let's go." Johann grinned at the children. Elsa sat up straight and clapped her hands. "Let's go down to our new home. We'll all be Wallachs for a time now, eh?"

The family camped the first night on the outskirts of the town. The following day, Johann located a piece of land on the road at the edge of town where he could build his inn.

It took a month of hauling timber from the mountains, of cutting, hammering, building, with almost no help, but in the end the *gasthaus* took shape. It looked oddly out of place, a Bavarian inn sprung from a Wallachian village, but the day Johann hung his sign above the door announcing the opening of the Rote Hexe, the villagers crowded around, making approving noises in a language Johann was beginning to speak more easily every day. The inn's name caused a few eyebrows, and in truth Anna had questioned her husband's odd sense of humor, but the crudely carved image of a rather silly witch with a long hooked nose, in a roughly painted red cape, forestalled any further objection.

The Rote Hexe—the Red Witch—had a large dining area, a kitchen in the back, and a small brewery building in the back. The second floor was the Hess family's living quarters: two bedrooms and a small area for bathing. Johann was proud of his work, all the more so since he wasn't trained in carpentry, but with some advice from some of the more experienced locals, he had managed.

One of those locals stood at the side of the road now, grinning up at Johann where he adjusted his hand-made sign from the hanger over the door. At eighty, Alexandru Lacusta was by far the oldest man in the village of Svato. A kindly man, Alexandru had taken it upon himself to befriend the Hess family, to help them learn the language and ways of the people living in the shadow of the Carpathians. He stood watching the final step of the construction now, clapping his hands as Johann clambered down the rude ladder.

"Well done, son, well done," the old man said. He strode to Johann, seized his hand, and pumped it. "It will be good, to have your inn here on the road—anything to coax a traveler to stop, to part with a little of his gold in our poor village."

"I'm not finished." Johann grinned at Alexandru. "In a few more weeks, my first batch of lager will be completed. Then, my friend, you'll see good reason for the weary traveler to break his journey here."

"I'm confident it will be so." The old man laughed.

Anna Hess poked her head out of the doorway. "Johann," she called, "the children and I have the dining area clean. Won't you invite our friends inside to see?"

Johann waved to the gathering crowd. "By all means," he called. "Everyone—come in! Come in to my Red Witch, see what we have built!"

San Diego, Earth, 2367 CE

Jonas Ortega was one of the best forgers in the business; he turned out Confederate identity cards that even the best agents in the Confederate Justice Department couldn't tell from the genuine article. He had also gone to the same school as Virgilio Garcia; he was pleased one rainy, dismal afternoon to look up at his door monitor to see his old friend standing there.

Ortega reached across his desk and tapped his speaker button. "Come on in, *amigo*," he called, and tapped the unlock pad.

A moment later, Garcia walked in, grinning. "*Que paso, ese?*"

"Same old, bro," Ortega replied. He got up, embraced his old friend "What's up with you? Want a beer?"

"Sure," Garcia agreed. Ortega walked to a shelf, picked two aluminum cans, and tossed one to Garcia. Garcia twisted the bottom of the can, which quickly turned frosty cold; he popped the top open and took a long drink as Ortega followed suit.

"Need one of your products," Garcia said as they sat down on the room's only couch.

"Thought you might," Ortega said. "All this news about El Machete and all that."

"Yeah," Garcia laughed. "Some deal, eh?"

"Some deal."

"Seriously, bro. I need new ID and Inter-Visas for Connie and me. I can provide hard funds for the Inter-Visa."

"I bet you can. Where you going?"

"Halifax," Garcia lied. With the sums of money he now controlled at stake, he knew there was no one he could trust—not now. "Who knows after that? I'll send you a message after we're settled someplace."

"I'll need to get Connie in for an image, too," Ortega replied. *Wonder where you're really going?* "Can do yours now, I suppose..."

"Connie and I will both come in tomorrow morning, if that's all right," Garcia said quickly.

"Sure, bro, sure. That's fine. Have another beer."

New ID *tomorrow morning*, Garcia thought, looking at his old friend over the rim of the can, *and on the semi to the Quito skyhook tomorrow afternoon. Perfect.*

Tijuana, the next day

"Get ready."

Mario Tamburo looked the flat's door over quickly, professionally. "Huh," he muttered. "Master Gee-Six electronic locks, three in sequence."

"Yeah? That it?" Paolo answered without looking away from the elevator.

"Sure is. Hell, why don't they just use duct tape?" Mario extracted a small black box from his sport-coat pocket, held against the door. It hummed for a moment before all three locks clicked open. Mario pushed the pad carefully; the door slid open. Pocketing the lockpick, he took another small device from another pocket, aimed it inside the open door and examined the unit's tiny display.

"Looks like they flew the coop," he said. "Nobody in here. No active electronics. No explosives."

"Let's have a look around," Paolo suggested.

"Sure."

Mario drew a tiny pistol from a holster under his jacket and moved catlike into the room. Paolo followed, closing the door behind him after one cautious glance down the hallway. The brothers split up, each into a different room in the tiny flat.

"Here," Mario called softly after a moment. Paolo entered the office a moment later.

"This is where his computer setup was," Mario said. "See," he pointed, "that's where the data cables came in. All the stuff's gone, though. El Machete has flown the coop, all right."

"The old man ain't gonna like that," Paolo warned.

"Can't be helped. We'll still find him. It's just going to take a little longer."

They left as quietly as they had arrived. As the brothers walked back through the main room, a pinhole camera hidden in the corner of an empty bookcase recorded good full-front images of both their faces and transmitted the images by a phased millisecond pulse to a receiver several miles away, where it was recorded in a hidden, encrypted directory on the main server of a shipping company in San Diego.

The Quito skyhook

"There's the bus, VeeGee." Constance pointed at the long, silver shape of the skyhook bus descending into the huge, octagonal terminal building.

"*Si.*" Garcia was staring intently into a small remote datapad. Constance craned her neck to look over his shoulder.

"Isn't that our old flat in TJ?"

"Of course—and those are the Tamburo brothers. It seems they found where I pulled off that net hack."

"VeeGee, that's frightening," Constance complained. "You said they'd never find us! You *promised!*"

"Don't worry, *querida*." Garcia patted her on the arm. "We have changed identities twice since leaving TJ, and we'll do so again when we get to Caliban—then we'll ship out immediately for Tarbos, and change again there. Everything's fine."

"I hope you're right." She looked uncertain. "Let's get on the bus."

Garcia took her hand, held it for a moment, and smiled. "Nothing to worry about, *querida*. I'll take care of you."

A moment later, they were on the bus, bound for the SS *Chippewa Valley*'s boarding shuttle and thence to Caliban. Garcia was confident that they couldn't be followed; he didn't know that the Tamburos were as good at tracking fugitives as he was at hacking banking institutions. It would take less than a year to find out the truth.

Chapter Two

The Tarbos skyhook, 2368

"Here, Mario. The bus to the surface."

"Good."

"I'm glad to get off that damn liner," Paolo Tamburo complained. "Let's get down to the surface and find that hacker."

As the Tamburo brothers boarded the bus, a small security camera panned over them, recording their facial profiles and running an instant check through the Tarbos main information systems to compare them against any 'persons of interest.' The Tarbos planetary database drew a blank, but one other did not. Another database, an unofficial and unauthorized one, also monitored the various Mountain View security camera net and ran routine facial recognition checks on new arrivals based on its own information base. That database found two matches and sounded a programmed alarm.

A penthouse apartment in Mountain View

A sudden, loud, grating buzzer startled Virgilio and Constance Garcia out of a sound sleep.

"What is it, VeeGee?" Constance asked, her voice thick with sleep.

"Un momento." Garcia got up from the expansive bed and walked into the next room, where his computer gear was set up. One look at the main monitor made his swarthy face turn pale. *"Madre del Dios..."* He ran back to the bedroom, pulling his nightshirt over his head. "Constance! Get up! We have to get out of here!"

"What is it, VeeGee?" Constance sat up, rubbing her eyes. "What's wrong?"

"The Tamburos! They are here, on Tarbos! They just boarded the skyhook bus, which means they'll be in Mountain View within the hour, and this is the first place they'll come. Don't ask me how, *querida,* but they found us!" He grabbed a bag from a closet and tossed it to the girl. "Pack our clothes and other things—quickly. I must move our money and take care of our data. Quickly, girl!"

Wide-eyed, Constance climbed out of the bed and began throwing clothes from the wardrobe into the bag while Garcia went back to his computers.

His foresight had paid off. Two quick pre-programmed commands dispersed their Tarbosian holdings to three smaller banks, from there to a small savings and trust company in the Warehouse district, and from there to a terminal account which hummed and spat out a certified transfer chip from the carefully modified terminal on Garcia's desk. Another command erased the hacked link to the Mountain View security net, and one final command loaded all of the system's data and operating software onto another small, detachable storage chip, which Garcia detached and laid on the desk. One final command, and the entire computer system began a purge that would leave all data and history as completely destroyed as though it had been dropped into Tarbos' sun.

The hacker picked up the storage chip and hurried back into the bedroom, where Constance was stuffing a few final items into the bag. "Dress now, *querida*, quickly!"

"Where will we go?"

"To see Stephan Griggs, for now—he owes me for tracking down that corporate espionage ring for him. After that, I don't know just yet—I'll think of something. Just hurry!"

"All right, VeeGee, give me a second to get dressed. Comb your hair out, honey, and put on good clothes, make it look like we've been out all evening."

"That's good thinking, *querida*." He kissed her cheek. "I'll do that. We'll have to leave Tarbos, you know that?"

Constance was already stepping into a sheer black skirt. "I know."

Five minutes later, they were gone, leaving another apartment and another life behind. An hour passed as they made their way cautiously through the bustle of the early-morning Mountain View walkways to the offices of General Systems and Robotics, a military hardware and security firm catering to the Confederate Marine Corps and other, less well known interests.

Garcia paused at the General Systems building's entrance to look up and down the street. His ordinary-looking sunglasses hummed briefly, imperceptibly to anyone more than a few centimeters away, as their lenses flexed to adjust magnification and a built-in fiber optic camera scanned the crowds. The glasses' microprocessor sent data over a personal wireless network link to the datapad Garcia held in his left hand; the facial recognition program on the pad remained silent.

He looked at Constance, who was wrapped up in a black wraparound cloak with a big black hat hiding her red hair. "So far, so good," Garcia breathed. "Come on, *querida*." He placed his sunglasses carefully in an inside jacket pocket and went inside.

The hacker was not surprised to see a humaniform android receptionist, rather than a human, behind the polished black polymer desk in the lobby. "May I help you?" the blonde haired, blue-eyed, smiling droid asked.

"Julio and Polena Fernandez to see Mr. Griggs," Garcia answered, using the name on his latest fabricated indent card.

"One moment," the droid purred, its voice pleasantly feminine, almost seductive. Garcia was reminded for a moment of the "pleasure droids" advertised on adult vid channels. He and Constance waited impatiently for several seconds as the droid sat there silently, no doubt communicating through its onboard wireless link.

"Please look into my eyes for retinal scan identification," the machine said at last. Garcia motioned to Constance, and she, then Garcia, each looked briefly into the droid's China-blue eyes.

"Identification and pass clearance confirmed," the machine said. "Mister Griggs will meet you in the fourth floor foyer." The receptionist droid pivoted and motioned towards the lifts.

"Thank you," Constance said as they walked quickly past the desk.

"You're welcome," the droid answered politely. "Have a pleasant morning."

Stephan Griggs, the President of General Systems, was waiting for them on the fourth floor as promised. A tall, spare man with thinning gray hair, Griggs had built his company from a small warehouse operation to a major supplier to the Confederate Navy Department and the security forces of several major Confederate worlds, largely due to several unique innovations in robotics.

"Mr. and Mrs. Fernandez." He greeted them, his eyes narrowed, his demeanor cautious. "Nice to see you. What can I do for you this early on a lovely Mountain View morning?"

"I need a favor."

"All right." Griggs stared at Garcia. "What kind of favor?"

"I need planetary scout probes sent to several locations I've been looking at, I need undocumented passage to Fortune, I need some people to help set up a private colony, and I need some security. I've got a bit of trouble."

Griggs' eyebrows tried to climb off the top of his skull. "*What?* You're talking about a couple of million dollars for the probes alone!"

Garcia felt Constance's hand suddenly grip his arm. He patted her hand to calm her. "I know. It will be worth your while."

"You have ten seconds," Griggs said, smiling, "to prove that."

Garcia pulled out a terabyte data chip and handed it silently to Griggs, who extracted a personal datapad from his jacket pocket and plugged the chip in. He examined the contents quickly.

"I suppose you've set this to be sent to the Confederate Bureau of Investigation unless a pre-arranged signal is sent, yes?"

"You guess right," Garcia agreed. "Actually, unless a signal is sent at an interval of two Standard Days, from now until I deprogram the setup."

Griggs looked at the datapad again. "Damn you. I never should have let you into our systems—you're no better than those hackers from Kona-Tech."

"You set the fox to guard the chickens, *amigo,*" Garcia said amiably, "and it worked, didn't it? I don't really give a damn if you do business with the pirate colonies on Last Chance and Wilson, myself—but the Feds sure would be interested. This was a last resort for me, Stephan, I never wanted to pull this string, but now it's a last resort for you, too. I suggest we work together."

"Well," Griggs said, "I can get you to Fortune well enough." He tapped his datapad. "We have a freighter leaving here tomorrow night for Zed, you can trans-ship there for Fortune. I can't help you with ID, but I may be able to provide you with some security help—a new toy we've been developing for the Marines. Picture a giant armored attack dog, but smarter—with guns."

"Sounds impressive. I'll need some people, too."

"There should be plenty of rough characters you can hire on Zed. It's a good place for that sort of thing."

"I can cover the ID," Garcia said. In truth, he already had it arranged.

"All right." Griggs tapped at his datapad again. "Go to the skyhook, level four, pier six, at nineteen tonight. You'll ship as supercargo on the *Julius Simmons*. Ask for Captain Hollister. There will be three crates in your name at the pier; you'll have to see they get loaded. Speaking of names..." He looked expectantly at Garcia.

Throughout their travels and the accompanying identity changes, Virgilio Garcia had faithfully maintained a Hispanic surname, out of respect for his parents and grandparents—or so he told himself. That had to change now.

"Give the names as Vincent and Contessa Giovenco," Garcia told Griggs, "of Palermo, Sicily, Earth." *If you can't beat 'em, join 'em.*

"You sure?"

"Yes." Garcia politely spelled the names out.

"All right. It's arranged," Griggs said. He pulled the terabyte chip from his datapad, tossed it back to Garcia—now Giovenco. "May I assume that we are even, now?"

"I will deprogram the notification routines once I'm safely at my destination," Giovenco assured him.

"All right," Griggs said. *And if you don't—well, there may be a surprise in one of those crates.*

The unmanned probe droids departed from General System's skyhook facility the next morning. Designed along the same lines as an expanded Navy reconnaissance proxy, each probe was a ten-meter-long titanium football. The probe body was crammed with sensors, given an independent AI brain and a hyperphone transmitter, and coupled to a small, underpowered but efficient Gellar drive. On launch, each probe fired maneuvering thrusters to boost away from the dock; a pre-programmed interval later, the Gellar drives activated to take the droids to their destinations.

An hour later, the General Systems freighter *Julius Simmons* departed for Zed with two undocumented passengers.

The day after that, the Tamburo brothers boarded a passenger liner for Earth. Their quarry, the hacker El Machete, had seemingly vanished into thin air. The brothers were uncomfortable in the knowledge that their father would be very displeased with their second failure to catch the hacker. They knew that the search would not end on Tarbos.

Wallachia, 1459 CE

Johann snapped suddenly awake.

He looked at the window. The pale December sky beyond the window betrayed the time, a good half-hour before sunrise. Frost glittered on the glass; the room was cold. It had been a dry winter, with no snow to soften the hard-frozen ground; the roads were hard as iron, the grass brittle and brown.

"What is it, Johann?" Anna's soft, sleepy voice came from under the thick comforter.

"Nothing," Johann said. "Nothing, beloved. Go back to sleep."

Johann stood up, shivering as his bare feet touched the varnished wooden floor. He pulled his trousers on over his long, skinny legs and left the bedroom, walking across the house to peer in the room where his children slept. Felix and Elsa slumbered on, quietly as children do, both wrapped up in their blankets like gophers in a winter burrow.

Johann smiled. The smile didn't last; something was bothering him. Shivering, he went downstairs to start the morning fire, when he realized what had awakened him.

Horsemen. On the road. Many horsemen.

The fire forgotten for the moment, Hess went to the front door of the Hexe and looked out. The horsemen were soldiers, presumably soldiers of the *Voivode* Vlad Tepes, whom Hess had heard were engaged in battle against the Turkish forces far to the south.

Why, then, were they here?

One horseman rode slower than the others. His horse limped, a forefoot lamed; the rider held his iron helmet in his lap, probably because of the bloodied bandage tied around his head. Long hair hung down his back. His face was heavily bearded, with long mustaches dangling.

"Are you Vlad's soldiers?" Johann called on impulse.

The wounded horseman reined his mount to the side of the road, looked down sadly. "Soldiers of the Impaler, aye," he said. "Returning from the fight, from the lost battle."

"Lost to whom?"

The horseman spat into the road. "The forces of the infidel Turk, Suleiman Bulut," he snapped. "They outnumbered us five to one, slaughtered most of our men. Only the few you see here escaped."

"I thought we were at peace with the Ottomans," Johann said.

"Until Vlad refused to pay further tribute to the Sultan. Until the Pope announced another Crusade against the Ottomans, that was only a few weeks ago. Who knows?" The horseman looked over his shoulder. "All I know is it's the noblemen that start the war, and us ordinary men that fights it."

"Where are you going?"

"North," the soldier said, "with Suleiman Bulut in pursuit, no doubt. If I were you, I'd take to the hills—take your whole village, if they'll go. The Turks can't be more than a few hours behind us."

Johann digested that recommendation with a thoughtful look. "To leave all I've built here, all my neighbors have here; they won't want to flee. I'm not sure I want to just run away."

"Suit yourself. German, aren't you, from the Holy Roman Empire?" Johann nodded; the man had noted his accent. "I wager you'll wish you'd stayed there before all this is done." The horseman touched his finger to his eyebrow by way of farewell and spurred his limping horse back into the column.

Chapter Three

Zed, 2367 CE

The landing shuttle settled slowly to the black surface of the landing pad.

Outside, it was nighttime. The landing field was illuminated by rows of blue lights, and by the great, shining silver disk of the larger of Zed's two moons. Looking out the view port, Garcia/Giovenco could see the edge of the tarmac, where banks of three-meter ferns bent away from the blast of the shuttle's landing thrusters.

After a few moments, the shuttle's door popped open. A waft of warm, humid air drifted in, carrying the inevitably odd smell of a new planet.

Constance—Contessa now—noticed it as well. "Every planet smells different, don't they, VeeGee?" she said, smiling at him from her bucket seat next to his.

Giovenco smiled back at her. "I suppose they do. Every planet has its own plants and animals, its own weather; I suppose that's why they all smell different." The hacker spoke more deliberately now in the attempt to school himself out of his habitual Tijuana accent and speech mannerisms. He stood up and began pulling their luggage out of the overhead compartments.

Zed was a wild world, wilder even than Forest. The planet's three continents were covered mostly by rain forest. The climate was hot, muggy, tropical; the flora was rank and persistent, the fauna numerous and Jurassic in form and temperament. The couple stepped out of the shuttle, wincing at the heat. They looked up at a flight of three odd, leathery creatures that flapped by overhead.

"Nice place, eh?" The shuttle pilot was emerging from the shuttle's hatch behind them. "Head over there to the terminal." He pointed to a low, flat building just visible past a stand of trees. "There will be a shuttle bus into town along in a few minutes. 'Scuse me, I have to go see the Port Authority. Good luck, folks." He nodded to them, turned and walked off.

Giovenco pulled out his inevitable datapad and looked at it. "The town," he read, "is called Fairview. Looks like it's the only city of any size on the planet, with a bunch of little villages and drilling camps set up all over the place. Main industry is extraction; the planet is loaded with hydrocarbons, and the jungle has lots of natural pharmaceuticals precursors. Nice."

"How long will we be here?"

"The *Hudson* will be here in three weeks," Giovenco said, "with a week layover—four weeks to recruit colonists." The hacker picked up their two large bags, all the material possessions they had brought with them aside from a datapad and a certified transfer chip bearing ten million Confederate dollars. The balance of El Machete's fortune was stashed in anonymous accounts in six different banks on Tarbos, New Albion, and Corinthia.

They walked quickly through the trees. The night creatures of Zed whistled and buzzed around them; in the distance, something roared with a deep, primal sound. Contessa grabbed Giovenco's arm in distress as the roar was repeated, closer.

"We'll get into town," Giovenco assured the frightened girl, "and get a place to stay. Don't worry."

"All right," Contessa breathed. "I'll be fine as long as I'm with you, VeeGee."

The couple walked more quickly then, entering the terminal building just as a beaten-up old skimmer bus pulled up.

San Francisco, Earth—the local offices of the Confederate Bureau of Investigation

"Lieutenant?"

Lieutenant Joan Carson, CBI, looked up from her terminal screen to see Special Agent Joachim Chen standing in her office doorway. "What is it?"

"I've got a curious little electronic money trail here you really ought to see, Ell-Tee."

"Curious? How?" Carson was immediately interested; her knack for unraveling complex money-laundering scheme had made her a lieutenant years ahead of the normal promotion schedule.

"Look here," Chen said, walking around the desk and placing his personal datapad on Carson's desk. "You remember we just got this tip, it involves the big Italian family, the Tamburos, that we suspect are involved in drug trafficking and money laundering, right?"

"Right."

Chen pointed at three transactions highlighted in red on the pad's screen. "I was going back over the records we've gleaned on them over the last few years. I got to thinking that we should look for patterns, rather than specific instances—but when I did that, I found these three instanced transactions that just don't make sense."

"Three transfers," Carson read. "To banks in Belize, the US, and Russia. The money was moved again almost immediately and…"

"…the records were wiped."

"The bank didn't do that," Carson said. "Serious legal problems for them."

"No. And look at the amounts, Ell-tee."

"Thirty million dollars."

"Count the zeroes again, Lieutenant."

Carson looked closer at the pad's tiny screen. "Thirty… *billion?* Thirty billion dollars. Holy shit."

"Transferring that much money and wiping it just doesn't make sense," Carson said. "The Tamburos aren't stupid, or they'd be in jail by now."

"You know what this looks like, don't you?"

"Yeah," Carson said. "It looks like they got hit by a hacker."

"A hacker that took them for thirty big." Chen grinned. "They've gotta be royally pissed about that."

"I'm sure they are. Try to find out where that wiped transaction went, Chen; talk to the managers of the banks, see if they have any hard electronic backups of the transactions on those dates. I want to know who this hacker was and where he is now. If he was that far into the Tamburos' systems, then he might be the key we need to shut them down."

"Already on it, Ell-tee," Chen said. "I dove into the planetary 'Net, did some research on the local hackers. Remember El Machete, the Robin Hood hacker from a few years back? He's the top candidate. He has the skill to pull this off, and he made a career of robbing crooks and corrupt politicians. There's one problem, though."

"And that is?"

"He's disappeared. Two possibilities: the Tamburos already found him and he's dead ..."

"In which case that thirty big would have reappeared some-place."

"...or he's flown the coop, and he's off-planet now. No doubt living high off the hog."

Carson looked thoughtful for a moment. "All right," she said. "The combination is right. Thirty big disappears, hacker disappears, and the money hasn't shown up in any of the Tamburo operations again. The hacker still has the money, and he's gone off-world. Find the money, and we'll find him. He's the key. We need El Machete to put the Tamburos away."

"That's how I see it."

"All right, you've got the job, Chen. Find him. You're lead agent on the detail; you've got Holtz and Juarez to help."

"Resources?" Chen wanted to know.

"Unlimited hyperphone use. See me if you need to go off-planet."

"You got it, Lieutenant. We'll find him." Chen grinned—it was his first time as lead agent on a major investigation—and left the office.

Lieutenant Carson followed him a moment later, announcing to the office appointment-droid that she was going to lunch. She left the CBI building, walked swiftly down towards the Bay, and in the safe anonymity of the noontime crowds, used her encrypted personal datapad to call a number in San Paolo, Brazil, that auto-forwarded to Milan, Italy.

Wallachia, 1459 CE

Mid-day and the residents of Svato were gathered in the town square.

The horsemen were gone; the last of them passed through the village only a half hour after the first. A cloud of dust on the horizon to the south heralded the approach of many more.

A boy, Stefan Niculescu, ran down a side street into the square. "I saw them," he shouted. "From the ridge above town."

"Calm yourself, boy," Alexandru Lacusta said. "Who did you see, and how many were there?"

Young Stefan took a deep breath. "As many as flies in a barn," he said. "There are far too many to count. Some are on horseback, some on foot. They carry a banner—green and yellow."

"Ottomans," someone called from the crowd. "Carrying the flag of Mehmed the Second!"

"We must flee!" came another voice.

"To where?" Alexandru Lacusta's voice was strong for his age, and his opinion carried much weight in the village. "Flee into the hills? Leave behind our homes, our supplies? What are we to live on, if the Ottomans provision on our poor village?"

"How are we to stop them if we remain?" Johann asked. "Alexandru, my friend, it makes no sense to stay here. We should at least send our women and children to the hills."

"I'm afraid it's too late for that," Alexandru said. Johann looked at the old man, whose gaze was fixed on something behind him. He turned.

Six horsemen, large, heavy men in mail armor, sat watching the villagers from a side street where it opened into the town square from the east. As the townspeople gasped, four more appeared on the north side of the square, then four more to the south. The cavalry of the Ottoman commander Suleiman Bulut had already surrounded the village.

One of the horseman cantered his mount into the square. He unsheathed his sword, waved it over his head. "You Wallachs! Nobody leaves!" he called in heavily accented Wallachian.

"What do you want?" Alexandru Lacusta asked the Turk.

"Not all that much," the Ottoman grinned, revealing crooked, gapped teeth. "Just all that you have. And perhaps more." He turned to the other Turkish soldiers. "Gather all the townspeople here, in the square. Suleiman Bulut comes! He will decide their fates."

Chapter Four

An unexplored desert planet, 2370 CE

A human being would have found the atmosphere almost unbearably hot and dry, the yellow-orange glare of the sun oppressive. For the little predator stalking the shores of a small, intensely salty sea, it was just another day.

The creature was about the size of an Earthly raccoon, but there the similarity ended. Its body structure was trilateral rather than bilateral; three heavily scaled legs projected from the three corners of its triangular body. Three eyes rose on stalks, one above the base of each leg. Underneath the flat, triangular, heavily scaled body was a round, jawless mouth equipped with teeth like chisels.

Rising high on its three legs, the predator stretched two of its eyestalks to peer over a small dune. Its quarry, a large trilateral herbivore, grazed on lichen-like plants with three companions. It was grazing just on the other side of the dune, within easy striking distance. The herbivore was twice the size of the predator and was likewise equipped with scaled armor. Two of its eyestalks focused on the ground, finding more food, while the third kept a constant vigil of the surrounding landscape.

The predator retracted its eyestalks. Creeping to the edge of the dune, it tracked its quarry now by the faint scratching sounds made by the creature's grazing, as the herbivore lowered its body to the wind-swept rock and used a rasping tongue to scrape lichens from the surface.

Crouching, the predator was about to spring when the shadow passed overhead.

Two eyestalks rotated swiftly to examine the sky. The planet had no large airborne predators, so no instinct warned the predator to seek cover. A large object, an unnatural round shape in the skies of this trilateral world, floated in the sky, growing slowly larger. The predator's tiny, flat, trilateral brain processed this information and spat out a conclusion based on millions of years of evolution: *There is no threat.*

The creature sprang then, its three triple-jointed legs unfolding in one bound that shot it over the dune to land neatly on the herbivore's main body segment. Teeth as hard as iron sheared through the herbivore's scales. A long, barbed tongue shot through the gap in the scales, found the herbivore's brain, shattered it. Uttering a low groan, the herbivore sank to the ground as its companions scattered.

Clicking its teeth together in satisfaction, the predator was preparing to feed when the wind hit it. A wholly unnatural wind, screeching from the flatlands just up-slope from the seashore, caught the predator and the carcass of its prey, flipping them both over and throwing them into the water as a huge, disk-shaped object settled slowly to the ground. Two more disk-shapes followed it down; the predator's eyestalks rose as it bobbed to the surface, and the little animal watched as the second and third titanic shape settled to the surface some distance away from the third.

A tiny opening appeared in the side of the nearest disk, then, and several figures emerged. Even as he agitated his limbs to swim to the shore, the little predator angled two of his eyestalks and rotated the crystalline lens of his eyes to increase the magnification of his sophisticated visual system. The figures that emerged were unrecognizable as life to the predator, standing oddly upright, with two lower limbs and two upper, and an odd projection on the top. They moved but were far too big for prey. Since they were neither food nor a recognized danger, the predator ignored them and concentrated on reaching the shore.

Its tiny, flat triangular brain was not capable of assessing the fact, but the predator's world was about to change dramatically. Man had arrived on this barren desert planet, and nothing would ever be the same again.

Nearby

The door to the cargo hull slid slowly open, and the once and former El Machete stepped out to survey his new domain. A bright yellow sun beat down mercilessly; a dull blue sea lapped sluggishly at its sandy shoreline a short distance away. The only other scenery was the endless expanse of yellow sand and brown rock.

The landscape was forbidding; for a moment, Virgilio Garcia cum Vincent Giovenco wondered at his own sanity for bringing his fledgling organization to such a barren place. Constance— Contessa—walked out of the ship and took Giovenco's hand.

"It's not very pretty," she observed.

The hacker looked down at the young woman. She was wrapped up against the glare of the sun; a white, robe-like gown hung past her ankles, long sleeves hung past her slim white hands. Her head was covered by a gray cloth and a large, floppy hat. Dark glasses protected her eyes.

"You look like one of those Arab women in the old vids," Giovenco teased her gently.

"You know how easily I sunburn," Contessa complained.

"I know. We'll have shelters set up soon. This was the best place, dear one."

"If you say so."

"We have to have time," Giovenco reminded her in a quiet voice. "I need time to build an organization to match the Tamburos. That's the only way we'll ever be safe from them. I'll have to beat them at their own game."

"You will, VeeGee," Contessa whispered. "I'm going back in the ship until we have a shelter."

"Of course." Giovenco watched her walk back into the huge cargo hull before turning to watch the sullen sea again. A moment later another voice interrupted his reverie.

"Boss?"

Giovenco turned to see the short, squat form of his executive assistant, Giorgio Berculioni, standing ankle-deep in the fine yellow sand of the dune. He held a datapad clutched in one pudgy hand.

"Yeah, what is it?"

"We've got the reactor set up and running," the would-be *consigliore* informed him. He pointed back towards the nearest grounded cargo disk, where heavy equipment raised clouds of dust as they rumbled out into the hot desert sunshine. "We're unpacking the service and assembly droids now. They'll get to work on basic infrastructure, water lines, power, all that. Desalinization plant will be running within the hour, and then we'll have the H-rig going to make hydrogen for the skimmers and air-cars. The first prefabs should be up before dark—I have one personal unit going up for you and Contessa, and a coupla bigger ones to use as temporary barracks. Scouts are looking over the terrain now— nothing much good for farming or grazing, really, and hardly any wildlife. We might be able to graze a few cattle along the coastline in a couple more years, if we can get any grasses to take."

"Great," Giovenco muttered. He shrugged; he had not planned to found an agricultural world in any case. "How long will our provisions last, assuming we find nothing here?"

"A year, maybe. Fifteen, sixteen months if we ration."

"That should do." Giovenco—he was getting used to thinking of himself by that name—regarded his new sidekick. When word had gone out on Zed that a Sicilian "Don" from Earth was recruiting for a new settlement, an amazing variety of characters had shown up—most of them fleeing something, no doubt, and an amazing number of them with Italian surnames. Berculioni was one such, a short, toad-like man with rheumy yellow eyes who nonetheless showed a remarkable knack for keeping Giovenco's business organized. He had the makings of an excellent advisor.

"Boss," Berculioni said, "I gotta ask—why this place?" He swept an arm across the horizon. "Ain't much here. Gonna be hard to get colonists to come here—no good farmland, nothing to look at."

"Where are you from originally, Giorgio?" Giovenco asked.

"Huh? Me? Originally Chicago—on Earth. I shipped for Zed just three years ago. Why?"

"Ever been to Las Vegas?"

"Oh hell yeah." Berculioni grinned. "Went there for my cousin Joey's bachelor party. We had a hell of a time."

"Then you remember, Vegas sits in the middle of a desert too, and it hasn't hurt them any. I'm not interested in farmers or sightseers. But we can't just put a big gambling town on any of the settled worlds, and I wanted us far enough off the trade routes so that the Confederates won't take too much interest in us—but close enough to draw tourists." Giovenco had another, more personal reason for wanting a remote location, but he left that unsaid. "We're going to found a place where the normal rules don't apply. This place may be dry and dusty, but the location is perfect."

"Fair enough, Boss." Berculioni consulted his datapad again. "Those geologists, Johns and Thompson, they think there's oil here. Not a lot, but their first seismic survey showed a couple possible domes in the area. Once we're set up, they'll sink a couple wells. If we have oil to crack for food, we can stretch the rations out with synthetics until we get some trade going. That might give us as much as three years."

"We'll be operating before then," Giovenco said. "We'll get some cash coming in and some trade going, and food won't be a problem, even if we have to import a lot of it." He pointed at a small plateau overlooking the small, salty sea. "First settlement's going right over there."

"What are you going to call it, Boss?"

"Nova Reno," Giovenco said with great conviction. "Good name for a gambling town."

"How about the planet, Boss? I figure you've got the right to name it."

"I've been thinking about that," Giovenco admitted. "I saw an old vid once that I liked. I think I'll name it after that. Why not?" He turned to his henchman and grinned. "Roman Holiday."

Parma, Italy, 2370 CE

It was Emil Tamburo's habit to gather his organization, his 'family,' together once a year in a formal meeting. This year's meeting had not gone well; the family's failure to develop good contacts inside the Confederate government had cost Emil and his sons some of their stature and resulted in a challenge to Emil's leadership from his cousin Joseph.

Joseph Tamburo was a tall, lean man with pale blonde hair, a legacy of his Swiss mother. He was known to be a ruthless operator, even in the circles in which the Tamburos routinely moved; his challenge, while only verbal, was threatening. Emil Tamburo's hold on control of the vast criminal enterprise was slipping.

"So," Joseph said as the first day of talks was winding down, "it's been six years since we started trying to develop contacts on Tarbos. You, cousin, you have people in governments of Russia, China, India, Britain, even the United States—but nothing on Tarbos." He tapped on the datapad lying on the table in front of him. "We moved fifty million dollars out of the Rim Worlds last year—out of the *Rim Worlds!* Mother of God, Emil, we should be moving ten times that off Tarbos alone, but you're saying we can't even get a toehold?"

"So far," Emil said evasively. He managed to hold back his anger.

"So far," Joseph repeated. "All right. All right."

"What are you saying, *cugino*? Maybe you think you could do better?" Emil's voice was dangerously even.

"Maybe I could at that," Joseph snapped. "You aren't doing so hot lately, Emil—first the issue with that hacker, that little *merda* that took us for thirty bees, and now this!"

"The hacker..." Emil gritted through clenched teeth. "El Machete, indeed, the hacker. We found him on Tarbos. We'll find him again."

"You found him a day late on Tarbos," Joseph shot back. "A day late, Emil. Just like you found him a day late in Tijuana. You have not had a clue as to his whereabouts for what—three years now? This hacker is making us look like fools—he's making you look like a fool, Emil."

"We have people on it," Emil said, looking around the table. Joseph Tamburo's was not the only face showing dissatisfaction.

"We'll have him within the year." *If we don't, with that much money, he could build an organization of his own—and we won't be able to touch him. He may have already done so.*

"A year?" Joseph Tamburo grinned now, his trap neatly sprung. "Very well, *cugino*, I propose we give you your year—and if we do not have our money back, then, I think, it will be a good time for new leadership."

A murmur of consent went around the table. Emil Tamburo wanted to take the small personal projectile gun under his coat and blow a hole in his cousin's chest, but he held the urge back— later, perhaps, but now was not the right time.

"Very well," he said, looking around the table. *I hope that* CBI *bitch knows what she's doing.* "One year from now, we will meet again—then, Joseph, we will see what we will see."

Chapter Five

Parma, Italy, 2372 CE

Joseph Tamburo, cousin of Emil Tamburo and aspirant to dictatorial control of the Tamburo family enterprises, now occupied a niche in an underwater canyon in the Aegean Sea.

Or, rather, what was left of him did.

Two years after Joseph's challenge at the annual family meeting, Emil Tamburo's hold on the family's enterprises was stronger than ever, in spite of his failure to produce the hacker El Machete or the thirty billion Confederate dollars that had evaporated from the family's accounts.

The reasons for Emil's resurgence were twofold. First was his ruthlessness in disposing of his primary rival, in which he was aided by his two vicious and unforgiving sons. Second was his announcement of a penetration into none less than the Confederate Bureau of Investigation itself. The Tamburos now had on the payroll a senior CBI officer in charge of investigations in financial matters. But the best development was one that Emil Tamburo was just now reporting to the family, once more assembled in conference.

"Our contacts in CBI," he said, "have a lead on that hacker, and on our money."

"Really?" a voice asked from the far side of the huge oak table. "After all this time? So, what are we doing about it?"

Emil smiled at the questioner, a second cousin, Antonio Genovese. "For the time being, nothing."

"*Nothing?*"

"Nothing. You want to know why, *si*? I'll tell you."

Tamburo pressed a contact on the table. A holographic map of the Confederacy swirled down from a tiny projector set into a ceiling tile. Tamburo used a laser indicator to point at a white dot just outside the Confederacy's southwestern border.

"Anyone know what this place is?"

"New colony," Antonio Genovese said. "Roman Holiday. Supposed to be a wild place—no Feds, none of the normal rules. Gambling, women, everyone's favorite vices rolled up on one planet."

"That's the place," Emil agreed. "The planet was founded two years ago by some clown calling himself Vincent Giovenco. He recruited a bunch of people on Zed, bought a couple of freighter loads of supplies, and just dropped in on this new place and took over. Now, our person in the CBI has found a couple of odd things out about this 'Giovenco.'

"First, the record on this guy is a little fishy. There's a birth certificate registered on Zed, but no biometric signature from the delivering doc. He's listed as a native Zeddan, but nobody there seems to know him. Kind of odd, given that there are only a few thousand people on the planet; you'd think someone would remember a guy rich enough to hire a hundred people and two freighters.

"Finally, the CBI can't turn up where he got all this money, but they do have some trail on him going back about three years— before that, nothing."

"Three years, eh?" Antonio Genovese muttered.

"Three years. Right about the time we got robbed."

"So, you think he's our guy?" Genovese demanded.

"I'm betting he is," Tamburo agreed easily.

"So, we're going to go get him, right?"

"Not so fast." Tamburo shut off the holo-projector and sat down at the head of the table. "There are a couple of things we have to consider."

Around the table, every eye was fixed on Emil Tamburo. He grinned at them and continued.

"One." He counted off his points on his thick fingers as he spoke. "This guy, this 'Giovenco,' he's in charge of a whole planetary organization now. Figure he's got some ex-military types working for him if he's got any brains, and he's obviously not stupid. We can't just muscle in on him. Two: by all accounts, Roman Holiday is fast becoming a very profitable enterprise— *very* profitable. Three: Giovenco has placed himself outside of Confederate law, and he's banking on gambling, hookers, booze, and drugs to make money—he's playing our game now."

"So, what will we do?" someone asked.

"We move slowly. I have four guys on the way to Roman Holiday now, by way of Tarbos, Caliban, and New Albion. They're all good boys, they're all faithful to the Tamburos. They'll get inside Giovenco's organization and keep us informed."

"In another year or two, I'll send a few more. Then a few more—infiltrate a few guys every now and then, until we have people close to Giovenco. Very, very close."

"Sounds good so far," Vito Genovese, Antonio's uncle and respected *consigliore* to two generations, agreed. "So, we get people inside, and when the time is right, we toss Giovenco under the bus."

"And in the meantime, I'm making arrangements. My sons and I are leaving Earth tomorrow. We have arrangements made with a private scout ship to take us to the colony on Jinx."

"Jinx? Rough place," Vito Genovese said. "Mostly pirates. Scum of the Confederacy."

"Pirates, indeed," Tamburo said. "Just the kind of people we need."

Roman Holiday, 2373 CE

Nova Reno's 'winter, such as it was, brought about fourteen planetary days of light rain and wind, following which the inevitable oven-like heat closed in again.

Construction went on through the brief cluttery spell, beginning with Vincent Giovenco's headquarters building—a veritable fortress of white chalcedony quarried from the badlands north of the growing settlement. Two private investors had already begun construction of gigantic hotel-casino complexes, and a fast-growing brothel had sprung up to attract Confederate dollars from the construction crews.

One afternoon after the return of the brutal heat, Giovenco stood out on the parapet of his 'villa' and looked out over the growing town.

"Gonna be a city before long, Boss."

Giovenco turned to see Giorgio Berculioni. He grinned at his *consigliore*; he had come to rely heavily on his advisor's rough-hewn counsel.

"Vice attracts business," Giovenco said. "Got a hyperphone message from an investment consortium on New Albion that's thinking about opening a racetrack and casino here, and the Palace on Tarbos is negotiating for space to put a branch here too. Things are starting to happen."

"Got another freighter just dropped out of subspace too, Boss," Berculioni said. "They're carrying a load of construction materials and food from Forest. Got some new workers coming in on the ship, too—about a hundred."

"Good. We can use them."

Berculioni looked around. "Contessa, she asleep?"

"Yes," Giovenco replied.

"Sleeps a lot during the day, don't she?"

"She does," Giovenco said, a bit startled at the realization himself—Contessa *did* sleep a lot during the day, but for some reason he'd never stopped to consider that fact before. "Why do you ask?"

"No particular reason, Boss, but it does bring up one other thing—we got no doctors to speak of here, no hospital, nothing other than a basic clinic and first aid station we set up when we landed. Something else to consider, eh? Ain't none of us gettin' any younger, Boss."

"True. You know, Contessa's always been a bit shy of bright light, but she seems to have gotten a bit worse since we came here. I hope it isn't a sign of anything."

Berculioni shrugged. "I doubt it, Boss—I mean, she's always looked perfectly healthy, just a bit pale from bein' indoors all the time."

Giovenco looked at his *consigliore*'s expression. "Was there something else, Giorgio?"

"Well, maybe," Berculioni began.

"Speak up," Giovenco ordered. "If you're worried about something, I want to know about it."

"Well ..." Berculioni looked hesitant for a moment, then shrugged and went ahead. "I'm just thinkin', Boss, we got a lotta new people coming in here all the time—and not exactly savory characters, *capice*? People coming here to party from all over, but the people we got coming here to live, out on the edge of no place, well, how do we know we can trust any of them? Escaped convicts and criminals, most of 'em, I reckon."

"You might be right."

"We might want to keep an eye on who and where we're recruiting, Boss. I'm just sayin'."

A thought occurred to Giovenco. *I wanted to build an organization to match the Tamburos in strength. I'll have to match them in wits, too. I wonder, if they find us here, will they come right at us or try to get someone inside?*

"You make a good point, my friend," he said at last. "Next time the senior staff meets, bring it up. We'll have to do something about that. I'm not having anyone in the organization getting any ideas about rocking the boat."

Or anyone outside the organization, either.

Wallachia, 1459 CE

Within a half hour of the arrival of his scouts, Suleiman Bulut himself rode into the town square.

The Ottoman commander rode a large, black horse. He was a large, broad man, swarthy, with thick black hair and a heavy black beard. His eyes were black, hard, and merciless. He wore an iron cuirass over a black shirt, black leggings, and boots, all covered with a long, black, hooded cloak. A sword hung from his saddle. Two massive men, lieutenants, moved in behind him, armed with swords and spears.

He rode once around the town square, examining the residents of Svato dispassionately. Finally, he barked orders at his men, in his own language; quickly, the Ottoman soldiers moved to separate men from women, children from adults. The men were held in the town square; the children and women were driven down separate side streets, out of sight.

When this was done, Suleiman Bulut addressed the men of Svato.

"Wallachs," he shouted. His use of the local language, while heavily accented, was understandable. "I am Suleiman Bulut, commander of the army that surrounds your town. I am appointed to command by the Sultan himself, and as such my word is law."

The men of the town stood silently in the cold, waiting.

"I will provision my men from your village. All foodstuffs, and whatever comforts you have here, are forfeit to the Sultan's army. You men have a choice." He leaned forward in his saddle, scowling at the villagers. "The first is simple: Join my army, fight as a soldier of Allah against the traitor Vladimir Tepes, and your women and children will be spared. The second choice is likewise simple—die here and now, and your families with you."

He sat back, grinning. "Allah is ever-merciful with the faithful. Join us, convert, fight with us, or die today, here and now. You must choose."

Three men stepped forward, all young men without families. Johann looked at them with contempt as they pushed through the crowd to surrender. Two of Bulut's soldiers moved them quickly away from the angry villagers.

"Well, three of you have good sense," Bulut snapped. "And the rest?"

Alexandru Lacusta answered for them. The old man strode proudly forward, stopping only feet in front of the Turk's black horse. With a contemptuous look at the Ottoman, he hawked and spat loudly on the ground.

Suleiman Bulut gestured, a single finger crooked over his left shoulder. One of the two lieutenants behind him cast his spear;

Alexandru Lacusta, struck through the heart, collapsed on the frozen mud of the street.

"He speaks for all of you, then?"

Silence.

"Perhaps," Suleiman Bulut said, addressing the men of Svato, "I have not been sufficiently persuasive. Perhaps you have not taken me at my word." He looked back at his lieutenants, then back to the villagers. "I think a demonstration is in order. "Kemal." One of his lieutenants stepped forward. He spoke to the man in Turkish for several moments.

The lieutenant grinned at his commander then and spurred his horse out of the town square, riding rapidly up the street where the children had been taken. Bulut gestured, and the remaining horsemen gathered in close, hemming the men in tightly. Swords and spears drawn, they formed into a tight circle around the men of Svato.

The apprehensive hush was broken suddenly by the scream of a child.

Tarbos, 2373 CE

Stefan Griggs stood up as the Confederate officials entered his office. One of them held out her hand as they approached his desk. "Lieutenant Joan Carson, CBI," she introduced herself. Without being asked, she showed Griggs her badge and ident card. "This is Sergeant Paula Ortega."

"Lieutenant," Griggs said, smiling in his most friendly and cooperative manner. "What can I do for you this morning?"

Carson handed over a datapad, the holographic display already on. "Please read this, sir, and acknowledge with your thumbprint on the pad. This is a warrant, issued by the Second Confederate

District Court in Mountain View, for all records concerning your dealings with one Vincent Giovenco of the unaffiliated colony Roman Holiday, and for records of all hardware, software, and other chattels transferred to his control."

"Oh," Griggs managed to reply, his smile fading as he read the warrant.

"We are particularly interested," Carson said, leaning forward, "in all information on a special operations combat droid that is missing from your reported defense systems inventory, and in the override codes for that droid."

Griggs looked up and managed to place his smile back on his face. "Of course," he said quickly. "Anything to help the CBI catch a bad guy."

Damn, Carson thought. *Tamburo's forgers really are that good. I never would have got a warrant from a real judge, not for this.*

She smiled, tightly, for just a moment. Once this job was done, a comfortable retirement on Avalon, funded by the Tamburos, awaited her.

Chapter Six

Roman Holiday, 2386 CE

Sixteen years had passed since the founding of Roman Holiday, sixteen years of building, of recruiting, of advertising for investors. Nova Reno had exploded into a center of gaming, prostitution, and other activities, some legal under Confederate law, and some not; Vincent Giovenco oversaw the whole thing personally for the first ten years until two smaller towns sprang up down the coast of the Sunrise Ocean. Giovenco appointed two "consuls," sub-bosses, to run those areas, while retaining overall control of the burgeoning planetary government that was becoming known as "The Organization."

The once and former El Machete was finding the administration of a city, a growing list of suburbs, and a planet taxing. "I'm spending all my time in meetings," he complained repeatedly to Contessa.

He was in one such meeting, in the expansive second-floor conference room of his Nova Reno headquarters, when the call came in.

"Next item," Vincent Giovenco was telling his assembled employees, "update on the skyhook. Leo, you were on that."

An engineer recently from Forest, Leo Capaldi—who had been born Leonard Campbell—made his report. "We have a shipment of nanotube precursors coming in on the next freighter from Tarbos, Boss. Construction of the base housing and pedestal will be complete in another month. It will take longer than normal to extend the tower to the asteroid we've captured, since we don't have a mountain to run it up from, but we should have the tower in place in four, five months—then another month to get track laid and the cables and support structure for the buses."

"How long to get the top-end station up and running?"

Capaldi consulted his datapad. "Six months, maybe seven—we don't have a lot of trained construction engineers, Boss. We'll have to do a lot of OJT to get our people in the groove."

"Make it happen," Don Vincent ordered. "Get more people in if we have to. We are losing a lot of business because of this. Fewer and fewer ships every year are coming with dirt-landing capacity. We need that 'hook operating."

"Yes, Don Vincent," Capaldi answered.

Giovenco looked up as Giorgio Berculioni entered the room. "Boss," the *consigliore* said, "we've got a call in the signals center you might want to take."

"A call? From who?"

"Hailing call, Boss, from a Confederate Navy frigate. They're in orbit now. The Captain wants to talk to the man in charge down here."

"The Navy? What the hell do they want?"

"Wouldn't say, Boss," the *consigliore* said. "Won't talk to anyone but the top man."

Wallachia, 1459 CE

The screams of the village children echoed through the square. One man sprang at a Turkish soldier and received a spear through the heart for his trouble. Johann Hess seized another's spear, tried to wrest it away; the soldier next in the rank struck with his sword, stabbing Johann in the shoulder before drawing back and slamming the flat of his heavy sword into Johann's temple. Dazed and bleeding, Johann collapsed.

The screams lasted for some moments before tapering away to a dread silence.

"Pity," Suleiman Bulut said. He adopted a mournful expression. "And all your fault, too. You could have saved them, you men; their lives would not have been pleasant, perhaps, but they would have lived. Now I'm afraid you all will have to forfeit far more."

"What do you mean?" Johann managed to get to one knee. His head was spinning. He could feel blood running down his chest, soaking his heavy winter tunic.

"My men have been long at war," Bulut said in a disarmingly friendly tone. "They have been long away from the comforts of their wives. *Your* wives will have to do to fill those needs for now."

"What do you mean?" a voice called from the village men.

"I'll show you," Bulut said in an agreeable tone. He gestured again.

A moment later, three of the village women were dragged into the town square. Soldiers held them, arms pinned behind them, where all the men of Svato could see.

"Osman," Suleiman Bulut called to one of his lieutenants who sat on his horse nearby. "You did well in the last day's battle against these infidel Wallachs. Take your pick of these three, as your reward."

The lieutenant saluted his commander with his sword. He dismounted rapidly, walked to the soldiers holding the three women. "That one," he said, pointing at Carmen Patrescu, the young wife of Nicolae Patrescu, an apprentice to the village baker.

Grinning widely, the soldier holding Carmen Patrescu shoved her to the lieutenant. "Who is this one's husband?" he called out.

When the village men remained silent, the lieutenant drew a long, curved-bladed iron knife, held it to Carmen's throat. "Who is it?"

"Me!" Nicolae Patrescu called in a panicked voice. He shoved forward through the group. "I'm her husband! Don't hurt her!" Nicolae pleaded.

Johann watched from where he sat on the frozen ground, weak and cold from blood loss.

"Hold him," Suleiman Bulut ordered. Two foot soldiers came forward, forced Nicolae to his knees. One held a spear in the small of Nicolae's back while the second laid a heavy, gauntleted hand on his shoulder.

"Let him watch." Bulut chuckled. "Let him learn the consequences of refusing me."

Carmen Patrescu gasped as the Ottoman lieutenant tore her blouse open.

The *Reuben James*, 2386 CE

Lieutenant Colonel Robert Patrick sat up at the tone. Reaching up from his stateroom's narrow bunk, he tapped a contact on the room's sole com-panel.

"Patrick," he said, yawning. The past few weeks stuck on a Navy frigate with nothing to do was wearing on him.

"Good morning, Colonel," the voice from the panel came back. "Commander Timmerman here. We have arrived in geosynch orbit over someplace called Roman Holiday. Would you join me in the shuttle bay? We're going to the surface."

"Sure thing," Patrick replied. "Five minutes."

"Very well." The com-panel clicked off.

Finally, he thought as he began to pull on his 'planetfall' lightweight khaki uniform, *Something to do besides watch old vids.*

It was a short walk to the frigate's shuttle bay. Patrick walked in to see Timmerman and two Marines waiting for him next to one of the ship's tiny landing shuttles. One of the Marines had the chevrons of a sergeant on his breastplate, the other, a lance corporal. The Marines were wearing battle armor and carrying carbines, while Timmerman had a holstered sidearm buckled on over his undress white jacket.

Colonel Patrick frowned. "A bit intimidating, aren't we?"

"You've seen the Ionescu files," Timmerman calmly replied.

"Sure. But we're just going down to talk to the guy running the show down there, right? We don't even know for sure that Hess came here."

"That's right. And we also know that this planet—'Roman Holiday,' indeed—is only marginally more civilized than the Rim Worlds, so I plan to be prepared for anything. The Marines will keep a low profile while we're talking with the honcho."

"If you say so. This old man, Hess, he's a sharp character. If we put on any kind of show of force, he'll blow, and we'll end up with an empty sack."

"Relax, Colonel." Timmerman smiled and clapped Patrick on the shoulder. "There isn't any ship in orbit other than ours, not even a parked drive tunnel. Long odds against him being here anyway; it's just the only inhabited planet along his last known course. There *are* a bunch of thugs in charge down there, though, and I figure on showing them we're serious."

Patrick frowned but let the matter drop. "Well, I'm ready."

"Good—if you'll just get on board, Colonel." Timmerman indicated the shuttle's open hatch. "We'll be on our way."

"All right."

The ride to the surface was rough, but nothing out of the ordinary for Patrick, who had logged over a hundred drop boat insertions; the Marines, too, sat through the battering, jolting ride with aplomb, having done it many times on exercises.

Timmerman was less comfortable. He made use of the small polymer 'barf bag' in his bucket seat's storage pouch twice on the trip down. By the time the shuttle floated to rest on the bright, hot, dusty surface of a landing field on the outskirts of someplace called Nova Reno, the Navy commander was weak, pale, and shaken.

Patrick climbed out of the shuttle first. The dry desert air hit him like looking into an open oven door. "Nice," he muttered. "Nice place." The sun was brighter, the air hotter than Jinx had been, but the dusty, dry planet looked all too familiar.

Timmerman came out next, squinting against the bright light. The Marines followed, one after the other, fading and almost disappearing as they activated their armor's microchromatophore stealth systems.

Patrick looked back. The Marines were only visible as a pair of hazy, shimmering distortions of the desert behind the shuttle. "I don't think you need the stealth systems, guys," he said.

"Yes, turn them off," Timmerman ordered. "Raise your visors. No point in overdoing it."

"Yessir," the Marine sergeant answered. Both Marines shimmered back into view and raised their face shields. The sergeant had a slightly smug impression; in their climate-controlled armor, the Marines scarcely felt the planet's blasting heat.

"That must be our ride," Patrick said. A large open air-car was floating towards them. One figure stood up in the air-car's passenger seat as it pulled up alongside the shuttle.

"You're all the Navy guys, right?"

"That's right," Timmerman answered. A slight breeze blew a skiff of dust across the paved surface of the landing field as the two men regarded each other for a moment.

The local finally hopped from the air-car. He was short, squat, with slicked-back black hair and a thin black moustache; his suit was impeccably tailored and impossibly clean for this dusty place. Yellow hoptoad eyes inspected the Confederate officers carefully, lingered on the armed and armored Marines for a few moments longer.

"Well," he said at last, "I'm Giorgio Berculioni. I work for Don Giovenco. The Don sent me here to bring you boys to see him, so climb on in, and we'll head into town."

"Very well." Timmerman and Patrick climbed into the air-car's back seat; after a moment's inspection, the Marines clambered into the small cargo bed at the rear, their polymer armor clicking and rattling against the aluminum of the air-car's body.

"Don't get many Marines here," Berculioni called over his shoulder as the air-car accelerated smoothly away from the shuttle. "Nor Navy either, really."

"You're pretty much off the trade routes."

The local turned to grin at Timmerman. "That's true. People who come here gen'rly want to come here, for one reason or another—nobody comes here on their way someplace."

"I suppose so."

"Damn right," Berculioni affirmed. "And there's good reasons to come here, trade routes or no. You know what they say—what happens on Roman Holiday, stays on Roman Holiday." He looked at Patrick and leered. "You fellas should stay down here over-night—you'd be amazed."

"We're not here for a party, Mr. Berculioni," Patrick said. "We're looking for a fugitive."

"You probably came to the right place then. Hell, half the people work for the Don need hangin'. People come here to *party* is one thing, but people who come here to *live*... that's something else."

"What about you?" the Marine sergeant called out.

Berculioni laughed a short, barking laugh.

Lieutenant Colonel Patrick watched with interest as the air-car rode smoothly into the outskirts of Nova Reno. The outlying areas consisted of a few obvious apartment complexes and even some houses; a few moments later they passed through a small warehouse district, and then into Nova Reno proper.

The main strip was impressive enough in the hot desert sunshine; Patrick looked up at the towering facades of several huge hotel-casinos, noting all the light outlets, and figured that Nova Reno's main drag would be several thousand times more impressive at night.

They passed another building with two guards outside a stout door; a large, explicitly illustrated sign proclaimed it to be "Paula's Pink Passions." Prostitution was legal in plenty of places throughout the Confederacy, but it was rarely advertised so plainly.

"Just another coupla blocks," Berculioni called out.

A minute later, the air-car floated to a stop in front of a large building built of some kind of white stone. The building was had very little by way of decoration; it was simply a huge, white monolith rising from the ground, pierced by large double doors at the front, and rows of windows on the upper level. *Built to be defended,* Colonel Patrick told himself. His trained eye spotted e-beam cutters on the corners of the building's roof, no doubt controlled by hidden cameras.

The building had another defense, one that showed itself as soon as Berculioni led them inside.

The main room took up much of the lower floor of the building. A fountain tinkled gently in one corner near an expansive bar; the floor was richly carpeted, the walls hung with tapestries, the air cool and faintly scented.

A rattle of metallic limbs betrayed the machine's presence before anyone saw it scuttling across the room. It was a large, heavy, tank-like security droid, six dull gray metallic legs supporting a crablike body with a round turret "head" mounted on top. Four arms surrounded the body, two with large metal grapples and the other two ending in small, rotary projectile guns. A variety of sensors protruded from the machine's "head," most of which were focused on the Navy men as the robot scuttled across the room.

"PLEASE DO NOT MOVE," the robot ordered as it slammed to a stop in front of them. "IDENTIFY YOURSELVES."

"Commander Raphael Timmerman, Confederate Navy, commanding the frigate *Reuben James*. This is Lieutenant Colonel Robert Patrick, Confederate Marine Corps. These two are Sergeant Jorge Aames and Lance Corporal John Simms, also Confederate Marines."

"RECORDED. THREE OF YOU ARE BEARING ARMS. YOU WILL SURRENDER THEM IMMEDIATELY."

"I'll be damned," the Marine sergeant said. "I recognize you. A General Systems Mark IV special operations droid." He turned to Berculioni. "Where the hell did you guys get that? There were only supposed to be three prototypes built."

"The Don, he has ways." Berculioni chuckled. "Sorry, guys, just a routine security thing—you'll get your weapons back when you leave the building."

"SURRENDER YOUR WEAPONS IMMEDIATELY," the robot repeated, raising its weapon-arms in an obvious threat. "THIS WARNING WILL NOT BE REPEATED."

"Do it," Commander Timmerman ordered. He unbuckled his pistol belt, handed it over. The Marines reluctantly handed over their carbines and watched with frowns as the robot opened a compartment in its crablike body and tucked the weapons inside.

Camera eyes regarded the Marines impassively. "TWO OF YOU ARE WEARING ENHANCED COMBAT ARMOR SYSTEMS. YOU WILL REMOVE THEM."

"What?" the Marines demanded in unison.

"Tinny," Berculioni asked the robot, "how's about the two Marines just wait here? I'll take the other two up to the Don."

The robot's head swiveled to regard Berculioni for a moment, and then cycled back to the Marines. There was a moment as the machine accessed its decision algorithms, and then: "ACCEPT-ABLE," it barked. "I WILL WATCH THEM."

"Fine. Boys, you can just sit over there at the bar, I'll send someone in to get you a drink—water or soda, I 'spose, you bein' on duty and all. Commander, you and the colonel here can come with me."

"SECURITY PROTOCOL TWO IS ACTIVE," the robot boomed out as its 'head' swiveled to watch the Marines proceeding to the bar. "UPPER LEVEL RESTRICTED TO BIOMETRIC IDENTIFICATION ACCESS."

"I hear ya, I hear ya. Come along with me, fellas."

Berculioni ushered them up a wide, curving stairway to what looked like a blank, white wall. The *consigliore* paused and then put his thumb on an unmarked spot on the wall, which faded away to reveal a long hallway with several old-fashioned wood panel doors.

"Come on in, boys," he said. "Boss is last door at the end."

"Tight security, eh?" Colonel Patrick said in a low voice.

"Yeah," Timmerman replied. "Real tight. Kind of paranoid, aren't they?"

Patrick nodded. He was watching Berculioni, who was speaking briefly into a panel outside the last door.

The door swung open into the office. "Please, come in," a voice called out from inside. The two Confederate officers went in, followed closely by Berculioni.

Lieutenant Colonel Patrick looked at the planet's boss with narrowed eyes. The Don was a slight man, clad in a dark silk suit, finely tailored; his shirt was gleaming white, his shimmering blue tie was carefully knotted. His thick black hair was slicked back on his head; black eyes crinkled at the corners as he smiled amiably. Patrick looked at the man's skin tone, his features, listened to his accent as he spoke a few formal words of greeting. His training in demographics and linguistics kicked in; *He's about as Sicilian as Pancho Villa.* He shook his head. Timmerman was already into the introductions.

"Commander Rafael Timmerman, commanding the CNS *Reuben James*," he was saying. "My colleague is Marine Lieutenant Colonel Robert Patrick, Navy Intelligence."

The Don nodded. "Don Vincent Giovenco," he said. "I'm the founder of Roman Holiday. You wanted the man in charge; I'm him. Please, have a seat." He indicated two plush chairs in front of the enormous polished desk.

"Thank you," the two officers replied. They sat down; Patrick was mildly startled when the chair warmed slightly and exuded a faint, pleasant scent.

"May I offer you gentlemen something to drink?" Giovenco was asking.

"Thank you, no," Commander Timmerman replied. "We won't take up but a few moments of your time."

"Impressive security droid you've got downstairs, Don Vincent," Colonel Patrick interjected.

"A gift from an old friend," Giovenco replied with a feline smile.

"Um. All right. Must be some friend—Force Recon has been trying to get some of those for about fifteen years now, Congress refuses to allocate the money—too expensive."

Commander Timmerman shot his Marine colleague a sharp glance. "Mister Giovenco," he said, noting the Don's blink at that form of address. "We're not here to talk about sec droids. We're here looking for a fugitive." He pulled a holocube out of his pocket and activated it; a three-dimensional artist's rendering of a scrawny old man with a shock of white hair swam into view.

Giovenco smirked. "Looks like a real rough character. What'd he do to make the Feds send the Navy after him?"

"That's between him and the Feds," Timmerman said. "We're just trying to locate him."

"You say so. Giorgio, this guy look familiar to you?"

"Never seen him before, Boss."

"You heard him," Giovenco said. "What do you boys want me to do? Look around for him?"

"The last data we had on this guy had him heading here," Timmerman replied. "If he's here, it would be in your interests to find him and hand him over."

Giovenco's eyes narrowed. He leaned forward in his chair. "You want to explain why?"

"There is a very strong possibility that he's carrying a disease," Patrick said. *What the hell,* he told himself. *It's actually more or less true.*

"Disease?"

"A new hemorrhagic fever," the Marine confirmed. "Something that's been spreading out of the Rim Worlds. The Communicable Disease Labs on Tarbos want a good look at it; they don't have any idea how to engineer a counter to it yet."

Giovenco looked past the Confederates to his *consigliore*. He shrugged. "Fine," he agreed. "Giorgio, take few copies of that holocube, show 'em around."

"Right away, Boss." He took the holocube from the Navy officer and left the room.

"Gentlemen," Giovenco told the two officers, "we'll see what we can do."

Timmerman handed over a chip. "The ship's comm code and my personal comm code, along with Colonel Patrick's, is on this chip. Please call us if you find anything."

Giovenco took the chip and nodded gravely. "Are you two staying down here any time at all? I'd be pleased to have you as my guests at the Golden Palace next door; it's my own personal enterprise, and I'm having a small gathering there tonight."

The officers looked at each other. "Thank you, but we will have to decline," Patrick said. "The Commander and I both have duties that will keep us aboard the ship for now. We will be in geosynch orbit over Nova Reno if you need to reach us."

"Perhaps another time then."

"Perhaps," Timmerman agreed.

Berculioni came back in then and handed Timmerman the holocube. "Made three copies," he said. "That all right with you guys?"

"Fine," Colonel Patrick said.

"We will be in orbit for several days. Don Giovenco," Timmerman said, rewarding the man for his cooperation by using his preferred title, "we thank you. We look forward to speaking with you again soon." The officers and Giovenco stood; Giovenco gravely shook hands with them both before pressing a contact on his desktop. "Louie?"

A deep voice rumbled from an unseen speaker. "Yeah, Boss?"

"Would you come in and escort my guests to the door? I don't want them to have any trouble with Tinny."

"Right away, Boss." A moment later, a tall, thick man in a dark suit walked in from a back room. He was large, swarthy, and had a lantern jaw covered with a thick, blue five o'clock shadow—manifestly a bodyguard.

"My sec droid's AI isn't all that acute," Giovenco explained with a smile. "He gets confused sometimes—it's generally better if you're with someone he knows."

"Perfectly understandable," Timmerman said. A picture of the heavy combat droid popped unbidden into his mind.

"Gentlemen," Louie held a hand towards the door. The Confederates filed out, the thug on their heels. The door swung slowly closed behind them.

Berculioni pulled a tiny device from a jacket pocket, swung it around the room. "Clean. They didn't leave nothin' behind."

"I don't trust them," Don Giovenco said. "There's something they aren't telling us."

"No shit!" Berculioni barked. "I mean—excuse me, Boss, but yeah. Something's fishy. Disease, my ass."

Giovenco looked thoughtful. He picked up one of the holocubes, activated it and looked at the wizened image for a moment. "Giorgio, call down, have the garage get out an air-car. I'm going to visit a few of the major owners myself. You can come along."

"You got it, Boss." He spoke a few words into his personal datapad. "Air-car will be ready when we get down there."

"Fine. Let's go." Giovenco picked up two of the holocubes and dropped them in a jacket pocket.

A moment after the two men left the office, Contessa Giovenco drifted in. She picked up the remaining holocube, activated it, looked at the image, and scowled.

Chapter Seven

Wallachia, 1459 CE

By mid-afternoon, five men of Svato lay dead in the square, all killed for trying to defend their wives or daughters. Sixteen of the village's thirty-nine adult women lay dead beside them. All had been raped repeatedly, then slain with sword or spear when they grew too weak to resist. The men were forced to watch.

Through it all, Johann Hess grew weaker. He lay on the frozen ground now; his shoulder wound's bleeding had slowed, but Johann sat in a frozen black puddle of his own blood. His head spun and lights flashed in his fading vision; he held the darkness away through force of will alone.

He knew Felix and Elsa were dead, with all the other village children. He knew also that his beloved wife, Anna, was still alive, still held with the other village women.

Suleiman Bulut was growing bored. Throughout the mass rapes, he had remained on his black horse. Finally, he ordered the torching of the village homes and buildings as a diversion; when that was well begun, he waved for another group of women to be brought forward.

Johann's heart sank when he saw his Anna in the group of four women brought forth for the Ottoman's amusement.

One of the Turks, taken with Anna's plump figure, seized her. The Ottoman tore at her dress, exposing her flesh to the cold air.

Johann forced himself to his feet. Adrenaline surged in him, giving him strength despite the blood loss. He forced his way through the crowd.

The Turk forced Anna to the ground, laughing as she screamed in protest.

Johann reached the rank of soldiers. Most of them, tired, bored, and awaiting their turn to take part in the raping, were diverted, looking away from the crowd. Johann moved towards one of them.

The soldier heard Johann's dragging, shuffling approach. He turned, but too late. With a strength borne of desperation, Johann seized the man's spear, tore it from his hands. With an accuracy borne of rage, he cast the spear. His aim was true; the spear struck home, piercing the heart of the Ottoman soldier that was about to rape his Anna.

Then the pommel of a heavy sword struck Johann's head, and he saw nothing more.

Roman Holiday, 2386 CE

The Golden Palace hotel/casino was one of Vincent Giovenco's personal indulgences, and a profitable one at that. The huge, four-wing building had forty stories of hotel rooms, with one wing reserve for 'professional companions.' The first floor was taken up with a gigantic casino, several restaurants, a nightclub, and a theater. No fewer than eighty thousand lights studded the outside of the building, glittering and flashing endless patterns of green, blue, red, and yellow onto the busy main drag of Nova Reno. An endless stream of fifty-meter high holographic enticements—women, liquor, and gaming—hovered a dozen meters over the main entrance.

The Don liked to hold court in the hotel's Evensong nightclub several evenings a week. His reserved table was at the back of the club, where he and Contessa had a good view of the huge dance floor, and where his bodyguard had a good view of the entrances.

This particular evening, Giovenco noticed, Contessa was quiet and a bit pensive. He leaned over to whisper in her ear.

"Something bothering you, *querida*? I don't like seeing you unhappy."

Contessa noted his slip back into Spanish, something he rarely did; it confirmed a suspicion she'd been harboring.

"You haven't told me about your day." She pouted. "I know you had some Navy men in to see you—I heard Tinny yelling at them in the lounge."

Giovenco picked up his wineglass and took a sip. "I did," he agreed. "It wasn't anything to worry about, dear one—they're looking for someone, that's all."

"Who are they looking for here?"

"Just some smuggler," Giovenco lied. "Don't worry about it. It doesn't concern you."

He looked up and smiled as the owner of the Lincoln Arms, a new resort hotel on the seashore, walked towards the table. "Tony," he greeted the businessman. "Sit down. Have a glass of wine."

In the casino

Christine Hess's mood had been sour, but improved rapidly once she moved inside, into the cool air of the casino. *Six days,* she thought angrily. *Six days on this miserable, blistering rock, and I only now manage to slip away from the old man for a few hours.* Outside, even an hour after local sunset, the air was still, dry and hot.

She had dressed carefully for her evening's hunt. A white button-down shirt, worn open but for a tie at the waist, over a black synthleather bustier and miniskirt showed off her Amazonian figure to best advantage. She wore spike-heeled, knee-high black boots, and her black hair, grown now to waist length, hung loose in soft waves. She carried a black cloak with hood, unneeded now but possibly useful should she be caught out too close to sunrise. She walked into the main part of the casino, where a hatcheck droid took her cloak. She strode through the enormous room, aware of the stares of most of the male patrons.

Her gaze focused on a young, thin man playing a vid terminal game. She went to him, leaned down a bit to emphasize her cleavage, and breathed, "Can you tell me where the nightclub is?"

Speechless, his mouth gaping open, the young man just pointed.

She reached out and laid her slim hand on his. "Thank you," she said.

"Uh huh."

She smiled at him and walked off towards the Evensong. The attention of most of the casino's patrons went with her.

The nightclub exceeded her hopes for the barren desert world. Large, dark, the club formed an oblong around a dance floor illuminated with lightbars and flashing lasers. Maybe fifty people were gyrating to synthmusic on the dance floor, while a hundred or so more sat at tables or stood around the floor. She took a deep breath, savoring the aromatic cocktail of sweat, pheromones, sexual excitement, alcohol, and blood.

Best of all, the club showed a distinct gender disparity; there were far more men than women.

Christine seated herself at a table, ordered a glass of red wine, and began to size up the room.

At the back, near the fire exit, sat a small, impeccably dressed, dark-haired man. Two obvious bodyguards stood nearby; Christine's analytical eye told her they were armed. A young girl, slight, pale, red-haired, sat at the man's right hand, turning occasionally to grin vapidly at him in response to some comment. *Looks rich, looks important,* she noted. *Wonder who he is? Not what I'm looking for now, anyway.*

An hour passed. She shared a drink with one man, danced with another; neither appealed to her needs.

He approached her from behind, just as she was thinking of trying her luck elsewhere. "Hey, darlin'," she heard the slightly slurred voice say. "You're new here."

She inhaled. He carried a strong taint of alcohol, but he was well-built; his scent was that of a man used to hard physical work, a regular drinker but not an alcoholic. She turned to look at him: tall, broad-shouldered, dark-haired.

You'll do.

"Why, yes." She smiled. "I just got in a few days ago. Won't you sit down?"

"Working around here?" He waved at a serving droid that was gliding past. He looked at Christine and cocked a questioning eyebrow.

"Red wine, please, and thank you. I'm not working yet, but I hope to. I've heard this place is growing quickly, I'm hoping to get in on the ground floor of something good."

"I'm Mark Tobias." He grinned, holding out his hand.

"Christine Hess." She smiled back, taking his hand. "What is it you do here?"

"Oh, I'm working on the Don's skyhook project. No 'hook leaves a planet kind of sucking wind these days, you know? Not many ships even carry landing shuttles any more. Hell, even Forest is getting a skyhook now. How 'bout you? What do you do?"

"Financial planning," Chris said. "The Don, you said? Who is he?"

Tobias nodded towards the man Christine had noted earlier. "That's him. Don Vincent Giovenco, boss a' this whole place. He's the founder. The lady with him, that's his wife Contessa. Guy claims to be from Sicily—that's on Earth—but who knows?" Christine caught the undertone, as well as the subtle change in his heartbeat and scent. "Ever'one here claims to be from someplace. Ever'one here's generally got something to hide."

"Is there anything you'd like to tell me?" Christine said and smiled.

"You never know," Tobias answered.

An hour passed as they ingested several drinks each; Tobias' speech grew more uncertain, and Christine let her words slur as well, even though it had been many decades since alcohol had much effect on her metabolism.

They were on the dance floor when Christine judged the time right to leave. Tobias was obviously thinking along similar lines; dancing close, Christine could feel his obvious physical reaction.

"I was thinkin'," he said, "that maybe we could get outta here, go someplace a little quieter."

"Quieter, eh?" Christine smiled up at him.

"Yeah, you know. Quieter."

She took his hand, kissed the back of it, turned it over and kissed the ball of his thumb—then bit it, only slightly, just enough to draw a little blood—which, in his drunken state, Tobias barely noticed.

"I think you're right," Christine murmured. "Come with me."

Wallachia, 1459 CE

A hard slap woke Johann.

He shook his head. Two Ottoman soldiers held him on his knees. One seized his hair, pulled his head upward.

"Look at me," he heard a voice say. He opened his eyes to see Suleiman Bulut.

"You killed one of my men," Bulut said in a conversational tone.

"Let me go," Johann snarled, "and I'll kill more."

"I've no doubt you would try," Bulut said. "Alas, I'm afraid I cannot allow you to try. It would hardly set a good example for your fellow villagers, would it?" He gestured. "That woman—your wife?"

Johann said nothing. A string of blood ran into his eyes. He tried to blink it clear.

"Ah." Bulut chuckled. "But of course, she is. You're not old enough to be her father. I confess, Wallach, I admire your courage. I offer you one last chance to join us."

Johann spat. "I'm not a Wallach. I'm a Bavarian. As to your offer—burn in hell."

Bulut laughed. "Ah, but it is a very personal hell I intend to create for you," he said. He turned to the three traitors, the three men of Svato that had agreed to join the Turks at the beginning of the day. "Which of these homes belongs to this man?"

One of them pointed at the slanted roof of the Rote Hexe where it stood at the edge of the town.

"Of course," Bulut said. "Bring him. Bring the woman."

Johann was dragged to the road in front of the Hexe. Otto-man troops with torches stood by. Suleiman Bulut appeared a moment later, dragging Anna with him.

"Now," Bulut said, "Bavarian, you may watch."

Anna wrenched her right hand free from Bulut's grasp and tore at his face with her nails. The Turk smashed his hand into her head, knocking her senseless to the frozen ground.

Then he bent, tore her clothing from her, and methodically raped her as two of his soldiers held Johann's head up by the hair. "Watch," the soldier said. "Keep your eyes open, Bavarian, and watch, or I'll cut your eyelids away."

Johann's heart was a stone.

After an interminable time, Suleiman Bulut finished. He stood up. Anna lay on the ground, barely breathing. A trickle of blood ran from the corner of her mouth.

"You, there in the wolf-fur hood, give me your spear," Bulut ordered one of his men.

The Ottoman commander stood, looked at Johann for a moment. "Torch his home," he finally ordered.

Three men kicked the Hexe's door open. One broke a window. Torches flew to the roof, into windows. Moments later, the inn was ablaze.

"Watch now," Bulut said to Johann. "A life for a life." He drove the spear through Anna's chest.

Johann screamed in rage, tried to struggle to his feet, but he was too weak. The Turks held him fast.

"Throw her in the building," Bulut ordered. "Knock him in the head and throw him in with her. There, Bavarian," he said, "there is your hell."

Chapter Eight

The _Reuben James_, 2386 CE

Lieutenant Colonel Robert Patrick walked into the _Reuben James'_ wardroom, hoping to find his first morning cup of coffee, and was surprised to find Commander Timmerman seated at a table, coffee and a large portable display terminal in front of him.

Patrick went through his coffee ritual and walked through the wardroom to the table where the ship's captain sat, stirring as he went. "Morning, Captain. Something up? You're usually on the bridge by now."

"Have been," Timmerman said without looking up. "Since about oh-four, in fact. I was looking over the transit track logs we were given with this mission. Look here." He tapped the terminal, switching the view from on-screen to 3-d holographic; a star map appeared in the space above the table.

Patrick sat down. "OK," he said. He pointed with his coffee stirrer. "There's Jinx, and here's Roman Holiday—I assume that white cone is the projected transit track?"

"Right—there's about a six degree margin of error at this distance."

"You're worried because there's no sign of a ship here, right?"

"He may have come here and left again," Timmerman said, "or he may have gone somewhere else—he could have even dropped out of subspace in mid-jump, replotted and gone somewhere else entirely. We're operating on awfully thin information here."

"True enough," Patrick said. He took a drink of his coffee. "Still. This place makes a lot of sense. Non-affiliated world, outside the Confederacy's border—just outside, but even so, a good place to hole up. You've seen it down there. There isn't much in the way of law. Just a self-styled *Mafiosi* in charge, ruling the place with a gang of thugs; perfect place for a guy like Hess."

"Funny we haven't found an orbiting drive tunnel. Even if we assume his ship is equipped for dirt landings, he can hardly take his Gellar tunnel down to the surface—it should be in low orbit, waiting for him to climb out of the gravity well and pick it up."

"Should be," Patrick agreed. "Hell, maybe he's got some way to hide it. Tethered to an asteroid or something."

"But you still think he's here."

"Setup's just too good for him. I suppose we could call in for orders, but we're out here a ways—hyperphone message would take, what, a week to get back to COMTASKFOR947, and then another week for the reply to arrive here—once the Commodore figures out what we should be doing?"

"I should call in," Timmerman said.

"You're the captain," Patrick agreed easily. "But, while you wait for a reply, what say I head down to the surface, look around a little on my own? I'm the only one who's seen this Hess and his sidekick in person, and I'm pretty good at blending into a thug society—had a lot of practice these last few months."

"The boss down there knows you," Timmerman pointed out. "A bunch of his people have seen you, too."

"Give me ten minutes with my prosthetics kit, and my own mother wouldn't recognize me." Patrick laughed. "Trust me on this, Commander—I am good at this business. Besides, I have absolutely no intention of going anywhere near Don Giovenco and his killer tank droid."

"I suppose we could use our shuttle, drop you on the edge of town sometime after local sunset. They sure aren't running any orbit control or traffic radars down there—they'll never know we did a quick down and up."

"That's the thing about gangsters and pirates," Patrick said. "Not very sophisticated. Jinx was pure chaos—no traffic control, ships coming in and leaving as they pleased. I saw three crackups in a year."

The frigate's commander looked at the wardroom's wall clock. "Local sunrise is in about three hours. If you can be ready in an hour, I can get you to the surface a good thirty minutes before sunup."

"I'll be ready in thirty minutes. Shouldn't be too many people moving around that time of day. If our guy is down there, I'll get a line on him."

"All right, then," Timmerman agreed. "You've got your two weeks, unless we hear something from Giovenco before then."

"Good," Patrick said. He took another sip of black coffee. "Hope they actually import some decent coffee here—you wouldn't believe what they passed off as coffee on Jinx. Terrible."

The wardroom comm panel buzzed. Timmerman looked up, saw the call light flashing, and answered it, speaking softly into the mike for a moment.

"We may have found him after all," he said a moment later, turning to grin evilly at Colonel Patrick. "A ship just came into orbit; an unregistered ship. They're keeping their distance, but we've confirmed it is mounting two P-beam emitters."

"Pirate ship," Patrick said. "Has to be one of the old man's."

"That would be my guess."

"If he's down there," Patrick said, "I'll find him."

Wallachia, 1459 CE

Johann awoke slowly. The smell of smoke assailed his nostrils; his lungs burned. He opened his eyes to see flames, smoke. On the floor near him lay another figure.

"Anna?" He knew it was pointless to call her name. She lay near him in what he finally realized was the Hexe's dining area, her eyes open and blank in death, her clothes in rags. The wound from the spear was red between her pale breasts. The remnants of her skirt were already afire.

Outside, Johann heard the guttural laughter of the Turks.

The flames grew higher. He yelped as his sleeve caught fire. He burned his hand slapping out the flames.

The cellar, he thought. The image seared into his mind as the inn burned around him—beneath the kitchen, the trap door to the cellar where he kept his barrels of lager. Too weak to walk, Johann crawled to where the trap door was set in the floor just inside the kitchen door. He pulled it open, pulled himself through, dropped into the miraculously cool cellar.

For a moment he lay, listening as the fire spread above. He couldn't hear the Turks anymore; all he could hear was the roar of the blaze. In a few moments, the cool cellar was noticeably warmer. *Can't stay here. The outside door...*

Waves of dizziness assailed him as he forced himself to his feet. He forced himself to stagger to the narrow stairs that led outside at the rear of the *gasthaus*. He managed to make it up the stairs and outside. The afternoon was already fading to early winter twilight. Johann looked around, but all the Turks seemed to have left the area, no doubt sure he was dead. Gathering what little remained of his strength, Johann stumbled into the trees.

Nova Reno, 2386 CE

It was nearing morning when Christine finally returned to the cheap flat old Hess had rented in the town's warehouse district.

"Ah," the old man greeted her. He was seated at the kitchen table, datapad in front of him, reading what passed for local news. "A late night, eh, child?"

"I have my needs, as well as you do," Christine said. The old man reeked of some doxy's cheap perfume, body juices, sweat, and blood. "And don't tell me you sat here all night."

"I did not," Hess said, "And you're quite right, we both have our needs. A weakness, perhaps?"

She shrugged. "I can't see how."

"Well, never mind. What have you learned about things here? Any useful information?"

Christine smiled. "I saw the founder—the man in charge here. Like old Hogmanay back on Jinx, except I think this Giovenco is smarter, less brutal; he is a businessman, not a pirate."

"I agree—I've been reading about him. Don Vincent Giovenco, indeed." Hess snorted in derision. "The cheek of the man, styling himself thus."

Christine shrugged. "It's basically a dictatorship here," she said as she took the chair across the table from the old man. "The man I spent the evening with has been here a local year—about fourteen Standard Months. There are two smaller towns along the coast, run by 'consuls' that answer directly to Giovenco. He keeps a tight grip on things. He may be justified in that; apparently, he personally funded the startup of the colony, and paid for promotion to bring businesses in."

"A man of considerable wealth, then. Is there any chance you might..." Hess raised his bushy white eyebrows in an obvious suggestion.

"He has a wife," Christine said. "I have no idea how willing a philanderer he is—his wife is attractive, but she doesn't look too bright."

"He may prefer it that way. Dictators rarely surround themselves with people competent to challenge their authority."

"True enough." Christine had thought of that already. She also remembered that, while she had read and studied history as a student in the Confederate Navy Academy, old Hess had actually lived through much of it, and had a good acquaintance with dictators.

Christine looked at Hess, noted his thoughtful expression. "Do you have some kind of plan?"

"Not at the moment. I'm more interested to see what kinds of opportunities present themselves here. We made a good profit on Jinx; I would like to turn some of that capital into a long-term enterprise that will yield returns for some time to come."

"We might want to keep an eye on our escape route. I'll give you fifty-fifty odds that the Navy was able to track our subspace jump, cloaking device or no."

"Perhaps." The old man didn't look concerned. "Our ship is safely hidden in a hangar, and our drive tunnel is cloaked; they won't find either one, even if they should come here looking for us."

"And if they do?"

"I've been in tighter spots than this. I know well enough how to throw hounds off the scent, child."

"As you say, Grandfather." She stretched and yawned. "I'm going to sleep now. I expect we'll be busy the next few days."

"I expect we will, yes," the old man agreed, showing his yellow, pointed teeth in a grin.

Wallachia, 1459 CE

Through the night, Johann staggered away from Svato. Flickering light behind him spoke eloquently of the Ottomans' destruction of the village. He stopped once to rest, and spent an hour crouched helplessly, sobbing for Anna and the children.

Then, grunting in agony, he forced himself to his feet and climbed higher into the Carpathians. He paused to drink from a stream and stared for a moment at his own reflection; his unruly hair was white as snow in the moonlight; his drawn and haggard face looked as though he had aged forty years.

The sky was beginning to show the first pale light of dawn when he collapsed in a small pass in the rocks, unable to go further. He lay on the ground, stunned, barely conscious, when the other came to him.

The man—if he was a man—was skinny, skeletal. His hands were hooked like talons, his eyes gleamed yellow in the pale light. He looked at Johann where the Bavarian lay helpless and yawned to show pointed teeth.

Johann closed his eyes. *Useless to fight any more. Useless to resist.* He lay back, more than willing to take whatever fate offered— until he felt the man's needle teeth fasten onto his wrist.

"By God," Johann roared, "I'll not be *eaten*! Whatever else has passed, not that!"

The skeletal figure hissed. Johann's blood dripped from his mouth. Johann tried to wrest his arm free, but the creature's grasp was like iron.

Desperate, Johann's free hand scrabbled on the ground, seeking anything—a rock, a branch. He found a weapon at last, a fist-sized rock. With desperate strength, he smashed it into the weird figure's head.

With a piercing shriek, the thing dropped Johann's wrist. Johann clutched the wounded limb to his chest and sat up, gasping. He still held the rock.

"Back off, creature," he said, "or by all that's holy, I swear..."

The skeletal figure crouched. It began to circle, slowly, hissing all the while. Johann watched it, warily, while trying to edge closer to the ledge of rock that bordered one side of the small pass.

Then, with startling suddenness, the first rays of the morning sun struck through the pass! Caught in the glancing rays, the creature let out a shriek of fear and agony. It scuttled backwards, out of the light, leaving a faint trail of smoke behind it, and fled down the western slope of the pass into the trees that still lay in darkness.

Drained, Johann crept further back into the rocks. A small cavelet in the rocks offered some shelter; he crawled in, his strength finally gone. As the morning broke bright, clear and cold outside, Johann looked out once as what he assumed would be his last sunrise before slipping into a sleep so deep that it bordered on death.

The *Reuben James*, 2386 CE

Timmerman was at the shuttle port to see Colonel Patrick off.

He almost didn't recognize the Marine; only the fact that he was the lone person at the port not in uniform gave him away. Instead of the lean, tightly muscled, forty-year-old Marine officer, he saw a portly, graying man with dark brown eyes and a hooked nose, wearing a baggy, ill-fitting gray coverall and an old, navy blue trench coat. Timmerman laughed.

"I told you I was good at this," Patrick told him.

"You are at that," Timmerman said. "Here, I've got something for you." He handed over three golf-ball-sized objects.

"Grenades?"

"UV grenades," the frigate captain said. "My chief engineer cooked them up. Like my grandpa always used to say, if you're going to go hunting, you'd better use enough gun."

"I suppose so. All right then—see you in two weeks."

"Be careful."

Patrick grinned, saluted, and climbed into the shuttle.

On the surface

The sun crept slowly over the horizon as Patrick made his way into town. He had a carrying bag full of cheap, worn clothing, a small toiletry bag that concealed a small prosthetic disguise kit, the UV grenades, a pocketful of Confederate dollars, a Callistan ident card in the name of William Parker, and a thumbnail-sized tight-beam neutrino transmitter.

He walked up the nearly deserted main drag of Nova Reno. As he expected, the ends of the strip of casinos held the cheaper, more run-down lodgings; he went into one of those, a dump inaptly named the Royal Arms. A few tired-looking patrons were still moving about the casino.

The lobby smelled of stale cigarette smoke and liquor, under-lain by the faint smell of a locker room. The carpet had been red at some point but was now mostly a pattern of odd stains and worn spots. Even now, at sunrise local time with most of the estab-lishment's patrons sleeping off the previous night's excesses, the casino was alive with whirling and blinking lights, the beeping, burbling, and clinking of the gambling machines. A service droid scuttled past with an empty drink tray.

Patrick walked to the check-in counter. A clerk sat at the desk behind a polymer screen, head laid on his crossed arms on the desk. He was snoring.

The Marine rapped on the counter. "Hey!" he called. "You back there, wake up!"

"Wha?" The man, a dumpy, pudgy, gray-haired man with the broken-veined face of a severe chronic drinker, stirred and looked up. "Whatcha wan'?"

"Need a room," Patrick said.

"Long or short term?"

"Couple weeks."

The old man grinned, revealing a forest of rotting teeth. "Long-term, then—short term's measured in hours, pally."

"Whatever you say. Long-term, then. How much?"

"Forty bucks a day, I need the first and last day in advance. Inter-Visa, cash, or other?" the man asked.

"Cash." Patrick pulled a few bills out of a coat pocket. He found a hundred-dollar bill, handed it over.

A steel tab slid out of the countertop. A small glass oval on the top of the tab glowed with a soft green light. "Thumbprint." The man yawned.

Patrick placed his right thumb on the screen, held it a moment; he wasn't concerned about the record—his current thumbprint belonged to a ninety-year-old woman in a long-term care facility on New Wichita.

The clerk looked at his terminal screen. "Fine," he said. He passed two ten-dollar coins over. "You're in four-oh-six. Lifts are at the back of the casino, fourth floor, turn right. Thumbprint pad on the door is your key."

"All right." Patrick pocketed his change, picked up his bag, turned, and walked through the casino.

Nothing much will happen until evening. May as well lie up and relax for an hour or so, then go out and get a look around.

The room was old and worn, but reasonably clean. There was a bed, a small round table with two chairs, a vidscreen/terminal, and a small bathroom with a static-jet shower. Patrick tossed his coat on the table, kicked off his shoes, and sat down at the terminal.

OK, he thought. *If I was Hess, where would I appear? I expect he won't be moving around much during the day.*

An image came to mind: Hess's 'granddaughter,' a tall, Amazonian woman with raven-black hair. *And where would she be hanging out?*

He opened a local directory on the terminal and searched through listings for a few moments. *They'll be looking to move into the planet's power structure somehow ... that means getting close to Giovenco. They'll try to initiate contact somehow.*

He looked at his search screen. One nightclub's name looked familiar. He tabbed to a local area map.

I'll be damned. Right next to the boss-man's HQ. That's right—he mentioned he had a club of his own. If Hess wants to move in, that's the place he'll have to start.

It was worth a try. Patrick went into the bathroom, drank a tumbler of water, and lay down on the bed to nap for a few hours before starting his reconnaissance.

Wallachia, 1459 CE

He awoke suddenly. Strangely alert, he examined his surroundings.

The rock walls of the tiny cave hemmed him in. He could see outside, where the long shadows bending east indicated a sun about to set. *I've slept a whole day here? Maybe more?*

Johann moved his arms and legs experimentally. The blood on his tunic was dried into a crust, but his shoulder did not hurt—nor his head. He pulled the collar of his tunic open, examined the wound, and was amazed to see only a faint, pale scar.

With a start he realized he wasn't cold. His pale skin felt cool to the touch, but the chill air of the late December alpine evening bothered him not at all. The memory of the weird, skeletal figure from the early morning came back to him, as something vaguely remembered from a dream, along with a word he had first heard from old Alexandru Lacusta:

Wampir.

He clambered slowly, cautiously out of the cave and stood in the shadow of the rock overhang. He felt fit, able, and strong. Half-remembered stories from the village made him slowly, experimentally extend one long, narrow hand into the pale evening sun.

Agony! The sunlight scalded him like boiling water. He snatched his hand back.

So, he thought, *fate has dealt this all upon me—my family has been destroyed, my life's work taken from me, my adopted home and my friends massacred.* He held up the hand that the sun had burned, saw the reddened skin already drying, flaking away to reveal healthy new skin underneath. He noted that his fingernails had lengthened, thickened, to look more like claws.

No, he decided at last. *Fate has not dealt harshly with me. God has not dealt harshly with me. What God could allow such a fate to befall such good people? No. Suleiman Bulut, the Ottoman, he is the one responsible. No fate, no God brought him here. No God made him do what was done there.*

He raised a hand to his mouth, felt his eyeteeth, which were sharp, more pointed than he remembered. *No God has visited this curse on me, this curse of dark power—but I will turn it back, turn this curse into a blessing. And when I am done, no God, no fate will save Suleiman Bulut from me. This much I vow.*

When the sun set at last, he set off down the mountain towards Svato. The journey that took him a full night before, wounded and in agony, he now reversed in a few minutes. A long-legged, distance-devouring lope took him swiftly through the night; leaning forward, he bounded over deadfalls, ran through the forest night like a wolf. The darkness proved no hindrance; he could see in the dark woods as easily as in a sunlit field.

Arriving in Svato, he surveyed the ruin of the town. All homes and buildings burnt; a pile of dead bodies still lay in the town square, stiff in the cold. He went among them, recognizing the bodies of friends. He looked once up the street to where the village children had been taken, saw the shapeless mass lying in a field at the edge of the woods, but the last, shrinking remnant of his humanity would not let him go see.

At last, he walked to the edge of the town, to where the Rote Hexe had stood. The inn was burned to its low stone foundation. Only the stones and ashes remained.

Johann Hess fell to his knees in front of the ruin. Grief had gone; rage filled him, rage and a lust for revenge. His eyes blazed red as he threw back his head and howled his fury to the black, star-shot sky.

Behind him, a faint voice called. "Brewmeister Hess.". He stood, turned, saw a slight figure. He went to find the only other survivor of Svato—a boy of thirteen years, Stefan Niculescu, the boy who had kept watch from the ridge.

"Stefan," Johann said. "What is this? How have you escaped?"

"When they were driving us up the street," Stefan said, "me and the other children, I managed to sneak off—I hid under my father's house. I was burned when they set fire to it but managed to escape to the woods." He held up one arm, the skin blackened.

"My side, too—I fear I cannot recover." As Johann watched, the boy collapsed on the ground. "I came back here to die in my home, found all burned... then I heard you here."

"No," Hess said. "You will not die." He went to the boy, guided by an infant instinct, gifted to him by the virus that rapidly multiplied in his blood, his bones, his organs, changing him. He took the boy's burnt hand, examined it. "You are badly hurt, Stefan, but you will live."

"How?" the boy asked in a helpless tone.

Johann Hess offered no spoken reply. Instead, he took the boy's unburned hand and gently, oh so gently, lifted it. He bit the boy on the ball of his thumb, drank a tiny amount of his blood, and passed some moisture from his mouth into the wound. Johann had no idea what a virus was, how to spread the condition, but some instinct told him what to do.

"You will live," he assured the boy. "You will need a place to sleep, a place where the sun will not find you. You will recover. When you do, follow me to the north. Suleiman Bulut, the Ottoman, he is responsible for all this—remember that, seek out his men, seek him out, and deal with him as best you can. Do you understand me, boy?"

"Yes," the frightened lad breathed.

Johann lifted the boy, took him to the open passage to the Hexe's cellar, and placed him inside. "Sleep now, rest, recover. Remember what I have told you."

"I will," Stefan said.

Johann nodded. He climbed the narrow steps, went outside, and looked up once more at the uncaring stars. He took a last look around the ruins of Svato—the ruins of his life as a mortal man—and set off at a ground-devouring lupine lope on the road north.

Roman Holiday, Hess's flat, 2386 CE

It was normally old Hess's habit to sleep through most of the daylight hours, but the prospect of a profit was always enough to keep him awake. He felt the prospects for Roman Holiday were excellent, perhaps even for long-term investment, and so he arose after sleeping three hours and began his research anew.

The planetary 'Net was still in its infancy but did include several local news services. A name in one of the Nova Reno server listings caught Hess's eye.

Giovenco. Christine mentioned him—the founder.

He tapped the story headline to read the rest. The story itself was of no importance—some drivel about a gathering to celebrate the anniversary of the first landing. It was the tri-di image of Giovenco that caught his eye.

"Don Vincent and Contessa Giovenco," he read the caption. He tapped his datapad screen to enlarge the image. "Well, well," he breathed. He tapped again, and the image sprang from the datapad's tiny screen to hover in mid-air in front of him. He squinted carefully at Contessa Giovenco's image.

"A surprise indeed," he breathed. *Why would she be with this man, come all the way from Earth? And who is he ... ? There is something about the timing of all this.*

Hess had a remarkable memory, one that held nearly a thousand years' worth of data. That thousand years had left him with uncanny abilities to reconstruct events from what would seem to be insufficient data. There was no human plot, plan, or cleverness that Hess had not seen before.

He reduced the image back to the screen, and brought up a search utility, linked it to the recently updated databanks in the main computer of the *Red Witch*, parked several kilometers away at the landing field.

An hour later, he knew everything he needed to know in order to take the next step.

Chapter Nine

Wallachia, 1461 CE

It was a bright, warm summer evening when Johann was brought before the great *Voivode*, the Impaler, Vladimir Dracul, who led the crusade against the Turks. A senior commander in Vlad's army, a Saxon from one of the autonomous Saxon towns, led Johann into a large dining hall in Vlad's palace at Târgoviște.

Rough men sat around the table, feasting on steaming-hot meats, swilling wine and ale, laughing at coarse jokes. The Saxon led Johann past them, to the head of the table. "This is the man, sire," he said to a tall, thin man seated there.

Johann bowed slightly from the waist, never taking his eyes from Vlad's. The prince was a tall man, with a high-templed, narrow face, sunken cheeks, and large, glittering eyes. A large mustache covered his upper lip. Seated in a rough chair covered in wolf furs, Vlad noted Johann's gaze.

"You bow before me, but do not avert your eyes," Vladimir Dracul said.

"I mean no disrespect, of course," Johann replied with a slight smile. "It is not every day one meets a legend, sire." His vampire instincts, full-blown now, were in play; flattery would get him everywhere with this prince.

Vlad laughed. "Indeed," he said. "Your accent betrays you. Are you from one of the Saxon towns?"

"I am not, sire," Johann told him. He could be this honest, at least. "I am from Bavaria, the town of Augsburg. I came to your lands to open an inn, but my inn was destroyed by the Ottomans. Since then, I have followed your army, serving as a leecher and sawbones."

"Quite a good one, indeed, that Ælfred brought you before me. He tells me that several men, wounded unto death, recovered completely in your care, when everyone else thought them to be goners."

"I have a talent for healing, Lord."

"You do at that," the Dracul said. He looked carefully at Johann, noting his glittering yellow eyes, his long fingers, his chisel-like nails, his pale, sallow skin. "Yes, I can see you do—this 'healing' you do I have seen somewhere before, yes? Never mind," he said, waving a hand, silencing Johann before he could speak. "Many are the tales of these lands. My people are an ancient people; they tell many strange stories. Perhaps you have heard some of them?"

Johann didn't trust himself to answer, and so just shook his head. *He knows. He has seen my kind before.*

"Well, never mind. I can make good use of you. You will serve me directly, go where I send you, and serve my army as needed. For now, I think, you will accompany Ælfred here into the lands at the foot of the mountains to the west; he is tasked with capture of the Ottoman thief and raider, Suleiman Bulut." The Dracul noted Johann's expression. "I see," he said, his voice heavy with irony, "that you know that name."

"I do indeed," Johann said. "It was he and his that burned my town."

"You will be well motivated, then."

Again, Johann said nothing, but his expression was more eloquent than words.

"Good," the Dracul said, reading the Bavarian's face. "Sit yourself down, then, and eat at my table. Eat well. You'll need your strength in the weeks to come."

Roman Holiday, 2386 CE

"There," Christine said, her voice inaudible to the normal ear over the Evensong's thumping music but easily heard by old Hess's enhanced senses. "That table, in the corner. That's them."

Hess glanced sideways for only a moment; it was enough. He grinned at Christine and toasted her with his wineglass. "Well done, granddaughter."

Christine regarded the old man. He was unusually well turned out for the evening, in a black dinner jacket, black trousers, and a dark red shirt and tie. His unruly white hair was smoothed down and combed, and a pair of dark glasses hid his yellow eyes. Christine was modestly dressed in jacket and slacks, as she and Hess were not on the hunt tonight—not for blood nor for sex.

"Well," she told the old man, "you wanted to see him. There he is. What now?"

"I'm not sure yet," Hess said. "I wanted to confirm a suspicion I had about Contessa; I had the seed of a plan, but we needed some leverage. I believe I have that now."

"I'm not sure what you mean."

"Leverage," Hess explained, "a piece of information, something we can use to persuade the Don to do business with us. We left Jinx with a considerable profit, and this seems an excellent place to invest that money to generate long-term revenue. The thugs running this planet welcome outside investment, but the terms offered most outside businesses are less than ideal; 'The Organization,' as they style themselves, take a large cut of every business' profit." He sipped his red wine and looked at her over the top of his glasses. "I propose to avoid having that cut taken from our efforts here."

"And so, you needed leverage, as you put it," Christine said, amusement in her voice. "You intend to blackmail him."

"To put it bluntly, yes," Hess said. "I have some information; this 'Don' is not what he seems, not even close."

He took another sip of wine and glanced around the nightclub. "A profitable enterprise, this. All these people, drinking and laughing. The sale of liquor on this planet, in this city alone, must be considerable."

"I suppose so. Is that your plan?"

"Ever since the Dark Ages, child, there has been vast potential for profit in any enterprise that caters to mankind's vices; this world is an excellent illustration of that. Why should we not get our share of the profit?"

"Is that what we're here for? Profit?"

"What else?" Hess grinned and then looked up at the nightclub's ceiling. "Wait, child, until you've lived nearly a millennium, as I have. Diversions become scarce, making money in an ever-changing society is one of the few real challenges left." Hess had long since realized that several hundred years of life qualified him to answer not just one question but a thousand, and challenges of any kind came few and far between.

He continued: "Some look at the night sky and see adventure, new worlds to explore, new creatures to discover. I see a sky of diamonds, child—a sky full of opportunities to further secure my, and now your, financial security. You have already learned that to travel as freely as we do is expensive; living the life we lead requires considerable resources. This is not my first long-term investment and will not be my last; you have already learned the value of anonymity in longevity, now you must learn the value of financial stability as well. That, child, is why I wish to take on this venture."

"Well, we do have the capital available," Christine thought out loud. "We should have more than enough to set up inventory and a distribution network. On a planet like this one, that could be a very lucrative long-term investment."

"My thoughts exactly." Hess's voice suddenly changed, his eyes flared red behind his glasses for the briefest of moments, casting a faint ruddy glow on his face. Something was wrong. He felt eyes on him.

"Child," the old man whispered after a moment, "get up, casually, walk to the main entrance, and walk out into the casino. Wait there for five minutes and then go back to the flat. I will meet you there."

Christine looked at the old man's face. "We have a tail," she guessed.

"Indeed. Someone familiar. I will go out the back door here into the alley; I suspect he will follow."

"And what will you do?"

"I shall politely ask him what he wants, child, of course. Go now. I will see you shortly."

Christine frowned but got up and strolled slowly to the nightclub's entrance. In the doorway she stopped, looked back once, and walked out. Nobody followed her.

Very well. Come, then, let's see what you're after. Hess got to his feet, drained the last of his red wine and walked briskly to the back door.

Across the room, a bulky figure got up and walked nonchalantly after him.

Wallachia, 1461 CE

December, and Johann traveled south with Vlad's army, forty thousand strong. They crossed the Danube and struck south into Ottoman lands, burning, killing, and raping as they went. The army went as far as the Black Sea, killing over twenty thousand villagers and soldiers.

Johann was cautious; he converted a few among the wounded, only those in which he recognized a particular passion, a strength, a lust for revenge. A boy, one Belos Ionescu, was one such; a Turkish lance had struck him a mortal wound, but Johann turned him, fed from him, gave to him, and set him on Suleiman Bulut's trail. Stefan Niculescu was another of Johann's 'children,' as he thought of his converts; he followed Johann's direction on his recovery and returned to fight at Johann's side for a while, until his growing strength forced a split. Stefan left Johann to serve a Saxon *boyar* then, and Johann heard no more from him.

Johann learned to love the clash of battle. The noise, the glory, the excitement! Most of all, the blood—as he grew stronger, more confident, as he honed his abilities, his thirst grew ever stronger as well. But he remembered how he had come to be what he was, and so preyed only on the Turks and their allies, only on the soldiers of the nation that had sent Suleiman Bulut raiding into Wallachia. The local villagers and farm people, he left strictly alone, and admonished his 'children' to do likewise.

Serving as Vlad's sawbones did not prevent him from fighting alongside the common soldiers. His name began to spread in Vlad's army; they called him the German Devil, Johann the Black, after his habit of always going abroad in a heavy black hooded cloak to protect him from the sun. He fought as one possessed, whirling a heavy broadsword like a child's toy. In one battle alone, he was seen to kill a dozen Turks in as many minutes, screaming his rage the entire time.

And so his legend spread.

Vlad Dracul's goal had initially been the old capital of the eastern empire, Constantinople itself, but the army fell short, returning to Wallachia in the spring in 1462 with a hundred thousand of Mehmed II's troops in pursuit.

The numbers of the Ottoman army were irresistible. In June, the Sultan's men marched into Târgovişte itself, forcing Vlad to flee. Johann was forced to escape into the high Carpathians. His rage was profound, but useless; for the time, his revenge would have to wait.

Ah, he reminded himself as he climbed into the mountains alone, *but time is on my side. Suleiman Bulut will grow old.* He paused to look at his reflection in a small pool; he examined his shock of white hair, his gaunt face, his hollow eyes glittering yellow in the pale light of the evening. *Despite whatever I may look like, I will not grow old. In time, I will take my revenge—or one of mine will.*

Roman Holiday, 2386 CE

Hess walked out the door into the night, stepped away from the door, and waited. It only took a moment. The voice from the shadows was strangely familiar.

"Johann Hess," the man said. "Or whatever name you're using now. Stop right there, please."

The side street was dark; only the slight glow from a street-light cast faint shadows into the alley. Hess inhaled, cataloging odor and voice both; both were familiar, especially the odd, metallic tang of scent. He recognized the man from observations he had made of Hogmanay's key people on Jinx.

"Imagine that," the voice said. "I came here looking for you, and *bang*, find you the first night. I should get a bonus for this."

"Paddy Toombs," the old man said without turning. "How interesting it is to find you here, so far from your dead master."

"Toombs," the voice said. "Yeah. About that."

Hess waited. He held his hands clear of his jacket and slowly turned to face the voice. He saw a stocky, older man in shabby clothes—the scent and voice matched, but not the appearance.

"I'm not Paddy Toombs," the man said. "Obviously." He didn't ask how Hess knew him by his previous cover name; he presumed the old man had resources that he, Patrick, wasn't aware of.

"Who are you then? Speak up! My time is valuable."

"Lieutenant Colonel Robert Patrick," the figure said in a low voice. "Confederate Marine Corps, working for Navy Intelligence."

"Ah." Hess wore a cat's smile now. "*You* were the Confederacy's mole inside Hogmanay's organization."

"Obviously."

"And you have followed me here to Roman Holiday, for what? You have no authority to arrest me. I've read the Confederate Constitution—the Navy and its personnel are expressly forbidden from interfering in law enforcement matters, and you are outside the Confederacy's territory in any case. Am I to believe you are here to try to kill me? Ah, but many have tried over the long years."

"I'm not here to kill you, Hess—at least, not yet."

"Not yet," Hess repeated. "Indeed. Say on, then—what is it you want?"

"You should know that there are charges against you in the Confederacy," Patrick said. "The Confederate government knows what you are—what you and your 'granddaughter' are. I am to tell you, from the president, that you are strongly encouraged to remain outside the Confederacy's boundaries for the foreseeable future."

"So? The president seeks an accommodation, eh? What am I offered in return?"

"Formal charges will be dropped. Your description and records will be expunged from the Navy and Confederate Bureau of Investigation databases."

Hess leaned back against the steel rails of the fence that ran along one side of the alley. "And if I break that agreement?" He reached behind him, plucked a centimeter-thick steel bar from the fence's frame, bent it in a tight horseshoe and tossed it on the alleyway in front of Patrick. "Will the Confederacy send someone like you after me?"

Patrick grinned. "Not someone *like* me, no. I'm sort of one of a kind." He picked up the steel bar, bent it straight again and dropped it on the pavement.

"Indeed." Hess laughed. He clapped pale, spidery hands together. "Bravo! You are not one of us—let me guess, cybernetics?"

"Full-body prosthetics," Patrick agreed. "Arms, legs, most of my chest and abdomen are all artificial. I have enhanced musculature and skeletal structure pretty much everywhere. The same kind of nanotube smart-fiber used in the adaptive armor the Marines wear. Even part of my brain is artificial, a quantum neural net like they use in independent AI robots.

"I was in a bad skimmer crash when I was nineteen—lost both legs, one arm, paralyzed from the neck down. The Navy Department offered me a deal. Volunteer for an experimental prosthetics program, in return for twenty years' service, should the operation succeed. As you can see," he held out his arms, "It succeeded."

"And so it did. I am surprised that they did not simply do a regeneration technique. Stem cell regen procedures have been routine for some time now."

Patrick smiled. "That twenty year arrangement I mentioned? I fulfilled that seventy-six years ago." He shrugged. "If I'm injured, or something fails, it's just a matter of finding a spare part. I like the work, it suits me, and so I kept going. Mandatory retirement ages don't really apply in my case."

"And yet the Cybernetics Act renders specimens such as you illegal," Hess pointed out.

"Passed two years after I was fitted with my first prosthetic body. You might say I was grandfathered in."

"Indeed," Hess nodded. He didn't look particularly surprised. "Let me ask you, Colonel—why is it in the president's interest to offer me this accommodation?"

"Predators serve a purpose," Patrick said. "Having you out here on the periphery could serve to keep things in check. The president has no illusions of being able to contain someone like you in a prison; therefore, he prefers to keep you out in the unaffiliated worlds, serving as... shall we say, a controlling influence... on the kinds of people that these planets attract."

"I will accept no authority over my actions outside the Confederacy," Hess offered. *Or anywhere else.*

"The president requests none. He presumes you will continue your usual activities once you return to the Rim Worlds; that is sufficient."

"Return to the Rim Worlds? What will become of Roman Holiday? I had not entertained any notions of returning to the Rim."

Patrick looked into Hess's eyes. "The Assimilation bill in Congress will have the Confederacy absorb this planet, along with a few other unaffiliated worlds. It's going to pass the House of Selectmen soon, and the Confederate Senate will approve it; what's more, Roman Holiday is in a strategic location. We need a Navy base here, and the president will make it worth the planetary government's while."

"I propose that your president will fail," Hess said. He smiled widely, showing pointed, yellow teeth. "However, I may be able to offer a counter-proposal." He explained for several minutes.

"I'll have to call this in," Patrick said. "It will take some time for a hyperphone message to arrive from Tarbos."

"I am," Hess said, "a patient man. After all this time, I could scarcely be otherwise."

"One other thing," Patrick said. "I'd appreciate it if you contacted whatever crew you left on your ship up there—tell them we're working a deal. It wouldn't do to have them get any ideas about the Navy frigate that's hanging up there in geosynch over Nova Reno."

Indeed. Hess chuckled inwardly, managing to hide his surprise. *This Giovenco, this boy, he must have left such an obvious trail.* "I will contact them," Hess agreed easily, "and inform them that they are to take no action against any ship of the Confederate Navy."

"Very well," Patrick said. "Then I'll leave you to go about your evening's business. I'll be in touch."

"Stay well, Colonel, and be cautious."

"Always." The Marine faded into the shadows.

Hess walked away towards the main street, well pleased with this turn in events. *I can use the signals suite in the* Red Witch *to contact that second ship. This will be interesting indeed.*

496

Wallachia, 1462 CE

Vlad had been captured and imprisoned in Transylvania, his army dispersed; his brother, Radu the Handsome, was installed on the throne. Johann Hess and his followers were known to have served Vladimir directly, and so the forces of Radu and of the Sultan Mehmed all sought them.

Johann took refuge in an abandoned castle on the Wallachian-Transylvanian border, in the hopes that the Dracul would return from exile. He restored the ancient pile, built in some long-forgotten time by some long-forgotten *boyar*, and furnished it. In this he had the help of a local Gypsy tribe. The Szgany Sandu seemed willing to serve him, and so Johann left them alone, feeding not on their blood nor taking advantage of their daughters; instead, he housed them in his castle and placed them under his protection.

It was the Sandu chieftain, old Yulian Sandu, that brought Johann a warning from a nearby village where he had gone for news.

"Master," the Gypsy had said, addressing Johann as he habitually did; the Gypsy 'king' seemed to admire Johann's tenacity, his strength, and willingly served as his eyes and ears in the Carpathians. "Master, word comes from the south—the Sultan has offered a reward for you, a substantial reward—enough for a man to buy a kingdom of his own! Radu the Handsome has offered lands, titles, gold, all to the man who brings you in. You and yours—your sons Belos and Stefan, your daughter Catherine, all of them."

Johann digested this news. "It would be unwise to stay here, then, so close to the Sultan and Radu. Perhaps we should move, my friend."

"Where will we go, Master?" the fawning old Gypsy asked.

Johann thought a while. "North," he said at last, "North and west. I'll return to the Empire, to Bavaria, for now." Too many knew him here in Wallachia and in Transylvania. Too many of the Sultan's men knew him by sight. An important lesson, that; Johann knew that it was within his power to live for centuries, but longevity would be synonymous with anonymity. He was destined to live always in the shadows, not only hiding from the sun but also from notoriety.

It was a lesson that would serve him well through the centuries.

The *Reuben James*, 2386 CE

Commander Timmerman was just thinking of a hot supper in the wardroom when the signals rating called out a message. "TBN transmission from the surface."

"Patrick," Timmerman muttered. "What's he want?"

"Voice channel to you, sir, private."

"Very well. Put him through here." Timmerman extracted a tiny headset from the arm of his bridge chair, put it on. "Go ahead, TBN, this is Romeo," he said, adhering to secure procedures even with the almost-impossible-to-track tight-beam neutrino transmission.

The faint crackling hiss of the TBN connection washed into the headset. "Romeo, this is Papa," Patrick's voice came in.

"Go ahead, Papa."

"Romeo, I'm sending up an encrypted message. I need you to forward it by hyperphone to Navy Intelligence at the Tarbos Fleet dock, under the code header 'Perfect Sunset.'"

Timmerman blinked. "Copy that, Papa. You all right down there?"

"Finer than frog hair, Romeo. Fleet will be sending an encrypted reply."

"We'll forward it on. Papa, clock's ticking. What's your status?"

"I'm going to need some more time," Patrick said. "Three weeks, minimum. I'll have to get that message back and act on it."

"Home base isn't going to like that," Timmerman complained. "They are only expecting us to be gone two weeks, tops. They're still cleaning up things at our last stop."

"Contact the mother ship," Patrick suggested. "Tell him Navy Intel requests your assistance for an additional thirty Standard Days, and give them that code header."

"Copy that, Papa. You need anything from us? Getting kind of dull up here."

"Any news on that pirate ship?" Patrick asked.

"In fact, yeah. They're just hanging out there, about a thousand kilometers east of us in geosynch; they have to know we're here, but they aren't doing anything. They sent a big shuttle to the surface about ten hours ago, it hasn't come back up yet."

"Probably taking something down to our boy. If you can sneak it in, tag those ships with an encrypted burst-transmission hyperphone beacon, but otherwise leave them alone. Other than that, I'm doing just fine. Thanks, Romeo. Papa out."

"Well, I'll be a son of a bitch," Timmerman said into the headset. He looked over at the signals rating.

"Encrypted message coming in on the TBN, Cap'n," the EMT2c said.

Later that evening

Christine's eyes went wide as a knock sounded on the door. Hess grinned at her, got up, and opened the door to reveal Contessa Giovenco.

"Good evening, Contessa," the old man greeted her. "Or should I say Colleen? Colleen—oh, let me think—Colleen Connelly. That is the last name I remember you using."

Contessa's usual vacant smile was gone, replaced by a cold, calculating look. "Jonas. Or is it Johann? Günter, perhaps?"

Hess looked up at the ceiling. "Günter? I do not believe I have ever used that name. Perhaps I should." He looked back at the girl in the doorway. "Hess will do, my dear. I've been expecting you. Will you come in?"

She said she would and did.

Contessa cast a sharp look at Christine before taking a seat on the couch. "One of yours?"

"Belos' daughter," Hess agreed. "My granddaughter." The old man sat in the room's only chair, across from Contessa. "What can I do for you this evening, Colleen?"

"I think you know," Contessa answered. "I want you to veer off. Don Vincent is *my* mark. I've been working on this for a long time now. I won't be moved in on, old man."

"I had no doubt of that," Hess answered calmly. "But I have information which you do not possess, and I may be able to help you with a problem you do not yet know you have."

"And in return?"

"The Navy seeks Christine and me, due to a small... miscalculation... I made on our last planetfall. They know we are here on Roman Holiday. You and Don Vincent will help us to disappear from the Confederacy's sight."

Contessa/Colleen laughed. "A miscalculation, old man? *You*? The notorious Hess, who calculates every move to the inch?"

Hess' grin faded. "We are none of us perfect," he snapped.

"Wait a minute," Christine barked. "Who are you, anyway, 'Contessa?' And how do you know Hess? Are you another of his 'children,' or what?"

Contessa laughed again. "*His* child? Me, who has known the mighty Chuhulain himself? No, I'm not one of his."

"Child, Colleen had been among the Elite for almost a thousand years before my time," Hess admitted. "She was among the very first."

The tiny red-haired girl's eyes flared red for a moment. She held her head high. "He's right. I knew many of the Ulaid—as the men they were, warriors of Ulster, not the demigods of children's fairy tales. I lived at Emain Macha; I knew the king Conchobar mac Nessa, the druid Cathbad, and oh, yes, I knew Chuhulain." She winked at Christine. "A remarkable man—a, shall we say, *gifted* man he was. For an ordinary man, anyway. But what was I but an ordinary girl, all those thousands of years ago?"

Christine shook her head. "Unbelievable. That was, what, two thousand years ago?"

"Twenty-four centuries ago," Contessa corrected. "Almost two and a half millennia."

"And here you sit," Hess quipped, "not looking a day over a thousand. You must have been keeping yourself well—how is it that you come to this place?"

"With Don Vincent, as you have seen," Contessa answered. "He is a man of vast means. I intend to inherit those means."

"Don Vincent, yes, this man who is not nearly what he seems." Contessa scowled at the revelation of information she did not suppose Hess had. "And the planet?"

"It is a private holding. Part of Don Vincent's estate, should anything... happen... to him."

"The Confederacy will absorb the private worlds in time, you know," Hess warned. "There is debate in the Confederate Congress to that effect even now."

"They won't act for some years yet," Contessa argued, "and the planet's economy will be well-established by then in any case. The income will still be considerable."

"Indeed. Be assured, Contessa, I have no designs on Roman Holiday's economy, except, perhaps, for a small concession? In return for the information I bear?"

"What did you have in mind?"

"Liquor and legal recreational drugs," Hess said quickly, "for the planet."

"For Nova Reno."

"Liquor, recreational drugs, and tobacco, for the city and for all surrounding areas in the district as they grow," Hess countered. "I'm sure they will grow."

"Importing only?"

"Importing and wholesale distribution."

"For how long?"

Hess just grinned.

"What do you offer in return?"

"My silence. Christine's silence. And our aid in dealing with the people that your hacker robbed. I suspect you do not wish Don Vincent to know your true nature, yes?"

Contessa looked thoughtful for a moment. "Very well, then. Done. You have your bargain."

"And you will have your information, and our assistance in dealing with your own problem." Hess said. "Set up a meeting with Don Vincent sometime in the next few days. Send for us when you have made the arrangements, and we will come to you with all of the details."

The small girl who had known the Irish heroes of the first century rose to her feet. "I will. I have your contact code."

"I thought you would." Hess chuckled.

Contessa turned to Christine. "A pleasure meeting you, my dear." She looked up. "Old man." She smiled sweetly at Hess and left.

Christine spoke up as the door clicked shut. "So how many are there?"

"Of us?" Hess asked. "Of the Elite?"

"Of course."

The old man looked thoughtful for a moment. "A hundred. Perhaps less. We have the capacity to live for a very long time, as you have seen, but remarkably few of us do."

"How do you know?"

"I do not, in truth." Hess walked across the room, sat down at the tiny desk. "You do develop a sense for these things." He tapped away on the small terminal on the desk, opening a series of queries into wholesale liquor prices.

Christine decided to let the matter drop. "Do you trust her to keep her end of the bargain?"

"Of course not. I trust no one—not even you, granddaughter. But in a situation of mutual benefit such as this, I see little chance that Colleen will betray us."

"If you say so. One other thing, Grandfather—Contessa, or Colleen, or whoever she is—she looks younger than me, and she is almost fifteen hundred years older than you. If she looks the way she does... well..."

"Why do I look like I do? Like a frail, scrawny old man?" Hess smiled.

"Well, yes."

"Survival, child—survival. Who would think such a feeble old man a threat?"

"Good point."

"You use your looks to your advantage," Hess pointed out. "And since I never have possessed your obvious… *charms*, I use my appearance to my advantage as well."

Christine digested that bit of information with a thoughtful expression.

"We will need to secure some storefronts in Nova Reno—three or four, I should think, to start with. Then we will need at least two more in the outlying suburbs. We will worry about the other towns later. Will you see to it, child?"

"Of course, Grandfather—I'll start in the morning."

Hungary, 1521 CE

Sixty years passed, and Johann again found himself in Hungary, fighting the Ottomans.

Suleiman Bulut was long dead, grown old and eventually dispatched by Johann's 'son' Belos Ionescu. Johann felt a great frustration at Bulut's death by hands other than his own, but decided he would have to accept his revenge by proxy; in the meantime, the culture that gave rise to Bulut, the Ottoman Empire, remained, and so Johann set himself to fight the Turks yet again.

In the interests of preserving his anonymity, he changed his name—easy enough in those times—and became Grigor Hess, a German mercenary in the army of the Hungarian king Louis II.

Hess, as he now thought of himself, fought alongside Louis II's men in the battle of Mohács and was forced to flee when the battle went to the Ottomans. He crossed the river at Csele, at the same ford where the king had drowned an hour earlier, weighed down by his armor. Hess crossed the river and, under cover of darkness, abandoned the army and headed north into Poland.

The following spring found Hess back in Augsburg, where his life began. Using monies earned as a mercenary for Louis II and from booty taken in that conflict, he set himself up as a merchant, dealing in wines and ales, and for twenty years lived in the town as Jonah Hess.

Augsburg had grown in the sixty years Hess had been gone, but he renewed some old ties, striking up a friendship with Adolph Guttenberg, a baker whose grandfather Hess had known before, when he was still merely a man.

It was Guttenberg who, indirectly, set Hess off on his first great round of wandering.

It was a quiet evening in Augsburg, and Hess was seated in a wooden chair in the courtyard behind his place of business when he saw Guttenberg's face appear above the back gate. "Jonah," the tall, lean man called. "Have you heard?"

"Heard what?" Hess answered.

"Rome is sacked. The Emperor Charles II and his men have taken the city."

Hess digested this news without much interest; his former faith had deserted him after the deaths of his wife and children, and sixty years of war had done nothing to renew his faith in the Church of Rome.

"The Pope is said to be fleeing the city. Who knows what will happen next? All Europe may well be plunged into war, my friend."

"Adolph," Hess said, "don't stand out there. Come in, sit down. I've just received a shipment of white wine from Tuscany, let me pour you a little."

Adolph Guttenberg was never one to refuse such an offer; he opened the gate and came in eagerly. Hess got up and went into the kitchen at the rear of his business, returning with two pewter mugs.

"It's bound to be trouble," Adolph said after tasting the wine. "England's King is married to Charles' aunt—he will be caught between the Empire and the pope. Martin Luther is teaching in Germany, and many in the Empire are beginning to listen to him. The emperor will have to either accept Luther and his followers or destroy him. I tell you, my friend, the Church and the Empire have never been at such odds. A fellow would have to go to the New World to escape the turmoil."

Hess started at that comment. His hatred for the Ottomans had not abated, but that crusade seemed impossible for the moment. Life as a merchant was proving dull. Perhaps a life as a pioneer would prove more challenging?

Within a month, Hess had sold his business and departed for Bremen, there to make his way to the New World.

Chapter Ten

Nova Reno, 2386 CE

"Don Giovenco," Hess began, moments after he and Christine were ushered into the planetary bosses' office, "you have a problem."

"And I suppose you have the solution." Giovenco chuckled.

"I do," Hess agreed.

"Well, then," the planetary boss said amiably, "please do sit down, and tell me all about it." He motioned to the two chairs in front of his desk. Christine took the chair nearest the door, while Hess pulled his chair close to the Don's desk. He lowered himself into it, looking like a pale, wizened scarecrow. Outside the thick plasteel window, the lights of a normal Nova Reno evening sparkled and flickered.

Hess reached in a jacket pocket, pulled out his datapad. "Do you follow Confederate news services?" He examined the Don carefully with glittering yellow eyes.

"Not really," Giovenco said cautiously. "We don't get much news out here—once in a while a passing ship updates our servers, but usually..."

"Usually," Hess guessed, "people who come here are not particularly interested in current events, yes?" He chuckled, a dark, oily sound. "Please, Don Giovenco, watch this story." Hess laid his pad on the desk, activated the holodisplay.

> The Confederate Congress is considering HS 1265-
> 09, a bill that would incorporate several unaffiliated
> worlds into the Confederacy, some say by force. While
> the exact provisions of the bill are as yet unknown,
> the main provisions allow for the expansion of the
> Confederacy's borders by twenty parsecs beyond the
> current recognized borders, with the exception of that
> area near the Grugell frontier.

Hess paused the playback. "How far are you, Don Giovenco," he asked, "from the nearest Confederate world?" Don Giovenco's face was creased with worry, rather more so than Hess expected.

The Don looked over his shoulder at a henchman, a small, squat, toad-like man who leaned against the back wall of the office. "Uh," the henchman replied, brows furrowed. "Not that far. That new world, Alcor, is the closest—about seventy-eight light-years, Boss, more or less."

"Well within the twenty parsec limit, then," Hess said. He started the playback again.

> Affected worlds would become subject to the legal
> requirements of the Confederate Constitution, includ-
> ing free and open elections for planetary offices, and
> full disclosure of all planetary officials and authorities.
> The bill was passed unanimously out of the House of
> Selectmen Internal Affairs Committee...

Hess shut the display off. "So," he said, "it seems you are going to be absorbed, Don Giovenco." Instinct told Hess this was precisely the card to play; Giovenco's swarthy face was pale, his breathing fast, and a sheen of sweat made his face glisten.

"What are the odds of that bill passing?" Giovenco asked in a low croak.

"You are of course free to verify my information with any current data you have," Hess replied, "but the president has already indicated his willingness to sign the matter into Confederate law. Because of their proximity to the Grugell frontier, the Rim Worlds are excluded, but it is no doubt due to recent activities in that sector that this bill has gained popular support." Those activities, of course, had been encouraged, aided, and abetted by Hess, although Giovenco had no way of knowing that.

The old man leaned forward in his chair. "I happen to know," he said, "that a ship of the Confederate Navy is in geosynchronous orbit over this planet even now."

"Yeah," the Don agreed. He wiped his face with the back of his hand. "They were in to see me the other day." A holocube lay on his desk; managing a weak smile, the Don activated it. Hess was mildly surprised to see a tri-di of his own face. "They were looking for *you*."

"As I suspected. I also know, Don Giovenco, that another ship is in orbit over this city; I know that this ship has already sent a shuttle to the surface, with at least ten men in it. Those men are now holed up in your city somewhere, and I suspect they mean to do you ill, my friend, or else why have they not gone to any of the local landing fields and registered as per your rules?"

Giovenco looked at his *consigliore*. "Any landings registered in the last few days?"

Giorgio Berculioni again consulted his datapad. "No arrivals in the last five days except for the Navy shuttle, Boss."

"I suppose you might be right," Giovenco agreed. He snapped his fingers. "Giorgio," he called. "Find out where they are. Fast."

"Yes, Don Giovenco." The henchman left quickly.

"Indeed," Hess said. "It seems we both have a problem, Don Giovenco. You do not want your true identity revealed to the Galactic population," he said. "My granddaughter and I do not wish to have the Navy find us, to know our whereabouts—neither here, nor anywhere else we may choose to go. There is a Navy ship in orbit, seeking us—seeking to impose their will on us—and there is another ship in orbit, bearing men of harsh business, who seek you. We can help you deal with these men and to avoid becoming known, Don Giovenco, and you can help us throw the Navy off our track."

Giovenco leaned back in his chair. He examined the ceiling with a thoughtful expression.

Hess picked up his datapad, dropped it back in the pocket of his baggy black pea jacket. "Well?" he asked. "What say you, Don Giovenco? Or, now that we are alone, should I call you El Machete?"

"*What?*"

"Oh, yes." Hess grinned. "Unlike you, Don Giovenco, I stay abreast of current events. I have read of the exploits of El Machete on Earth, the famed Robin Hood hacker. I also read how he disappeared, right after the rumored theft of a great deal of money from an organized crime ring. The final clue was the manufacturer of some specialty hardware on my ship, General Systems on Tarbos—the president of General Systems is, let us say, a confi-dant of mine."

"Griggs," Giovenco breathed, "sold me out..." His voice trailed off on a despairing note.

"He did not give up the information easily," Hess assured him. "But I have spent a great deal of money with Griggs, having some special work done; he is loath to antagonize a good customer, and I must say, he did seem displeased with you."

"I guess he has reason to be," Giovenco said.

"Now," Hess went on, "there is the other matter—a matter of that ship in orbit."

"Who are they?"

"I do not know that," the old man admitted. "They are un-communicative. However, with your hacking skills and the signals suite in my yacht, which is parked at the landing field on the outskirts, we may be able to find out."

"Unless they've got a system I've never seen before," Giovenco mused. "But that's not very likely—I've stayed pretty current. Never know when the old hacker touch may come in handy."

"Useful skills such as that can save you," Hess agreed.

Giovenco's face hardened. He stood up. "All right. Let's go."

Canada, 1675 CE

"You've been to Spanish Florida, then?"

Hess nodded agreement. Outside his small Fort Nelson home, a blizzard howled. "Some years ago—horrible climate. I came through the English colonies and ended up here five years ago, just as Radisson established the fort. Warmer in the Floridas than here, of course," he told his guest, "but the summers are awful. How many Spaniards are dying there in the summers of miasmic fevers is anyone's guess." Hess neglected to mention that he had passed through Spanish Florida over a hundred years earlier. He had passed through the Colonies slowly, stopping wherever his interest was piqued, moving on when he grew bored. After moving through a dozen identities, he was now Fredrick Hess, a native of Mannheim.

"Wanderlust, yes. It does get into one's blood, yes?"

Hess stood up, poured another glass of lager for himself and his guest, and sat back in his chair. His small two-room house, a cabin really, sat on a small rise overlooking the Nelson River. For five years, he'd made a living brewing beer for the small settlement, and satisfied his unusual hungers and lusts by means of an occasional visit to the local Indian tribes. A minor legend was growing around those visits, attributed to some superstition the Indians had of a supposed cannibal spirit called the Windigo. The legend made Hess wonder if, perhaps, he was not the only one of his kind in the New World.

His guest, the British trader Paul Smith, held no such suspicions. The only thought he had for the Indians was to relieve them of their furs for as little as possible. He was a ruthless, mercenary man, and Hess found his utter unscrupulousness intriguing.

"Rumor has it that Radisson and Des Groseilliers have once again sworn allegiance to France," Smith was saying. "And, I suspect, they'll eventually open an enterprise of their own to compete with the Hudson Bay company."

"That will cause trouble," Hess observed.

"Of course!" Smith barked. "Bloody French. They'd love to take over all of Canada. It will lead to fighting, soon enough."

"Fighting, yes," Hess agreed. He admitted to himself that he missed the clash and fury of war; now, in the modern seventeenth century, muskets and cannon would surely lead to greater slaughter than mankind had ever known—and for him, greater opportunities for feeding, and for gathering booty. "I suppose you are right. British and French, here in Canada—it will doubtless lead to trouble."

Smith was looking at his friend with a keen expression. "Seen it before, have you?"

"In '66 and '67," Hess lied easily, "when the English fought the Dutch, yes."

"It won't be like that here," Smith said. He took a long pull at his lager mug. "No big ships, no cannon. It will be bands of rough men with muskets, pistols, knives, and hatchets, fighting in the woods. English traders against French *couriers*, God knows whose side the Indians will take."

Hess smiled. War again—it seemed mankind could settle its differences no other way.

Roman Holiday, 2386 CE

The pirate ship *Edwin Hayes*, late out of the Rim World Wilson, had a fairly recent signals suite for its class, only about twenty years out of date. The *Hayes* had escaped Wilson only a day ahead of the Confederate bombardment of that world, driving to Corinthia to find an encoded message awaiting them—a message that the *Hayes'* Corinthian captain had been expecting for a matter of years.

His orders had been simple: Go to Earth. Pick up thirteen men there; take them to the new unaffiliated colony at Roman Holiday, land ten of them on the surface, and wait in orbit for further orders.

Orlando Teale wasn't very happy with his passengers. The old man, Emil Tamburo of Sicily, was an unpleasant, overbearing sort; his arrogant sons were patently cut from the same cloth. The ten men that were, thankfully, now on the surface were obvious thugs, no doubt practiced killers.

That didn't bother Captain Teale. In his tenure on the Rim, he had dealt with their kind, and far worse. That experience had taught him one thing: the value of keeping scrupulous records of all communications, all requests, all orders given to him and his by clients. The Tamburos were no exception; all exchanges, down to surreptitiously recorded conversations in his ship's wardroom, were stored in a secure, encrypted directory in his ship's computer.

The Tamburos, of course, knew nothing about Teale's records. Nobody did, Teale thought, not knowing that was about to change.

On the underside of Teale's ship was its hyperphone transmitter. That transmitter responded to a brief interrogatory routine that was used to initiate receipt of an interstellar beacon signal. On the surface, Vincent Giovenco was at his terminal, sending just such an interrogation to the *Hayes*.

"What cover are you using for your signal?" Hess asked, curious.

"It's the equivalent of an interstellar wrong number." Giovenco smiled, oddly glad to be back up to his old tricks. "The United Container ore transport ship *Indiana* has a hyperphone ident code only a digit off from this ship; I'm sending a message in United Container's format, looking for a schedule update. The *Hayes'* computer won't even forward that to their signals panel; it will be refused, and a refusal code sent back."

"How does that help you?"

"It's hard to explain," Giovenco said, leaning back in his chair while the signal processed. "I'm kind of flying by the seat of my pants here. I'm hoping that the *Hayes* will have one of the older microswitch computers that holds the hyperphone transmitter open for standard acknowledgement, but that it's current enough to have direct computer control. That gives me a doorway... Ah, there we are," he said. The terminal screen in front of him lit up with a scrolling list of seemingly senseless numbers.

"Standard Universal Dynamics 202 encryption system," the hacker said, "with 256-bit encryption. Why do they even bother," he grumped. "This *mierda* was obsolete twenty years ago." He spun his chair to a second terminal and tapped rapidly. "Yeah, knew I had the key."

"Can you get into their main data?" Hess asked. He was impatient but fascinated; he enjoyed watching a master at work.

"Easy," Giovenco agreed. "I'm scrolling through directories now. Look." He pointed at the screen. "Here's the captain's personal directory. Hyperphone messages, audio files, all sorts of crap. I'm going to copy this to my local system, so we can look at it later—don't want to stay connected too long, always the chance they'll detect us."

"Excellent," Hess said.

"Yeah," Giovenco said, "it's just great—here's a name I recognize. Emil Tamburo. He's on that ship. He's up there overhead right now." The hacker's swarthy face paled a little.

Hess laid a pale, scrawny hand on the man's shoulder, making him flinch a little. "You have nothing to fear from the Tamburos," the old man assured him. "You and I have a bargain, my son, and I intend to carry through. The Tamburos have men on the surface. Find out where they are."

"Sure," Giovenco said. He bent back over his terminal.

"They have a safe house," he said after a moment. "That means..."

"That the Tamburos have men inside your organization," Hess finished the thought for him, "and have had them here for some time." The old man looked thoughtful. "How many men?"

"Ten, according to this," Giovenco said. "Just like you said. Tamburos' regular shooters—these guys will be killers."

Hess shrugged. "Christine?"

"Piece of cake," the seemingly young woman replied. "Get me the location. I'll do it later tonight."

"Then," Hess told the hacker, "we shall take our leave now, Don Giovenco; my granddaughter will need time to prepare."

"Prepare for what?"

Hess told him.

"Her?" Giovenco's face was incredulous. "A woman? One woman? Against ten of Tamburos' hired killers?"

Christine's temper flared; it had been many decades since anyone had questioned her abilities. "A former Force Recon Marine," she snapped, "and two-time kickboxing champion at the Confederate Navy Academy. I've qualified Expert with every personal weapon in the Corps' inventory, and I taught unarmed combat at the Academy for three years." She thought it best not to mention her other abilities, the skills and abilities gifted her by Belos Ionescu and honed by countless lessons from old Hess.

"All right." Giovenco held his hands up. "No argument from me, lady."

Hess grinned at the hacker and led the way out of the building.

On the street outside, the old man pulled his datapad out of his jacket pocket, consulted it briefly. "I'll be informing that Marine Colonel, Patrick, of this."

Christine's eyes shot wide. "What? Why?"

"I have my reasons. Playing the Navy against the Tamburos suits our goals for now, child; if Giovenco fails to stay in control of this planet, then all our plans here will come to nothing. If the Navy gains too strong a foothold, given this bill in the Confederate Congress, our freedom to operate here will be strictly limited." He smiled, extending an arm to indicate the way to their parked skimmer.

"And our potential for profit will be limited as well, right?"

"Yes," Hess agreed easily. "There is great potential here; if we can make this conclude as I hope to, we should be able to set up an enterprise here that will generate income for us for a century or more."

"While we look for opportunities elsewhere," Christine guessed, "inside the Confederacy and out."

"Indeed. I have no intention of allowing the Confederate president to place restrictions on our movements. We will travel as we please, seek opportunities wherever it suits us. No man, in almost a thousand years, has denied me this."

"I hope you know what you're doing, old man," she muttered.

Hess did not reply.

Canada, 1759 CE

Militiaman "Walter" Hess climbed the cliff swiftly, even in the dark, even burdened with musket, bayonet, powder, and ball. He soon outdistanced the other soldiers of the British general James Wolfe, and was first to scramble over the top to see the encampment of the French army spread before him.

It would be sunrise soon. Hess pulled the hood of his non-regulation cloak over his head and crouched in the high grass of the Plains of Abraham, peering into the darkness. A man walked past, fifty yards to his front—a sentry, or just a bored soldier on a stroll, Hess neither knew nor cared. He wore the white jacket of a French regular, and that made him fair game. Hess sprang, taking the man down quickly and feeding on his pulsing bloodstream. He was careful not to let anything of himself get into the man, lest he be converted; Hess knew that, in his youth, he had converted too many, too carelessly. Anonymity required caution.

He lifted his head away from the Frenchman's corpse. He pulled a handful of grass loose, wiped his mouth with it. Grunting and scrabbling noises behind him told him that the other British soldiers were gaining the top of the cliff. Hess drew his hatchet, dipped it in the pool of blood under the Frenchman's neck. When the other British troops approached, he grinned broadly and held the bloody hatchet over his head.

As the sun rose, the British troops held the top of the cliffs. The small camp ahead of them held only forty or fifty men, French troops under the command of Captain Louis de Vergor. The camp was captured in a matter of minutes.

"Walter—oy, Walter!" Hess turned to see an old British sergeant, John Landon, grinning at him. "Be ready, lad—we're going to march on Quebec City, count on it!"

"Keen on it, are you?"

"It's a short life, but a merry one." Landon laughed. "May as well grab a bit of glory."

Short for you, perhaps, Hess said to himself.

Gradually, French militia began to filter into the area, exchanging shots with the British. Several houses were set afire. Hess was sent on a scouting mission to find the French regulars that the British general Wolfe knew to be nearby. He loped through the trees and brush on the northwest side of the field; his black cloak hid him in the shadows of the trees, and his unnatural speed prevented the French from identifying him as a British scout. Within the hour he was back to the British line.

"French troops approaching in column," he reported to General Wolfe's aide. "At least three thousand. Mostly regulars, some militia, some Indians."

Armed with this information, the British were in formation and waiting for the French. Two British volleys set the French into a full retreat.

Within the week, Quebec was under British control. Following the capitulation, "Walter" Hess learned he was to be awarded a citation by the British authorities for his scouting mission.

Public acclaim and public scrutiny, he thought on hearing the news. *Not desirable for one such as I. Once the fighting is over, British*

Canada's soldiers will again be the unwanted orphans. Perhaps it is time to move on. That evening, Hess packed up his personal effects and vanished into the night, bound for the colonies to the south.

Chapter Eleven

United States (Union) 1862 CE

Night had fallen at last. Captain "Abraham" Hess pulled off his slouch hat, ran long fingers through his white hair, and looked up at the stars. *An interesting day,* he mused. *Chasing General Johnston's troops up the Peninsula. McClellan, he is an egotistical incompetent. We have almost twice the men Johnston has, and at every turn the Union army blunders along.*

Hoofbeats behind him, growing swiftly closer, interrupted his thoughts. He turned to see Lieutenant Abner Dean, one of the regimental commander's staff, riding up behind him. As he approached, Dean's horse suddenly shied away and snorted in alarm.

Dean dismounted, shook his head, and led his nervous horse a few yards away, where he tied it to a tree. He walked over to Hess, slapping dust off his dark blue trousers. "Sir," he said, "I begin to appreciate why you walk everywhere."

"Horses have never liked me." Hess chuckled. *Even a dumb animal can sense a predator.* "What can I do for you, Lieutenant?"

"The colonel would like to see you at his headquarters as soon as possible," Dean told him. "We'll be moving west tomorrow again, towards Seven Pines."

"Very well. My compliments to the colonel; I will be along presently." Hess put his hat back on.

"With respect, sir," the lieutenant began.

"Yes?"

"We've been in the field for some time, sir, the spring sunshine has been most pleasant, and you're still pale as death. Are you sure you're quite well?"

Hess was amused but did not show it. "I'm very well, Lieutenant, thank you. I have a medical condition, a photophobia; my skin and eyes are very sensitive to light."

"Ah," Dean said. "The hat and cape."

"Indeed." Hess glanced up once more; the stars seemed particularly compelling tonight. "Very well. Ride ahead, Lieutenant; and inform the colonel that I am on my way."

Dean saluted, mounted his horse and trotted away through the darkness.

Hess walked down the trail after him. Horses and dogs always reacted badly to his presence; horses shied and even reared away, and dogs growled and snapped. *One day an animal will give me away.*

A worry for another day, he decided. Tomorrow or the next day would bring another confrontation; Confederate troops lay in wait for them down the rail line, somewhere near Fair Oaks. In the confusion and clash of battle, Hess would surely find an opportunity to feed, but the mere intake of blood was no longer as satisfying as it had been only a hundred years before.

There must be more to immortality than this; to live forever, to care for nothing but gorging myself like some animal. Always I have served in men's armies as a common soldier or, as now, a minor functionary. Why should this be, when I am among the elite of mankind? Why should it be this way, when four hundred years of life have equipped me not to follow, but to lead?

Anonymity is synonymous with longevity, he reminded himself. *But perhaps notoriety can be exchanged for a new obscurity when my immediate purposes are served; I have the ability to force my will over my flesh to some degree. Perhaps moving from one life to another, one identity to another, I can achieve more—more material success, more power in the world.*

It was something to consider. For now, though, there was this war, this American civil war; and just ahead, down this path that ran alongside the rail line, his commander awaited his presence. He pulled the brim of his hat down over his eyes, adjusted his revolver belt, and walked into the darkness under the trees.

Nova Reno, the safe house, 2386 CE

Enhanced abilities or no, Christine knew there was danger for her in facing a minimum of ten armed men, so she planned and equipped herself accordingly.

It was an hour past midnight as she crept towards the safe house. A black synthetic bodysuit hid her from visual detectors as well as shielding her from infrared scanners. A belt around her slim waist held two flash-bang grenades, a ten-millimeter automatic pistol, and a large, titanium fighting knife. Her head was covered in a black balaclava, her eyes shielded by goggles that protected them from any UV radiation as well as enhancing her already excellent night vision. Black combat boots and fine black leather gloves completed her combat gear.

She paused under a window to listen. Several voices were audible; several were still awake. *I'll have to be careful.*

A second-story window was slightly open to let in the night air that was marginally less hot than usual. Christine looked up, gauged the distance, and leaped, lithely, soundlessly. She caught the sill, slid the window open, and flowed inside.

Someone was in the room; the soft breathing pattern of sleep was as plain as the clash of cymbals in Christine's ears. She moved forward slowly, softly, unsheathing her knife as she went.

A moment later, the breathing stopped. The strong smell of spilled blood activated Christine's hunger, but she fought the urge back—*time enough for that later.* She moved out of the room, listened in the hallway. Two other rooms contained a total of three sleeping men. Christine moved from room to room like a ghost. A minute later, the two rooms contained three dead men, and she was ready to tackle the group on the main floor.

Christine looked up and down the second floor's main hallway. There was a lift shaft at one end; she slipped down the darkened hall and listened to the voices at the bottom of the lift shaft.

"Man," one of them was saying, "I thought this was going to be a fun gig, but I'll tell you—I'll be glad when tomorrow is over with, get that hacker done and get back to Earth. This place stinks."

"I hear you, bro," another voice, lower, guttural, came back.

Tomorrow. As soon as that. Well, they got close.

Christine listened carefully, cataloging voices, heartbeats, breathing—six men were in the large room downstairs, watching some vid programming that involved a woman repeatedly moaning in loud bursts. She scowled, took a flash-bang grenade from her belt, activated it, and dropped it down the lift. As soon as it detonated, she stepped into the shaft, let the grav field drop her gently to the lower floor.

A large, swarthy man was struggling to his feet a meter away. Christine let him have a spinning kick, driving her combat boot into his larynx and shattering it. The man collapsed.

Across the room, two others were on their feet, dazed but functional. Christine drew her pistol, fired twice. Both men dropped.

Christine dropped and rolled. Pistol bullets whined through the air where she had stood a second before. She came to her feet and lunged, flying across the room to a thin, hard-looking man with a large projectile gun. He tried to swing his gun to cover her, but failed, as she stepped inside the arc of his arms and slammed her hand into his solar plexus. As he doubled forward with a grunt, Christine drove her knife into his neck, withdrew it, spun and rolled again.

Two men were rushing her from across the room. Christine grinned inside her mask, leaped, grabbed a light fixture on the ceiling and spun her body to land *behind* the charging pair, fired her pistol once, twice. Both men dropped.

A pair of arms grabbed her from behind. This man was large, strong, healthy, and well trained; he nimbly stepped away from Christine's boot as she slammed it down and back, seeking his instep. His arms wrapped around her chest and squeezed, seeking to crush her. Both of her arms were trapped. The man shook her.

"Kill you, bitch," he hissed, his breath hot in Christine's ear.

"Oh," she said, "I don't think so." Her right hand still held her pistol; she fired down and back, the bullet striking the man's thigh. He let go of her, howling in pain. Christine spun away, aimed, put another bullet into the man's forehead, and fell into a defensive crouch.

There was one more.

His thudding heart gave him away. He was hiding behind a large, overstuffed chair in the corner of the room. Christine strode to the chair, grabbed it, tossed it aside. Behind it, a slight, pale man raised a pistol; Christine grabbed the muzzle and turned it to the side as the man fired. She winced as the bullet passed through her hand, tore the pistol away from the thug, tossed it.

The survivor cowered on the floor. "Who the hell are you?"

Christine reached up, removed her goggles and balaclava. She took the glove off her wounded hand, held it palm-outward towards the little man. "You hurt me, you son of a bitch," she said, her voice deceptively calm and sweet. "But not very badly. See?"

The thug goggled. The wound in Christine's hand stopped bleeding as he watched, the flesh closed up, and pink new skin grew over the injury.

"You came here to kill Don Giovenco," she said amiably. "I'm afraid we can't allow that."

"He crossed Emil Tamburo. Nobody does that and lives."

"You crossed Don Giovenco, little man," Christine informed him. "Sauce for the goose." The scent of hot blood was all around her; she could contain herself no longer. The surviving thug watched in horror as Christine's eyes flared red, as her jaws elongated to house a hell of serrated teeth, as her hands turned to talons. She fell on him then, her teeth meeting in his throat. The last sound the thug heard was the gurgling of his own blood through the ruin of his gullet, and Christine's hissing as she finally fed her raging hunger.

Satisfied at last, Christine finally stood up. Her arms hung at her sides, her breath came short and fast. She stood still for a moment, then spun and sprang at the corner of the room.

An unseen hand caught her, threw her back. She hit the far wall hard enough to shatter the paneling, fell to the floor, and crouched there, hissing. Blood dripped from her fangs. Her eyes glowed like coals. She held her hands out wide, talons ready to strike.

"Calm down, girl," a voice came from nowhere. There was a shimmering in the air, and the form of the Marine Colonel

Patrick swam into view. He wore only a black polymer bodysuit, carried no gear. "Sorry if you're still hungry, but there isn't enough blood in me to feed a horsefly these days." He held up a hand. "Microchromatophore stealth system, built right into my chassis. Some days, being mostly synthetic ain't all bad."

Christine straightened up slowly, slipping back to her normal form as she did so. She stepped to a fallen thug, stripped the shirt from his corpse, wiped her face with it. "What are you doing here?"

"I've got an interest in this too, you know. You, alone, against ten armed killers? I wanted to make sure you were covered."

"You were worried about me," Christine said, her smile deceptively charming. "How sweet." She moved close to him, smiling. "I suppose I should be flattered."

"Don't be." Patrick pushed her back. "And don't try your usual crap with me, girl. I haven't had the urge or the ability for anything like that in almost a hundred years." He tapped his chest. "Prosthetic, remember?"

"Pity," Christine said.

"Are you done here?"

Christine looked around the room. "Yes, that's all of them."

"There's a terminal over there; let's see what they were up to." Patrick stepped to a desk along the far wall, examined the terminal. He tapped a key on the keypad. "Hrm. Encrypted local storage."

"Too bad."

"Don't be hasty. I can get around that. I've probably got algorithms for every encryption scheme ever thought of."

"Really?" Christine asked. She looked pointedly at Patrick's empty hands. "Where?"

"In here," Patrick grinned, tapping the side of his head with a forefinger. He held up his left arm, opened a small portal and extracted a data cable, which he plugged into the system's dataport. Data began scrolling across the terminal's screen.

"Interesting."

"Yes?" Despite herself, Christine was intrigued.

"They've been in contact with Emil Tamburo. Too recently for the signal to have come from Earth…" His voice trailed off.

"Well? What is it?" Christine demanded.

"He's here, all right," Patrick said. "In the system. Emil Tamburo himself. Your hacker was right. That armed pirate ship here in the system, the *Hayes*, he's on it, just like the boss-man said…" Patrick scrolled through the messages, reading at an impossible rate. "These thugs were supposed to send a code signal if they succeeded. If they don't, well, if I'm judging the message traffic right, I expect the Tamburos will bombard the planet from orbit. There's a reference here to some number of thermonuclear bombardment canisters—where the hell did they get those?"

"Do they know your ship is up there?"

"Unless they're stupid or incompetent, they'd have to," Patrick said. "The *Reuben James* is up there in geosynch orbit over Nova Reno, in plain view of everyone, and I'd have to think the Tamburos will have run a recon into the system. The *Reuben James* spotted them some time ago—when the we spotted the first one, we thought it was yours."

"Obviously not. The Navy is prohibited from engaging them here, outside the Confederacy, except in direct self-defense, isn't that right?"

"Exactly." Patrick looked at Christine. "That abort code was inside one of these thugs' heads. There's no way to send it, no way to stop Emil Tamburo, and the *Reuben James* is forced by Navy regs and Confederate law to just sit up there and watch it all happen."

"I have to tell the old man," Christine said. "We can't just let them nuke the city, regulations or no regulations. We'll have to do something. Our ship isn't armed, but maybe we can get Giovenco to do something—he must have some forces. The old man will know what to do." She smiled. "He always does."

"Yeah. You do that. I'm heading back to my hotel, I have to talk to the *Reuben James*. Maybe, between the three of us, we can come up with something."

Germany, 1920 CE

The Great War had given Hess a unique opportunity.

Serving with the 7th Bavarian Field Artillery, he had struck up a friendship with a young man that shared his last name, along with his height and slim build. "Rutger" Hess had managed to force his unruly white hair to grow thick and black, like that of his new companion, and it had not escaped his notice that young Rudolf Hess was roughly his height and shared his square-jawed, rather gaunt face and slim build. When the young man was killed by a severe chest wound, it was easy enough to change places with the young soldier by the simple expedient of swapping identification papers. Therefore, it was "Rutger" Hess that went to the cemetery, and "Rudolf" Hess continued his career after the war ended, returning first to his native Bavaria, and then on to Munich.

It was in Munich, in a small beer hall, that he first heard the man that was to change the course of his centuries-long life.

The man was a failed artist, a veteran of the Great War, a recent dischargee from a Bavarian regiment. While Adolf Hitler was unimpressive physically, Hess recognized something in him, a certain talent for polemics, an instinctive feel for stirring the baser elements in the society of a defeated, post-War Germany.

The man's antipathy towards Jews, Hess estimated, was just another element in his political strategy. After one particularly rousing speech, Hess took the time to introduce himself.

"Rudolf Hess," he told the man, offering his hand to the somewhat wild-eyed man after a particularly bombastic speech. "I am impressed by your words, Herr Hitler." He briefly considered converting Hitler, decided he could control the unstable and somewhat dimwitted man without that. "I would like to learn more of your movement."

"I would be glad to talk more of the German Worker's Party with you, Herr Hess," Hitler told him. "I will tell you this—we require one thing of our members, and that is absolute loyalty." Hitler's dark eyes glittered; Hess knew there was more going on behind those eyes than he was admitting.

Germany is defeated, in turmoil, her currency worthless, her people disheartened. This man may be able, with some guidance, to change all that.

That guidance, of course, "Rudolf" Hess was uniquely suited to provide, with five hundred years of experience in manipulating people and events. Hitler, he was certain, would surround himself with besotted incompetents, as would-be dictators usually did.

"*Jahwohl*, Herr Hitler," he agreed.

Hitler favored him, briefly, with a tight grin. "We will speak more, then," he said, and moved on to the next admirer.

Nova Reno, 2386 CE

Lieutenant Colonel Patrick woke easily after four hours sleep, which was all the remaining organic portions of his brain and body seemed to need any more.

He walked to the bathroom of the cheap hotel flat and ran a glass of water. Opening a can of sugar, he stirred as much sugar into the water as it would hold, then drank it down—fuel for his internal bio-battery. He repeated the process twice more.

That, and a quick swipe of a comb through his hair, was all the preparation he needed for the day to come.

He looked at his chassis—he'd stopped thinking of the mostly mechanical frame as a 'body' decades earlier—and shrugged. *Guess there's no point in disguises any more.*

He held up his right forearm and opened an access panel. He slid his left index finger across the tiny screen in the compartment; his graying hair returned to a more normal brown. Next, he extracted a small needle attached to a length of tubing from his prosthetics kit, inserted it into an aperture in the panel, and tapped a contact; the silicone that he had loaded into his chassis to simulate a slightly overweight, middle-aged man began to run out into the sink.

Patrick turned on the hot water to run the thick silicone run down the drain, and watched as his stature returned to its normal, lean form. With this done, he detached the line, rolled it, and placed it back in the case. Finally, he ran his finger down another slider, returning his eyes from dark brown to their normal steel-gray.

Finished, he regarded himself in the mirror. What he thought of as his 'default' form was much like he had looked when the skimmer accident had robbed him of a normal life, although he had 'aged' himself by fifteen years or so, to look the age a lieutenant colonel of Marines should look. The chassis looked enough like a normal body that few would look at him twice in singlet and running shorts, and few did, as Patrick generally made a physical training regimen part of his routine while on assignment, even though the cybernetic body made it pointless.

Everything comes with a price, Patrick frequently reminded himself. His cybernetic body was no exception.

Shrugging, he walked out into the main room, pulled on a faded gray shipboard coverall. He flipped back his left thumbnail to use his tight-beam neutrino transmitter.

The *Reuben James*, 2386 CE

Commander Timmerman laid his headset back in the receptacle on his bridge chair.

Patrick had solid information; Timmerman had no reason to doubt him. This "Giovenco" that ran the planet was actually the Robin Hood hacker El Machete, and the pirate ship in orbit belonged to neither him nor old Hess, but to an Earth-based *Mafiosi* family bound to destroy the hacker. To that end, one of the ships was carrying a set of orbital nuclear bombardment canisters. It took only moments for the *Reuben James'* scanners to verify that.

"Signals," Timmerman ordered, "prepare to copy a message to COMTASKFOR947. And Weapons, I want an inspection on all missiles and pee-beam projectors."

Just in case, he told himself.

Germany, 1945 CE

Seated in the docket next to Hermann Goering, a man he despised as a dimwitted lackey, "Rudolf" Hess was, for the first time in five hundred years, at a loss for what he should do next.

The words of the chief prosecutor of the Nuremberg Tribunal echoed hollowly in Hess's ears. "In the prisoners' dock sit twenty-odd broken men." The American prosecutor's eyes were hard, his lips tight with contempt.

Contempt we all have earned, Hess told himself.

The American prosecutor, Jackson, continued: "Reproached by the humiliation of those they have led almost as bitterly as by the desolation of those they have attacked, their personal capacity for evil is forever past. It is hard now to perceive in these men as captives the power by which as Nazi leaders they once dominated much of the world and terrified most of it. Merely as individuals their fate is of little consequence to the world."

The previous day, when asked for his plea, Hess had managed to mutter only "No."

I tried to rein these men in, he thought for the hundredth time. *I flew to England, tried to negotiate a peace. The British know I tried. I underestimated that little Austrian worm Hitler. Now his country, my country, lies in ruins. Now I am captured, a prisoner along with these others, these dogs, these scum—Goering, Von Ribbentrop, Keitel, Bormann, Speer, and the others.*

The purpose of the trial was obvious. Mankind was beginning to mature. No longer would the machinations of ruthless men in positions of power be tolerated by the great powers. Hitler was dead, and Hess supposed Stalin would not last long either, in this new age.

Three weeks later, as Hess sat in a semi-torpor, listening to the testimony of the SS General Ohlendorf, a sudden realization shook him fully awake.

Ohlendorf was replying to questioning by an American Colonel Amen, describing his part in Hitler's "final solution." "After the registration," he said, "the Jews were collected at one place; and from there they were later transported to the place of execution, which was, as a rule an antitank ditch or a natural excavation. The executions were carried out in a military manner, by firing squads under command."

Colonel Amen asked him, "In what way were they transported to the place of execution?"

Ohlendorf replied, "They were transported to the place of execution in trucks, always only as many as could be executed immediately. In this way it was attempted to keep the span of time from the moment in which the victims knew what was about to happen to them until the time of their actual execution as short as possible."

"Was that your idea?" the American asked.

"Yes," Ohlendorf replied.

We were no better than the Ottoman scum that butchered my family, Hess thought. *Anna, what would you think of me now? Felix, Elsa, how proud you would be of your father!*

He thought briefly of his latest son, Wolf, not a 'child' of conversion, but rather his child by a woman. Marriage to Ilse Pröhl had been part of his pose, but Hess had exercised care to avoid infecting the innocent woman with the virus that teemed in his blood, and so the son Wolf was nothing more than human. *Wolf, you spent too much time among these men. You too will suffer a fate similar to ours, no doubt.*

I will survive this, Hess promised himself. *I will survive imprisonment; I will survive anything the Allies can hand me for punishment. Henceforth, I will not serve with or for men like these. Instead, I will hunt them. I will not again forget the lessons Suleiman Bulut and Vlad Dracul taught me, all those centuries ago.*

Early the following year, the Tribunal found "Rudolf" Hess guilty of crimes against peace and conspiracy to commit crimes against peace. He was given a life sentence by men who had no idea what that meant to such as Hess, but he decided not to bother himself with that. *I will use this imprisonment to my advantage,* Hess decided. *I have learned an important lesson from all this. Now, I have time to carefully plan my next steps. The world will never be lacking in Hitler's kind. All too many men fancy themselves predators—once I make my way back to freedom, I will teach them what it means to meet a* true *predator.*

Never again will the innocent suffer at my hands. For Anna, for Felix and Elsa, I vow this.

Roman Holiday, 2386 CE

Emil Tamburo stood on the pirate ship's bridge and regarded the main viewscreen impassively. Below the hired ship, the yellow-brown orb of Roman Holiday turned slowly. A few degrees above the planet's rim, the gray form of a Navy frigate hovered.

"Still no message from the surface," Emil heard the voice of the *Hayes'* captain behind him say.

"They've failed, then," Tamburo said.

"Looks that way. Sure you want to go through with your fallback? Damn little of that city will be left if you do."

"The family has forced me to it," Tamburo said quietly. In the last family assembly, a growing aggressiveness on the part of the group had forced Emil to agree to destroy the hacker if he could not easily take over.

The pirate ship captain pointed at the screen. "And the Navy?"

"We're outside the Confederacy," Tamburo said. "Their own regulations prevent them from interfering." He smiled. "Unless, of course, you fire on them first."

The pirate laughed. "Damn little chance of that. I'd just as soon ride one of those nukes down to the surface."

Chapter Twelve

Roman Holiday, 2386 CE

Giovenco's headquarters were as safe as anywhere for a meeting, so that is where the group convened. Giovenco himself, his *consigliore* Berculioni, old Hess and his granddaughter, and the Marine Robert Patrick formed the group that would decide how best to prevent a holocaust.

"What I find confusing," Patrick said after drinks were passed out and normal amenities observed, "is that Tamburo is pissed off enough to nuke the planet over this."

"I took him for thirty big," Giovenco admitted. "That would be enough to piss anyone off."

"Enough to commit an atrocity like this?"

Hess held up a skinny hand. "It is… unusual behavior, even for a thug such as this. One must assume he is under pressure from other sources; he is the leader of a criminal enterprise, and must have others among his subordinates that would relish an opportunity to overthrow him, to take over. Therefore, he must show himself to be more ruthless than they."

"None of this will get him his money back," Patrick said. "That's got to be a big concern."

"Unless he means to take over the planet itself. The profits from operations here alone would serve to recoup what Don

Vincent took from him, many times over, within a short time—ten years at the outside."

"He can't recover anything if the planet is a radioactive ruin," Giovenco objected.

"Colonel," Hess said, "best guess, what capability does Tamburo have in his weapons?"

"Well..." Patrick paused for a moment while the cybernetic portion of his brain accessed data he hadn't had cause to examine before—in other words, knowledge he hadn't known had been programmed into his firmware until he looked for it. "Assuming he has devices manufactured in the Confederacy, any orbital bombardment device he has will have three settings: suborbital, for massive EMP damage to disrupt communications; high-altitude neutron burst, that will kill animals and plants and blow out some electronics but leave buildings intact; and low-altitude air burst, which would pretty much flatten the city. That's a thumbnail; I've got a lot more data."

"That's plenty," Giovenco said. "He wants to neutron-burst all my people and take over our operation."

"That's the logical conclusion," Patrick agreed.

"You people aren't going to just sit up there and let him, are you?"

"The Navy can't do anything about it," Patrick told the Don. "Confederate law prohibits us from interfering in local matters unless we're attacked directly."

"What about what you did on Jinx?" Christine asked.

"Ordered by legal authority—the president, authorized by Congress—in response to direct attacks on Confederate shipping and Confederate Navy ships by units that came from Jinx."

"Yes," Hess interceded, "yes, we're aware of that, just as you, Colonel, are aware that we came here from Jinx. That's not relevant at the moment."

Christine looked up from her datapad. "Can the *Reuben James* place herself physically between the pirate ship and their targets?"

"That would be *legal*," Colonel Patrick said, "but unlikely—Commander Timmerman isn't going to place his ship in front of a nuke. No captain would. If the pirates opened fire anyway, that would give the *Reuben James* shaky legal ground to fire back, but only after they had a nuke launched on them."

"On the other hand, the pirates aren't stupid enough to open fire on a Navy frigate—there are lots of easier ways to commit suicide," Christine pointed out.

"Don Vincent," Hess asked, "what are the chances you could gain access to the Navy ship's data banks?"

"Not very likely," Giovenco said. "Navy systems are pretty damned secure, and I'm a few years out of date. Old systems like on those pirate ships are a piece of cake, but the Navy? No way, *ese*."

"Your ship wouldn't happen to be armed, would it?" Patrick directed the question at Hess.

"No," the old man answered. "The original *Red Witch* was," he said with unusual candor, "but not this one. My first ship required a crew of twenty; I wanted to be able to operate this one myself."

"Times change," Patrick agreed.

"Our strengths," Hess said, "are as follows: Don Vincent can gain access to the pirate ship's databanks. We have one unarmed ship that can achieve orbit, and can perhaps interfere in the pirate's operations." He didn't mention his ship's stolen cloaking device. "We have advance warning of Emil Tamburo's intent, and we know that he is personally present on one of those ships."

"You know," Christine said, "if we can destroy the ship Tamburo is on, we stand a good chance of ending this once and for all. The rest of the Tamburos may well decide to cut their losses.

Thugs aren't generally too anxious to fight an opponent that's shown they can fight back."

"A trick," Hess said, "a deception is what we need here."

"We'll need it fast," Colonel Patrick said. "They may be getting ready to launch even as we speak."

"Christine," Hess said, "please, go to the landing field, prepare our yacht for departure; I'll meet you there shortly. Colonel Patrick, please contact the *Reuben James*, warn them of the pirate's intentions."

"They can't do anything," Patrick objected.

Hess grinned. "Trust me. You have a transmitter in your hotel room, yes?"

"Sure," Patrick agreed. He suspected he was being maneuvered into leaving the meeting; he looked at his thumbnail for a moment, but was unwilling to give away the presence of a signals device so neatly concealed. *I wonder what all the old man is really up to.*

"Time may well be of the essence," Hess said smoothly. "The pirates may be preparing to fire even now. Hundreds of thousands of lives are at stake, Colonel."

"All right." Patrick looked from the old man to the Don, back again. "I'll go now." Frowning, he left the room.

Hess waited a moment, and then turned to Don Vincent Giovenco. "Don Vincent, can you once more gain access to the pirate ship's system?"

"Easy," Giovenco said.

"Another thing," the old man continued. "Would you happen to have a small satellite booster?"

Germany, 1987 CE

Over his years in captivity, he had allowed his hair to grow white again, his face to grow more gaunt, to give the appearance of aging as a mortal would. It had been long enough, Hess decided; forty-five years in captivity was more than enough.

He took the lesson to heart; seeking power was not the path he wished to walk. Let others, with their fleeting, mortal lives, seek power over the destiny of others. Hess would remain in the shadows, profiting from the misfortunes of others. His time in Hitler's company had reminded him of the evil men were capable of; and while they thought of his kind, the Elite, as evil, Hess knew the truth—that men themselves visited far more brutality on each other than he and his kind were capable of.

He thought often of his lost family, of his wife Anna, the children. Evil men had taken them from him. He had taken his revenge, however indirectly, on those men, and now the Ottoman Empire itself was only a memory. But the lessons of World War II were not lost on Hess; evil men still walked the world, and always would.

And if I serve these evil men, how then am I better than they? If I have learned nothing else from Hitler, I have learned that.

Hess set himself to his new purpose with a will. First, he would have to regain his freedom; then, he would set himself to prey on those who fancied themselves as predators, and in doing so, amass resources to help him hunt more efficiently, over a wider range.

But he could do nothing within the walls of Spandau Prison.

For months, "Rudolf" Hess practiced a new art. In the dark of his Spandau cell after lights out, he practiced slowing his heart, reducing his breathing to near-nothing, until at last he could force himself into a state of torpor that was as close to death as was possible for his altered metabolism.

At last, he was ready. August 17th, 1987, and he was allowed into a small summer house in a garden area of Spandau. It was simple enough, to tie an electrical cord around his neck, then around the window latch, and slump to the floor. He slowed his heartbeat to nothing, slowed his respiration to an imperceptible level, and 'died.'

Once his body was placed in a coffin, it was simple enough to revive himself. He seized a guard of roughly his size and stature, fed from him, placed his corpse in the coffin, and fled.

Chapter Thirteen

Roman Holiday, 2386 CE

"Ready to launch, Grandfather," Christine announced.

"Proceed."

The *Red Witch*, sans Gellar drive, lifted smoothly from the landing field and arced towards low orbit. A small, cylindrical device hung beneath the yacht.

"Stay as low as possible," Hess ordered, "and come up beneath the drive from below. Drop the cloak from the drive unit as soon as we dock."

"I hope the Navy won't be tracking us," Christine worried aloud. "Won't it look kind of funny if we just disappear and reappear again?"

"We'll be over the horizon from the *Reuben James*. They won't break off contact with the pirate ship to track us."

"We should find a way to remotely activate and deactivate that device."

"All in good time," Hess told her. "All in good time." The old man tapped on the co-pilot's console in front of him, bringing up a global traffic radar. He smiled when a contact appeared; the ident code showed it to be a Confederate Navy shuttle, bound for the landing field they had just left.

On the surface, Vincent Giovenco sat at his personal terminal. A pre-set series of commands activated his link to the planet's hyperphone transmitter.

"Is this dangerous, VeeGee?" Contessa asked from behind him. For a brief moment, Giovenco imagined he was back in Tijuana. "Everything I've done in the last fifteen years has been dangerous, *querida*," he said, "but at last, this time, I really do know what I'm doing."

"Worth the deal you had to make with that old man?"

"We couldn't pull this off without him," the hacker said. On the terminal, interrogatory codes scrolled past. "If this works, we'll keep the Feds off our backs, we'll get rid of the Tamburos, we'll keep our operations. That's worth handing him a liquor concession."

The Hayes

Emil Tamburo strode onto the pirate ship's Bridge. "Is it local morning yet?"

"About four hours out," Captain Teale replied.

"Launch so that the devices detonate at local sunrise," Tamburo ordered.

"That Navy ship is moving in on us," Teale reported.

"They can't do anything." Tamburo smirked. "That's not legally a Confederate planet down there."

"If they've got one guy on the surface," Teale observed, "then they could conceivably call that a direct attack on Navy personnel."

"They'd have to know that we were attacking their people directly," Tamburo said. "A high-altitude neutron burst can't be targeted against a few people."

"Contact coming up from the surface," the technician at the scanning console called out. "Looks like a small private ship. They're arcing away from us, heading over the horizon. I show a Navy shuttle heading downwards."

"To pick up their people," Tamburo gloated. "They're getting ready to leave. Don't worry about it. The Navy can't touch us, Teale, not even if we fire on the planet. They won't try. They can only interfere if we shoot at them directly, and we're not going to do that— right?"

"You say so." The pirate captain looked doubtful, but Tamburo's tight expression discouraged further discussion. *What the hell*, Teale thought, *his contract has him paying for any damages we take. If we survive.*

The *Reuben James*

"The shuttle reports Colonel Patrick on board, Captain," the signals watch called out. "They're returning to the ship, ETA thirty-nine minutes."

"Very well," Rafael Timmerman answered. "Helm, close on the pirate ship, put us on station five hundred kilometers forward of them. Weapons, stand by on shields."

"Standing by," Weapons reported. "Pee-beams and missile bays report all weapons ready."

"Very well."

The Red Witch

Hess extracted his personal datapad from a jacket pocket and brought up a holo-display. "Steer nineteen by fifty," he said. Beside him, in the pilot's seat, Christine adjusted the controls.

"Your man Giovenco didn't have much time to program this thing we're carrying."

"One must respect a true master of any craft," Hess said, his eyes still locked on his datapad. "The boy knows his business. I believe he will hold true to his end of the bargain. We must now worry about ours."

Christine frowned but held her silence. She glanced at the instrument panel, tapped a contact to activate the Geller drive's onboard locater beacon. The signal came back almost instantly; they were only a few kilometers away.

Old Hess tapped his console to open an encrypted burst-transmission signal to the surface. He spoke into the wand mike, saying simply, "Are you ready?"

"Yes," came the monosyllabic reply.

"Very well," the old man replied. He tapped the contact off. "Engage the cloak. Move in behind the pirate ship."

"Moving in now," Christine responded instantly. Beneath the deck, there came the Gellar drive's characteristic rumble.

The *Reuben James*

Commander Timmerman went to the shuttle docking bay to welcome Colonel Patrick back on board; both officers proceeded from there to the bridge, where events were beginning to pick up.

"The signal from the nukes have gotten stronger, sir," Scanning reported as soon as Timmerman strode into the bridge. "Looks like they've been loaded into launch tubes."

"Nukes?" Timmerman asked. "Plural?"

"Two, sir. I'm getting better returns now that they're preparing to fire; looks like Mk II canisters. On the high-burst setting, they'll kill every living thing in a thirty-kilometer radius. Figure overlapping burst zones, maximum coverage."

Timmerman stared at the scanning rating for a moment, then looked at the screen, where the dented, chipped shape of the pirate ship floated. "Very well. Weapons, raise shields. Arm pee-beams and forward missile bays. Just in case."

"Shields are up, pee-beams and missiles armed."

"You can't shoot unless they shoot at us," Patrick reminded him.

"I know," Timmerman snapped. "But there is one thing I can do."

Patrick looked at him with a questioning expression, but the Navy commander remained silent.

Oh, shit, Patrick said to himself as an idea occurred to him. *We never thought of that. I never had to make that deal with the old man... Damn it!*

The Hayes

"Weapons are programmed and ready for launch. Optimal launch time to burst at sunrise local is 0942 ship time—that's sixteen minutes from now."

"Program it," Teale ordered. He turned to Emil Tamburo, who watched from the vacant executive officer's station. "That's what you wanted, right?"

The *Mafiosi* looked thoughtful for a moment. "Yeah," Tamburo decided. "Make it a hell of a sunrise for them, eh?"

The Red Witch

"We are in position, Grandfather," Christine reported. "Cloaking device is engaged." The yacht came to a halt, relative to the pirate ship, about ten kilometers aft.

"Good, child. Hold here for now."

"They may be preparing to launch," Christine said. "Local sunrise is in about 15 minutes—it wouldn't surprise me if they made that their time on target."

"Exactly what I would suspect, child; you're learning. Hold here for now," the old man repeated. He consulted his datapad. "Watch the local time. Let me know when sunrise is ten minutes out. Timing is everything."

"As you wish, old man."

Nova Reno

Vincent Giovenco—he was beginning, for the first time in many years, to think of himself once more as El Machete—was once more in the *Hayes'* main computer.

There's the commander's direct control access, he read from his terminal screen. *If I can take remote control of his personal terminal in his quarters, I may be able to get control of their weapons console—at least for a few moments.*

That captain better be on the bridge. If he's in his quarters for all this, we may be screwed.

The hacker looked at the clock on his terminal screen. *Fourteen minutes to go. I hope we can pull this off.*

Roman Holiday, 2386 CE

"Time, Grandfather."

"Launch the device."

Christine pushed a contact. Underneath the cloaked *Red Witch*, a small, modified satellite booster powered up its ion drive and launched, activating a small radar transponder in the process.

On the planet below, Vincent Giovenco—El Machete—selected a command prompt from the *Hayes'* masters' personal terminal. Far above, in geosynchronous orbit, the pirate ship's shields went up.

"Move," Hess ordered on the *Red Witch*. "As planned—go six hundred kilometers north on full drive, de-cloak, and run in as though to block."

The yacht responded like a thoroughbred, accelerating hard away from the launch point of the decoy.

The *Reuben James*

It was the last thing Timmerman had expected. From the sound of the scanning technician's shout, no one had. "MISSILE LAUNCH FORWARD," the ScM2c screeched. "PIRATE SHIP IS RAISING SHIELDS!"

"Target pee-beams," Timmerman ordered. "Missile first."

"Targeting—locked," Weapons ordered.

"Fire!"

The Hayes

"What the *fuck*!" Captain Teale leaped out of his chair, staring at his personal console in shock.

"What is it?" Emil Tamburo demanded.

"Our shields have gone up! Someone's in our computer... How the hell?"

"What?"

Teale spun on the *Mafiosi*, his face a mask of rage. "You didn't tell me you were after a *hacker*, you son of a bitch," he shouted. "He's set us up! Raising shields, the Navy will see that as hostile, and you can guess what he'll do next, can't you?"

"He can get into your ship's computer? How?"

Tamburo was interrupted by a shout from the pirate ship's scanning station. "Captain, I've got a missile launch from aft—I can't see any ship! Just an inbound missile, a hundred kilometers, fifty..."

Teale toggled the ship's announcer. "ALL HANDS BRACE FOR IMPACT," he shouted.

But there was no impact.

"What happened?"

"The missile," the scanning tech breathed, "it gave us a haircut, missed by a few centimeters, I swear... Cap'n, it's headed for the Navy ship."

"Launch the devices," Teale ordered.

"What?"

"You heard me, damn you! Arm the devices and launch!"

The pirate ship shuddered as the nukes left the launch bays.

The *Reuben James*

The frigate's powerful particle beam emitters made no noise and produced no recoil effects on firing; only the weapons rating's report made the results known. "Missile hit," she said coolly. "Targeting the pirate ship's drive now."

"Fire when ready," Timmerman ordered. "They're fair game now."

"I'm showing two canisters launched," Scanning reported.

"Shift fire," Timmerman said. "Take out those nukes."

The Red Witch

"As I suspected," Hess breathed. "All right, decloak, take us in as planned, full drive."

The *Reuben James*

"New contact, came outta nowhere," Scanning called. "Designate Bogie-Two—he's chasing the nukes, sir, he's diving on the nukes."

"Hold fire," Timmerman ordered. "Signals, get me an ID on that ship."

"Confederate ident codes," Signals replied, "private yacht *Red Witch*, registered to Joachim Hess, Earth."

"Hess—the old man, the one we're after? What the hell is he playing at?"

"He's trying to take out the nukes—but why?"

"He's not armed," Scanning reported. "He can't stop them."

"Not without ramming," Lieutenant Colonel Patrick announced as he strode into the bridge.

Nova Reno

El Machete smiled when he saw the report on the pirate ship's weapons log. He opened the device's control utility, looked for a certain prompt, found it, selected it.

The Red Witch

Hess watched his console clock, counting down seconds. *Four, three, two...* "Now, child, come hard right, full drive, raise full shields, engage cloak. And, dear, brace yourself—this is going to be close."

The *Reuben James*

"Holy shit!"

On the frigate's main screen, the diving *Red Witch* disappeared into a ball of nuclear flame.

Timmerman's face reddened. "Target two Shrikes on that pirate ship. Blow his ass out of the sky. Scanning, what happened to that yacht?"

"Nothing, sir, not even wreckage—before the blast, they weren't running shields or anything. Private yacht probably didn't even have anything more than navigation shields for micrometeors and other such trash. No good against *that*."

"We'll check on that." Timmerman turned to the Marine colonel. "Well, that solves your little chase, doesn't it? Looks like your man is scattered atomic dust."

The Hayes

"Two missiles incoming," the pirate ship's scanning tech reported sadly.

Emil Tamburo jumped out of his chair, bounded to the signals station. He held a datachip out to the signals technician. "There's a code on this chip," he said quickly, "and an AM radio frequency. Send it to Nova Reno, as much power as you can, tight-beam on the city."

"Why?"

"Last resort," Tamburo said.

He looked up at the pirate ship's main screen. The two missiles from the Navy frigate were visible now, racing in from the front. The pirate ship's particle beam projectors reached out, but the fire control system was out of date; the missiles dodged and jinked...

"They're gonna both hit," Tamburo said.

The *Reuben James*

"Two hits," Weapons reported unnecessarily. On the main screen, the pirate ship puffed into a rapidly expanding ball of gas and debris.

"Well," Timmerman said, "two birds with one stone. Signals, take a message for COMTASKFOR947. The prime target is dead, the secondary target is dead, and we—legally—prevented a holocaust in the process."

He looked around the bridge. "Not a bad day's work, people. Not bad at all."

Chapter Fourteen

Roman Holiday, 2386 CE

"Well," Don Vincent Giovenco said in a satisfied tone after his screen went dark, "that takes care of that."

He shut off the utility he'd used to hack the pirate ship. *Finally,* he told himself, *the Tamburos are taken care of. I can stop worrying...*

His thoughts were interrupted by a noise from the floor below. *Gunfire?*

His office door burst open. Pete Amece, one of his bodyguards, burst in. "We've got to get you out of here, Boss—it's Tinny, he's gone nuts! Shooting the place up!"

Giovenco looked at the back door to the office, which led to the roof. "Is my air-car on the pad?"

Amece looked back out the door. "Yeah, it should be ready..."

The bodyguard's head exploded in a shower of blood, bone and brains. With a rattle of metallic limbs, the special-operations droid appeared in the doorway, weapon-arms raised.

"DO NOT MOVE," the droid boomed. "AND THIS WILL BE QUICK."

The landing field

The *Red Witch* coasted to a light landing in front of a large hangar, where several of Don Giovenco's men were waiting to rush the yacht under cover.

"That was too close," Christine said as she climbed down the ship's boarding stair. She looked up at unmistakable blast damage on the yacht's fuselage. "We've got a bunch of electromagnetic pulse damage to repair, not to mention the blast damage, before we can go into subspace again."

"Not to worry," Hess said. The ship had been hit hard indeed, but he had paid to have it built tough—this was not the first time the ship's robustness had proved worth the expense. "What, four to six weeks to repair this? There are local people who can do that. I would say Don Giovenco owes us that much."

Giovenco's headquarters

The droid took a step forward and leveled the rotary cannons on its rear arms. Giovenco closed his eyes.

The cannons fired, but instead of scattering the planetary Don into pieces, they chewed holes in the ceiling above him. Giovenco flinched as ceramic and polymer tiles rained down on him; he opened his eyes and was sure his mind had snapped.

Contessa Giovenco—Colleen O'Hara—was astride the droid, pulling its weapon-arms upward. The girl's face was twisted into a savage snarl; her arms showed muscles like corded steel as she strained against the struggling droid. As Giovenco watched in disbelief, she managed to wrench one of the droid's cannons loose, tossing it into the hallway behind the machine.

"YOU ARE ORDERED TO CEASE RESISTANCE," the machine boomed. It reached over its back with one of its forward arms, seized Contessa in a steel grapple and threw her hard on the floor in front of it. The remaining weapon arm raised and fired, but Contessa had dodged away—she ducked to the side, seized the droid's forward right leg, and yanked, snapping the leg off at the knee joint. The droid stumbled. As Contessa stepped away from the tank-like robot, Giovenco saw her face—her unbelievably distorted face, fangs jutting from a gaping mouth, eyes flaring red!

The droid crashed through the office's double doors, aiming its surviving weapon-arm at the Don. Contessa yanked it to the side as Giovenco dove for the floor behind the desk. Bullets slammed into the wall behind him, into the desk, chewing away at the polymer armor in the desk itself.

"YOU ARE ORDERED…" the machine boomed again, stopping suddenly in mid-sentence. Cowering on the floor behind the desk, Giovenco heard the snapping of metal, a rending noise, and then a crash.

He peeked slowly, cautiously over the top of the desk. The security droid lay on the carpet, a pool of machine oil spreading black around it. Contessa crouched, catlike, atop the fallen machine, eyes gleaming crimson.

"I'm sorry, my love," she hissed through a cave of sharklike teeth, "but I'm afraid I can't allow you to remember this."

Her eyes flared brighter still, holding the hacker in place like a fly on flypaper.

"You've seen me for what I am," she crooned, her features flowing back to normal but her eyes remaining horribly red. "This will leave you with a headache you won't forget, I'm afraid—but you will forget what else you've seen."

She bounded from the fallen droid to the desk, seized Giovenco by the shirt collar, and held him up. Her eyes, burning crimson, seemed to burn into his brain.

Chapter Fifteen

Roman Holiday, 2386 CE (Six months later)

"It has all worked out so very well!"

Christine looked up from her packing as the old man walked into the rented flat. "It has?"

"Of course!" The old man looked positively joyful. "Exactly as I had hoped. Our liquor and recreational drug chain stores are opening as we speak. The import and distribution network is in place. Toler, the man we hired to manage the business, is an irredeemable scoundrel, but he won't cheat us; he is anxious to keep his position. We're paying him more than he could earn anywhere else on this scabby rock." The old man seated himself on the small couch, the room's only remaining piece of furniture. "It will be easy enough to transfer ownership to any 'descendants' of ours as time goes on. Long-term, this enterprise alone will finance our travels for the foreseeable future, and our holdings here provide us a safe haven—a home, if you will, for whenever travel is unsafe or impractical. That may be useful, even if the Confederacy does not seek us directly."

"The Navy thinks we were destroyed in orbit," Christine agreed. "With that new Status of Forces agreement they were forced to negotiate with Giovenco, Confederate interference in the planet's affairs will be minimal for some time to come. We're free to come and go as we please, without worry of the Feds looking for us. You were right—that deal the president offered you turned out to be unnecessary after all."

"A deal made with one Confederate president is not useful," Hess noted. "The next occupant of the office may well rescind the arrangement, and seek once more to hunt us. Better they think us dead. Now we can travel as we please."

"Speaking of which, we're almost ready to leave," Christine said. "The *Reuben James* is long gone. There won't be another Confederate ship here for weeks, not until the engineers show up to begin construction of the new Navy base. If we're going to go, it's a good time to do it."

"Alcor," Hess said after a thoughtful moment. "A new colony. I propose we go there, see what opportunities present themselves. If none do, then at least we can see a new colony. It's not even a long trip from here. What do you think, child?"

Christine blinked. It was the first time the old man had asked her opinion on anything outside of technical matters concerning her military expertise. "Well," she said slowly, "it's as good a place as any, I suppose. I hear it's expected to boom—it's supposed to be rich in power metals and petroleum."

Hess clapped his hands together once. "Done, then. We'll leave as soon as we can be ready."

Christine smiled. "Tomorrow, then?"

"Tomorrow."

Earth, 2220 CE

"Johann Hess," the scrawny old man said, extending a narrow, long-fingered hand.

James Chandler of Chandler & Wright Shipwrights shook the hand carefully. "Jim Chandler. What can I do for you this morning, Mr. Hess?"

"I wish to commission an interstellar ship," Hess said.

"And whom do you represent?"

"Myself." Hess grinned. "This is to be a private yacht."

Chandler did his best not to laugh. "Sir," he said, "I'm not sure you understand the costs involved. Even a small private yacht will cost you over a hundred million dollars."

"I'm aware of this," Hess said. He handed Chandler a datachip. "I'm easily capable of paying for my ship, Mr. Chandler. My financial bona fides are on that chip, along with my ship's requirements."

Chandler took the chip, shot Hess a suspicious look, and stuck the chip into the terminal on his desk.

"Well," he said after a moment. "Please accept my apologies, Mr. Hess. You do indeed have ample resources. This ship, though..."

"There is no law against arming a private ship, is there?"

"No," Chandler said. "It's legal. Hell, there's not really any law outside the Earth-Luna system anyway; all the colonies are privately owned and operated, mostly by Off-World Mining. You'll need a crew of at least twenty for a ship this size."

"As I planned," Hess said.

Chandler punched a button on his desk. "Jenny, will you send down to the cafeteria for some refreshments please? Coffee for me." He looked at Hess expectantly.

"Green tea, if you would be so kind," Hess said. "It has health benefits, you know; it aids longevity." He grinned.

"Green tea for my guest," Chandler said, and turned the 'com off. "Well, Mr. Hess, let's get the contract paperwork started, so my people can get to work on your ship." He turned to his terminal, began to open various screens. "Oh—have you a name for your ship?"

"Yes," Hess said. "I'll call it the *Red Witch*."

"John Wayne and Gail Russell," Chandler said, "1949."

"Eh?"

"A movie," Chandler answered. "An old word for a vid—a 'moving picture,' they called them."

"A movie? I wouldn't know," Hess said. He smiled again, showing yellow, oddly pointed teeth. He ran a hand through his shock of unruly white hair. "The name appeals to me for other reasons."

"As you wish," Chandler said, laughing. "Let's get this ship started."

Roman Holiday, 2386 CE

Contessa Giovenco took a moment out of her preparations for the evening to look in on the Don, who was finishing up one final project in the rebuilding of their headquarters.

"VeeGee," she piped, smiling broadly as the Don looked up from his terminal. "Will you be able to reprogram Tinny?"

Giovenco looked up at the girl and smiled. "Of course, *querida*. The manufacturer left an Easter egg in the programming I never thought to look for—an override code, accessible through the droid's built-in radio transceiver. It was..."

"VeeGee"—she cut him off, laughing—"you know I don't understand all that technical jibber-jabber."

Giovenco smiled at her, then looked back at the repaired security droid—rebuilt, but 'dead' until its rewritten firmware was installed. "Well, dear, let me just say that yes, Tinny will be back, and he won't be going insane on us again."

"Too bad about Pete Amece," the girl said.

"He died defending his Don," Giovenco said sadly, "and if he hadn't dove on the droid with that grenade, it would have killed me. His family will never want for anything, I've seen to that."

"You're a good man, VeeGee." Contessa smiled again. Her expression was carefully vacant, maybe a bit stupid, but in the dim light of the workshop, as Giovenco looked back to his terminal, her eyes flashed red, for just a moment.

Epilogue

The Red Witch

Hess awoke with a start. He looked around for a moment, disoriented, finally recognizing his tiny stateroom in the *Red Witch*, the second ship to bear the name.

"Anna," he breathed. After almost a thousand years, the dream still came back to him.

His Anna, in the yellow dress he had given her at their wedding, standing in the kitchen of their Augsburg home. She turned, smiled at him. "Johann," she said, "have you any idea how much I love you? Such a good man, such an honest man. I have the envy of every woman in Augsburg."

The dream ended as it always did, in a kaleidoscope scene of fire, destruction, death.

Anna, the old man said, silently. He raised a skinny, clawed hand to his face; it came away wet. *Felix, Elsa—my long-lost dear ones. How I miss you all still. A thousand years, and still I grieve.*

Underneath his narrow bunk, the low *thrum* of power from the yacht's Gellar drive told him they were still under way. Forward, in the pilot's cabin, his 'granddaughter' would no doubt be watching the controls. Through the centuries it had amused Hess to refer to his converts as his 'children,' but he always knew it for a sham. *It cannot be the same,* he thought. *It will never be the same.*

Somewhere ahead lay the new colony of Alcor. Somewhere ahead lay new opportunities, new adventures, new diversions. Hess rolled over, tried to go back to sleep. Tried to avoid the ghosts of a millennium past. Tried to forget.

He knew he never would.

If you haven't read the first book in the Galactic Confederation series
The Crider Chronicles

When humanity ventures off earth, they assumed they were the galaxy's only colonizers. The farthest outposts would soon discover they were wrong. After moving from the mountains of Idaho to the depths of space, Mike Crider finds himself in the center of the action. From guerrilla battles through the wilderness of Forest, to the struggle to establish an intergalactic government, to the First Galactic War, the Crider family paves the way for a new galaxy.

Keep an eye out for the Exciting Conclusion of the
Galactic Confederation Series

About the Author

Anderson Gentry grew up in the hills and trout streams of northeast Iowa's wooded uplands, gaining a keen interest in wildlife, camping, hunting, fishing, and the outdoors.

Gentry served in the U.S. Army in the last years of the Cold War, including service in the Persian Gulf War. Captain Gentry concluded his military career by serving on the staff of the Command Surgeon, U.S. Army, Europe. Along the way, he obtained a bachelor's degree in Biology.

Anderson Gentry's first major novel, The Crider Chronicles received a 2005 Preditors & Editors Reader's Choice Award for Top Ten Science Fiction Novel. The Galactic Confederacy series has continued with the 2008 release of Sky of Diamonds. A spin off work, Barrett's Privateers was released in 2008.

His fast-paced, hard-hitting style combines a unique blend of outdoor savvy, real-world military experience, and realistic character development.

Read more at https://andersongentry.com

Also by Anderson Gentry

The Galactic Confederacy Series
The Crider Chronicles
Sky of Diamonds

Nova Roma Series
Nova Roma 1: De Itinere in Occasum
Coming soon -Nova Roma 2: Quaestu pro Nova Terra

Barret's Privateers

Find more about
Crimson Dragon Publishing's Books,
sign up for news, sneak peeks,
giveaways, and more!
https://crimsondragonpublishing.com